THE DRAGON THREE
by Victoria Perkins

The Dragon Three
Victoria Perkins
Cover art by Victoria Perkins

Thanks to:
Buddy and Alice for sharing the Enfield twins,
and Buddy for being the model for Corakin;
my HLA people, Jozy, Rob, Amber, Henry, Jason,
Marci, Alexis, Sarah, Dede, Monica, Lacilla, Lawanda,
Janet & Julie, for their support & inspiration;
my last WCS study hall for their constant entertainment;
Christa and Jen for letting me use Zoe & Asha as
flabotnum, and Meredith who is just as responsible
and awesome as Sophie

Special thanks to Stacy and Sincerely Photography,
and to models Alexis and Kristen.

Also, special thanks to those who were willing to wade
through all of the junk to help me find the polished
product, those who took the time to write reviews,
and to AEC for first giving The Dragon Three a home.

For my amazing family: my parents, brothers,
awesome sisters-in-law, the best nieces and nephews
in the world, as well as the nephews I never had
the privilege of knowing, Gary and Bert who have
always been part of the family, and my unbiological
sister Krystal for her constant support and love.

PART ONE: DRAGON EYES

Prologue: Hope a Little Harder

For centuries, evil had slept deep under the earth. Now, it rumbled, eager to return and destroy. Only One could survive against it, but the ancient scholars who had held the necessary knowledge had all but disappeared. And should the One prevail, the battle would have only just begun, for the creature was the beginning, not the end. Little hope remained that anyone could find the secrets needed to save the world, much less interpret them, but little hope was better than none, for without hope, the world would be doomed.

Chapter One: Just Breathe

Brina Tri Fine was no ordinary girl, for Brina had a secret. It was this secret on which she dwelled, resting her forehead against the cool glass of the backseat window. The outside scenery flashed by as the vehicle sped past, fields of corn and wheat, grazing garflags and cows. Bright yellow sunflowers and purple masnaeds bobbed in the breeze side-by-side. The sweet-smelling nosidam tree was in full bloom, its red flowers in stark contrast to its pale blue leaves. All in all, it was a beautiful day, but Brina didn't register any of it. Her thoughts were already miles ahead, dreading what was to come. She'd begged her parents to drive her to school, wanting the time to prepare. Not that it would make much difference, she knew. She was just putting off the inevitable.

Brina glanced at the reflection in the window, studying the solemn face looking back at her. It was a pretty face. Not extraordinary like her older sisters, Barika and Basha, but pretty enough for people to notice. Tendrils of dark red waves framed her heart-shaped face, and the rest of her hair hung down her back in a waist-length braid. She'd gotten her hair color from her father. The twins closest to her age, Bem and Bae, were also red-heads. The other four had their mother's blond hair. All of them had dark brown eyes – mother, father, six brothers and sisters. All except Brina. No one knew where her light violet eyes had come from; no one in either her mother's or father's families had eyes like hers. But, then again, no one in either family – no one in the whole world for that matter – was like Brina. She'd long since given up asking Elsali, the Creator, why she was different, and tried to focus on what she could do rather than what she couldn't. Unfortunately, school probably wasn't going to be one of those things.

"We'll be arriving shortly." Vani Fine's voice cut through Brina's thoughts.

"Thank you, Mother," Brina replied automatically.

Fifteen years younger than her closest sibling, Brina had been raised more like an only child than the youngest of a large family. Her parents had doted on her, or so it had seemed to the outside world. Brina had been kept at home for her first fifteen years, taught basics by tutors who believed her parents were schooling her in the magical arts when they got home from work, which was understandable when one considered her parents' skill.

Her father, Ziven Fine, was Principal of Audeamus Elementary School, the most elite elementary boarding school in all of Ortus. Most considered it the greatest one in the country, and all of the Fine kids, except Brina, had attended. Vani Issa-Fine had followed in her own father's footsteps, teaching botany at the Seriatim School of Higher Education. Seriatim was a good school, but not as good as the Audeamus School of Higher Education. Only the best of the best achieved acceptance and most of them were graduates of the Audeamus Elementary and Middle Schools. A few, like Brina, were accepted based on the exceptional talent of generations of family members. It was for this reason, and this reason alone, that Brina Fine was on her way to Audeamus.

"Are you wearing your uniform?"

"Yes, ma'am," Brina didn't add how her mother could have turned around and seen for herself that Brina had already fastened her dark blue summer cloak around her neck. Instead, Vani chose to ask and keep her eyes focused on the road ahead. Brina sighed. It wasn't like her parents were mean or cruel to her, they just didn't seem to know how to behave around their abnormal child. Sometimes, she even felt sorry for them. This wasn't one of those times. She had enough going on in her head without having to worry about how her parents were dealing with everything.

"And you have everything you need?" Vani continued.

Brina almost smirked, but managed to keep herself in check. "Yes, ma'am." She bit the inside of her cheek to refrain from making a snide comment. Sarcasm and a quirky sense of humor – often combined – were her go-to defense mechanisms, and she was definitely on the defensive at the moment, what with her certain doom looming ahead. At least, she thought, the required school uniform was simple enough. Modest clothing, sensible shoes and, for classes and formal occasions, dress cloaks. It was the only simple thing about this entire situation. From one of her side pockets, Brina withdrew a long, thin piece of wood. *Hemlock*, she thought with a wry smile. *There's irony for you.* She twirled the wood between her fingers.

"Brina, don't!" Vani had finally turned around. "You could..." Her voice trailed off as she realized what she'd been about to say.

"I could do what, Mom?" Brina's voice was soft. Her hand stilled, gripping the wood with enough force to turn her knuckles white. "I could do what? Poke myself in the eye, because we all know that's about all the damage I can do with this."

Vani studied her daughter for a moment, a mixture of wariness and sorrow in her dark eyes. "You know I'd help you if I could," Vani almost whispered the words.

Brina felt a surge of guilt and reached out to touch her mother's arm. "I know, Mom."

Vani searched for something to fill the silence. "Did you remember your mirror?"

Brina nodded. Tucked away in her bag was a communication mirror. Most people preferred wand messaging when a *Rasha Harma* spell wasn't necessary, but it wasn't too strange to use another method. The main benefit was the lack of magic needed to make it work. The device itself was enchanted. Even someone like Brina could use one.

"We're here," Brina's father, Ziven Fine, spoke for the first time.

Brina's heart thudded in her chest and she took a deep breath to try and calm herself.

Vani returned to her original position as her husband pulled the car up to a set of large iron gates. She made a jabbing motion with her wand. "*Ilak Ahcor.*" With a loud creak, the gates swung open, allowing the car to pass through. The driveway was long and winding, more like a road cutting through a grove of golden trees than a path leading to a school. As they rounded the final turn, the trees gave way to gently rolling grasses leading right up to the walls of Audeamus.

The mansion itself sprawled over almost three acres and rose nine stories into the bright blue sky. Out of sight were the four underground levels, which were rumored to have been built over a series of natural caves that ran beneath the entire campus. Behind the mansion, Brina knew, were numerous outbuildings housing some of the on-site staff or serving as classrooms for classes involving exotic plants and animals, as well as other functions. Though she'd never seen the school before, she knew most of the layout of the building and grounds from the stories her parents and siblings had told. She might've had her one huge shortcoming, but she did have some things going for her, not the least of which was her excellent memory.

Ziven parked alongside another family who had just arrived. Brina noted, with a silent sigh of relief, how her parents had timed everything perfectly. They'd wanted to reach the school at the peak of busyness and blend in with everyone else. Brina didn't wait for her parents, eager to stretch her legs. The butterflies in her stomach had tripled in the last few seconds and some movement would distract her even if it wouldn't quiet them.

"Ziven! Vani!"

Brina didn't turn as she heard her parents' names. Instead, she busied herself with retrieving her luggage. A few minutes later, her mother called her over. Standing with her parents was a tall man about their age, if not a few years younger. His strawberry blond hair was thinning, but his face was youthful and his light blue eyes sparkled. Immediately, Brina noticed the gold trim at his collar, sleeves and the hem of the dark blue robes he wore over his dress slacks and shirt.

"Headmaster." Brina smiled and held out a hand.

"Good eye." He returned the smile with a genuine one of his own, knocking about ten years off his age. "I've been looking forward to meeting you."

Vani's smile faded a bit. "Brina, this is Headmaster Manu. He's an old friend of your father and I."

"I hope you're referring to the length of friendship and not age." Headmaster Manu chuckled.

Brina felt the butterflies settle a bit, the banter putting her at ease.

The headmaster looked down at Brina. "Where's your room?"

Brina pulled out the letter even though she really didn't need it. She'd been staring at the letter almost every waking hour since it had arrived. "Room thirteen seventy-four."

"Very good. My oldest son, Corin, is in thirteen seventy-nine."

"How old is he now?" Vani interjected.

"Seventeen. Tyl and Sadra are, as you two know, still too young for Audeamus. But how time flies. It must seem like just yesterday you were here with Baka."

"His son and Barika's second daughter are twelve already. Barika's oldest, Genevieve, will be old enough to apply next year." Vani referenced her oldest grandchildren and Brina could tell her mother was hoping that talking about the other members of the Fine family would keep the headmaster from asking too many questions about Brina. "Time does move quickly."

"Audeamus is never the same without a Fine." Headmaster

Manu motioned for the Fines to follow him. "I'll show you the way, Brina, although I'm sure Ziven and Vani remember where everything is."

"That's really not necessary, Roderick," Vani protested.

"Nonsense. I insist." He turned to Brina. "Just bring your things."

Ziven intervened. "I'll get them. Brina, you go ahead with your mother and Headmaster Manu. I'll catch up."

"Thank you." Brina fell in step next to her mother as her father opened the trunk of the car and began to float her bags out.

The trio had barely gone five paces when a small brown creature darted out in front of them. Immediately, a figure followed, shouting, "Ziege, come back here! Bad Ziege! Bad badger!" The man skidded to a stop in front of Headmaster Manu.

Brina looked down. The animal in question sat at her feet. It was, indeed, a badger, but one with such an intelligent face Brina felt it could almost talk. She knelt down and held out a hand. It sniffed her hand and then allowed her to scratch its head.

"Thank you, Miss." The owner retrieved his pet.

"Problems with Ziege, Corakin?" The headmaster didn't seem surprised by what had just happened. In fact, he appeared to be mildly amused, even if a bit patronizing.

As Brina stood, she took a good look at the man who now chided the animal he held in his arms. He was several inches taller than her, but not quite as tall as her father, and much thinner. His short brown curls were a mess from his dash across the grounds, a pair of glasses perched crookedly on the bridge of his nose, and his robes were splattered with mud. The bronze trim told Brina he was a professor even though he didn't look much older than she was. She guessed his age at around twenty-five, if that.

"Corakin Gibberish, meet Vani Fine and her daughter Brina." Headmaster Manu patted the badger's head, the expression on his face suggesting he'd rather not touch the creature, but rather that it was expected of him. "Ladies, this is our Foreign Languages professor, and his pet badger, Ziege."

"Nice to meet you." Corakin smiled, and then looked puzzled. He glanced up at the headmaster. "Fine? As in–"

"Yes." Headmaster Manu nodded. "Brina is the youngest of Vani and Ziven's children. It's her first year at Audeamus."

"*Molto buono, molto buono.* Very pleased to have you." Corakin attempted to extend a hand, realized his arms were full of badger, and stopped. "Very pleased. Now, if you'll excuse me, I need to return Ziege home." He turned and headed back in the direction he'd come, muttering to either himself or the badger. Brina only caught part of what he was saying, "*Quam magis lubrico uncta mustela,*" before he was too far away to be heard. She was pretty sure the phrase meant '*more slippery than a greased weasel,*' but it was possible she was mistaken.

"A bit odd," Headmaster Manu said. "But an excellent professor. Highly intelligent and great with the students." He motioned behind the women where Ziven was approaching with Brina's luggage. "Ah, Ziven, you've caught up with us. Shall we?" Once again, the group started off toward the school. The headmaster kept up a steady stream of talk, showing Ziven and Vani the changes that had been made since their last visit a decade ago. Brina fell behind, letting the conversation flow above and around her. "And, if you were to go down to the Fuhjyn field, you would see we've been able to completely redesign it, courtesy of Barty Decker."

"Barty Decker?" Vani glanced at her husband. "Wasn't he a year behind us in school?"

"That was his brother, Erasmus," Ziven corrected. "Barty was quite a few years younger. He's the one who married Felicity Remmington, the wandmaker's daughter."

"You're right," Headmaster Manu interjected. "As you know, the Decker brothers were the only heirs to both the Decker fortune and the Firestorm Carriage fortune. Erasmus died about ten years ago, and since he never married or had children, everything went to Barty. When Barty's daughter started here, he made a huge contribution to the school and we were able to hire a top designer for the field." He glanced back at Brina. "I believe his daughter will be Brina's roommate."

Brina disguised her surprise as she followed her parents through the front door. She'd forgotten she'd be sharing a room. Well, it looked like she'd be home earlier than she'd previously thought. She figured it was just as well, since any child raised in a family that rich would probably be a horrific roommate. The Fines may have been well-known, but they weren't rich. Well off, but not rich. At least, not in the old-money Decker family sense. Based on what the headmaster had just said, her roommate was the only living descendent to three of the richest families in all of Ortus.

Suddenly, Brina realized the headmaster was talking to her. "Up one staircase and then to the left is the main auditorium, used for special occasions, holidays, that type of thing. Any all-school meals or assemblies are held in there. To the right is the exit nearest the stables. Usually the shortest route for anyone taking outdoor classes. If you need to get to the greenhouses, take the exit on the far side of the auditorium." He motioned toward a large, rectangular mirror on the wall. "And these are located throughout the castle." He took out his wand and tapped the mirror. He took care to enunciate as he spoke again. "Room thirteen seventy-four."

Brina watched as their reflections swirled and disappeared. Instead of the mirror's shiny surface, a detailed map appeared. A little stick figure stood next to the words "You are here." A red line appeared, going up several staircases, right through a corridor, through a room and into another corridor. It went up a short flight of stairs to the left and stopped. Another group of letters floated into existence. "Got it?"

"That's convenient," Ziven was impressed. "I'll have to speak to the school board about getting one of these for my school. I constantly have students showing up late to class because they were lost. Or so they claim."

"Yes, yes, Mirror Maps are a nice bit of magic," Headmaster Manu started walking once more, following the directions from the mirror map.

"Do the room numbers correspond with the floor?" Brina asked as the headmaster began to walk up the wide stairwell.

"Yes, just be sure to remember the school's main entrance is actually on the fifth floor, so if you come in here, remember to start counting at five. But there's no need to worry about going too high. You're at the top."

"Great," Brina forced a smile. Now she'd have to carry all of her things down eight flights of stairs when she was expelled. Maybe she'd get lucky and someone would throw her suitcases down the stairs. Although, she supposed, eight was better than thirteen.

Headmaster Manu either didn't notice the tightness in Brina's voice or didn't care, because he continued speaking. "Obviously, any students who have passed their Transportation Test can bypass all of the stairs." He glanced at Ziven and Vani. "And we've managed to iron out the problems with transporting off of school grounds." He chuckled.

"What's so funny?" Brina asked, more because it seemed expected than actual curiosity. She was still trying to decide if she liked the headmaster or not. He didn't seem to have a lot of depth.

"Your sisters tried to sneak out one night after they first received their Transportation license." The corner of Vani's mouth twitched up in a half-smile as she answered. "Back then, Roderick was in charge of discipline and he'd done a Tailing

Charm so he'd be able to find anyone who transported out of the school without permission."

"Good thing too," Ziven continued the story. "Barika and Basha had made a slight navigation error."

"Where'd they end up?" Brina'd never heard this story before and had a difficult time picturing her sisters, almost twenty years her senior and oh-so-serious about life in general, behaving like teenagers.

"Malafide." Headmaster Manu paused at the top of one flight of stairs.

"Isn't that almost a hundred miles away?"

Vani nodded. "And very dangerous. After that, the girls never tried transporting further than twenty miles, and never at night. I think they're still wary about transporting long distances."

They all stopped on a platform and Headmaster Manu motioned toward the two corridors leading in opposite directions. "This is the first level of dormitories. Everything under level ten are classrooms, with the exception of the assembly hall and the living quarters at the back of the ground floor where my assistant, Mr. Stryka, lives."

"Ahne Stryka returned this year?" Ziven fell in step with the headmaster as they began to climb again. "I thought he would have left after you were appointed Headmaster instead of him."

"Ahne wasn't too happy about it," the headmaster admitted. "But he's come to terms with his position and is looking forward to taking a hand in the disciplining."

Brina's attention wandered once more as the headmaster and her father began discussing disciplinary policies. Other students and families were passing the Fines on their way back down the stairs. Several others were following behind Brina, their luggage bouncing unevenly up the steps from students attempting levitation on their own. A few parents had decided to forgo the annoyance of bobbling trunks and had their own wands out to steer. Brina felt a surge of pride at her parents' ability. Not everyone could keep a spell going with such little effort. Then her stomach clenched at the thought of how embarrassing it was going to be for them when everyone discovered her secret.

"And here we are." Headmaster Manu pointed toward an arched doorway to their right. Intricately carved into the wood above the frame were the words: *Veritas Lux Mea.*

"*The truth is my light,*" Brina murmured.

"Ah, you know your Latin." A smile spread across the headmaster's face. "But, from your family, what else would I expect?"

Vani and Ziven managed small, nervous-sounding chuckles as they followed Headmaster Manu through the doorway. Brina took a deep breath and continued after her parents. It was so close now. A few moments later, they came out into a long, narrow room, about three times the width of the corridor and twice as long. Tables stretched from one side of the room to the other, all beautifully crafted wood with complex designs and patterns along the edges and down the legs. Benches of equal length ran along either side. Several older students looked up in surprise as Headmaster Manu waved a greeting. It would seem he didn't make a point to escort every new student to their room. Apparently, Brina thought, the extra attention was just one of the many perks of being a part of the Fine family.

"The dining area for Level Thirteen. It also serves as a common room when so needed." The headmaster slowed a bit, waiting for Brina to catch up with her parents. "Rooms one through sixty-nine are back through the left archway and branch off from the corridor. Rooms seventy through ninety-nine are through that door." He pointed to another arched doorway directly across from the one they'd just come through. "There are three hallways, one for the seventies, one for the eighties and one for the nineties. We want the one to the left." The headmaster motioned for two students to come forward.

The girl was Brina's height, with an athletic build and a classically beautiful face. Her straight black hair cascaded down her pale rose-colored cloak almost to her waist, not a single stray hair to be seen. Her eyes were a rich dark brown, her skin dusky and flawless. She was one of those girls that people would watch walk by without even realizing they were doing it. She gave a small smile and held out a hand without waiting for an introduction. "Hi, I'm Ananda Spruce. I'm the girls' Floor Captain."

Brina shook her hand, feeling an instant liking. She turned toward the young man and wasn't entirely sure what to think. He was tall, almost towering over Brina's five feet, ten-inch frame, which wasn't something to which she was accustomed. His brown hair was short, slightly curling at the edges. An expensive dark gray cloak was fastened with an even more expensive-looking gold clip. He was an attractive person, but the look in his light blue eyes was disconcerting, as if the expression he showed was at war with what he was really thinking.

"I'm Gray Plumb." His pale eyes swept over Brina, assessing the fine weave and pricey fringe of her cloak with a critical eye. He held out a hand as his gaze returned to her face. "I'm the Floor Captain and head of the Thirteenth Floor's Fuhjyn team."

Headmaster Manu completed the introductions. "Ananda, Gray, this is Brina Fine."

Ananda's eyes widened just the slightest bit, and Gray's eyebrows shot up. Brina saw something pass across Gray's eyes, but it was gone too quickly for her to put a name to it. "It's nice to meet you both."

"And you." Ananda's smile grew, showing just a hint of even, white teeth.

"If you have any problems at all, Ananda and Gray are the ones to whom you will want to go." Headmaster Manu nodded toward the pair as he motioned for the Fines to follow him. He walked directly across the room, stopping in front of a set of long curtains. He pulled one of the drapes aside and motioned for the Fines to go first. He waited until Brina's luggage followed her before stepping through and letting the curtain fall shut behind him. The hallway was wide with doors on either side. Each door had golden numbers written above them. "Ananda and her sisters are in seventy. Gray and two others are in seventy-one. You're right next door in thirteen seventy-four." He paused in front of the door and retrieved his wand. "You share your bathroom and sitting room with the pair in thirteen seventy-five." He tapped his wand against the door. "Each door recognizes the wands of the students who live there. Only yours, your roommate's and staff wands will open the doors. No incantation needed."

Brina breathed a small sigh of relief. At least she didn't need to worry about being locked out of her room. That would be an embarrassing way for her secret to be revealed. While wands were used to direct and channel a person's magic, their registration didn't require magic to work, but was rather a charm on whatever was doing the registering, like the door.

The door swung open and the headmaster stood aside. Brina let her father move her trunk through the door before following it inside. She stopped just inside the doorway. Her parents stayed in the hall.

"Do you need help unpacking?" Vani's voice was tight.

Brina shook her head. It was time for the awkward parting, made all the more awkward by knowing she'd be seeing them again soon. "I'll be fine."

"Then we'll let you get settled." Ziven avoided his daughter's eyes.

"We'll talk to you soon." Vani glanced at Brina and then away again.

"Okay."

An awkward silence fell.

Brina broke it. "Well, good-bye then."

Her parents returned the sentiment and disappeared down the hallway, following Headmaster Manu back through the curtains and out through the common room. And just like that, Brina was no longer under the protection of her parents.

Chapter Two: The Unknown

Brina turned toward her room, trepidation tying her stomach in knots. She took two steps inside and realized she wasn't alone. On the bed farthest from the door sat one of the smallest people she'd ever seen. At least a foot shorter than Brina herself, this girl had straight black hair, neatly braided into two long plaits, creamy white skin and dark blue eyes. She looked like she was twelve. The girl smiled and her entire face lit up, transforming her from pretty into beautiful, though not making her appear any older. She bounced off the bed and practically skipped across the room.

"Hi!" She said brightly. "I'm Thana Decker. I'm fifteen and this is my first year here, but I've been away at school for ages. I've always wanted to come here because Audeamus is the best school around, but I'm sure you know that, and I'm so excited to be here, aren't you?" She said everything in one long breath and Brina's jaw dropped. Without waiting for a reply, Thana continued. "I've been here for two weeks already because Daddy had important business and wanted to bring me himself and it was the only time he had free for a while so he figured better early than late." She paused to take a breath. "What's your name?"

"I'm Brina," Brina grinned. "Brina Fine."

Thana's eyes widened. "Wow, one of *the* Fines. I wonder if Headmaster Manu put us together on purpose since we're both from pretty well-known families though I'd rather be known for strength of magic than money, wouldn't you agree? I'd say the only one here with more money than my family is the Plumb family, but I don't think they're very nice, do you? Have you met them? Daddy's known them for years so Gray and I grew up together. Unfortunate name, isn't it? But I think he deserves it." Thana smirked and Brina was now certain she was going to like her roommate. "I know, I'm talking too much. I tend to do that."

"It's okay." Brina unlatched her trunk and began removing things. "I don't mind. It's generally too quiet at home."

"But don't you have, like, a ton of brothers and sisters? I mean, Daddy always said the Fines were a big family."

Brina nodded, frowning slightly at the thought of her talented siblings. "There are seven of us, but they're all a lot older than me. In fact, they're all married and have kids."

"Really?" Thana bounced on the corner of her bed. "So, you, like, have nieces and nephews?"

"Twelve nieces, eleven nephews." Brina's mouth twitched to a smile as her roommate stood up. "And all of them closer to my age than my brothers and sisters. I was raised more like an only child."

"That's me." Thana rocked back and forth on her toes, as if the mere thought of standing still was too much for her. "I'm an only child. Good thing, Daddy always says, because one of me is enough. Goodness knows I'd talk the ears off of a garflag if I had half the chance. Do you want any help?"

The change of subject caught Brina off guard and it took her a moment to process the question. "Thank you. Which closet is empty?"

Thana pulled her wand from her pocket and gave it a flick. The closet doors on the left swung open. "I can take care of the clothes. I always manage to get them put away neatly." She grinned as she saw Brina glance at the unkempt half of the room. "I can do it, I just don't generally bother. Hope you don't mind. I thrive on organized chaos."

"No problem. Thanks again for the help," Brina began to make her bed as Thana waved her wand and muttered a spell. One by one, Brina's clothes danced from the trunk over to the closet and draped themselves over the hangers. Her shoes skipped along behind them, making a straight line across the back of the closet. Her jeans and dress pants zoomed across the room, still tightly folded, and stacked themselves on the shelves at the far right side of the closet. By the time Brina finished the bed, everything else had been put away. Already Brina's half of the room was tidier than Thana's.

"Great, now we're both done and we can go exploring." Thana linked her arm through Brina's, an accomplishment considering the difference in their heights. "Maybe we'll run into the guys from seventy-five. I haven't met them yet, but Ananda told me they're around here somewhere. Where do you want to go first?"

Brina shrugged, unable to keep herself from smiling. "Wherever you want to go."

"Great! We're off to seek adventures," Thana declared, marching toward the door and dragging Brina behind her.

As the girls passed into the hallway, Brina retrieved her wand and tapped the door behind her. A polite voice came out of the door. "Brina Fine, hemlock and Manticore tail dart, room thirteen seventy-four. Your wand has been recorded." Brina slid her wand back into its pocket. When someone was expelled, she wondered, did they have to un-record the wands?

"Let's check out the grounds. It's absolutely gorgeous today, don't you think?" Thana led Brina through the living quarters, either ignoring or oblivious to the gazes following them across the room. Just as they reached the door, a hand grabbed Brina's wrist.

"And where are you ladies off to this afternoon?" Gray's smile didn't quite reach his eyes.

"We're going to take a walk around the grounds." Thana answered, glancing over at Gray's hand which still gripped to Brina's wrist. "No accompaniment necessary." Her voice had cooled considerably.

Noticing where Thana had been looking, Gray released Brina's arm, something dark flitting across his face before disappearing behind practiced politeness. He spoke to Brina, his tone indicating that Thana wasn't included in his invitation. "I know this place as well as my own home – well, two of the houses my family owns, at least. It is hard to keep up with all of them. I'd be happy to show you around the grounds."

"No, thank you." Brina kept her tone cordial. "I'm sure Thana and I can find our own way around."

A scowl appeared momentarily and then vanished. "Let me know if you change your mind."

Thana tugged on Brina's arm. "Come on."

The pair disappeared into the corridor. They passed several more families as well as older students obviously comfortable with arriving by themselves. No one paid the pair of first years any mind. It was different than Brina had imagined. She knew the purpose of schools like Audeamus was to assist the transition from child to adult, allowing the mid-age of fifteen to twenty to have responsibilities and privileges while still providing structure and discipline. She'd heard her parents say so hundreds of times. She just hadn't expected to go from the confines of her home where she rarely ventured in public, and never alone, to this heady freedom.

"Watch this." Thana grinned, extracting her wand from her pocket. She paused on the tenth-floor landing and waited for it to clear. Once everyone else was out of sight, she tapped the wall just under the Mirror Map and muttered something Brina couldn't quite make out. With a whisper of wood against wood, the panel to the right of the map slid back to reveal a staircase. Thana motioned for Brina to follow her. Once inside, the panel slid shut again.

"*Fiat lux.*" Thana's voice was hushed. A ball of light appeared in front of her.

"What's this?"

"Found it last week. It'll take us straight to the back garden."

"You found it?" Brina fell in step beside Thana as they descended the stairs. "What'd you do, go around tapping the walls and muttering random words?"

"Not exactly." Thana's eyes sparkled in the dim light. "I found out, if you ask a Mirror Map very specific directions, they can show you hidden passages."

"So, a lot of people know about this?"

Thana shook her head. "No. Like I said, very specific. I just asked for the quickest and most secret way to get from our room to the outside, back of the school."

"That simple?" Brina raised an eyebrow.

"Yeah." Thana giggled.

Brina couldn't help but smile. Normally, she detested giggling girls, but Thana's laugh was child-like, innocent, not vacuous or flirty. She paused for a moment, watching her new friend bounce down the last couple stairs.

"Right here," Thana touched her wand to the blank wall in front of her. "*Aruza.*" The paneling slid open. A faint stream of sunlight cut between the trees hiding the doorway, illuminating the base of the staircase. Together, the girls slipped through the opening and the panel shut behind them. "The garden's cut off from the rest of the yard and kids used to sneak inside for some, uh, privacy. So now, the entrance from the yard into the garden is enchanted so Assistant Headmaster Stryka knows whenever anyone is in here, but, if you come through the back way, no one knows."

"How do you know all of this?" Brina asked.

"Do you really want me to answer?" Thana gave the taller girl a wicked grin and Brina shook her head. "Actually, it was just part of what I asked the Mirror Map."

Thana ducked behind a pair of trees. Brina followed. A moment later, the girls emerged into a secluded area of the back garden. A hedge grew around a small section, offering peace and quiet. A fountain stood in the center, water bubbling over white marble. Brina stepped closer, intrigued by several markings she couldn't quite make out. As she drew closer, she realized they were letters, but not any letters she recognized despite her proficiency at languages.

"What's that say?" Brina couldn't take her eyes from the strange carvings. She'd never really had much interest in the school or its history, though she was surprised she hadn't learned about the fountain in Ortus history. Something like this, she thought she'd remember.

"No one knows." Thana strolled over to Brina's side. "This fountain's been here as long as anyone can remember. It's why they built the school here. Legend has it that it says something really important, like a big secret or something. No one's ever been able to crack it, not even the greatest wizards. Finally, they just stopped trying and everyone just forgot about it."

Brina nodded, still transfixed by the unknown writing. She didn't know how long she would've stood there if Thana hadn't tugged on her sleeve.

"C'mon." Thana's bubbly demeanor softened and a worried note crept into her voice. "Let's check out the rest of the grounds."

"Hmm?" Brina looked down, the movement seeming to break the spell. She shook her head and her eyes focused again. "Oh, right. Let's go."

The girls followed the sinuous path and, a minute later, exited the garden. Here, the grounds were open, and the occasional tree dotted across the gently rolling slopes. Well-groomed paths were stripes of brown across the green. Most of the students out and about were on these paths. Once in a while, the statelier professors appeared, hurrying along with some urgent business in mind. The lone exception was a thin young man, too old to be a student, but almost too young to be a professor. He stood at the base of a tree, peering upward and muttering to himself. Brina recognized him almost immediately.

"What's Professor Gibberish doing?" Brina gestured toward the anxious-looking individual.

"Oh, you've met Corakin." Thana started walking in the direction Brina had pointed. "His oldest sister and Daddy are great friends. I don't like her much. I think she's a bit too fond of Daddy. Corakin's all right though. A really nice person." Thana called out to the professor as she skipped down the hill. "Hello there, Corakin!"

Corakin jumped, apparently startled by the sudden greeting. He spun around, searching for its source, an anxious expression on his face. However, as soon as he saw the girls, he smiled. "Thana, how wonderful to see you. And I see you've met the newest student from the Fine family."

"We're roommates."

"Ah, *sehr gut..., sehr gut...*" Corakin's smile widened. "I'm sure you're quite the pair." The worried look reappeared on the professor's face.

"What's the problem, Professor?" Brina asked kindly.

"It's Ziege."

"He escaped again?" Brina couldn't quite contain her smile.

"No." Corakin looked up, expression glum.

The girls followed Corakin's gaze. Brina could just make out the brown fur of the creature in question among the bright blue of the esum leaves.

Thana asked the question Brina was thinking. "How did your badger get in a tree?"

"BD," Corakin scowled. "Floated Ziege right up into the tree."

"Can't you just float him back down?" Brina didn't know who or what BD was, but she didn't think it was someone or something she'd like.

Corakin shook his head. "BD put a bubble charm around him to shield from any spells. Once I have him back, she and I will be having a serious discussion."

"Okay." Brina stepped up to the tree and grabbed a low-hanging branch.

"What are you doing?" Thana sounded more curious than anything.

"Getting Ziege." Brina swung herself up onto the branch.

"Be careful!" Corakin called.

Brina didn't answer as she made her way up to the tree. This she could do. She'd spent many happy childhood hours in the woods behind her family home, climbing the trees and pretending she was in a world where she belonged. It didn't take her much time before she was face-to-face with the same intelligent animal she'd seen earlier that day. She held out a hand. "Remember me, Ziege?" she murmured. The badger leaned forward and sniffed Brina's fingers. "Now, I'm going to pick you up and we'll make our way back down to the ground, okay? Back to Corakin?" The little creature's eyes sparkled at the name.

Brina wedged herself against the tree and held out both arms. The badger willingly went to her and crawled up onto her shoulder. It perched there, snuffling around Brina's ear as she slowly made her way back down the tree. As she reached the bottom branch, she swung her legs over it, steadied herself and plucked the badger from her shoulder. She leaned down and passed it off to Corakin's waiting arms.

"*Gracias.*" Corakin cradled the badger, cooing to it in yet another language.

"No problem." Brina smiled again.

Suddenly, a loud crack cut through the air and the branch Brina was sitting on broke free of the tree, crashing to the ground. Brina fell with it, landing with a sickening thud. Her right arm twisted under her and a sharp flare of pain went through it.

"Brina!" Thana darted forward.

Brina struggled to sit up, face white. She held her arm gingerly. "Arm's broken."

"Guess you should've kept your fat butt on the ground." A

mocking voice made the trio look up. A haughty-looking young woman stood several feet away, surrounding by a giggling gaggle of girls. Her wand was drawn, held between two delicate fingers.

"Belladonna Juniper," Thana spoke between gritted teeth. "It's not enough you put Ziege up there, you had to almost kill Brina too?"

"Me?" The stunning brunette didn't quite manage to sound innocent. "I don't know what you mean."

Thana stood, pulling herself to her full, though unimpressive, height. "You broke the branch, BD."

"Prove it." Her blue eyes darkened.

"I saw you cast the spell." Another voice came out of nowhere.

Everyone turned toward the sound. A handsome young man walked up the hill, bright green eyes sparking. His blond hair was wild, as if he'd run his hand through it too many times for it to remember how it was supposed to lay.

"Hi, Aidan," BD's voice was sugary sweet as her bright eyes devoured the young man.

"Professor Gibberish, I saw BD cast the spell." The young man reached down and helped Brina to her feet, careful not to jar her injured arm. His eyes met hers, and he smiled a crooked and grim smile that didn't quite reach his eyes.

"Come on, Aidan. It was just a joke." The girl next to BD protested, a carbon copy who was obviously BD's younger sister.

"Not a very funny one, Damiana," Thana said and Brina saw her friend's hand twitch towards her wand before appearing to remember about the professor.

"I'll deal with this." Corakin turned toward Brina who was still cradling her arm in her opposite hand. "Get Brina to the healer."

"I'll show you the way," Aidan offered. "This way."

As the trio walked away, they could hear Professor Gibberish scolding the group of girls, every other sentence in a different language. Before passing through the entryway into the cool interior of the mansion, the shrill voice of one of the Juniper sisters cut through the relatively still air only to be cut off by a loud "*satis*" from the professor.

Aidan motioned for the girls to follow him through a side door. "I'm Aidan Preston, by the way."

"Thana Decker." Thana still hadn't smiled since the branch had broken.

"Brina Fine." Brina spoke through gritted teeth, every step jostling her injured arm.

"Wow, pretty important families." Aidan sounded more amused than impressed which Brina immediately liked. Then his voice darkened. "What'd you two do to get on the bad side of Belladonna Juniper before school even started?"

"Rescued a badger." Brina shrugged and then winced at the movement.

Aidan chuckled as the group reached a set of double doors clearly marked "Healing Wing." They swung open.

"Someone hurt already?" An attractive young man in his early twenties appeared as the girls followed Aidan into the spacious room.

"Fell out of a tree." Brina gave Thana a sideways look, clearly saying to keep the details quiet.

The young man's face didn't register any surprise as he motioned Brina forward. His name tag read Jacen Raphael, Head Healer. His dark hair was short and clean, neatly brushed back from his face. Pale gray eyes studied Brina's face for a moment before he spoke. "All right, if that's all you want to tell me." He took Brina's arm and pushed her sleeve up to her shoulder, examining the injury.

Brina's face grew even paler and she swayed. Aidan stepped up, placing his hand on the small of Brina's back. His free hand pulled his wand from his pocket. "*Arua* chair." A chair slid to a stop next to Aidan and he helped Brina into the seat.

"Thank you, Aidan." Jacen didn't take his eyes from Brina's arm. One hand held her wrist while he extracted his wand. He muttered something and splints appeared, holding Brina's arm in place. "*Arua Nohya*." A small bottle flew across the room into the healer's open hand. "Take one capful of this every hour for twenty-four hours, starting at dinner. And, yes, you'll need to wake up every hour tonight to stay on schedule. It'll be weak for a day or so, but you should have full use of your wand arm in forty-eight hours."

Brina took the bottle and obediently drank a capful. She grimaced at the taste, but didn't complain.

"Rough luck for your first day of school." Healer Jacen commented.

"Yeah." Brina nodded in agreement, but felt a surge of relief. It looked like she'd last at least a couple of days. She'd spent so much of her life away from others her age that she craved their presence, if not their companionship. She felt a flush creeping up her cheeks.

"Brina, are you okay?"

It must've been the concern in Thana's voice that drew the healer's attention away from the chart he was marking because Brina hadn't yet realized anything was wrong. Healer Jacen's eyes widened and he grabbed at his wand. Brina started to speak, but found she couldn't draw in enough air. Her face flamed and she gasped, trying to breathe.

Jacen pointed his wand at Brina. "*Rallvah*."

Immediately, Brina felt her throat open and cool air flooded her lungs. The heat in her face faded away as she focused on slowing her breathing to a normal speed.

"What happened?" Aidan looked to the healer for an answer.

"Allergic reaction. It's rare, but it does happen." Jacen put the back of his hand on Brina's forehead. He directed his question to her. "How do you feel now?"

Brina nodded. "Better." She handed the bottle back to the healer.

Jacen frowned as he took the medicine. "I'm sorry, but this means your arm has to heal without magic."

"Without magic?" Thana sounded more horrified than Brina felt.

"It can be done. It just takes much longer."

"How long?" Brina tried to stifle the hope suddenly blooming inside her.

"At least a month. Maybe a week more."

"That's awful!" Thana turned to her friend.

"And I'll need to see you every few days to see how you're doing. You should be able to get the brace off by mid-Animus," Jacen said.

"Of course." Brina didn't trust her voice to not give away the surge of joyful emotions rushing through her. She had an excuse for not doing magic for at least a month. She could stay for a month. She said a silent prayer of thanks to Elsali.

"Do you want me to contact your parents?"

Brina shook her head. "I'll do it."

"Are you sure?" A deep ringing interrupted anything else the healer was going to say.

"Dinner bell." Thana explained to Brina. "Do you need any help?"

"I'm good." Brina stood, catching a glimpse of herself in a mirror. Though her face was still chalk-white, she was steady on her feet.

"This way, m'ladies." Aidan grinned and gave a bit of a bow.

"You're a little peculiar, you know that, right?" Brina couldn't help but smile as she passed by.

Aidan's smile widened. "Nope. I'm a lot peculiar, but I don't mind the mistake." He fell into step on Brina's other side.

Halfway down the corridor, he grabbed Brina's elbow. "Shortcut." He pulled Brina to the left toward what looked like a window.

Brina gasped, sure they were going to break through the glass. A moment later, they emerged into the far eastern corner of their dining hall. They stepped out from behind a large glerna plant and joined their floor-mates in finding seats. The trio sat at the far end of the closest table, the one with the least amount of people.

"Thanks for not telling the healer about BD." Brina settled herself between Thana and Aidan. "I don't need any more problems with her."

"No problem," Aidan said easily.

"Okay, I have to know about the window." Thana leaned across Brina to speak to Aidan.

"Oh, that." Aidan waved a dismissive hand as food appeared on their table. "Found it last year about halfway through the term. It scans your wand and sends you to the dining hall for your floor. Convenient little shortcut."

"Sure is." Thana's eyes sparkled.

"So, this is your second year here?" Brina reached for a basket of rolls with her good hand.

Aidan nodded, his mouth full of food. He swallowed and elaborated. "Turned sixteen on Fidelis twelfth. You're both first years, right?"

Thana and Brina both nodded. Thana added, "But I've been away at school for years. Not around here, but all over Ortus. Daddy thought it best for me to get a well-rounded education. I never really minded, but I must say I'm glad to be in a place for more than one year. What about you, Aidan? Where did you go to school before here? Was it near your hometown and where's that exactly?" Thana paused, waiting for Aidan's response.

The young man just stared, one hand clutching his glass, mouth slightly opened. It seemed he'd forgotten all about eating in the midst of the verbal onslaught, not that Brina could blame him. She chuckled. "You'll have to excuse Thana. She does that sometimes."

Aidan found his voice. "Known each other long, have you?"

Thana answered. "Nope, we just met today. About fifteen minutes before you, as a matter of fact. I already warned Brina that I talk too much. Sorry. I really do try to be quiet, but I have all these thoughts and questions and they just come spilling out, and–"

Brina interrupted with a grin. "You're babbling, Thana. Why don't you eat something and let Aidan answer some of your questions?"

"Oh, eating, right! I almost forgot! I'm famished. I always eat a lot even though I'm so little. Daddy says he doesn't know where it all goes."

"I guess it takes a lot of energy to fuel your mouth." One side of Aidan's mouth tipped upward.

Thana nodded, having already crammed her mouth full of fried chicken. She didn't seem bothered by Aidan's half-factitious speculation.

"To answer your questions," Aidan continued. "I just went to a local school in Aliquantulus. I grew up just outside the city with my parents, three older sisters and a younger brother. My dad owns an odds-and-ends store, and I helped him manage it after school. The dorms were actually closer to the shop than our house." He glanced at Brina. "What about you? Where did the rich and powerful Fines send their youngest child?"

"Mom and Dad kept me home." Brina focused her attention on spearing a piece of chicken with her fork. "They taught me themselves."

If either Aidan or Thana thought the response was strange, they didn't show it, instead moving on to other subjects. The trio kept up a steady stream of small talk as they finished their meal. Just as they were pushing back from the table, a magnified voice echoed into the room.

"All students and staff will report to the main auditorium in twenty minutes for the welcome assembly."

"I just want to brush my teeth first." Brina looked down at Thana.

"Good idea," Aidan cheerfully agreed. "Where's your room?"

"Thirteen seventy-four." Both girls answered together.

Aidan let out a peal of laughter. "Talk about fate. I'm thirteen seventy-five."

Brina and Thana's faces brightened. If Aidan was one of their suite-mates, sharing wouldn't be so bad. The trio crossed through the common room.

"Who's your roommate?" Brina asked as they made their way through the corridor.

"Sigurd Maldve. Nice kid. A bit quiet. We've been at the same school for eight years and have roomed together just as long. His family lives four houses down from mine."

Aidan and Thana pulled out their wands and tapped their respective doors. Brina followed her new friend into their room. A minute later, all three stood at the extended sink. Five minutes after that, Aidan knocked on the open door connecting the girls' room to the bathroom.

"Come on in." Thana was rummaging through her desk for something.

"Why don't you just summon it?" Brina watched from where she sat on her bed as Thana tossed aside several paper airplanes, a half-full bottle of blue bubbles, and a folded poster of a scene Brina recognized from a show about sisters trying to find their father while they solved crimes, or something like that.

"It has an anti-summoning charm on it," Thana explained, making a face at something unrecognizable that might have once been a bunch of grapes. She threw it into the garbage and continued her search. A moment later, she straightened, a triumphant expression on her face. "Found it!" A thin silver chain dangled from her hand, and at the end of it, swung a small silver box.

"What's that?" Aidan asked from just inside the doorway.

"It records what specific people are saying. Great for taking notes when you really don't want to listen." Thana dropped the chain over her head and tucked it under her shirt in two smooth movements. "I have a really bad memory when it comes to speeches or lectures. I just can't seem to pay attention. Do either of you have any gum? I'm partial to peppermint."

Brina and Aidan shared the first of what Brina was sure would be numerous amused glances.

"No?" Thana sounded disappointed.

"Ready then?" Brina looked away from Aidan first, her stomach twisting in a not entirely unpleasant way.

"Sure. Let's go!" Thana fairly bounced out the door.

"Any shortcuts to the auditorium?" Brina asked Aidan as she watched her new friend skipping in front of her.

"Not ones I've found." Aidan, too, kept his eyes on Thana for the most part, though they occasionally darted back to Brina. "The auditorium's the most secure place in the whole school; there are hundreds of enchantments around it. Only certain wands can work in there and direct Transportation is impossible. A lot of magical stuff won't even work there, so it's a lot like the Fuhjyn field."

Brina felt a spark of hope. She'd forgotten there would be places in this mansion where she wouldn't be quite as abnormal. She even had a momentary desire to inquire about tryouts for the Fuhjyn team, then pushed the thought away. She wouldn't last long enough to get the chance to play. Suddenly, she realized Aidan had asked her a question.

"Sorry, what was that?"

"I asked if you liked to play Fuhjyn." Aidan stepped around a lost-looking first year as Thana fell back to join in the conversation.

Brina nodded. "I haven't really been able to play much. Just when my family visits since that's the only time there are enough people around to play."

"I'm pretty good." Thana spoke without the slightest hint of arrogance. "I'm small, but fast."

"You must be a Praelia." Aidan led the girls into the auditorium and steered them toward seats in the back. "Going to try out for the team?"

Thana nodded. "Yes to both. What about you two? What positions do you play?"

"Custos," Aidan answered. Both turned to Brina.

"Latet." Brina's voice was slightly embarrassed. Not many girls played the dangerous position. Without magic to repel the ball, most Latets had to be either incredibly fast or incredibly good at hiding. And, of course, they needed to be able to take a hit without breaking stride – or a bone. Pick a small, fast player, odds of contact went down, but odds of a wipeout went up. And when a Latet was on the ground, the game was lost. Even the fastest Latet couldn't run from a prone position. Most teams went for a medium to big guy who could hide well. No matter the size, most Latets spent the entire season black and blue.

"Impressive." Aidan eyed his suite-mate with a new appreciation. "You should try out for the team. Our Latet's awful."

"Who is it?" Thana asked as the trio followed a large group of students into the auditorium. One or two of the students shuddered as they passed through the entrance, Thana included. "I hate magic canceling enchantments."

"I barely notice anymore." Aidan maneuvered the group to the far corner of the room. Once seated next to Thana, he spoke again. "Gray."

"What?" Both girls looked puzzled even though Brina was the only one who'd spoken.

"Gray's the Latet for the Thirteenth Floor."

"There goes any chance I had, even if my arm was healed by then." Brina felt an odd mixture of disappointment and relief wash over her.

"Why?" Thana asked.

"Gray's the Captain. He's not going to assign me his position."

"I don't know about that." Aidan smiled, a devious light glinting in his eyes. "Give me some time."

"What–" Brina's question was cut off by Headmaster Manu coming to the stage at the front of the auditorium.

A hush fell over the room before the headmaster began speaking, so he didn't need to quiet the crowd. Nevertheless, he raised his hands and gestured for silence, as if the movement was part of the speech. When he spoke, his voice echoed back to the corners of the room, magically amplified to reach every ear. His magic, it appeared, was allowed.

"Greetings, students and staff of Audeamus. I am Headmaster Roderick Manu. For those who have returned, welcome back. For our newcomers, welcome. We're pleased to have you." The headmaster gave a wide smile. "I trust you've all been well fed and watered, and are now ready to be introduced to your future professors."

"After which we'll be treated to an exciting recitation of our school rules." Aidan muttered under his breath. "Unfortunately, the singing pandas weren't available this year, so you'll just have to make do with the same old speech."

Thana stifled a giggle, and Brina grinned. She knew she shouldn't be amused – her own father being a headmaster and all – but she couldn't help it. The off-beat sense of humor was very similar to her own.

"Something funny, ladies?" An annoyingly familiar voice came from Brina's other side. Gray seated himself in the empty seat, turning slightly so he was facing Brina. His gaze fell to her arm. "What happened?"

"Fell out of a tree." Brina glanced sideways at Thana, and then focused her attention on the headmaster who was halfway through introducing the line of professors.

"Our Botany professor, Mrs. Echinacea Fennel," Professor Manu said.

"Well, if you need assistance for anything." Gray leaned closer and whispered in Brina's ear as a professor with short, wild-looking golden hair waved at the students. "Anything at all, just let me know."

Brina replied, lips barely moving in her effort to keep from giving a sharp retort, "I'll do that."

Apparently satisfied, Gray leaned back in his seat, arms crossed over his chest.

Brina stared straight ahead, not really seeing or hearing Headmaster Manu. Hundreds of thoughts had been buzzing through her head all day, and Gray's fascination with her wasn't helping. Was it too much to ask of Elsali for the short time she had here to be drama-free?

Chapter Three: First Day of My Life

All was quiet in the dorm room. Brina lay back on her bed, staring at the ceiling. She'd survived her first day. But that hadn't really been much of a shock. No classes, no magic needed. The most she could hope for was to stay until her arm healed. After that, it was only a matter of time before she was found out.

As Brina listened to Thana's rhythmic breathing from across the room, she felt a pang of regret. She, Thana and Aidan would've become great friends, she was sure of it. And, there might have even been something more with Aidan. Now, she'd never get the chance to find out. Tears leaked from the corners of her eyes, but she didn't wipe them away. She'd cry now so when her secret was revealed, she'd be able to stay strong. Even the pain in her arm couldn't distract her from her misery. It was well past midnight before she finally fell asleep.

It felt like only a few minutes had passed before Thana was shaking her shoulder. Brina rolled over, squinting her eyes against the bright, early morning sunlight streaming through the window. Thana was already chattering.

"Our schedules were posted on our door this morning. I hope you don't mind, but I brought yours in too. It looks like Audeamus sticks with a normal school schedule, two full weeks of work and then a week off, scheduled around holidays. I like this way better than breaking the weeks into two five-day halves like they tried doing in Vosescrus. So, it looks like we have all the same classes. Our first one's in ninety minutes and I didn't know how much time you needed to get ready so I'm glad you're up. I wasn't sure if I was going to have to wake you. Aidan's already at breakfast because his first class starts in forty-five minutes, and Sigurd's been gone for a while because his first class is at six, so the bathroom's free."

Brina sat up and groaned. "You're a morning person, aren't

you?"

Thana grinned, her face lighting up. "Course I am. I've been up since dawn. Beautiful sunrise this morning. You'll have to come see it with me sometime."

"You're insane. You know that, right?" Brina climbed out of bed, thankful she'd showered the night before. Despite her broken arm, it took her only a few minutes to get dressed and gather her things. After a quick sweep of the room to make sure they hadn't forgotten anything, the girls headed for the dining room.

Aidan was finishing up his pancakes, but scooted over so Thana and Brina could take a seat next to him. Thana kept up a steady stream of chatter, allowing Brina and Aidan to exchange greetings and little more. Surprisingly, between the outflow of words, Thana managed to consume three pancakes before Aidan had to excuse himself to go to his Astronomy class. Thana and Brina both waved as he headed off to class. Thana continued her monologuing while finishing five more pancakes, two bowls of fruit and three large glasses of milk. Brina had long since finished her meal and continued sitting at the table, nodding and adding the occasional word to the conversation. She was almost as fascinated by Thana's ability to talk and eat as she was by anything else she'd seen so far. By the time Thana was done, most of the other students had left and they had only fifteen minutes to get to their class.

"Did you pass your transportation test?" Thana asked as the girls returned to their room to brush their teeth. Brina shook her head and Thana continued. "Too bad. I passed last week. Guess we'll just have to rely on my superior knowledge of the quickest ways through the school."

"Sounds like a plan." Brina smiled and followed her friend back into the hallway. Instead of turning toward the dining hall as Brina expected, Thana headed for the opposite end of the corridor. "Where are we going?"

"History." Thana grinned. "Watch this." At the end of the hall was a full-length mirror. She pressed her hand against the frame and spoke, "Third floor, room seven." She grabbed Brina's left hand. "Come on."

Before Brina could react, Thana pulled the two girls through the mirror and into a secluded corner of the third floor, just a few feet from their classroom. As the girls stepped out of the corner, Brina had the oddest feeling no one was seeing them until they took a few extra steps to join the crowd of students. Brina waited until they'd squeezed into the far back corner to question Thana.

"Will that mirror take you anywhere in the school?" Brina kept her voice low even though the chair next to her was empty.

Thana shook her head. "Only to classrooms. There are corners on each floor enchanted so no one can see you arrive, and each level with dorm rooms has a mirror. Apparently, it's for PA's to get to their classes if they're running late."

"Any Professor Assistants on our floor?"

Thana wrinkled her nose in clear distaste. "Gray. He helps Professor Belva. Apparently, business is his focus and he thinks a lot of math courses are going to get him there. Thinks he's going to double the family fortune or something like that."

"What's your focus going to be?" Brina was honestly curious as to what career her perpetually happy roommate would choose. She hadn't ever given a career path any serious thought. By the time she'd been old enough to stop wanting to be a butterfly or unicorn, she'd understood the likelihood of her being able to work anywhere was slim.

"I'm not sure. There's so much I like to do." Thana took a deep breath and began counting off subjects. "I've thought about Healing, but it takes years of studying after Audeamus and I'm not sure I could handle more school. Then I thought about Astronomy because I love the stars, but I'm definitely not a night person. Now I'm thinking about something in the entertainment industry. Probably acting because I'm not a very good singer."

Brina grinned. "I think you'd be a great actress," she replied truthfully.

"What about you? What's your focus?"

Fortunately, Brina didn't have to answer the question because a tall, slender woman suddenly appeared at the front of the room. As the professor called the class to order, Brina gave an inaudible sigh of relief. She couldn't tell Thana that she doubted she'd ever be able to declare a focus, or be able to compete in any area beyond the Fuhjyn field. Employment would be limited in her future, even if potential employers didn't find out about her little 'problem.' She turned her attention to the professor.

"I am Professor Clio Penah and this is history."

Professor Penah was pretty and almost as young-looking as Corakin. With her dark hair and eyes, and dusky skin, she had an exotic look to her, as if she was from another era. She spoke clearly, without a hint of an accent, her eyes slowly moving over each student as if she was gathering information about them with just a look. Brina suppressed a shiver as those dark eyes lingered on her. She felt almost as if the professor had seen right through her.

"I know most of you have been thoroughly educated in the basic and immediate history of Ortus and our largest cities. Names and dates, surface events. This class delves deeper into some of the darker areas: the mysteries and mythologies of our people. We will attempt to sort out fact from legend and to bring to light our deepest truths."

"I think I might like history here," Thana whispered, eyes dancing. "Secrets and mysteries. I love it!"

Brina managed a half-smile, her stomach churning at Thana's words. She suspected her secret was a far bigger mystery than anything Thana would find in class.

"Now, when I call your name, please raise your hand."

***

"Having both Law classes back to back is really going to make the morning drag out," Thana said to Brina as they left their third class of the morning.

Brina nodded in agreement, not trusting herself to speak. Argumentative Law might be a bit on the dry side, but she knew it was Practical Law that would probably be the first to reveal her secret. Less than five minutes into class, Professor Kali Geryan had assured the eager class they would be learning numerous defensive and offensive spells. The butterflies in Brina's stomach had exploded and multiplied at that moment and they'd yet to calm down.

"Ah, here we are." Thana pointed to the door at the far corner of the ninth floor.

The last of the classroom levels was virtually deserted, telling Brina they were as late as she'd thought. She made a mental note to tell Thana no more 'snack' stops between classes.

"Over here." A welcomed voice called over the pre-class chatter. Aidan waved at the girls from the far back corner.

The girls exchanged smiles and made their way through the haphazard groups of desks.

"Gray," Thana muttered.

"What?"

"Gray's watching you." Thana clarified as she slid into the seat on Aidan's left.

Brina took the desk on the right as she rolled her eyes. "You're delusional."

"Okay." Thana's tone clearly said otherwise. "If you say so."

"What's Gray doing here anyway?" Brina settled into the seat. "Didn't you say he was almost eighteen? Isn't he a bit old for this class?"

"He must not have taken his two required Language halves."
A funny look crossed Aidan's face. "And Thana's right. Gray's
watching you."

Brina stole a glance at the young man in question and
flushed. Gray's pale eyes met hers, the expression on his face
unreadable, or at least, it wasn't something Brina wanted to
read. She quickly looked away. Before Thana or Aidan could
comment, however, a side door opened with a bang and
Professor Gibberish appeared.

"Welcome, welcome all of you fabulous students of
Audeamus." The class quieted as the professor began to speak.
"I am Professor Corakin Gibberish and this is Basic Language I,
where we shall look at the rudimentary structure of our
language. Should you wish to proceed past Basic Language II,
my upper level courses progress into the language of your
choice. As it is the language on which we base our spells as
well as many of our world's languages we shall begin with
Latin." He spoke over the soft groans of his students. "By the
end of the half, your language skills in Latin should be enough
to get you through the rest of your education. Now, if you'll
take out your notebooks, we shall begin."

"Um, Professor." Thana raised her hand. "Shouldn't you
take attendance?"

"Quite right, quite right. Sorry." Professor Gibberish smiled,
completely nonplussed by the fact that a student had just
pointed out a mistake. "I do get ahead of myself. Thank you,
Thana." His gaze shifted to Brina. "And how is your arm,
Brina?"

"Better, Professor," Brina gave a half-smile. "Though I
won't be using it for a while." Off of Corakin's puzzled look,
she added, "I had an allergic reaction to the potion, so my arm
has to heal without it."

"*Niri maitea, hau da, nahiko penagarria.*"

Brina knew enough to know that the professor was saying

her injury was unfortunate, but couldn't quite get the verbatim translation.

"I truly am sorry to hear that." He glanced at Thana. "Will you be taking notes for Brina then?"

Thana nodded and Brina caught some movement out of the corner of her eye. Thana had her hand firmly wrapped around the silver chain hanging around her neck. "Of course, Professor." Thana glanced at Brina and winked.

"Now, where was I? Ah, yes, attendance." Corakin turned toward his desk and picked up a piece of paper. He raised his voice so everyone could hear him. "Tap your wand on your name. For the rest of the half, as you enter the room, the doorway will check your wand. Do not think you can send your wand with a classmate as there is an enchantment in place to prevent that."

"We've done this in other classes, you know." Gray's voice carried across the room.

"Then even you should be able to do it correctly." Thana's snide comment was equally as loud.

The door slamming shut stopped any retort Gray may have made. All eyes turned to see a pair of girls enter. Brina stifled a groan. She'd been so sure she was going to like this class. Gray she could handle. BD and Damiana, on the other hand, were just a recipe for trouble.

"You're late." Corakin pointed to two empty seats at the front of the room.

To the surprise of pretty much everyone in the class, neither BD nor her sister complained as they made their way to the seats.

"He must've gotten them in serious trouble for them to be quiet," Thana muttered. Brina and Aidan both nodded their agreement.

"Now," Corakin clapped his hands together once. "*Oportet procedere in spectaculum.*"

An hour and half later, the trio followed the crush of students through the doorway and into the hall. Once there, the crowd thinned out as everyone went their own way. The girls and Aidan headed for the stairs.

"How good are you two at foreign languages?" Aidan sounded glum.

Thana shrugged. "Passable, I guess."

"I'm pretty good." For Brina, any subject not requiring magic was fairly easy. In addition, her excellent memory and good ear for sound made languages a cinch. She downplayed her talent. "I studied some Latin before."

Thana's eyes sparkled. "Great! We can have a study group."

As they climbed past the tenth floor, they heard a shrill giggle from behind them. A familiar voice, breathlessly distorted in an attempt to be flirtatious, followed the laughter. "Gray, you're so funny."

"Damiana," Aidan muttered to his companions. "She's had a crush on Gray since last year."

"I'd say they deserve each other." Thana's voice was low.

"Somehow, I doubt Gray shares your sentiment," Brina said dryly.

Aidan glanced at Brina and then changed the subject. "What do you have right after lunch?"

Thana answered for both of the girls. "Botany."

Aidan's face brightened. "Me too."

The group from languages was one of the first into the dining hall, which meant they had their pick of the tables. The trio gravitated to the back corner again. Aidan sat across from the girls, his back to the wall. Suddenly, his face tightened and a moment later, the girls knew why.

"This seat taken?" Gray slid into the empty spot next to Brina. Looking rather annoyed, Damiana plopped herself down on Gray's other side. BD went around the table to place herself next to an unhappy Aidan.

Brina shook her head, unable to bring herself to be entirely rude to Gray. He hadn't actually done anything that warranted a less than pleasant response from her. "No one else is sitting here."

"Good." Gray's smile reached his eyes, making them glint in a way Brina didn't want to acknowledge.

Maybe she shouldn't have been so polite.

"I see you're milking that arm for all it's worth." BD spoke over the noise of everyone ordering their meals.

Brina flushed, biting her tongue to keep back a sharp retort. Thana, however, didn't have any such reservation.

"Shut it, BD," the girl snapped. "Brina wouldn't be in this situation if you hadn't broken the branch. Or put Ziege in the tree to begin with."

"You broke her arm?" Gray looked at BD, eyes flashing dangerously.

"It's not my fault she climbed up a tree for a stupid badger," BD scowled at Gray.

"Besides, there's no proof BD did anything to the branch," Damiana interjected, trying to draw Gray's attention back her way. "Maybe Brina was just too heavy."

Brina felt her face grow hot as her temper rose. She opened her mouth to speak, but was beat to it by Gray.

"Damiana, BD, why don't you two sit somewhere else?" Gray returned his gaze to Brina. "I don't really feel like listening to you talk."

Damiana recoiled as if she'd been slapped. BD, furious, spit out a response. "We're allowed to sit where we want."

"Maybe," Gray didn't bother looking as he responded. "But it doesn't mean I want you here."

"Brina." Thana nudged her friend.

With a start, Brina realized her mouth was still open. She shut it with a snap but no one else seemed to notice. To cover her embarrassment, she took a bite of her sandwich.

"What did the healer say?" Gray's tone made it clear he wasn't talking to anyone else.

Brina swallowed the bite she'd just taken and answered. "A month, minimum."

Gray's eyebrows disappeared under a fringe of hair. "That's crazy. You should go see the Headmaster. Healer Jacen isn't doing his job if it's taking you so long to heal."

Brina shook her head. It came as no surprise that Gray hadn't been paying attention in language class when she'd told Professor Gibberish what had happened. "No, that's not it. He did everything he could. I'm allergic to the potion so my arm has to heal naturally."

"That sucks." Gray leaned forward. "You'll probably need help with your classes. I can ask Headmaster Manu to be excused from my classes so I can–"

"I'm in all of Brina's classes," Thana interrupted. "I'll be helping her."

"So will I." Aidan put in. BD gave him a hurt look and then glared at Brina.

Gray scowled, eyes moving between Thana and Aidan before coming to rest on Brina again. "Well, if you ever want help from an older student, just let me know."

"Thanks." Now thoroughly embarrassed, Brina turned her attention back to her lunch. After a few minutes of uncomfortable silence, Gray stood and walked away. Damiana immediately followed though Gray didn't even acknowledge her. BD gave Aidan a scorching look which he completely ignored. With an annoyed exhalation, she went after her sister. Without taking her eyes from her plate, Brina muttered, "Does Gray always take an interest in helping the injured?"

Thana snorted laughter. "Hardly. A couple summers ago, I shattered three bones in my foot and broke my leg in four places. Gray tripped me when I was on crutches."

"That's mean." Aidan stabbed at a piece of chicken with

more vengeance than necessary.

Thana wore a grim smile of satisfaction. "When I got my cast off a couple days later, I chased him down the road and hexed him. It was two weeks before his hair started growing back."

The half hour bell rang and several older students rushed out. The trio turned their attention back to their meals which they finished in an unusual silence, each lost in their own thoughts. Brina couldn't decide what was worse, the constant worry that someone would somehow figure out she was different, or dealing with the drama of Gray thinking of her like the shiny new toy. The quarter hour bell rang and the three stood.

"Four more classes," Thana groaned. "I hope every day doesn't go this slow."

Aida shook his head. "Just wait until you start getting the work piled on. You'll be wishing for more than thirty hours in a day."

"Great," Brina muttered as she followed Thana back to their room to empty their bags.

An hour later, the girls found themselves halfway through their Botany class. Despite Brina not being overly fond of plants, she knew she'd be enjoying class with this professor. Professor Fennel's enthusiasm and fast pace more than made up for the dry material. Up close, she looked even younger than she had when Headmaster Manu had introduced her, but Brina knew she had to be at least in her mid-thirties since the youngest of the professor's three children had just started at the Audeamus Middle Academy. Brina had a feeling Professor Fennel was one of those rare professors who, no matter her age, would always find a way to connect to her students.

Regardless of how good the professor was, Brina felt her attention wandering as Professor Fennel extolled the virtues of the sharfang plant. Without the focus required by note-taking, Brina was finding it very hard to concentrate. She heard something about stewing the petals, but couldn't quite make out why this was necessary. Since Practical Botany didn't start until the second half, the class was on the seventh floor, a corner room with large windows on two sides. Out of one picture window, Brina could see the ridge of mountains dividing northern Ortus from its southern half. The tallest of the mountains glimmered with snow. Brina stared at it and the reflecting light mesmerized her. The sunlight sparkled, throwing diamonds back to Brina's dazzled eyes. It reminded her of something. Of what, she didn't know, only that it was important. Something was important. They–

"Ms. Fine?"

Brina jumped, startled more by Thana's elbow to the ribs than she was by her name.

"Brina, would you care to answer the question?" Professor Fennel arched one pale eyebrow. She sounded mildly amused.

Panicking, Brina glanced beside her. Aidan, on the other side of Thana, nodded his head minutely. Brina took the cue from him and answered. "Yes, Professor."

"Thank you, Brina. I'm sure Aidan feels fortunate to have claimed such an attentive partner." The professor looked mildly amused, but didn't say anything else.

As soon as Professor Fennel turned her attention back to the rest of the class, Brina whispered to Thana. "What was that all about?"

"Since you can't write, Professor Fennel asked who'd be your partner for tests. You were agreeing to her choice."

"Oh," Brina stole a glance at Aidan. He caught her looking and winked. Her face burned, partly in embarrassment at being caught daydreaming, but also because of the way Aidan made her stomach twist. She leaned back into her seat, feeling extremely foolish. She was never this easily distracted. Gritting her teeth against the impulse to return her attention to the window, Brina faced the professor and didn't take her eyes from petite Professor Fennel until the class ended.

"Something on your mind?" Aidan asked as the trio headed for the stairs. Their next class was one of only a few on the fifth floor.

"Hmm?" Brina only half-heard the question. Her mind was repeating the shimmering image of sunlight on snow, trying to figure out why it intrigued her so much.

"You seem a bit flustered," Thana glanced at Aidan as she spoke. His expression indicated his agreement.

"It's nothing." With great effort, Brina pulled her thoughts back to the present. "What class do we have next?"

Chapter Four: Stronger

The next few weeks were the happiest of Brina's life. She didn't need to make excuses for doing things the 'hard' way, didn't have to constantly worry about someone realizing they'd never seen her do magic. For the first time, Brina had friends. The only shadow on an otherwise great time was the occasional feeling she was missing something – a clue, an omen, some foreshadowing of things to come – but, try as she might, she couldn't actually grasp the idea and it continued to be pushed to the back of her mind as other things came up.

The first break at the end of the month of Vir, Fuhjyn tryouts, had been held. Despite the slight twinge of jealousy and regret, Brina had been truly happy when Aidan and Thana had both made the team. Aidan, with a mysterious smile, had insisted Brina not give up on the idea of playing for the thirteenth floor, but had been unwilling to provide further details. Whenever Thana and Brina had tried to get him to talk about it, he'd clammed up, but both girls had the strangest suspicion that Aidan had been planning something.

Brina had all but forgotten about Aidan's previous comments regarding Gray and the Fuhjyn team when he approached her after lunch. It was their second week off and the professors had loaded everyone up on homework. Brina was just trying to figure out what subject to work on next when Aidan entered the dining hall. He and Thana had been at practice – their first – so Brina was eating alone. Aidan plopped down across from her, muddy and sweating, a grin on his face. Brina assumed Thana was in the shower.

Without so much as a greeting, Aidan said, "We're running a scrimmage this afternoon. Want to play?"

"Um, Aidan?" Brina lifted her arm. She'd been wearing only a light brace since the first of Animus and was supposed to go back to the healer in two days to get it taken off, but it wasn't like she was anywhere close to top form.

"Come on, you can play with that." Aidan's eyes sparkled and Brina felt her resolve weakening.

She tried a different tactic. "What about Olcan Klar? Isn't he the back-up?"

Aidan shook his head. "Gray split the team in half for the scrimmage. Each team has positions to fill. He's leading one, I'm the captain of the other."

"Gray made you the other captain?" Brina was momentarily diverted by the surprise. Gray had made it pretty clear how he felt about Aidan and it was far from warm.

"The team voted," Aidan explained. "Anyway, Olcan refused to play under me, so I need a Latet."

Thana rushed up to Brina, hair still wet from the shower. "Did you hear? Aidan challenged Gray and now we get to play for—"

Brina turned from Thana to Aidan. "You did what?"

Aidan flushed and looked down. "I merely suggested Gray might not be the best choice for our Latet."

"He's a good captain though." Brina surprised everyone by defending Gray. "I mean, he chose you two, didn't he?"

"Because we blew by the competition," Thana countered. With a mischievous glint in her eyes, she added, "And I think he was hoping that picking the two of us would earn him points with you."

"Which it obviously did." Aidan glowered at a spot on the table that had apparently offended him.

Brina glared at him. "Fine, I'll play." She stood. "But if I break my arm again, you're doing my homework."

"Deal." Aidan's smile reappeared. "Go change your clothes and then Thana and I will take you down to the field to meet the rest of the team." Suddenly, he seemed to realize Thana was clean. "Why'd you take a shower? We're going to be playing again in a half hour."

"Because," Thana pulled herself up to her full height. "I, unlike some people, find that being smelly and disgusting during a meal tends to ruin the appetite, even one as substantial as mine."

"Huh." Aidan shrugged and shoved another biscuit into his mouth.

Thirty minutes later, Brina and her two friends stepped through the gates and onto the field. Brina caught her breath as she looked around.

"Beautiful, isn't it?" Aidan steered the trio toward a clearing.

Brina could only nod in agreement. She'd seen the Fuhjyn field at her father's school, but this one made the other look small. She knew both were the regulation five hundred square feet, surrounded by bleachers two hundred feet in the air so the audience could see over the various obstacles. But the similarities ended there. The other field had looked planned, the trees and rocks strategically placed over the terrain. This looked like a park had sprung up in the fenced-in area, a strange forest straight out of a fairytale. Trees of every possible type towered overhead, casting an odd bluish-green tinge to the floor beneath. Boulders and shrubs dotted the landscape. A bubbling sound nearby told Brina a stream was flowing through the field about ten yards away.

"When Daddy asked what I thought he should donate money to the school for, I immediately said this," Thana said. "And I'm so glad I did. It's the best non-professional field in all of Ortus."

"I think it's nicer than some professional fields." Brina couldn't stop staring.

"If it wasn't for the dis-magic enchantment, I'd come here all the time." Aidan sighed.

Brina started. She'd forgotten all about that part of the game. As soon as they'd stepped through the gates, Thana and Aidan had lost their magic. They were on equal footing now. Before she could dwell on the thought, however, Aidan greeted several newcomers. Brina recognized the handsome blond from the room across the hall. The other two she'd seen in the dining hall, but they were older than she was and she'd never gotten their names.

"Jordan Dyson, Mirabelle–"

"Just Mira, please." The young woman smiled at Aidan, her bright green eyes dancing, but not flirtatious. Her entire countenance said she enjoyed life and everything about it. Brina instantly liked her.

"Sorry. Mira Visu and Kane Lalloc. All Praelian." Aidan returned Mira's smile and turned to Brina. "This is Brina Fine. She's our Latet."

Jordan grinned. "I think you're in the room across the hall from me."

"Thirteen seventy-four."

"Thirteen seventy-three." He held out his right hand for Brina to shake. "Latet, huh? Is that how you broke your arm?"

Brina shook her head. Before she could answer, Mira spoke up. "You're the girl who fell out of the tree on the first day here."

"Not exactly," Brina muttered, ears hot.

"BD hexed the branch," Thana interjected.

"Yeah, that sounds like my cousin." Kane's tone was dark. Brina looked at him, startled.

"Don't hold it against me." The young man's olive-green eyes were open and honest. "I'm sure you know what it's like dealing with family." He raised one dark eyebrow. "Miss Fine, is it?"

Brina grinned. He was right. She was the last person who should judge someone based on their family.

Less than ten minutes later, Brina was surrounded by the rest of Aidan's hand-picked Fuhjyn team. Other than Thana, Aidan had brought only two from Gray's team: Kane and the Custos backup, a fifteen year-old named Rose Hanover. The rest were people he'd remembered from tryouts. Most were students Brina recognized but didn't actually know. A few, like Rose and a fiery girl named Harper de la Vega, were in many of Brina's classes. The rest were older students like Mira and Kane, but none had a problem deferring to Aidan's leadership.

Case in point, Aidan was now addressing the entire team, and no one's attention was wavering. "Even though we haven't practiced together, we have the better athletes and we know Gray's team. We can beat them." He looked at each person individually. "Let's not worry about plays or anything complicated. Let's just have fun and see what we can do."

"Nice players, Aidan." Gray's voice cut through the air. All eyes turned toward his voice to watch as Gray sauntered across the field, leading his team. His tone dripped sarcasm. "Looks like you got the best of the best." His gaze came to rest on Brina. "Maybe there's truth to that after all." His eyes returned to Aidan. "Didn't take you long to fill the roster."

"Or you." Aidan's normally warm voice had cooled considerably.

"Here." Gray tossed a thin leather strap to Aidan. "Who's your Latet?"

Aidan kept his focus on Gray. "Thana, help Brina put that on."

"She's got a broken arm." A petite girl behind Gray spoke up. Her gray eyes flashed and she ran a hand through her short-cropped orange hair. Brina recognized her from a room down the hall, and had a vague recollection of being the subject of one of the girl's scathing glares for some unknown reason.

"She's going to get hurt." Gray directed his comment to Aidan.

"I'll be fine." Brina hoped her voice didn't reveal her jumbled nerves. She glanced down at her ankle. The leather strap fit snugly around the ankle. In the center of it, a small blue light glowed, signaling the game hadn't yet begun.

"I saw Professor Geryan on my way over and she said she could referee for us." One of the eighteen year-old Caw twins – Brina still couldn't tell Alhena from Almeisan – tossed a ball to Gray.

Brina immediately noted the color. Each team had a ball with which to tag the opposing Latet, and each ball was the color of the team, or for a school team, the floor's color. Since they weren't a professional team, the ball used to score was striped in the Audeamus colors rather than the field colors. In this case, it was dark blue and silver. The ball in Gray's hand was a bright yellow. Behind him, Brina caught a glimpse of the lime green that represented the Thirteenth Floor.

"I borrowed the Twelfth Floor's ball from the Knight twins." Gray threw the yellow ball at Aidan a bit harder than necessary.

Aidan caught it and then tossed it behind him to a petite Praelia named Katie Wright. The brunette caught it with a smile, and immediately began to spin it on her finger.

"All right Captains." Professor Geryan's voice boomed from the speakers mounted around the stadium. "Shake hands."

Aidan and Gray gripped each other's hands with enough force to whiten their knuckles, but neither one flinched.

Professor Geryan continued. "You have two minutes to situate your teams. The Latet's band will beep a ten-second warning. After that, the light goes green. Remember, if the light goes red, you've lost your team fifty points. Good luck to you both."

Aidan gathered his team together, but before he could start issuing directions, Brina spoke up. "If Thana can tell me a quick layout of the field, I can get a head start."

"Good idea." Aidan nodded once and turned his attention to the rest of the team.

Thana picked up a stick and quickly sketched a square in the dirt. She pointed out the main landmarks: the stream, the biggest boulders – including the one that looked like a giant guinea pig – the ancient oak tree towering over the center and, of course, the goal posts for both teams.

"Thanks." Brina turned to go.

"You'll remember all that?"

Brina grinned and tapped her temple with one finger. "Photographic memory." Then, with a graceful stride, she disappeared into a thicket. Once out of sight, Brina turned sharply to the right, heading for the stream. Since she only knew the basic layout and wouldn't be able to move as freely as usual, she'd have to think faster, a challenge she relished. An idea had struck her, but she wasn't sure if it would work, or if she could get there fast enough. Just as she jumped from the last rock to the opposite bank, the band around her ankle beeped loudly. A few feet away, another Latet alarm sounded.

"Over there!"

Brina heard someone call out and darted behind a bush just as the light on her band turned green and Professor Geryan announced the start of the match. Relying solely on instinct, Brina tucked herself into the bush, hiding her long braid in her dark clothes. She began counting as she heard Gray's team rush by. Years of practice had taught her to keep two counts and she did this now. One for the numbers passing by and one for the seconds she had left.

"I'm telling you, I heard the ten-second warning." One of the twins was just outside Brina's hiding place.

"Stay here." Gray's voice was softer. "Listen for the beeps. If you can trap her, great." He took a few steps and then stopped. "Try not to actually injure her."

Either Alhena or Almeisan snickered, then one of them spoke, "Don't want your pretty girlfriend all bruised up?"

"Watch the attitude. You can be replaced." Gray's voice was cold. A moment later, Brina heard the captain's footsteps fading away.

Brina knew the young man was out of hearing range when

one of the twins spoke, "I don't know why Gray is wasting his time with the Fine girl. The family may be big news, but she isn't anything special."

"And consider the company she keeps."

Brina took a slow, deep breath, pushed the comments out of her head, and prepared to run. By her count, only the twins remained nearby. She couldn't tell the two of them apart, but it didn't matter which one was which, only that they were there. Brina picked out her mark – a cove of pine trees thick enough to protect her back as she ran – and gave herself a three second countdown. A moment later, Brina got the distraction she needed.

Professor Geryan's voice boomed out. "Thana Decker takes possession for Aidan's team."

Before the first syllable died away, Brina burst from her hiding spot in a full sprint. The cursing behind her told her two things. One, the twins had spotted her, and, two, she'd caught them off guard. She heard them start pursuit as she zig-zagged across the clearing. Just before she reached the trees, a dull thud on her shoulder knocked her off balance. Instead of fighting it, Brina allowed her body to spin completely around. Even as the twins yelled, the amplified voice confirmed the hit.

"The Caw twins strike Aidan's Latet. Score is fifty to zero, Gray's team in the lead."

Brina cut between two trees, ignoring the throbbing in her shoulder. She could hear the twins breaking through the underbrush. She sprinted across the next clearing and, instead of going through the kilter trees, ducked behind a boulder and waited. Seconds later, the twins emerged from the pines. As Brina had hoped, the girls went through to the second cove without breaking stride.

"Jasper Pressman tags the Latet. Aidan's team ties Gray's team at fifty."

Brina grinned as she cut back through the clearing. She was

almost there.

"Mirabelle Visu scores. Aidan's team leads fifty-five to fifty. Amos Watson takes possession of the ball for Gray's team."

From the corner of her eye, Brina caught a flash of color. She didn't know which team it belonged to, but pushed herself forward even faster. Her sharp eyes took in everything as she ran. Just as she'd hoped, a smaller tree stood in the shadow of the towering center oak. Without missing a step, Brina veered slightly, heading for the smaller of the two trees. She grabbed a branch with her good hand and pushed off with her feet, using her momentum to swing her up onto the branch.

"Foul by Flanagan Laise on Kane Lalloc. Penalty shot to Lalloc."

Brina took a few seconds to catch her breath before standing up, balancing gracefully on the branch.

"That's probably not a good idea." Nineteen year-old Becca Davenport had spotted Brina.

Brina just grinned and pulled herself up higher. Now she could see over the boulder and caught a glimpse of Gray's hair. She gestured to Becca who nodded.

"Kane Lalloc scores on the penalty shot. Aidan's team leads sixty to fifty. Anard Faust takes possession for Gray's team."

"Harper!" Becca's blue eyes didn't move from their lock on Gray's position. "Hurry up–"

A shout behind Brina cut through the rest of Becca's sentence. "Their Latet's in the tree. Get the twins!" Buck Posey called behind him as he ran past.

"Brina, get out of here!" Thana was right behind Buck.

"Foul by Devon Murphy on Gilbert Hanover. Penalty shot to Gray's team. Retaliatory foul by Persephone Asgard on Devon Murphy. Penalty shot and change of possession to Aidan's team."

By the time Professor Geryan finished her announcement, the Caw twins had arrived, and Brina had scrambled up several feet. She could see little now through the thick foliage, but could hear the twins calling to each other as they circled the base of the tree, trying to find a place where they could get a clear shot.

"Save by Aidan. Score remains sixty to fifty in Aidan's favor."

"You'll have to come down soon," one of the girls called up. "Or you'll lose points for not moving."

Brina paid them no mind as she studied the tree across from her. She'd been keeping count almost without thinking and knew she had only a few seconds to make a decision. Beneath her, she heard the teams heading for the opposite goal. A half grin came to her face. She braced herself against the tree, and tensed muscles she'd developed over years of doing things the hard way. "Here it goes." She muttered to herself and pushed off. She heard exclamations from below as she soared across the empty space between the trees. A stab of pain shot through her arm as she grabbed at a branch. For one terrifying moment, she thought her grip would fail, then her hold tightened and she found herself colliding with one side of the old tree.

"Devon Murphy scores. Aidan's team leads sixty-five to fifty. Thana Decker takes possession for Aidan's team."

"Did she just jump into the tree?"

Brina grinned at the incredulity in the voice of the twins below her. She risked a quick glance below her to make sure the Cleptas didn't have a clear shot. Then, she balanced herself and began counting.

"Save by Sterling James. Score unchanged. Aldis Watson takes possession for Gray's team."

Brina shook her head in annoyance. Sterling James was huge, easily six and a half feet tall, and almost half as wide as the goal. He would barely need to move to cover most of the net. It was pretty smart of Gray to pick someone so big, but once the team figured out Sterling's weak spots, it was all over.

He'd never be able to move fast enough.

"Harper de la Vega steals the ball from Aldis Watson and passes off to Katie Wright."

Brina quickly scaled the next few branches, moving the necessary five feet to keep her alarm from beeping.

"Katie Wright scores. Becca Davenport strikes the Latet. Aidan's team leads one hundred twenty to fifty. Gilbert Hanover takes possession for Gray's team."

Below her, Brina could hear the Caw twins shouting to each other and to whoever else was nearby. Neither one seemed pleased with their inability to find an opening to Brina. Halfway up the tree, Brina kept counting.

***

"Brilliant! Absolutely brilliant!" Thana threw her arm around Brina's shoulders. "I wish I could've seen those twins gaping up at the tree like a couple of *macchas*." Thana fairly danced up the path. Aidan and Brina couldn't stop grinning. A few yards in front of them, the rest of Aidan's team was cheering and hollering. Gray's team had cleared out immediately following the final buzzer. Brina was fairly sure the story of their match would be cast in a less than truthful light by the time her team reached the school, but it didn't bother Brina because, for the first time, she felt like a normal person.

"I've never seen anyone do that before." Aidan walked on Brina's other side, his eyes sparkling. "I thought Gray was going to have a fit when he heard the final score."

Brina shrugged. "Yeah, I doubt he'll be offering to help me again any time soon."

Aidan's smile widened. "That's okay. With Thana and I around, you won't need his help."

"Don't sound so pleased," Thana muttered. Aidan glared at her, but Brina didn't acknowledge the exchange.

"Brina!" Professor Geryan hurried across the grounds. Apparently, she'd been waiting for the team to return.

"Professor?" Brina allowed Aidan and Thana to pull ahead a few paces.

"Quite an impressive feat you accomplished." Professor Geryan's dark eyes shone. "Where'd you play before?"

"Just at home." Brina and the professor followed the others into the mansion.

"Really?" The professor sounded surprised. "Then where did you get such a creative defense?"

Brina shrugged. "It just made sense. I needed something simple and, since I didn't know the terrain, the tree seemed like the best shot."

"Why didn't you try out for the team?"

Brina raised her arm.

"It didn't seem to slow you down today." The professor walked up the stairs next to Brina. Thana and Aidan had fallen back a couple steps from the rest of the group and were acting like they weren't interested as they listened intently to the conversation.

"Gray's the captain and the Latet. No way is he giving up his position." Brina could feel the professor's surprise at her nonchalant tone.

"We'll see," Professor Geryan said. She ignored the look of surprise Brina threw her way. "I'll see you kids later."

"What was that all about?" Thana sounded perfectly innocent, but Brina wasn't fooled. When Brina merely raised an eyebrow, Thana smiled guiltily. "Well, what are you going to do about it?"

Brina shrugged off the question. "How much time until dinner?"

"About three hours before the dining hall opens for the earliest dinner," Aidan answered.

"*Quod sugit.* I'm starved," Brina scowled.

Thana chuckled and Brina threw her a dirty look. Thana grinned in response. "I've got some food in our room."

"Really?" Brina was startled out of her annoyance.

"Dad had the new cook send some snacks yesterday."

"That's what was in that big box you got?" Brina followed Thana into the dining hall. She'd already learned that, for the Deckers, having servants was more to keep Thana's father from accidentally burning down the house while trying to cook or clean than because they didn't want to do their own work. Thana loved telling the story of how her dad had caught the curtains on fire when she was seven because he'd been convinced he could do the spell to clean them.

Anything else Brina might have thought was drowned out by the thunderous applause that greeted them. About half of the Thirteenth Floor were gathered in the center of the room, cheering. Aidan smiled as Thana took a mock bow. Brina attempted to hide behind Thana, which just amused the others even more. In the background, Brina caught a glimpse of Gray in the shadows, a vicious scowl marring his handsome face.

Chapter Five: Time Has Come Today

The corridors were deserted as Brina headed back to her floor. As soon as she'd left the healing wing, she'd realized she'd left her wand in her room, which meant she'd have to take the long way around rather than using the mirror shortcut. The extra time didn't bother her; she rarely thought about stuff like that anymore. She almost felt normal, but had a bad feeling all of that would be coming to an end soon. She flexed her hand and frowned. It didn't hurt, but it was pale and weak. None of it mattered though. What did matter was she'd be expected to do her own wand work now. She was still running things over in her mind when she reached the dining hall. It was already packed and she scanned the tables.

"Bri!"

Brina smiled despite herself when she heard Aidan's voice. Thana was waving one hand. The other was busy keeping the girl's mouth full of whatever was for dinner. Aidan called her name again, and Brina wove her way through the tables and students. She slid into the empty seat between Thana and Aidan, eager to hear about the rumor of a complaint Gray had supposedly lodged against Aidan. Dinner was fried chicken and, judging by the pile of bones on Thana's plate, several birds had already been devoured.

"Thought you weren't getting your brace off for a couple more days." Aidan gestured to Brina's arm.

"Figured if I could play Fuhjyn, I could get rid of it." Brina tried to make her voice sound relieved. Aidan appeared to buy it, but the look Thana gave said something else. Brina ignored it. Instead, she turned to Aidan and asked, "So what ended up happening with Gray?"

Aidan grinned and took the bait, filling in all the blanks from the hour before. Thana interjected occasional comments to add flavor, but kept darting sideways looks at Brina as both girls ate. When Aidan excitedly explained to Brina that Professor Geryan was questioning Gray's validity to captain, Brina's smile became genuine. She really was glad Aidan would get his chance to lead, even though it would be after she was gone. Suddenly, the reality of what she was losing washed over her and she wasn't sure she could keep up the charade.

"I've got some homework I need to finish." Brina interrupted Aidan. She ignored the startled expressions on her friends' faces and bolted from the table.

***

"What was that about?" Aidan's eyes widened as he watched Brina practically flee from the dining hall.

"I don't know for sure." For once Thana was somber. "But I have an idea." She bit her lip, internally debating something. "I'll talk to you later." She left Aidan looking even more bewildered than before.

A few moments later, Thana quietly entered her room and stood in the doorway, watching her roommate taking clothes out of her closet and tossing them on the bed. As Thana watched, her sharp eyes found something that confirmed her suspicions. It took her almost more time to process the information than it did to act on it, which was saying something. She stepped into the room. "Need help?"

Brina started and spun around. "Oh, Thana. Hi." She swiped the back of her hand across her eyes.

"Going somewhere?" Thana kept her voice light as she crossed to Brina's side.

Brina looked away, apparently unable to meet her friend's eyes. "It's not what–"

"Not what it looks like?" Thana's tone was uncharacteristically soft as she reached down, picking up the item that had caught her attention. "Really? Cuz it looks like you're planning on leaving because you can't do magic." She stretched out a hand toward Brina, the slender hemlock wand held between delicate fingers.

Brina's jaw dropped. "How... what... how?"

"It wasn't so hard." Thana perched on the edge of her bed. "Well, if you're me."

"Did you...?"

"Your secret's safe with me." Thana smiled. "I didn't tell anyone and I don't plan to."

Brina's expression went from unreadable to puzzled in a split second. "Why?"

It was Thana's turn to look shocked. "You're my friend, Bri." Thana jumped up. How could she sit still when so many exciting things needed to be done? "Now, the question is, how do we keep this from everyone else?"

***

The classroom was already half-full when Brina and Thana reached it. At the door, Brina began to turn. Thana grabbed Brina's arm. "It'll be okay. Trust me." Brina nodded once and followed Thana into Law class. The girls wound their way through the desks until they reached their usual back corner.

"All right, all right." Professor Geryan raised her hands to quiet the class. "Pair up for wand work."

Students quickly moved to stand by their usual partner. Brina felt the knots in her stomach tighten, and her hand clenched around her wand. Thana put a hand on her arm, but the gesture failed to soothe her nerves.

"Today we're going to work on incapacitating spells." Professor Geryan stepped out from behind her desk. "What spell would be the best for this?"

Brina raised her hand. She and Thana had agreed that Brina's knowledge of what to do would go a long way in selling the act they would be playing. It also made Brina feel better about getting her friend involved in all of this.

"Ms. Fine?"

"*Moratorium.* The hindrance spell."

"Excellent, Ms. Fine," Professor Geryan said. "And what would the practical application of this particular spell be?"

Brina raised her hand again and the professor nodded at her to continue. "Either for protection to prevent an attack or for law enforcement to detain a suspect."

"Very good. Now, who will demonstrate this spell for us?" Professor Geryan looked around the room and then pointed at Thana. "Ms. Decker. Thank you. Please cast the spell on your partner."

Thana grinned. "All right, Brina."

Brina took a step toward Thana.

"*Moratorium.*" Thana flicked the tip of her wand and Brina's legs locked in place.

"Excellent, Ms. Decker." Professor Geryan smiled. She waved her wand, and Brina felt her muscles once again under her control. "Now, in pairs, practice the spell on each other."

Thana motioned for Brina to follow her further away from the rest of the class, giving them a bit of extra time before they'd be graded. A quick study, Thana mastered the spell before Professor Geryan made it around to the pair. As the professor approached, Brina and Thana switched places and performed the choreography they'd rehearsed the night before.

"Very good, Ms. Fine." Professor Geryan praised Brina. "It's nice to see your wand work wasn't effected by your injury."

"No ma'am." Brina managed to keep her expression and tone neutral.

"Keep up the good work." The professor moved on.

"I can't believe she bought it." Brina waited until Professor Geryan was out of earshot before whispering to Thana.

"I told you it would work." Thana smiled. "I'm an excellent

actress."

"One class down, only a couple more to go." Brina wasn't quite as optimistic as her friend. "Do you really think we can get away with this?"

"Of course." Thana's eyes sparkled. "Besides, the risk is what makes it fun."

"Glad you're having fun," Brina said. She'd never found anything so not fun in her life.

As Thana opened her mouth for another retort, the bell rang and students scrambled to pick up their books. Thana grinned and followed Brina to their next class, which was fortunately with their favorite professor. Corakin lifted a hand in greeting as the girls crossed to their usual seats, but didn't say anything. He seemed preoccupied with a bowl of shiny silver bead-like things he was poking with his wand while muttering under his breath.

"Have fun in class today?" Aidan directed the question at both girls, but his eyes barely passed over Thana before settling on Brina.

The tiny girl smirked and Brina shot her a glare. Brina started to respond, but an exclamation from the front of the room distracted everyone. As did the silver flames now covering Corakin's desk.

"*Hoc est non bonum!* I've accidentally made napalm." Corakin clapped his hands together and raised his voice. "*Achtung, achtung*! If everyone would please move to the adjacent classroom, I will be with you shortly."

***

Thana bounded into the room with more energy than anyone should have rightly have before dawn had fully come. Her smile, though, was infectious and Brina found herself grinning in spite of the unseemly hour.

"What?" Brina couldn't take the waiting, particularly

because it was accompanied by Thana bouncing on the foot of Brina's bed.

"Professor Geryan just posted a notice in the dining hall." Thana jumped to her feet. "There's going to be a re-vote for Fuhjyn captain next week. They're even going to cancel afternoon classes for it. Aidan versus Gray, and if Aidan wins, there'll be new tryouts!" Thana practically squealed. "You can be on the team too!"

"Don't get your hopes up." Brina wasn't sure if she was talking to Thana or herself, "Gray's good."

"You're better," Thana said. She winked and smugly added, "Besides, Aidan prefers you."

Brina felt her face grow hot under the double meaning. She didn't want to think about that. She kicked aside her covers and swung her legs over the side of her bed.

Thana's tone softened. "You care about him too. I know you do."

Brina gave her friend a look she hoped said she didn't want to talk about it. The message must've gotten through because, mercifully, Thana didn't say another word. Brina headed for the bathroom, feeling a sudden need for a very hot shower to relax her now-tense muscles.

When Brina emerged from the bathroom, slightly less sleepy and far less rumpled, Thana had apparently decided not to broach the subject again because all of her chatter was about anything but Aidan. Brina relaxed as they headed down the hall. As usual, Aidan had saved them seats. He waved, greeting them both by name, but only lighting up when his eyes landed on Brina. Thana snorted in amusement as she sat on one side of Brina, earning a dirty look from the other girl. Brina just hoped Thana would leave it there. She had enough to worry about without trying to figure out whatever this was between her and Aidan. Besides, she couldn't base a relationship on a lie and there was no way she would be telling him the truth any time soon.

Chapter Six: Dirty Little Secret

"One of the most ancient secrets of Ortus has its origin here, on our very grounds," Professor Penah walked the length of the classroom, every eye on her as she spoke. She never yelled, rarely raised her voice even, but she never needed to. She had the gift of keeping her students' attention with little effort on her part. "Can anyone tell me what it is?"

Thana raised her hand and the professor nodded at her. "The fountain?"

"Correct," Professor Penah nodded. "It has many names: Fountain of Words, Fountain of the Unknown, and Key of the Guardians, to name just a few. There is no record of its creation and thousands of theories as to who made it and why."

Brina raised her hand. "What about the words on it?"

The professor's dark eyes gave Brina an appraising look. "No one knows what they say, leading many to believe they are written in a lost tongue. Others hold to the theory that the words are part of an ancient prophecy and only the one about whom the prophecy was made will be able to read what is carved into the stone."

As Professor Penah turned away, Brina found herself thinking about the fountain and those mysterious words. If she could just study it, she'd be able to figure it out, she was certain, no matter what theorists said. Unlocking the secrets of Ortus's greatest mystery. Now, that would be something her parents could be proud of, magic or no.

Days later, Brina found herself there, at the fountain yet again. Something kept drawing her back, that much she knew. What troubled her was not knowing who or what it was. Every time, she would stare at the letters for hours, feeling as if she'd seen the characters before. Perhaps in a dream. She shook her head and resumed her pacing. Something obvious was there, something she just wasn't seeing.

"Couldn't sleep?"

Brina stopped, mid-stride, at the low voice. The soft tones were familiar and she turned. The shadowed figure took a step forward.

"I like it here," she said, crossing her arms over her chest. "It's peaceful."

"That it is," Gray agreed, something very un-peaceful in his eyes. He took another step, closing the distance with his long strides.

Brina moved back, coming to an abrupt halt when her legs came in contact with the edge of the fountain. A jolt of electricity shot through her body, making her limbs go rigid, the hairs on her arms stand on end. The sensation was unlike anything Brina had ever experienced, a mixture of pain, pleasure and pure energy exploding through every cell, and it didn't stop or lessen. After almost a full minute, Brina's body began to absorb it. Her muscles unclenched and her eyes refocused. Her heart was pounding.

Gray's face was only a few centimeters from her own. And moving closer.

Without a conscious thought, Brina side-stepped, breaking contact with the cool stone at her back. The loss was nearly as startling as the initial shock and Brina stumbled. In the second she took to right herself, Gray was at her side. His hand closed on her upper arm, steadying her, but, as she straightened, his grip didn't loosen.

"I'm fine. You can let go now." Brina kept her voice mild, eyes locked on Gray's hand. When he didn't respond, she spoke again, voice harder. "Gray, let go."

"Come on, Brina," Gray's voice was silky, sensual... and dark. "We could be amazing together. Two of the world's most powerful families, joined." His head bent toward her, pale eyes locked with Brina's violet ones.

"Gray, no," Brina pushed against Gray with her free hand,

twisting her other arm in an attempt to break free.

"Brina, yes." Gray's tone was mocking. "I'm the best offer you'll ever get." His lips brushed against her cheek as she turned her head away. He swore and grabbed Brina's chin, forcing her to turn her face back towards him.

Brina's temper flared at the combination insult and assault. Before she could consider the possible ramifications, she clenched her fist, drew back, and let go, landing a solid hit against Gray's jaw. The force and surprise broke Gray's grip, and he stumbled backwards, hand now at his face in shock. "*Kahaba*! You hit me!"

"That's no way to speak to a lady." A deep voice came from the garden entrance, and Aidan stepped forward, eyes blazing, wand out. "If you don't back off, I'll hex you, and it'll be less pleasant than an aching jaw, I promise you."

Gray's eyes darted from Brina to Aidan and back again, loathing etched onto his handsome face. With a scowl, he hurried away, still holding the swelling side of his face.

"Are you all right?" Aidan crossed to Brina's side as soon as Gray disappeared.

Brina nodded, then winced as she unclenched her fist. Aidan reached for Brina's hand even as he pocketed his wand. He examined her knuckles, tips of his fingers brushing over her soft skin. Brina shivered at his touch; a feeling similar to the one she'd experienced coming in contact with the fountain spread out from where his skin touched hers.

"Doesn't look like you broke anything," Aidan looked up from his examination.

"Too bad," Brina quipped. "I was hoping for at least a cracked jaw."

Aidan, however, didn't smile. "What were you thinking, punching Gray like that?"

"I was thinking I didn't want him kissing me and he wasn't taking no for an answer." Brina jerked her hand away from

Aidan.

"I meant," Aidan's tone softened. "Why did you hit him instead of cursing him? Your wand arm was free."

"Oh." Brina ducked her head so Aidan couldn't see the expression on her face as she sought for a plausible lie.

"Brina," Aidan hooked a finger under Brina's chin and lifted her face so their eyes could meet, but he didn't hold her there like Gray had done. "What's going on? I know something is up. I see how you and Thana look at each other, as if you're hiding some big secret. Is there something wrong with your magic?"

Brina chuckled, a low, bitter sound. "That's not possible." A puzzled expression crossed Aidan's face. Brina sighed. She didn't want to hide from Aidan anymore, even if it meant exposing her secret. She was so tired of lying to the people she cared about. "It's not possible because I don't have any magic. Never have."

Myriad expressions crossed Aidan's face in quick succession, starting with disbelief and ending in admiration. "You do everything without magic."

"Yeah, I'm a freak that way." Brina blinked back tears. Her emotions were all over the place tonight.

"Not a freak," Aidan's eyes blazed. He slid his hand around the back of Brina's neck, thumb resting at the base of her jaw. "You're something unique, special. Something, someone, amazing." He bent his head and Brina put a hand on his chest. He hesitated, unsure if she would push him away as she'd tried to do to Gray. Instead, she clutched at the front of his shirt and pulled him the last few centimeters needed for their lips to touch.

A quarter of an hour later, Brina tried to make it back into her bed without waking Thana. In one sense, she succeeded. She didn't wake her friend because Thana wasn't sleeping. Instead, the tiny teenager was curled, cat-like, on top of Brina's comforter. Thana took one look at Brina's flushed face and sat up immediately. "Tell me everything."

Brina stretched out on the chaos that was Thana's bed and propped her head up on her arm. Face flaming, Brina started with Gray's appearance and ended with an embarrassed trail off. To her immense relief, aside from a wicked grin, Thana didn't acknowledge the romantic interlude, instead focusing on Brina's reason for being in the garden in the first place. A focus that Brina was all too happy to follow.

"There's something about the writing on the stones. Something I feel like I should recognize. Like I could see it out of the corner of my eyes if I just tried a bit harder." Brina clenched her hand in frustration, ignoring the throb of pain from her bruised knuckles.

"I think," Thana's normally cheerful voice was surprisingly grim, "it's time to do some research about this fountain thing."

"Research?" That hadn't been what Brina was expecting from her action-oriented roommate.

Thana sighed, a truly exasperated sound. "Really, Brina?" She tucked her legs under her sparkling pink and purple bathrobe as she continued. "You're the only person in the history of the world to be born without any magical ability, yet you have this strange connection with one of our world's greatest mysteries. I, for one, don't believe in coincidences. Or," she added as an afterthought, "leprechauns."

Brina smiled. "I don't believe in leprechauns either."

"Good. Then we'll head to the library first thing."

As Brina watched her friend skip back to the other side of the room, she commented, "Is it bad I completely understood the connection between the leprechauns and the library?"

"Nope." Thana grinned. "Now get some sleep because we've got a busy day tomorrow." Her eyes sparkled as she succumbed to temptation. "I would wish you sweet dreams, but I'm sure you won't need any wishing on my part."

Brina stuck out her tongue. "*Troshitje.*"

Thana chuckled and crawled under her blankets. Less than five minutes later, she was sound asleep. Brina, however, took much longer to drift off, her mind replaying the night's events in a strange swirl of emotions. Her final thought before finally drifting off to sleep was of how Aidan, so fair that one would think of sunlight and spring, smelled of cedar and Spanish moss and things Brina immediately associated with the night sky. She smiled. Her nighttime musings always got a little poetic. Her subsequent foray into dreamland proved Thana right: dreams beyond sweet. They were, in fact, so saccharine that when, several hours later, Thana burst out of the bathroom, singing at the top of her lungs, Brina buried her head in her pillow, eager to return. Unfortunately, Thana's choice of song had succeeded in banishing the images of a pleasant picnic for two, and Brina rolled over with a resigned groan. She'd never understand her friend's obsession with the Dark Wonder's song "Get Off My Goat."

Hours later, while safely sitting in the back of Language class, Thana and Brina explained to Aidan why they hadn't met him for breakfast. In the background, Professor Gibberish was testing each student on the proper pronunciation of specific phrases. This task seemed to be as pointless as the research the girls had done over the past couple hours.

"No, Mr. Plumb, you are not correct. You said, 'I am the battle beaver.' Try again."

Brina covered her mouth to muffle a snicker as Gray massacred another incoherent sentence. A few others in the class laughed as Corakin explained that the use of 'I am not a trash monkey' could result in turning oneself into said monkey rather than the desired spell to augment sight and understanding. Thana tucked her notebook under her language notes as the professor turned. The trio arranged their faces into what Brina hoped were entirely innocent expressions.

"Ms. Fine, perhaps you could give us the proper

incantation." If Professor Gibberish had noticed anything odd about the friends' behavior, he didn't mention it.

Resisting the childish impulse to smirk in Gray's direction, Brina said, "*Permissum mihi animadverto quod audite.*"

"*Valde bonus.*" Corakin clapped twice as he spun to face the rest of the class. "Now, the rest of you together." He held up his hands to conduct the chorus and Thana returned to her summary of what she and Brina had found in the library that morning.

"There's probably three to four hundred myths about the fountain alone." Thana kept her voice low. "And another couple hundred about the writing. So far, the only commonality we've found is they're both ancient and no one knows their origins."

"Has anyone else had a," Aidan searched for the right word, "reaction to the fountain?"

Thana shook her head as Brina felt blood rushing to her cheeks. Part of it was the memory of what she'd felt when she'd touched the fountain. The rest came from remembering the event following the contact. Based on the heat in Aidan's eyes, he was thinking along the same lines. Both blinked when Thana snapped her fingers between their faces.

"Time for that later. Let's focus." Despite the smile, Thana's tone was stern.

"Focus on what, Thana?" Brina sighed. "There's nothing here."

"And you don't think that's suspicious?" Thana's voice dropped to a whisper.

"Never knew you were a conspiracy theorist." Aidan glanced toward Corakin who had turned his attention to eighteen year-old Zoe Bohr and her utterly disastrous attempt at speaking Latin.

"Unless, Miss Bohr, you intended to refer to yourself as a crying cross-eyed cat, you need to try again."

"I'm not one of those nuts who think Mazzie Greene is still alive or Ethan McGee was killed by his girlfriend and buried in their backyard." Thana rolled her eyes as she mentioned two of the more popular urban legends at the moment. "I just think there's something a little strange about the lack of substantial information about something so old."

Whatever else Thana had intended to say was abandoned as Professor Gibberish stopped directly in front of their seats as he addressed Zoe's best friend, Asha Kirke.

"Perhaps, Ms. Kirke, you could now explain to the class why you just said, 'the girl with the pirate hat was doing pirouettes.'"

The topic of the mysterious writing wasn't broached again until the class ended and the students made their way down to the dining hall for lunch.

Thana picked up the conversation on whatever train of thought she'd been having when the bell rang. "The theory with the most plausibility is that the fountain and the writing are some sort of protection."

"Protection against who?" Aidan fell in line behind Brina.

Even Thana looked worried. "Or what."

***

"This is pointless." Thana threw down her book in frustration. "Every single one says the same thing: nothing."

"If the most exceptional minds Ortus has ever known haven't been able to figure this out in thousands of years, did you really think three teenagers would crack it in three weeks?" Brina raised an eyebrow.

"No," Thana reluctantly admitted. "But I was hoping."

"Well, it was time to take a break anyway." Aidan stood and stretched. "Fuhjyn practice."

"Yes, my captain." Thana saluted as Aidan helped Brina to her feet.

"If we don't win our first match, Gray's going to dispute my position." Aidan reminded Thana, his anxiety clear in his voice.

Aidan had won the vote for Fuhjyn captain by a landslide, but Gray and the rest of the old team who hadn't been selected during the new tryouts had taken every opportunity to disparage him. The fact that Aidan's girlfriend and one of his best friends had made the team just made matters worse. Those on the team knew Brina and Thana were outstanding in their positions, but Aidan still worried about what others would think. The first match would be on Gnaritas twenty-first, just a few days away, kicking off the Fuhjyn season. There would be two matches a week during the third week of the month from Gnaritas to Otium, ending with the final between the top two teams on Otium twenty-ninth. The beginning of Fatum usually brought about the first major snow of the year and the ground wouldn't be seen again until the beginning of Lumen. While Audeamus didn't get hit with the worst of the snow, it did get enough to make playing safely next to impossible.

Brina gave Aidan's hand a comforting squeeze. "We'll be brilliant." She turned to Thana to address the previous statement. "After a couple of millennia, I doubt a few days more will make much of a difference."

"I suppose." Thana sighed, following her hand-holding friends out of the girls' bedroom and down the hall.

Quarter of an hour later, Aidan was directing his team onto the field. As Brina continued to familiarize herself with the various obstacles and niches throughout the terrain, including but not limited to, trees, rocks, streams, vines, and thorns, Aidan organized his players in various defensive and offensive positions.

"Brina, Thana and Aidan," Professor Penah interrupted Aidan's description of an original play he'd named The Harvelle Distraction after his favorite Fuhjyn players, twin brothers Joseph and Allen Harvelle.

"Yes, Professor?" Brina was honestly puzzled. If it had been one of the practical professors, she would've been worried they'd caught on to Thana and Aidan's classroom assistance, but history was one of the classes in which Brina's accomplishments were all her own. Still out of the corner of her eye, Brina saw Thana and Aidan exchange worried glances.

"Step over here for a moment, please."

With the eyes of their teammates on them, the trio walked toward their professor who waited patiently for them to join her. "It has come to my attention," she began, "that you three have been spending inordinate amounts of time researching the fountain in the garden."

Brina's puzzlement rose to complete confusion. She hadn't heard of any rule saying they couldn't do that. "Yes, ma'am."

Professor Penah studied Brina for a moment, dark brown eyes serious. A strange expression, one Brina couldn't identity, crossed the professor's face. "My grandmother was a historian and did quite a bit of digging into the fountain. I can send for some of her work, if you'd like."

"Uh, sure," Brina stammered. She didn't need to look at Thana or Aidan to know they wore identical expressions of surprise. An offer for resources hadn't been where she'd thought this conversation was going.

"Very good. I'll let you know when I have them." Professor Penah turned her attention to Aidan. "Good luck in your match."

As the professor headed off of the field, Brina turned to her friends. "That was weird, right?"

"Yeah," Aidan agreed.

"Little bit." Thana's tone was thoughtful. "Maybe a lot bit."

Chapter Seven: Every Rose Has Its Thorn

"They're backwards!" Brina exclaimed.

"What?" Aidan looked up from his Fuhjyn playbook. Their fourth match was in less than twenty-four hours and Aidan's nerves were beginning to show. He'd been staring at the same page for twenty minutes, which wouldn't have been odd if said page had actually contained a play. It was, however, just the cover page and bore only the words "Thirteenth Floor Fuhjyn Team." They'd won the first three matches, but this was the first rematch for a team they'd played before, which meant they'd lost the element of surprise, and Aidan was freaking out again.

"The reason everyone thinks the words are in some unknown ancient language is because the letters are written backwards." Brina held up her language notebook, showing where she'd written the first couple words. "Like a mirror image, see? It was probably so simple no one thought of it before. I mean, if you know the thing's ancient, of course you're going to think 'ancient language' before trying a mirror."

"I'll be right back." Thana leaped to her feet and dashed through the connecting bathroom into her and Brina's bedroom. She returned a moment later, small mirror in hand. Thana knelt on the floor next to Brina and Aidan set aside his book with a half-hearted sigh. The girls exchanged eye rolls and smirks as he moved from the chair where he'd been sitting to a spot on the other side of Brina. Half an hour passed before they were able to reverse the entire inscription. Now, the letters were recognizable, but the words themselves still didn't make sense.

"I really thought that would do it." Brina ran her hands through her hair in frustration. The answer was so close, she could almost touch it.

"Professor Gibberish." Thana stood. "I think he's our best bet. If anyone knows what weird language this is, it'd be him."

Ten minutes later, the trio entered the language classroom

and approached Corakin's desk. The young professor was bent over an ancient-looking manuscript while scribbling notes on a notepad. He was so intent on his work that he didn't appear hear the kids until they were just a few feet away, and then he let out a brief, high-pitched shriek before recognition dawned in his eyes.

"Uh, sorry, Professor, we didn't mean to startle you," Aidan said.

"*Nie, nie.*" He waved his hands as he set aside the manuscript and the notepad. "I'd just heard Professor K's first year Zoology class accidentally lost half a dozen enlarged spiders and I thought you were them." He gave them a sheepish smile. "How am I able to help my favorite students?"

"Could you take a look at something for us, Professor?" Brina handed the paper to the professor and tried not to think about the enlarged spiders that may or may not be loose in the school.

Corakin studied the words intently, brow furrowed in concentration. After nearly a full five minutes, he turned to his students, an expression on his face Brina could only describe as 'someone kicked my badger.'

"What's wrong, Professor?" Thana asked.

Corakin sighed. "There are fish in my head where the words should be."

Thana glowered down at the paper as she followed Aidan and Brina down the hallway. Brina didn't blame her. She'd been so sure Professor Gibberish would be able to solve the problem she hadn't even considered what she'd do if it didn't work. She was so disappointed, she couldn't even muster up concern about those spiders. The trio turned a corner and headed for a usually-empty classroom for further discussion. As they stepped through the doorway, all three stopped and stared.

Zoe Bohr and Asha Kirke were at the front of the room, doing a strange dance that seemed to involve hitting themselves

on the top of their heads, while sixteen year-old Paschal
Kuryakin twirled in circles, yelling "I am not a pole on which to
dance." Two first year students, Shawna Oakes and Alyce
Wellington, were doing handstands in front of the Knight twins,
Peg and Piper, who appeared to be performing continuous
somersaults. Laying the center of the room, with her hands over
her head, was first year Serenity Madison. Every few seconds,
she yelled, "Battle stations!"

Before Brina or her friends could gather their thoughts
enough to do anything but gape, someone spoke up from behind
them.

"Excuse me," nineteen year-old Sophie Landers stepped
around Aidan. "*Fiat.*" She turned back around and shook her
head as the chaos around her abated. "Someone thought it'd be
funny to put makati juice on the desks. This is the fourth study
group I've been to that's doing things like this. One of them was
an entire room of students trying to dodge the bubbles that
Ruby Mann was making."

"Any idea who's responsible?" Thana asked.

Sophie scowled and tossed her long blond braid over her
shoulder. "I'm almost positive it was Gray, but Headmaster
Manu is going to take some convincing." The sound of tinkling
bells interrupted whatever she'd intended to say next. Sophie
muttered a few words under her breath and a gold ribbon shot
out of the end of her wand and formed letters. Sophie scanned
the message quickly before hurriedly excusing herself and
exiting, heading for yet another makatied classroom.

"Would Gray really do something like this?" Brina watched
the dazed students return to some semblance of order. "Too
much makati juice can cause permanent damage."

"Unfortunately," Thana answered, "Gray's never really been
what you'd call a long-term thinker."

"Still, it seems more like something BD would do, not
Gray."

Brina saw a flash of jealousy cross Aidan's eyes, but he managed to keep it out of his voice. "They are two peas in a pod. Or," a grin twitched up the corner of his mouth, "two apples rotten to the core."

Thana snickered and even Brina had to grin. Brina reached out and took Aidan's hand. "Come on, we can go to Thana and I's room to do more research."

"Um, our room might be a bit difficult to get into." Thana had the good grace to blush.

"Why?" Brina wasn't sure she wanted to know.

"Remember when I went to get the mirror? Well, I kinda didn't take the time to clean up."

Brina groaned. She didn't need a further explanation. Thana had received several packages from her father that morning for her sixteenth birthday. She'd shoved all of the wrappings into a drawer, promising to throw it away after dinner. Brina had a feeling the mirror had been in the same drawer.

"Back to my room it is, then," Aidan chuckled. "Sigurd is at the library all day today anyway."

As they walked, Brina tugged Aidan closer to her. "You do know I wasn't actually defending Gray. I just don't like to believe the worst of people. You don't need to be jealous."

Aidan flushed, his grin sheepish as he looked down at Brina. "That obvious, huh?"

"Little bit."

Aidan pressed a kiss to the top of Brina's head and slid his arm around her waist. Ahead of them, Thana shook her head. "Come on." Amusement tinged her voice. "We've got work to do."

***

Brina crouched in front of the fountain, index finger hovering over the words. She didn't quite dare to touch them again even though the proximity sent a thrill through her.

"Elsali," she prayed. "Show me what I'm missing."

She shifted and her movement, combined with the late afternoon sun, threw her shadow across the white marble in stark contrast. Brina's eyes widened and she tipped precariously. Righting herself, Brina scrambled away from the fountain and onto her feet. She darted through the hidden passage, up the stairs and into her and Thana's room.

"I solved it."

Her announcement was met with silence. The room was empty. As Brina turned, her gaze fell on the cat clock sitting on Thana's desk. It glared at her accusingly.

"*Sranje!* The match!"

Brina grabbed her uniform from her bed, wishing that, for once, she possessed enough magic to get herself out of this mess. Still pulling on parts of her uniform, she darted out of the room and headed for the field. She skidded to a stop just inside the locker room door, completely out of breath, face flushed, but in uniform. All eyes turned toward her, but Aidan didn't pause in his speech.

"After the last time we played the tenth floor, the entire team is going to be gunning for Brina, which means we've got a bit of an advantage." Aidan motioned to the lines and squiggles on the papers he'd passed out. "This strategy plays to each of our strengths and is designed to work against this team. Remember that Stana Scofield likes to stay near the edges of the field. She never goes to center. Emily Foreman and Priya McDouglas are the fastest of the Praelian and their main scorers. They have good defense, but our Praelian are better. Let's show them just how much better."

The team started to leave, Brina among them. Aidan's voice stopped her. "Brina, a moment please."

Thana glanced back at the pair as she followed the rest of the team from the locker room, a concerned look on her usually cheerful face. Brina caught only a glimpse of Thana's expression as she turned toward Aidan.

"Sorry I'm late. I solved…"

"You know how important this is to me, Brina." Aidan's eyes darted from Brina's face to the ground.

Brina apologized again. "I know, Aidan, and I'm here now. I'm sorry I was late."

"And it's not just the match." Aidan kept going like he hadn't even heard a word Brina had said. "If you're late, what does it look like to the team? I mean, you're my girlfriend and it looks bad if you can just stroll in any time you want…"

"Excuse me?" Brina's temper flared. "I earned my place on this team without any help from you, and in case you weren't listening, you *trottel*, I apologized. I was trying to tell you something important, more important than your precious game. I figured out the inscription on the fountain."

Aidan's eyes widened at Brina's outburst and he took a step forward. "Brina, I…"

"Don't." Brina held up a hand. Her voice was tight with anger. "We have a game to play."

Brina's natural reflexes and the extra energy fueled by anger kept her from falling victim to the tenth floor's offensive strategy, but it was close. As it was, she sustained two hits when backed into a corner, with only Thana's assistance keeping the situation from getting any worse. The glare her best friend sent her way had cleared Brina's head enough to finish the game with her usual skill.

When the final tone sounded, signaling the end of the match and the Thirteenth Floor's victory, Brina didn't join her teammates in the revelry. Instead, she snatched the band from around her ankle and tossed it toward Aidan. She wanted to quit, to scream at him, but she bit back the words and ran from the field before she could embarrass herself further. Out of the corner of her eye, she caught Thana smacking Aidan in the back of the head, but she didn't look back to see what happened next. She just wanted to get out of there.

***

Thana had been prepared to find Brina crying, yelling, throwing things, anything but calmly preparing to shower. The tiny girl stood silently in the doorway, watching her friend strip off the dirty uniform, drop it into a nearby basket, pull clean clothes from the closet and head, barefoot, toward the bathroom. A few seconds later, Thana heard the water start and she moved from her place at the door. She settled in her desk chair, unease twisting her insides as she anticipated the awkwardness and tension to follow.

Twenty minutes later, a dry-eyed Brina emerged from the bathroom, a billow of steam in her wake. Her gaze came to rest on Thana and she held up a hand before her friend could speak. "I don't want to talk about him. We have more important things to discuss."

"But, Brina…"

"He made perfectly clear where his priorities are." Brina's normally pleasant tones had bite to them. "And I don't want to talk about it." Brina began brushing out her hair with a visible vengeance, sending a fine spray of water into the air.

Thana nodded, refraining from commenting on the abusive treatment Brina was currently giving her hair. She had a feeling Brina might throw the brush at her if she made one of her normal quips. "What's this more important thing, then?"

"I figured out the inscription on the fountain." Brina set aside her brush and grabbed a piece of paper from her desk. She wrote as she spoke. "*Drekinn ceithre nevidna neem augu oighear eno lewe; moyo drwg blyskavka hana hasinzii yn codi prenyzuye jugneuda.*"

"So, what language is it?" Thana crossed the room to look

down at the words on the paper.

"It's not one language, it's eight."

"What?"

Brina pointed at the different words. "We couldn't figure out the language because the words aren't from one specific language, but from eight separate languages, ones that are similar to but not quite the same as ones we know now. They must be some ancient form of them, from thousands of years ago. Each language has two words, but since the words aren't next to each other, the pattern is hard to see. Once I saw the pattern, it all clicked."

"All right, what does it say?"

Brina studied the paper for a moment. "As far as I can tell, it's pretty much word salad. If you translate each word separately, it says: 'Dragon fire unseen takes eyes ice one life; heart evil lightning one slumbers rises pierces dies.'" Frustration and fatigue crept into Brina's voice.

"Yeah, that doesn't really make much sense." Thana began pacing. "How did you figure out it was different languages?"

"I was standing by the fountain and the sun made my shadow obscure the words so I saw *drekinn* and *moyo* at the same time. I realized they were the same language even if the other words weren't. They were also the closest to our modern language."

Thana grinned. "Maybe that's the key."

"Not following."

"Maybe the words that are from the same language belong together. It changes the order and could make more sense."

"Can't hurt to try." Brina took her pen and began rearranging the words. After a few minutes, she sighed.

"Did it work?" Thana was bouncing on the balls of her feet. She'd been quiet for over three whole minutes, a personal record when she wasn't otherwise occupied by food or Fuhjyn.

"Kind of." Brina read off what she had. "'Dragon eyes fire

and ice unseen, one takes life; heart slumbers evil rises lightning pierces one dies.'"

"So, it's a riddle. *Mirus*," Thana said. "I hate riddles."

A knock on the door interrupted whatever Brina was going to say in response. Brina and Thana exchanged glances, both knowing who was on the other side. After a moment's hesitation, Brina opened the door.

"What do you want, Aidan?" Brina's voice was flat.

"I came to apologize." Aidan visibly bristled at Brina's question.

"Alright." Brina motioned for the young man to continue.

"Maybe you should go first." Aidan crossed his arms and watched Brina with an expectant look on his face.

"Excuse me?" Brina's eyebrows shot up. "I already apologized for being late to the match. What more do you want?"

"What about how you acted after the game was over?" Aidan set his jaw. "Throwing the timer at me and stomping off?"

"You're lucky that's all I did." Brina clenched her hands into fists.

Aidan snorted in bitter laughter. "Come on, Brina, what else could you have done? Hexed me?"

Color drained from Brina's face as a hurt gasp escaped her lips. Before she could move or speak, Thana darted forward, her dark blue eyes almost black with fury. Despite the height difference of more than a foot, Thana managed to land a loud, open-handed slap across Aidan's cheek before slamming the door in his face.

"Brina! I'm sorry. I didn't mean it." Aidan's pleas were punctuated by his hands pounding against the door.

Without taking her gaze from Brina's wounded expression, Thana spoke, each word clipped. "Go away, Aidan, or I'll show what it really means to hex someone."

"Brina." Aidan's words were tinged with desperation.

"Please."

Only Thana responded, "I'm serious, Aidan. Go away or you'll spend the next week as a two-toed sloth."

Silence.

Footsteps.

The door to the neighboring room shut.

"Brina, I–" Thana started.

"Don't." Brina shook her head. "Thank you for what you did, but I don't want to talk about it right now, or ever." She pressed her lips into a thin line, emotions warring on her face. "Let's just see if we can get this riddle figured out."

Chapter Eight: Don't Dream It's Over

Brina had never been more miserable. Not when she'd thought her secret would be discovered and she'd be sent home in disgrace. Not even when, as a child, she'd overheard her parents discussing her abnormality and their fear she would never be 'normal.' Sheer stubbornness and a deep-seeded sense of commitment kept her from quitting the Fuhjyn team, but every practice was emotional torture, soothed only by the physical demands that led to a few hours of dreamless sleep. When her waking mind wasn't plagued with the repetitive loop of Aidan's cruel barb, it was filled with the nonsense of the fountain riddle. Even her dreams were a restless mix of the two, with occasional glimpses of puzzling images of mountains, snow and dark caverns full of mysterious shadows. She couldn't even manage to pray for more than a few sentences before her mind would be drawn back into chaos. Only Thana's presence kept Brina's schoolwork from suffering and, even then, she struggled to maintain her secret. Fortunately, the news of Brina and Aidan's argument and subsequent estrangement had spread through the school and most attributed her lethargy and haggard appearance to relationship troubles. It was a bit embarrassing, but Brina preferred it to the alternative.

"Miss Fine." Professor Gibberish snapped his fingers in front of Brina's face.

Brina blinked, banishing flickers of gold and steel from her thoughts. Heat poured into her face. "I'm sorry, Professor."

"That's quite alright, Miss Fine. Now, if you could please repeat the first part of the incantation one uses to protect a moving vehicle?"

"Um, '*Mihi sis crustum Etruscum cum omnibus in eo*'?"

Professor Gibberish sighed and shook his head. "*Nej*, Miss Fine. I believe you just ordered a pizza with everything on it."

The class tittered as the color in Brina's cheeks increased.

"I'm sorry," she apologized again.

Professor Gibberish nodded once and turned to the rest of the students. "*Lautlos*! Now, Mr. Cohen, perhaps you can provide the proper phrase."

When the bell rang, Brina grabbed her books and hurried from the room before anyone could tease her about her mistake. As she headed into the dining hall, Professor Penah approached. "Brina, could I have a minute?"

As Brina followed her professor off to one side of the hall, she racked her brains, trying to remember if she'd taken a history test in the last few days and how badly she could have failed for the professor to come find her. "Is something wrong, Professor?"

Professor Penah smiled. "No, I just received those books I said I would loan you."

Brina frowned. What in the world was the professor talking about?

"My grandmother's books about the history of the fountain."

"Oh!" The memory rushed back. "Thank you so much."

Professor Penah handed Brina three heavy, ancient-looking tomes. "Just be careful. These are very old."

"Of course." Brina felt a familiar surge of curiosity and anticipation as she added the volumes to her stack of school books. "Thank you again."

"It is my pleasure." Professor Penah's voice suddenly grew serious. "And, Brina, do not hesitate to ask for my help if you need it, no matter how odd your questions may seem."

Brina nodded, concealing her puzzlement over the change in the professor's tone. Before she could think on it any longer, Thana was at her side and Professor Penah was walking away.

"What are those?" Thana asked as she watched the professor depart.

"Books about the fountain." Brina grinned, all thoughts of her classroom embarrassment pushed to the back of her mind.

The answer she'd been waiting for might well be in her hands. "Let's take lunch into our room so we can start looking through them."

"Sounds good to me." Thana agreed, relieved to have a reason to avoid the awkwardness of being in the same lunchroom as Aidan. Aside from the obvious strain between him and Brina, there was still the unspoken tension regarding Thana's defense of Brina. During Fuhjyn practice, he refused to speak directly to either girl and they sat as far apart as possible in their shared classes.

Thana and Brina weaved their way through the crowded hallway, heading for the mirror that would transport them back to their floor. When the ground first began to move, Brina thought she'd been caught up in a waking nightmare. It wasn't until Thana grabbed her arm, eyes wide, that Brina realized the threat was real. Students screamed as some of the more level-headed ones darted for the doorways, Thana and Brina among them.

Panes rattled in the windows before finally shattering under the pressure. The walls shook, chunks of stone dropping to the cracking floor. Rock and glass rained down as the floor shifted and broke. The earthquake lasted for almost ten full minutes as people clung to each other, mindless of animosity or indifference, which was how Brina and Thana found themselves sharing a doorway with Gray. One final bone-wrenching jolt threw Brina into Gray's arms.

"I didn't think this area had earthquakes." Brina was shocked by how shaky her voice sounded, and even more so when she realized her legs were trembling.

"It doesn't." Gray's voice was just as unsteady as Brina's, his usual swagger gone. "Quakes are generally west of the mountains, near the coast."

"All students, please report to the main auditorium," Headmaster Manu's amplified voice managed to rise above the cries and exclamations of the young adults. "If you are injured and unable to move, please send a message to Healer Jacen. If you find a student injured and unable to send a message, please do so for them. If you are able to do so, please make your way to the main auditorium." The headmaster repeated the message again.

Brina turned to go, and then realized she was still in the circle of Gray's arms. She looked up, tensing for a fight. Instead, the vulnerable expression on Gray's face caught her off guard and she hesitated.

"About before," Gray released Brina from his hold. "I'm sorry." A crooked grin appeared. "I don't get told 'no' very often."

"Spend time with me and you'll hear it a lot more." Brina's smile took the bite out of her words.

"Brina, we should head for the auditorium." Disapproval colored Thana's voice as she took her friend's arm.

"You're right." Brina nodded. She looked up at Gray. "Come on."

The trio turned, and found themselves face to face with a pale, wide-eyed Aidan. "Brina, are you okay?"

"She's fine." Gray answered, only a hint of smugness in his tone. It didn't seem to have taken him long to regain his composure.

Aidan's eyes darted toward Gray and then narrowed. A sudden flush of color stained his cheeks. "I thought I told you to leave her alone, Gray."

"From what I heard, that's not your decision anymore." Gray's eyes flashed.

"*Facitis et stolidi!*" Thana exclaimed, a sentiment with which Brina whole-heartedly agreed. All eyes turned toward the smaller girl. "Can we save the manly display of testosterone poisoning until later?" She made a noise of disgust and pulled Brina down the corridor without looking to see if either of the boys was following.

The trip from the ninth floor down to the auditorium was total pandemonium. Professors patrolled the hallways, herding students in the correct direction while trying to assess the full extent of the damage. By the time the girls reached the auditorium, they'd seen giant holes in almost every wall, as well as gaps in the ceilings of almost every corridor. Brina and Thana entered the auditorium and gasped. Intricate designs decorated the walls as cracks made their way from the floor to the ceiling, or what remained of it. Huge parts were missing, revealing the cloud-covered sky. Professors directed students to the center of the room where the debris had been cleared and nothing was left overhead to endanger the huddled masses. The girls followed Professor Penah's instructions, but edged their way closer to the headmaster. Once in place, they watched the last of their schoolmates straggle in, both Aidan and Gray among them. Gray headed in their direction while Aidan, Brina noted with a pang, was comforting a seemingly distraught BD. Fortunately, Brina was saved the embarrassment of either Thana's platitudes regarding Aidan's appearance, or Gray's mostly unwanted attentions by the headmaster calling for attention.

"Everyone please stay in the center of the room, and speak to a professor if you are hurt." Headmaster Manu's voice was strained. "We need to determine the nature of everyone's injuries." He turned to the healer and lowered his voice, though Thana and Brina could still hear him. "Jacen, how bad is it?"

"No fatalities, but we have three seriously wounded and about a dozen with broken bones. The majority are just banged up and scared."

"Headmaster, I need to speak with you." Professor Penah put her hand on the headmaster's shoulder.

"Yes?"

The professor turned her head slightly to mask most of what

she was saying, but Brina managed to catch enough to understand. "Two students are missing."

"Missing? How could they be missing? Didn't you use *aperio*?"

Professor Penah raised her eyebrows. "Of course I did. Asha Kirke and Zoe Bohr are nowhere on the grounds."

The headmaster opened his mouth and then closed it again. After a moment's silence, he tried again. "Take Kali and Corakin, find Heimdall, and search the grounds on foot. There are soft spots here that could've prevented the spell from working." Headmaster Manu used the common term for an area where magical energy was naturally negated. Professor Penah nodded and headed off to find the other two professors and the groundskeeper.

"Headmaster." Assistant Headmaster Stryka shuffled toward the front of the room, glaring at any student who happened to get in his way. "Ama and I have finished the initial analysis of the building's structure." Stryka referenced the head of the housing staff, Ama Waldburg. "The living quarters have sustained the least damage, but they'll need to be fixed before we can send anyone back. We recommend releasing the students onto the grounds with the understanding they are to stay out of any buildings, and to return only when we've announced it's safe to do so. If we have the majority of the staff working, we should be able to repair the living quarters and the major damage before night fall."

"If they're sending us outside anyway," Brina whispered to Thana, careful to pitch her voice low enough so Gray couldn't hear her. "Let's slip out now and head for the garden." Off of Thana's questioning look, Brina added, "I have the strangest feeling this is connected to whatever the riddle is about."

Thana nodded and glanced around. Sliding her wand from her pocket, she flicked the tip in Gray's direction and muttered, "*Pulvis et umbra sumus.*" As Gray's eyes turned from the girls toward something only he could see or hear, Thana gestured toward the exit and followed Brina from the room.

It didn't take the girls long to reach the garden, even with the debris-littered hallways. As soon as they entered the garden, Thana began placing protective enchantments around the entrance to prevent anyone from seeing the pair sitting near the fountain. It appeared to have suffered no damage. In fact, the entire garden looked like the earthquake hadn't touched it. Certain they would find answers in the books Professor Penah had given them, Thana and Brina settled on one of the benches and began to read. Before they'd waded through more than the first forty pages or so, they heard voices just outside the hedge.

"What were Asha and Zoe doing at the Fuhjyn field in the middle of the day?" Professor Kali Geryan's words held something neither Brina nor Thana had heard in the tough woman's voice before. It wasn't until the others spoke that the girls realized what it was. Grief.

"We must first address what we are going to do. What will we tell the others? The girls' parents?" Professor Penah's voice broke on the last word.

"*Arduum sane munus.*" Corakin murmured. "To have to share their children are dead is bad enough, but not to be able to say what killed them…" He trailed off.

"What could do that?" Professor Geryan asked. "They looked like the very life had been drained out of them."

"I don't know," Corakin's voice started to fade as the professors moved away from the garden. "I don't know."

Chapter Nine: Start to Run

The entire school spent the following weeks in shock. A few of Zoe and Asha's closer friends took time off, returning to their homes immediately after the school's memorial service with no news as to when they would return. The Fuhjyn finals were put on indefinite hold as a specialized team of investigators spent days at the field, trying to determine the cause of the girls' deaths. Brina and Thana happened to overhear Conner O'Brien, head of the unit, tell Headmaster Manu the team had found no evidence to support foul play, and no explanation as to why Zoe and Asha had died. They could only rule that it had been a freak accident of unknown origin.

As the month of Otium ended and Fatum began, things slowly began to return to normal, although a more subdued version. Classes resumed their normal pace and Fuhjyn was scheduled to return in just a few days, with the finals scheduled at the end of the month. Brina and Thana spent every free moment in the garden, continuing their research and avoiding Aidan and Gray, neither of whom either girl wanted to see.

Brina stared at the page, words swimming in front of her eyes. Her mind was far away, in the mountains where snow shone red under the Fatum sun and caverns held dark, dangerous secrets. She could feel something pulling at her, drawing her, warning her. Thunder rumbled and lightning flashed, bright and jagged across a midnight sky, casting a silhouette of bones and skin in stark shadows.

"Brina!" Thana shook her friend's arm, calling her name.

Brina blinked, feeling a strange pressure around her eyes. "Thana?"

The other girl's face was pale. "What was that all about?"

"What do you mean?" Brina shook her head, trying to clear away the cobwebs.

"You were reading the book and suddenly, you went all

dreamy, staring off into space. I said your name four times before you snapped out of it," Thana paused, shifting uncomfortably before she added, "And your eyes went all weird."

"Weird? How?" Brina felt a chill wash over her. What was happening to her?

Thana moved so she was facing Brina, sober demeanor telling Brina the seriousness of what Thana wanted to say. "Your pupils got long and thin, like a cat."

"Or a dragon." Brina whispered the words, not knowing why she said them, only that they were true. "Thana, what's happening to me?"

"I don't know." Thana admitted. "What were you reading when it happened?"

Brina indicated the page in front of her and Thana took the book, reading the passage aloud. "'Of all the creatures in mythology to be thought to have at one time roamed this land, the dragon holds the greatest threat. People so fear this beast's powers that to speak of them is considered a curse upon the speaker's entire household. For the sake of generations to come, we shall take the risk and reveal the true nature and peril involved.'" Thana glanced up at Brina for a moment, then continued, "'Though its exterior is fierce, with razored claws and teeth, and scales too dense for any weapon to penetrate, the greatest threat a dragon poses is its source of energy. For though a dragon may feast upon flesh and bone, it draws its strength from magic itself, the very essence of our lives. Any person who ventures too close to a dragon's lair will find themselves weakened, and if they do not flee, will perish.'"

"Keep reading." Brina's tone was flat. She clenched her hands together, knuckles whitening with the force. She didn't remember reading the words, but knew what was coming next anyway, as if the words had been imprinted in her mind.

"'It is believed the Guardians, to protect their people from these creatures, constructed a device that would charm the dragon into a deep sleep. In a cavern of stone and ice, the beast will slumber until the Unseen One arrives. She will bear a mark of the dragon, and will be unique among her people. Her very nature will weaken the protection and wake the creature as she alone will possess the ability to slay the creature."

Thana set the book down carefully and turned to face her friend. "Brina, this is just crazy. You aren't seriously thinking…"

"It's under the field, Thana." Brina's voice was soft, but stopped Thana's stream of words with its weight. "That's what killed Zoe and Asha. It's what makes the field negate magic. It's all true. I know it. I can feel it."

Thana opened her mouth and closed it again. Her brow furrowed in thought for almost a full minute. Brina watched in silence as a thousand scenarios played across her friend's face. Brina could only imagine what each of them could be.

"We have to tell someone." Thana's voice trembled. "This is bad, Brina. No one's safe…"

"That's not entirely true," Brina put her hand on Thana's knee, stopping the flow from turning into a babble.

"We're not talking about weird words on a piece of rock." Thana stood, voice rising. "This is fangs and claws and fire…"

"I know what a dragon is." Brina kept her tone mild, surprising herself with how composed she sounded. "Relax. I'm not planning on running down there tonight with nothing but my trusty sidekick."

"Well, that's reassur…" Thana paused, eyes narrowing. "Did you just call me your sidekick?"

Brina grinned, Thana's indignation pushing back her own trepidation.

"Okay then, Miss Dragon-Hero, what's the plan?" Thana began pacing back and forth. "What do we do next?"

"You come to dinner with me."

Both girls jumped at the sound of Gray's voice. Brina shot Thana a dirty look. Thana's eyes widened guiltily and she mouthed "sorry" in Brina's direction. Apparently, she'd forgotten to place the concealment charms around the garden this time.

"Sorry, Gray." Brina thought quickly. "We have a Fuhjyn meeting in the dining hall."

"Without your captain?" Gray raised an eyebrow.

"What?" Brina felt her stomach knot at the mention of Aidan.

"I just saw Aidan heading down toward the Fuhjyn field," he added the next bit with a hint of malice. "I wouldn't be surprised if he was meeting BD down there. They have been spending an awful lot of time together."

Thana moved so quickly that neither Brina nor Gray saw her. "*Minus habens. Adidem.*" Thana dropped her hand to her side, but didn't pocket her wand. Gray's frozen stare continued to focus on where Brina had been even as the girls hurried from the garden. Neither of the girls spared Gray a second thought as they ran across the deserted grounds toward the Fuhjyn field, skidding to a stop just outside the entrance.

"How are we going to find him?" Thana asked, her words breathless.

"You go up in the stands. I'll get to a high point on the field." Brina instructed.

Thana nodded in agreement and darted up the stairs just inside the entrance.

"Elsali, help me find Aidan and please let him be okay," Brina breathed the prayer, then headed inside.

The field was a disaster. Between the earthquake and the investigators, everything was in disarray. Trees were uprooted, boulders smashed and pieces scattered. Rebuilding the field, Brina thought, was going to take more than just a few days. She made her way toward the large oak she'd climbed during her first match, intending to use its height to see over the rubble. As she stepped into what had been the clearing, she stopped. The tree was on its side, and where it had once stood was a gaping hole.

Instantly, she understood what had happened. The earthquake, caused by the waking dragon, had torn the tree loose, creating a doorway into the creature's cave. Zoe and Asha had been in the field for some reason during the earthquake. When the tree had revealed the entrance to the dragon's lair, some of the beast's power had been released, sucking the life from the closest magical beings.

Brina felt two tugs toward the dark opening. One was physical, a pull from every cell in her body. It was low, base, a steady thrum in each of her atoms. The thrum, she instinctively realized, was what drew people to it. A part of her responded to the call, but it was easily resisted. Whatever made her different from the others of her kind lessened the creature's thrall. She supposed because her presence wouldn't contain enough of what the dragon needed, she was lower on the food chain. Aidan, however, had exactly what the dragon wanted.

The second tug she felt was deeper and stronger than the first. It was a longing, a desire, something she'd felt before. It was like every fiber in her body was crying out for Aidan.

Brina glanced up toward the stands as she sidled toward the hole. While she was terrified of going in alone, the thought of what the creature could do to the people she cared about scared her more. She dropped into the hole more quickly than was probably wise, not wanting Thana to see and follow. After a moment, her eyes began to adjust to the darkness. First, she could see a few inches in front of her face and darker shadows she supposed were walls. Then, she felt a change happen. It wasn't painful, just a strange pressure around her eyes. After a moment, everything became clear.

"Well, that was interesting." Brina muttered as she inched

her way forward, relying on the pull in her bones to tell her she was going the right way. Deeper and deeper into the earth she went, through twists and turns, over grounds both smooth and rough. She ducked through corridors that would've been too short for even Thana to stand straight. Other caverns were so large she could barely see the top. She felt a strange sense of circling as she walked, as if the tunnels were taking her deeper, but not outside the Fuhjyn field. The air grew heavy, moist, and warm. The cracks in the walls and floor widened and grew in number as if she were nearing the epicenter of the quake.

Then came the smell.

Brina's twelve year-old nephew Misha, son of Brina's eldest brother Baka, had once forgotten an egg and tuna sandwich in the backseat of Ziven's car. After four days of ninety-degree weather, Ziven had gone to the car for something and nearly passed out. Brina gladly would've traded that smell for this one.

Survival instinct screamed at her to run, overriding the attraction the creature emitted. Only Brina's desire to rescue Aidan, to save him as no one had saved Zoe and Asha, kept her moving forward. Exactly how she was going to save him, she hadn't yet worked out.

A sound from her right drew her attention. Huddled in the shadows, Brina would've missed him if it had not been for her new, strangely enhanced sight. Aidan was pale, barely conscious enough to groan. As Brina crossed to Aidan, a roar echoed from inside the next corridor, shaking the cavern. Brina struggled to stay on her feet on the rolling floor as rocks dropped from the ceiling. She fell to her knees, not feeling the impact of her knees on the ground or the rocks hitting her head and shoulders. One particularly sharp shard scraped her cheek, leaving a bloody scrape, but she didn't care.

"Aidan?" Brina kept her voice low.

She stretched out a hand, fingertips lightly brushing Aidan's pale cheek. His skin was cold, far too cold considering the heat in the tunnels. Begging Elsali for strength, Brina pulled Aidan to his feet and began to drag him away from the darkness behind her. Another roar erupted from behind them, shaking their surroundings. The floor heaved; the walls cracked. Pieces of ceiling pelted Brina and Aidan as they staggered along. Later, Brina was never sure how long she and Aidan were trying to get out. It seemed like years since she'd seen the sun, smelled something other than the fetid odor clinging to the air far longer than it should have. Finally, a dim light appeared in front of them and Brina found the energy to continue. A rumble sounded from behind them and the ground renewed its shaking with more intensity than before. As Brina and Aidan emerged from the hole, pure instinct prompted her to throw herself and Aidan away from the entrance.

Brina sensed the dragon's approach seconds before it burst from the ground, its deafening roar drowning out everything else. She rolled onto her side, shielding Aidan's body as best she could with her own, feeling the creature searching for magic.

"Elsali, protect us," she prayed as she looked up over her shoulder.

With her newly-found vision, Brina found she could see every detail of the beast's body as it launched itself into the air, leathery wings stretched to an almost seventy-foot wingspan. Foul-smelling wind buffeted Brina's face as the dragon flapped, straining to catch a current. The setting sun threw rays of orange and red against the copper and bronze scales hiding under centuries of grime. Dirt and dust showered down on the field, coating everything as the dragon rose.

It screamed, the piercing sound echoing over the school grounds. Brina gritted her teeth, clamping her hands over her ears as the shriek reverberated off of the surrounding stadium. Even with her eyes narrowed in pain, Brina could see the open mouth, count the wickedly curved teeth, some blackened with age. Two horns, easily the size of Brina's entire body, protruded from the dragon's forehead, matching the spikes that lined thirty feet of heavily muscled tail, the smallest of which was at least three feet tall. A burst of flame shot out of the dragon's mouth, instantly reducing a section of the field to ashes. With a final screech of triumph, the dragon whirled in the air and flew away.

Brina watched until even her raptor-like sight failed her. She felt pressure building at her temples and knew her eyes had changed back to normal. All at once, the adrenaline that had been keeping her going drained away, and everything went black.

Chapter Ten: Everything Has Changed

"Maybe splash some cold water on her?"

"You will do no such thing, Thana Decker!" Assistant Healer Amari Julius snapped. "Brina will wake when she's ready."

"Just a suggestion."

The voices pierced the darkness enveloping Brina and she fought her way toward them. She blinked, eyelids heavy as stone, and her surroundings slowly came into focus. The Healing Wing was dark, pre-dawn moonlight shining through a crack in the curtains. At the foot of her bed, Brina saw two indistinct shapes, one tall and thin, the other so small Brina knew it was Thana. The other figure spoke again.

"And you shouldn't be out of bed yet yourself."

"What happened?" Brina's voice was rough.

"You're awake!" Thana ignored Healer Amari's protest and bounded toward the head of the bed. She seized the water pitcher from the bedside table and poured Brina a drink.

Brina pushed herself into a sitting position, amazed at how drained her entire body felt. She took the cup and drank from it greedily. Water had never tasted so delicious.

"What happened?" Brina repeated, her voice almost normal.

Thana shot a glance at the Assistant Healer. "We're not entirely sure."

"By the time Professor Penah found you, all three of you were unconscious and there was a giant hole in the Fuhjyn field." Healer Amari asked. "Was there a localized earthquake?"

"Excuse me, Healer Amari." Professor Penah's voice came from the doorway. "May I have a word with Brina?"

Healer Jacen appeared behind the teacher. "Just a few minutes, Professor. I don't want them to be taxed."

"How's Aidan?" Thana's eyes were dark with worry.

The grim expression on the healer's face made Brina's blood turn to ice.

"He'll live, but I don't know how or why. I've never seen anything like this before. It's like all of the magic was drained from his body. It should have killed him."

"Like Asha and Zoe?" Brina spoke through numb lips as images of Aidan flashed through her mind.

Both Healers started, but it was Jacen who spoke. "How did you–"

Professor Penah interrupted. "A word, please."

Jacen nodded, though his puzzled expression said he didn't understand what the professor wanted The Head Healer gave Brina an equally curious look before following his assistant from the room.

Professor Penah stood in the same spot, penetrating gaze so focused on Brina that the girl squirmed, wishing the professor would just speak.

"Millennium ago, an Order was formed to guard our world's most dangerous secret. To guard and to wait. '*Drekinn ceithre nevidna neem augu oighear eno lewe; moyo drqg blyskavka hana hasinzii yn codi pronyzuye jugneuda.*'" Professor Penah crossed to Brina's bed, something ancient and wise burning in her dark eyes. "I have been waiting a very long time to meet you."

Brina kept her face expressionless. "Why should the words on the fountain mean anything to me?"

The professor smiled. "'Dragon eyes fire and ice unseen, one takes life; heart slumbers evil rises lightning pierces one dies.' The one with the dragon eyes will cross fire and ice to slay the evil creature that sleeps in the heart of the earth. Only one who is unseen by the beast can wield the weapon needed to kill it."

"How do you know what it says? What it means?" Brina swallowed hard. Her heart was racing and she was finding it difficult to draw air into her lungs.

"Because I was there when it was written." The professor's statement hung in the air, too big, too heavy, to dissipate.

"But, you're young!" Thana blurted out, bringing a half-smile to the professor's face.

"Am I?" The professor raised an eyebrow.

Thana and Brina stared at their professor, mouths open and eyes wide.

"If either of you mind your history lessons, you may know me better by the name Jael."

"Not..." Thana stammered. "You aren't..."

"The woman mentioned in the Baibel? Yes, I am." Jael's serene expression and matter-of-fact tone did nothing to lessen the impact of her words.

"You'd have to be..." One could almost see the numbers flying through Thana's mind. "How old are you?"

"Old enough." The two girls continued to gape at their professor. "We do not have the time right now for details, but I needed to inform you of my true identity and involvement with the dragon. And, I must warn you not to speak of the creature to anyone else. Once you have been released from the healing wing, we will speak at a greater length. There is much I need to share."

A soft knock at the door preceded the healers' re-entrance to the room. "If you're finished, Clio," Jacen addressed the professor. "My patients need their rest."

"Of course." Clio / Jael nodded. With a final glance at each of the girls, the professor exited the room.

Jacen turned to the girls. "Thana, you need to return to your bed. Both you and Brina need to sleep." He glanced at his watch. "Sunrise isn't for another hour or so. I don't expect to see either of you awake until at least nine, at which point we will re-evaluate your condition to determine if you're ready to be released."

Brina saw her own questions echoed in Thana's eyes, but

knew they couldn't go through any of them now. Based on
Thana's frustrated expression, she understood the problem as
well. They couldn't risk being overheard. The girls held each
other's eyes for a moment before Thana complied with Jacen's
request.

Brina didn't go to sleep. Instead, she lay awake until all was
silent, filled only by the rhythmic breathing from the other side
of the curtain where Thana lay. Brina had heard Jacen leaving
Amari in charge before he retired for a few hours of sleep, and
then Amari had bustled about for nearly a quarter hour before
peeking in to see if the girls had done as they'd been told.
Through narrowed lids, Brina watched Amari return to her
office and settle in her chair, novel in hand. While not quite as
sharp as it had been in the tunnels, Brina found that her vision
was better than it had been before. With it, Brina was able to
make out the title of Amari's book, *My Immortal, 'm Cara*, from
her bed. When she was satisfied the healer was fully immersed
in her reading, Brina slipped from her bed.

Aidan was in the adjacent room, still and pale under the crisp
blue school sheets. Keeping one eye on Amari's door, Brina
crept into Aidan's room and up to his bed. Her heart constricted
as she stood over him. The bruises and scratches were even
more conspicuous against the stark whiteness of his skin than
they would have been had Aidan retained his tan, but it seemed
the dragon had taken that as well. Her hand trembled as she
brushed her fingertips over Aidan's discolored cheek.

"Brina?" Aidan stirred, her name a whisper in the still air.

Brina grabbed his hand, reminding herself to keep her voice
low. "Aidan? Can you hear me?"

Color seeped back into Aidan's face as his eyelids fluttered,
then opened. "Brina, you're here."

Brina felt the hot trail of tears run down her cheeks, but
didn't bother to wipe them away. "I'm here, Aidan."

Aidan smiled, eyes sparkling. "So, you forgive me for being

a *trottel?*"

"You idiot," Brina's voice cracked. "Of course I forgive you for being a jerk." She bent her head and gently brushed her lips across his. A familiar jolt of energy shot through her. From the widening of his eyes, Brina guessed Aidan had felt it too. "What was…?"

Aidan interrupted. "No more questions tonight, please. We can spend all day tomorrow analyzing everything that's happened. For right now, I just want to be here with you."

Brina smiled. "That sounds good."

Aidan moved himself to one side, trying to hide a grimace as his body protested the movement. Brina climbed up next to him, tucking herself under his arm and resting her head on his chest. She felt Aidan press his lips to the top of her head as she slid an arm around his waist. As she gave in to sleep, she heard him murmur against her hair, "I'm sorry."

She opened her mouth to tell him it didn't matter, but sleep claimed her before she could utter a word.

The pair were woken only a few hours later when Amari made her rounds. Her exclamation brought Thana running, though Amari found the situation much less amusing than Thana did. Amari shooed the girls from the room with less of a scolding than they'd expected and proceeded to fuss over Aidan's seemingly miraculous recovery.

By the time Jacen arrived and was updated by a still-flustered Amari, all three students were ready to return to their rooms. Jacen, however, insisted that the trio remain in the healing wing until their parents arrived, with Aidan still on bed-rest until then. The healer did, however, consent to letting them change from the healing gowns into their own clothes, which he summoned from their rooms. The clothes they'd been found in had already been put into the school laundry. After much begging and cajoling from all three, he also allowed the girls to pull chairs into Aidan's room so they could all talk. Amari sniffed her disapproval of the whole affair before heading home for some self-proclaimed well-deserved rest. After Jacen had disappeared into his office to study Aidan's various test results, Thana turned to her friends, smile wide and eyes sparkling.

"I take it the two of you are back together?"

Brina shot Thana a dirty glare, and Aidan just looked sheepish. Thana let the silence stand for a minute, appearing to savor it before changing the subject. "So, Professor Penah is actually Jael from the Baibel? What's up with that?"

"Wait, what?" Aidan turned his attention to Thana, everything else apparently forgotten.

Both girls laughed at the total bewilderment on Aidan's face, then Thana gave the brief and speedy synopsis, glossing over the garden interaction with Gray, much to Brina's relief. The last thing they needed was more tension between Aidan and Gray.

"So," Aidan slowly said. "Brina's some mythical, non-magical superhero, Professor Penah's thousands of years-old and there's a dragon on the loose, draining people of their magic, which can kill them, but somehow didn't kill me or Thana."

Thana and Brina looked at each other, nodded, and Brina said, "That's about it."

"Uh-huh." Aidan scratched his head with the hand not clasped with Brina's. "And we're sure I'm not still unconscious?" Brina chuckled and squeezed Aidan's hand. Both started as a shock went through them.

Thana's eyes narrowed. "What was that all about?"

Brina opened her mouth to explain, but was interrupted by a knock on the door.

"Thana?"

"Daddy!" Thana threw herself at the gruff-voiced man in the doorway.

Aidan and Brina stared. They couldn't help it. Barty Decker

was as large as his daughter was small. Easily over six and a half feet tall, he would've towered over most people, but his bulk made him seem even more massive. In stark contrast to Thana's black hair and dark blue eyes, Mr. Decker had short-cropped white-gold curls and eyes a rich brown. Then, as he gently placed his daughter back on her feet, Brina and Aidan saw him smile. That was all Thana.

"You must be Brina and Aidan." Mr. Decker crossed the room in two large strides, Thana skipping along at his side. He stretched out one enormous hand, first to Brina, then to Aidan. "Thana's told me all about you."

"I'm sure she has," Brina said with a grin.

"Brina!" Vani Fine hurried into the room, followed closely by an ashen-faced Ziven. They went straight to their daughter, barely sparing a glance for anyone else.

"I'm okay." Brina assured her mother. Ziven grabbed his daughter's hand. Brina repeated her statement to her father. "I'm okay." She felt tears well up in her eyes and pushed them back. She'd always wondered how much her parents actually loved her. They'd always been so distant that Brina'd never considered how upset they'd be if something actually happened to her.

"Thank Elsali." Vani brushed Brina's hair back from her forehead, hand cool and trembling ever so slightly. "We were so worried."

"Does anyone know what happened?" Ziven's voice was as pale as his skin.

With their parents so closely paying attention, the girls didn't dare look at each other. Thana let Brina answer.

"Not really." Brina felt a rush of relief that Professor... Jael hadn't yet filled her in on the details. Plausible deniability was a wonderful thing.

Before anyone could press the matter further, the door opened again and a woman entered. Even if they'd been in a

crowded room, Thana and Brina would've known anywhere
who belonged to her. Aside from her rich mahogany hair, she
looked as much like Aidan as Thana was unlike her father.
Without a word, she gathered Aidan in her arms, her grip so
tight her entire body was visibly tense.

"Shh, Mom, it's okay," Aidan murmured, extracting himself
by maneuvering his mother into his embrace. "Shh."

"I thought..." Rosemarie Preston's voice was choked and
hoarse. "I thought I'd lost you like I lost Adalayde. Like your
father."

"Shh, Mom, I'm right here."

Thana and Brina turned away, giving Aidan privacy as he
comforted his distraught parent. Taking their cues from their
children, the Fines and Mr. Decker turned their attention to each
other. Thana filled her father in on a play-by-play of everything
she could without breaking the promise to Jael. Brina prompted
her parents with questions about her siblings and their families,
learning about how Bem's nine year-old twins Rory and Rhys
had painted their cat green, and how the youngest of the next
generation, four year-old Zack, had taught himself to add. It was
all simple and mundane, and exactly what everyone needed.
When Jacen entered the room a quarter of an hour later, Aidan's
mother had calmed considerably and the Fines were almost
back to their normal selves. It was then the parents turned to the
healer for answers.

"All three of your children were found on the Fuhjyn field
unconscious. I ran every test I could think of, but could find no
cause for their state. Nor could I wake them. About an hour
after being brought to the healing wing, Thana woke on her
own. Brina followed about two hours later. Aidan woke up
sometime during the night after I'd left and Healer Amari had
taken over. None of them appear to be experiencing any lasting
side effects." Jacen's gaze flickered to Brina for the briefest of
moments and she knew Amari had told him that she'd been

with Aidan when he'd woken. She felt a rush of gratitude at the healer's discretion. She caught Aidan's expression of relief as well and hurriedly looked away, lest their faces betray them. They hadn't done anything wrong, but it still wasn't anything either of them wanted to explain to their parents.

"Do you think this is related to the deaths of Zoe Bohr and Asha Kirke?" Ziven's voice was much steadier than it had been, but he still didn't release his daughter's hand. "Their parents said it didn't appear to have been the earthquake…" He let his voice trail off.

"You'd need to speak to the team of investigators about their findings." Jacen carefully skirted the question. "As for these three, I am comfortable enough with their health to release them." He gave each of the trio a sharp look. "Provided, of course, they take it easy and find me immediately should they experience anything out of the ordinary."

"We promise." All three chorused in unison.

Ziven and Rosemarie both looked doubtful, but Jacen briskly pushed forward. "Now, if you'll excuse me, I still have quite a lot of paperwork to catch up on. I've fallen behind over the last few weeks." Without waiting for anyone to protest, Jacen exited the room.

"We really need to get back." Brina filled the awkward silence. "We've got loads of homework to finish. And I doubt all of the professors will cut us slack for being in the healing wing all night."

"Perhaps I should speak with Roderick," Vani began.

"It's all right, Mom." Brina smiled, insides warming at her mother's concern. "We can get it done if we head back now. Besides," she glanced at her friends, "we wouldn't want anyone thinking any of us had gotten preferential treatment, would we?"

"I suppose not," Vani reluctantly agreed. "You're sure you're okay?"

"Positive." Brina forced herself to sound worry-free and cheerful, though she was feeling neither of these things. Aidan and Thana immediately chimed in, their own false heartiness ringing truer to Brina's ears than her own.

Almost half an hour passed before the parents agreed to allow their children to return to their rooms unsupervised. Once the trio had left the healing wing and their parents had reluctantly departed to their various places of employment, Brina turned to the other two. "We need to find Prof – I mean, Jael." Thana and Aidan nodded in agreement and the three headed for the professor's office.

"Does anyone know if the professor lives on or off campus?" Thana asked.

"I don't know, but since the off week is almost over, maybe she'll be here getting ready for next week." Brina's words sounded as doubtful as she felt.

"I think one of the on-campus houses belongs to her." Aidan chimed in. "Professor Gibberish would know for sure. He's lived here since he started teaching a couple of years ago."

After finding Professor Penah's classroom and office empty, they decided to head to the on-campus houses to speak with their language professor. They quickly went through one of the PA mirrors and emerged on the third floor where a second shortcut through a doorway pretending to be a fichus plant deposited them a few short steps from the back doors. Professors who lived on campus were located in a neat row of seemingly small cottages at the base of a rolling hill at the very edge of the campus. Each house appeared to be a single-storied, plainly adorned white cottage with black trim. Were it not for the small basket with bright, sparkly blue letters spelling "Ziege" on the porch of one of the houses, Corakin's residence would have been impossible to distinguish from the others. Their arrival was musically announced as they stepped onto the porch, and almost immediately, the door opened and a thrilled

Corakin greeted them. "*Salvete, salvete.*"

All three stopped just inside the door to remove their shoes as was only polite, looking around as they did so. Like many on-campus dwellings, the cottage was much larger inside than it was on the outside. As eager as they were to speak with Jael, Corakin's interior decorating gave them pause. They were in a spacious foyer with rich mahogany paneling, and to their right was an elegant spiral staircase with an ostentatiously carved railing, though where it led, Brina could only imagine. From the vaulted ceiling hung a brass chandelier with sweet-smelling candles burning with everlasting, fire-safe flame.

"Professor," Brina was the first to be able to speak. "We can't stay."

"*Sielewi.* I thought you needed to speak to Professor Penah." Corakin looked fairly surprised, then confused. "Didn't I mention she's here?"

"Um, no, Professor," Thana said.

"Apologies." He stretched out an arm to invite them to walk down the hall. "The sitting room is this way." With a grand gesture befitting his blue silk dressing gown, Corakin led the way down the hall.

The first door they passed appeared to be a library with stacks of books teetering precariously as they neared the ceiling. A door to the left allowed a glimpse of a bright and shining kitchen, all white and silver and black. Directly opposite was a door bearing a brass plaque reading: "*Vita sine libris mors est.*" Brina mentally translated: 'Life without books is death.' Then, finally, Corakin took them through the doorway at the very end of the corridor. The room was a pale iceberg blue, the floor a dark wood partially covered by a thick, expensive-looking rug woven from the blue and silver hairs of a wild visil. Three overstuffed couches curved in a U-shape around a dark, low table. In the center couch sat the former Professor Penah.

"Brina, Aidan, Thana," Jael addressed each of them in turn.

"Glad to see you're up and about."

"Sit, sit." Corakin gestured to the remaining seats. "Refreshments? I have the most marvelous peach-mango green tea."

"Glasses all round, then, Corakin." Jael's voice was soft. "And something to eat if you don't mind. I daresay, after their adventure, our young friends are quite hungry."

"*Foarte bun.*" Corakin vanished, humming happily as he went. "I shall return shortly."

"Does he know?" Thana asked the question they were all thinking.

"Who I am?" Jael shook her head. "No. But he does know about the dragon as well as much of what I will be telling you. I have needed his help with some translations these past days and will likely need it again before our journey's end."

Corakin returned well-prepared with floating teacups and a tray laden with crumpets, cheese and tiny cucumber sandwiches, but the food was no match for Thana. She bounded from her seat, relieved Corakin of the tray, snagged one of the levitating cups of tea and settled back into her seat next to Brina before anyone else had the opportunity to react. After she'd shoved an entire sandwich into her mouth for a second time, she seemed to realize everyone was staring. She swallowed. "You should know by now I don't share food." A third sandwich disappeared.

"I'll make more." Corakin grinned and exited the room again.

As the door shut behind her colleague, Jael addressed the remaining three. "I will start to explain the situation, but once Corakin returns, my own history must become a bit vague."

The trio nodded, Aidan and Brina understanding the press for time, and Thana too busy clearing the tray to speak.

"Most of our kind, all in fact, save a very precious few, assume we were created with our magic, though the first usage of what we call magic doesn't appear until Abram and the angels rescued Lot's family from Sodmorah."

Brina and her friends nodded. It came as no surprise that they knew their Baibel stories as well as she did.

Jael continued. "But the reason nothing was recorded prior to Abram is that these abilities were not common until then. In fact, people without magic didn't fully disappear until after the birth of Jakob and Esau. The ability of certain combinations of wood and other elements to channel these abilities was not discovered until well into the time of Danyel and the fall of Jerusalem. Before that, only the most powerful of our kind could produce magic of any strength, and they were rare." Jael glanced toward the door. They could hear Corakin humming as he approached. Jael quickly added, "Understand when I refer to the Guardians, I am referring to myself among them. Only you three will know this truth. Others must believe what I am about to tell you has been handed down through the generations."

Four trays, heavy with sandwiches, cheeses and breads preceded Corakin into the room. Apparently, he'd assumed only one additional tray wouldn't satisfy Thana which, based on the way she was eyeing the incoming food, had been quite an astute observation. The additional trays joined Thana's now-empty one on the coffee table. Brina and Aidan quickly grabbed some food before Thana could start filling her napkin.

"Please, Clio, continue."

It took all three students a moment to realize that Professor Gibberish was speaking to his colleague. Jael simply took a sip of her tea and went on with her story, as if this was the way she'd been telling it all along.

"You are, I assume, familiar with the Baibel story of the Great Flood?" Jael gave a small smile of approval when the kids nodded. "Then you remember that Elsali commissioned a man named Noah to build an ark, but he refused. Two of his three sons, Shem and Japneth, chose to follow Elsali's design. They were joined by their friend, Raziel. Only these three men and their wives survived. As our race began again, a recessive gene, specific to these six people, started to manifest itself in the form of what we call magic. As the years passed, magic became stronger and mankind once more, became corrupted."

"The Tower," Thana apparently couldn't help herself.

Jael nodded. "By this time, the population was equal parts magical and non-magical. When The Tower was destroyed and the nations scattered, they segregated themselves into these two groups, with smaller tribes made up of common languages. But something else happened when The Tower fell. A chasm opened in the earth and a great beast was released." Jael's cadence and tone had become rhythmic, lyrical, as she shared her story. "Mankind fought against the beast, tribes uniting as best they could, but they were no match for the dragon. It slaughtered magic and non-magic alike. When it became obvious that the magical were dying, not from wounds, but from the creature absorbing their magic, those with magic fled, leading the non-magical into a trap and then leaving them to fight alone as a distraction." A shadow passed across Jael's eyes. "Only one magical tribe, the smallest of them, remained. Half died helping what few non-magical people had survived the dragon's wrath. Those with magic who had survived tried, as best they could, to protect the non-magical. They were ultimately unsuccessful and the last of the non-magical tribes was destroyed, though the story of their protectors remained. The remnants of that magical tribe came to be known as the *Starateli.*"

"The Guardians." Corakin's eyes widened. "I thought they were a myth."

"Well, that was a myth-stake." Thana chirped. All eyes turned to her. "Not the time? Right, sorry. Go on."

Brina rolled her eyes and saw Aidan struggling to conceal a smirk. Neither Corakin nor Jael, however, paid their responses any mind as Jael answered the professor's question. "The *Starateli* have become myth over the centuries, but, I assure you, once upon a time they were very real."

"Were?" Brina caught the past tense.

"The *Starateli* bargained with Elsali to save their people, all of the people, magic and non-magic alike. Because they had included the tribes who had betrayed them in their prayer, Elsali honored their request, but it came with a price." Jael paused, taking another sip of her drink. "Though they would have help over the years, the nine surviving Guardians alone would trade their lives for everyone else's. They would be given the means and knowledge to defeat the dragon, though they themselves would be unable to wield the final blow. That would come much, much later." Jael stood and crossed to one of the windows. "Three *Starateli* – Adah, Casta and Talas – lost their lives imprisoning the dragon beneath the earth. Twins, Sileas and Chaim, died creating the lock to contain the creature."

"The field and the fountain," Brina whispered, tears forming in her eyes as she realized what Jael was telling them. These weren't names learned from a book or by word of mouth. Jael had known them.

Jael's head tipped in acknowledgement of Brina's words though she didn't move from the window. "Tavish and Ceana gave their lives forging the sword to kill the beast. Lakyn took the sword to hide it from those who would seek to destroy it."

"Destroy it?" Thana cut in. "Who'd want to destroy the sword if it was the only way to kill the dragon?"

"Some who sought to deify the creature, to worship it." Jael turned her head slightly so her profile was visible. "Others believed they could harness its power for themselves, use it against their enemies."

"That doesn't make any sense," Thana protested. "It sucks magic from everyone."

"When it comes to power," Jael's voice was soft. "Mankind

shows very little sense."

A moment of silence fell before Aidan asked a question. "The final *Starateli* was left to guard the fountain, wasn't... he?" If Corakin noticed Aidan's hesitation on the pronoun, he didn't comment.

"Yes, she was," Jael corrected the pronoun, but didn't offer her name. "She was to guard the fountain and wait."

"Wait?" Corakin leaned forward, excitement on his boyish features.

"For the one who could use the sword to kill the dragon." Jael returned to her seat. "One with no magic."

"But you just said the last of those without magic had died long ago." Corakin's puzzlement was written on his face.

"They had." Jael turned her gaze to Brina, giving her the choice.

"It's me, Professor." Brina's voice was low, clear, betraying none of the chaos inside. Aidan threaded his fingers through hers, offering her the strength and support she needed to say the words. "I don't have magic."

Corakin's eyebrows shot up. "*Elsali misereatur!*" He looked from Brina to Jael and back again, as if hoping one of them would declare the entire thing a joke. "You can't mean that Brina is to take on a dragon?"

"I'm the only one who can." Brina gripped Aidan's hand more tightly.

A look of fierce approval settled on Jael's face. "We have a lot of work to do."

Chapter Eleven: Born This Way

"Aidan, can I ask you something?" Brina slowed to allow Thana to pull ahead as the trio made their way back to the dorms. Something had been nagging at her all day and she wasn't sure how to broach the subject.

"She was my sister." Aidan kept his eyes focused straight ahead. "My twin."

Brina bit back the questions that wanted to spill forward, knowing Aidan would provide the answers in his own time. She wasn't wrong.

"My biological father was Staff Sergeant Ferdinand Enfield. Like many of the soldiers in the Great War, he didn't return home. He and my mother had only been married for a month before he was deployed. He was gone for four months when he was assigned to Deigratia."

Understanding dawned on Brina's face. Everyone in Ortus knew what it meant to be in Deigratia during the Great War. "Animus Ninth." Only ashes had been left after that day.

Aidan nodded, expression tight. "When my mother heard about the attack on the city, she went into an early labor. By the time Major Anderson came to confirm my father's death, my mother had just emerged from a two-day coma, a widow and a new mother. I was in intensive care and my sister was dead." Aidan stopped and looked down at Brina, his normally sparkling eyes flat. "We were nearly two months early. My sister was stillborn. I barely survived. I was in the hospital for almost six months before I could go home. Adalayde had been cremated before my mother woke up. Later, her ashes were buried next to what they could find of my father."

Brina reached up with her free hand and cupped Aidan's cheek. "*Amado*, I'm so sorry."

Aidan placed his hand over Brina's, his eyes softening. "It's okay. I didn't know either of them. It just bothers me when my mom gets sad. She married my step-dad when I was still little. He's been my father, his daughters my sisters. Blood doesn't matter to us. And, my mom's been better since my little brother was born, but she's still really protective of all of us. Drives the girls and AJ crazy." He gave a half-smile and she squeezed his hand.

"Come on!" Thana called from higher up the path. "I'm starving!"

Mood dispelled, both Brina and Aidan hurried to catch up to their friend. They needed some normalcy for their brains to be able to process all of the crazy information they'd learned in such a short period of time. It wasn't until later that night, after Aidan had returned his room and Thana was fast asleep, that Brina allowed her mind to return to another part of the day's conversations, the part she'd been trying the hardest to avoid thinking about.

"If I'm the only one who can kill the dragon," she had asked, "why did it make me pass out? I mean, Thana woke up before I did, so it obviously affected me more than her."

Jael had looked from Aidan to Brina, surprise written across her face. "You don't know what you did?" Brina's blank expression must've answered for her because Jael had continued. "The dragon did not drain you, Brina. Aidan did."

"What?" The pair had asked the question in unison.

"Aidan was dying. The energy that gives him magic also keeps him alive. Your body is sustained by a different type of energy that can't be absorbed by the dragon. Your desire to keep Aidan alive, however, allowed you to transfer your energy to him. Enough to give his own body the necessary time to regenerate his magic, and enough to force your body into an unconscious state to renew itself."

"She could've died," Aidan's voice had been soft, shaking, as he realized what had almost happened.

Jael's dark eyes had spoken volumes.

Those eyes and their solemn, ancient emotions followed Brina into a restless sleep. When Thana's traditional morning song pulled Brina from a dream where she was being chased by a shadow who kept telling her it would kill her before she could kill it, Brina gave up rest as a lost cause and climbed out of bed.

"Ready to head back to classes?" Thana asked as she emerged from the bathroom in a billow of steam.

Brina groaned.

"I'll take that as a no." Thana stepped aside to allow Brina to enter the bathroom.

"I think I'd rather face the dragon." Brina's voice came through the door slightly muffled. "I forgot to do my language homework."

It appeared, as the girls joined Aidan at breakfast, they hadn't been the only ones neglecting their schoolwork. All over the dining hall, students were poring over papers. In fact, it seemed only a handful of people weren't immersed in a text of some kind.

"I'm surprised." Brina slid into the empty seat at Aidan's side. "Usually there aren't so many people rushing to do their homework at breakfast." She grabbed a piece of toast as she opened her language book.

Aidan's eyebrows disappeared under a fringe of fair hair in desperate need of a trim. "You haven't seen?"

"Seen what?" Thana spoke up from Aidan's other side, her fourth wrangleberry muffin almost half gone.

Aidan motioned to the newspaper laying in front of him. He leaned back so both of the girls could get near enough to read. He kept his gaze on Brina's face, his hand making comforting circles on her back.

Brina's eyes grew wider and wider as she read the colorful article, full of detailed descriptions and eyewitness reports. According to *Sinmun* reporter Camden Ryans, a large reptilian creature had consumed a dozen sheep and three woobies before vanishing into the mountains. What no one was able to explain, however, was why or how the two shepherds watching the animals had died. Neither of the bodies were marked and Healers could find nothing physically wrong with either man.

"What I don't understand," Thana finished reading first, "is why it didn't just go to the area with the highest population. More people to suck the life out of."

"Because it's smart." Brina's voice was low. She kept her eyes on the paper as she continued, but she wasn't reading anymore. She didn't know how she knew this, but she did. "It knows not to gorge itself, to make its food supply last."

"Is that a good thing or a bad thing?" Aidan's hand cupped the back of Brina's neck.

Brina considered the question before answering. "Good since fewer people are at risk early on, but bad because the smarter it is, the harder it'll be to kill."

"Good thing we're pretty smart too." Thana consumed her second plate of scrambled eggs. "Eat up, Brina. You're gonna need your strength for our, uh, extra-curricular activities today." Thana returned to her breakfast with frightening enthusiasm.

Brina stared down at the table, stomach in too many knots to consider eating. Aidan bent close to her, voice soft in her ear. "Brina, *amado*, eat something. You'll feel better." His lips brushed the hollow behind her ear and she felt her cheeks warm. "The fight's not today. Enjoy the time we have, and we'll worry about what's to come when it does."

Brina took a deep breath and nodded. "Okay. One step at a time." She looked over at Aidan and brushed back some of wayward her hair. She'd have to put it back in a braid or something before they went to Jael's.

"First, eat." Aidan handed Brina a plate of pancakes. "Then, class."

"And after that, all I have to do is slay a dragon." Brina muttered.

"One step at a time." Aidan repeated. "Breakfast, then homework."

This time it was Thana who groaned. "Can I fight the dragon instead?"

Thana's desire for combat rather than class became quite obvious when she was called on to share her homework answer to the question 'What occupation would you like to pursue after leaving Audeamus?'

"Unless, Miss Decker, you are intending to be a comedian," Corakin allowed himself a smile. "I do not believe your ambition is to become 'a baby squid in a tiny puddle.'" His voice was kind. "Be sure to practice a bit more diligence on tonight's homework, as tomorrow, you will not have the valid reason of a stay in the healing wing to excuse the poor work."

"Yes, Professor." Thana nodded, relieved he hadn't asked her to read any further. She had a sinking feeling she'd written 'Where are you taking baby' as her favorite vacation spot.

By the time the trio reached math, they weren't sure how they would manage to get all of their classwork completed before their training session with Jael that night. And no matter how vehemently Brina insisted her friends stay behind to do their work, they refused. After all, as Thana pointed out, they'd be going together anyway. Brina didn't respond, knowing it'd do no good to argue that she wasn't going to let them anywhere near the dragon. Besides, she reasoned, she could always sneak away without telling the others, though the thought of parting from either of them, especially Aidan, made Brina's heart ache.

"Brina!" A voice hailed her as she exited the classroom. The growl from Aidan confirmed who it was before Brina spotted Gray coming her way. She smiled as Aidan threaded his fingers through hers, pulling her closer to him in a possessive manner.

Brina squeezed his hand and murmured, "Be good."

Aidan just glared as Gray stopped in front of them. Gray's pale eyes darted from Brina's face to where her hand and

Aidan's were linked and back again.

"I heard you were sick." Other than a brief shadow passing over his face, Gray gave no indication he'd seen either Aidan or Thana. "I just wanted to make sure you were okay."

"She's fine, Gray," Aidan snapped, eyes flashing.

"I wasn't talking to you, Aidan," Gray sneered.

"Aidan," Brina kept her tone gentle, now more understanding of Aidan's reaction to anything, or anyone, who threatened to take someone he cared about. Finding out about his sister made his overprotective nature easier to deal with. At her voice, Aidan's tensed muscles relaxed. She addressed Gray, voice cordial, but nothing more. "Thank you for your concern. I'm feeling much better."

An uncomfortable silence settled, as if Gray were waiting for Brina to say something else. Finally, Thana broke the tension. "We'd better get going. Lots of homework to do."

"Oh, well, I guess I'll see you later." Gray awkwardly shifted his weight from one foot to the other, then abruptly turned and walked away. The corridor was virtually empty, allowing the trio to watch as Gray disappeared through a mirror.

"Maybe Gray should come with us to find the dragon." Thana's eyes danced mischievously. Aidan scowled and Brina started, shock evident on her face. "After all," Thana's grin widened. "We may need bait."

Aidan snorted inelegantly as he swallowed his laugh. Brina didn't look amused. Thana winked in their direction, and began to lead the way back to their floor. Before Aidan could move to follow, Brina tugged on his hand. Expecting an argument or reprimand, Aidan was reluctant to turn. His reluctance transformed to surprise, however, as Brina raised herself on her toes and brushed her lips over his. The shock that passed between them made them both smile. Aidan ran his free hand up Brina's arm and she shivered. His smile widened. A somewhat discreet cough from a nearby doorway brought color to both Aidan's and Brina's faces, though only Aidan looked smug about it.

"Sorry, Professor Idun." Brina mumbled.

"You might want to get started on your homework." Professor Erato Idun seemed to be struggling to contain her amusement. "I'm sure Professor Belua gave you plenty in math, and I doubt he was the only one."

"Yes, ma'am." Aidan's lips still wore a smirk as he and Brina hurried after their friend.

Aidan's high spirits lasted through the tediousness of homework, providing entertainment for both the girls. Aidan either didn't notice or didn't care as he grinned at his math paper, non-writing hand resting at Brina's elbow, fingertips lightly brushing her arm when she moved. Every so often Brina's pencil would skid across the page and Aidan's whole arm would twitch as another jolt went through them both, causing Thana to shove whatever food was in her hand into her mouth in an apparent attempt to keep from laughing out loud. Brina still didn't know what was causing the shocks, but she couldn't say she disliked them.

"Attention please." Headmaster Manu's voice echoed through the dining hall. What little conversation had been going on ceased as everyone waited to hear what the headmaster had to say. "The school board and myself have decided, based on the events of the past few weeks, that the remainder of the Fuhjyn season will be canceled." A collective groan and murmured complaints made the headmaster's next words more difficult to hear. "Until further notice, the Fuhjyn field will be off limits. Trespassers will be disciplined. Thank you."

"Maybe it's for the best," Thana piped up. "Now there's nothing to distract us from the drag..." Her voice trailed off as Aidan turned his incredulous face toward her.

Brina stifled a snicker. "You can tell you don't have brothers."

Aidan's eyes narrowed.

"Right. I forgot." Thana couldn't resist a good-natured taunt. "Men must throw ball, beat chest. Sports good."

"Come on, that's a bit of a stereotype," Aidan protested. "That's like saying all girls are like 'Ooo, pretty pink glitter. Let's accessorize and prance around with unicorns.'" His falsetto made both girls giggle.

"He's right." Brina smirked. "Plenty of girls like sports. And I'm sure there are just as many guys who like pink glitter and unicorns."

The trio's chuckles turned into full-blown laughter as Professor Gibberish, who'd wandered over to their table, happily interjected, "Contrary to popular opinion, only the rarest of unicorns are pink and none have glitter." He waited patiently for the trio to calm themselves before continuing, completely nonplussed at their mirth. "Professor Penah wanted me to ask that the three of you go to her house after dinner tonight. She's busy right now getting things ready." He smiled. "She lives two houses to the right of mine. The one with the blue-leaved ecaribu tree in the front window." He gave a little wave. "*Nawguralek.*"

"*Merci.*" The trio chorused in unison as the professor left, their levity fading away.

"This is really happening, isn't it?" Brina's voice was soft. She wasn't sure if the professor's wish for good luck made her feel better or worse.

Aidan brushed back a stay lock of her hair, tucking it behind her ear. "Scared?" he asked.

Brina lied to herself as much as to him. "No."

***

"This is awesome." Thana's voice echoed off the high ceiling.

Brina and Aidan could only gawk. They'd all found Jael's house easily enough thanks to the bright blue leaves peeking from behind old-fashioned lace curtains. The interior of the house was fairly spartan and nothing extraordinary. Then Jael had opened the door to the basement. A long stone staircase disappeared into blackness only pierced by the torches on the wall. The fire-safe flame burned only a step ahead and a step behind, both leading and following Jael and her charges down into the dark. Upon reaching the foot of the stairs, Jael uttered a single word and torches all around the room blazed to life. Hewn from rock, the room looked more like the dragon's cave than part of a house. Floor and walls were rough, uneven, and unadorned except a few feet of the furthest wall. On it, from various hooks and chains, hung myriad weapons of all sized and shapes.

"*Kazhah*! Nun-chucks!" Thana bounded across the room, intent clearly written on her face.

"Thana." Brina's voice stopped the smaller girl in her tracks. "No." Thana looked back at her friend, expression hopeful. Brina shook her head. "Just... no."

Thana turned, countenance and demeanor plainly stating that Brina had completely destroyed any chance Thana had at happiness. Brina and Aidan, however, exchanged glances of relief at a potential disaster averted. Thana may have been proficient on the Fuhjyn field but, for some reason, her skill failed to transfer to other areas. This had become glaringly obvious when, just after Zoe and Asha's deaths, Headmaster Manu had required all students to attend a two-day self-defense class. Thana ended up sending fifteen year-olds Maury Reaser and Enoch Buckley to the healing wing with black eyes when the right-left combination she was aiming at Brina went impossibly wild. Only Becca Davenport and Katie Wright managed worse injuries when Katie's overly enthusiastic throw landed Becca in the trashcan with a broken arm and pulled a muscle in Katie's back. Needless to say, self-defense training had come to a definitive halt after that.

Jael cleared her throat and the trio turned toward their professor. "I agreed to allow you two," she directed the statement at both Thana and Aidan, "to join us as you both intend to accompany Brina on her mission. I believe your companionship will be beneficial, and as magic will be useless against the beast, you must know how to defend yourself in other ways. However, my primary objective is to teach Brina so, when the time comes, she is able to slay the dragon. Should either of you prove to be a distraction, I will ask you to leave. Are we clear?"

"Yes, ma'am." Aidan and Thana answered, instantly serious.

Brina felt the tension in the room spike as the mission became deadly real. Jael apparently sensed the change in atmosphere as she gave her students a tight smile. "Good." She crossed to the wall of weapons and retrieved a sword. It was plain, a broadsword too heavy to be effectively wielded with a single hand... or so it originally appeared. Jael held it in her right hand, pivoting her wrist so that the blade sliced through the air as she walked back to where the three waited. She stopped a few feet in from Brina and spoke again.

"This isn't fencing for sport or entertainment, but it isn't exactly sword-fighting either."

"What do you mean?" Thana interrupted. "Isn't Brina going to be fighting a dragon?"

"And do you suppose the creature will be carrying a sword?" Jael sounded stern, but Brina could see the corners of the Guardian's mouth fighting against a smile. Thana had that effect on people.

"Oh. Right." Thana curled her fingers in the air. "Claws. Rawr."

After a moment of awkward silence during which Thana realized she should lower her hands, Jael handed the sword to

Brina, hilt first. "What you will need to learn is balance, grace and strength."

Brina took the sword in hand, surprised at the weight of it. She let the point rest on the ground as Jael continued.

"This is the same size and weight of the sword you will be using against the dragon. I've dulled the edges to prevent any serious harm, but every blade, whether dull or sharp, is dangerous. This one is no exception. It can break a man's arm with one swing. Do not fear your sword, but do not disdain it either. To treat a weapon with disrespect is to risk your well-being." Jael motioned for Brina to raise the sword. "To control your blade, you must build your strength. You are an athlete, but to use a sword, one must train different muscles." Jael placed her hand under the blade and maneuvered Brina until the girl's arms were extended, both hands on the hilt, sword pointed straight ahead. "Now hold."

"For how long?"

"Long enough." Jael remained cryptic. She turned to Aidan and Thana. "Aidan, time her. Thana, you are to watch the sword. If the point of the sword moves at all, even a waver, she is done. When it moves, tell Aidan. We will do this every day, increasing the time with each new session."

"Um, Professor?" Thana raised her hand slightly.

"Yes?"

"I don't understand how this is going to help Brina against a dragon."

Jael studied Thana for a moment before answering. "Most people think they should only fear the obvious on a dragon. The teeth, claws, fire."

"Don't forget the magic-sucking thing." Thana interrupted. Off of Jael's raised eyebrows, Thana apologized and motioned for Jael to continue.

"Yes, Thana, and the 'magic-sucking thing.' But every part of a dragon is dangerous. Their scales are harder to penetrate than the strongest steel, their skin tougher than the most battle-hardened leather, their bones more durable than rock."

"Brina needs to strong enough to get the sword into the dragon." Aidan answered Thana's question.

Jael nodded. "The blade must pierce the dragon's heart, for only then will it be able to do what it was made for."

"Which is?" Brina surprised herself at how steady her voice was. The muscles in her arms were starting to burn already, but she didn't want it to show.

"The reason no other weapon can kill the dragon, why no other person can wield the sword." Jael's dark eyes held a spark of something fierce and old. "It is not the piercing of the heart that will slay the dragon, rather what happens next. The sword was made to drain all magic from the dragon and channel it into the person who held it. Someone with their own magic wouldn't be able to contain it. But, someone with your unique chemistry, will be able to take the magic into yourself and survive."

"You mean," Brina fought not to drop the sword. "After I kill the dragon, I'll have magic?"

Jael nodded. "Yes, Brina. All of the magic you take from the dragon will be yours to keep."

Chapter Twelve: This Kiss

Brina bit back a whimper as she stepped into the shower. The hot water pounded into her sore muscles, painful and soothing at the same time. She'd been standing, sword in hand, with arms outstretched for three hours every day for the past five days with very little rest in between fifteen minute sessions. Each morning, she woke with stiff muscles. Last night, her arms had been unable to take any more abuse and the sword had dropped. The abruptness had pulled or torn something, and even the smallest movement was agony. The hot shower last night had helped at the time, but the lack of movement while she'd slept had made things worse.

Brina turned off the spray and reached for a towel, swallowing another pained sound as she wrapped herself in the soft cotton. Her hair dripped onto the floor and Brina let it. She couldn't raise her arms enough to dry her body, much less her hair. A billow of steam followed her into her room where she swapped her towel for a robe, allowing the thick material to absorb the liquid on her skin. She sat on the edge of her bed, twisting slightly to allow most of her hair to fall over her shoulder. As much as her limited usage of motion allowed her, Brina began to squeeze excess water from her hair.

A soft knock came at the door. "Brina." It was Aidan.

"Come in." Brina pulled her robe tighter around her.

Aidan stepped into the room, looking as freshly scrubbed, though more pain-free, than Brina. Without a word, he crossed to the bed and sat at her side. He took the towel and began to dry Brina's hair. They sat in silence, Aidan's hands working through the material to draw moisture into the cloth. When Brina's hair was sufficiently dry, Aidan leaned close, his voice low in Brina's ear. "Brush?"

"On the dresser." Brina's own voice was quiet as she watched Aidan retrieve her hairbrush. With a start, she realized this was the first time they'd been alone together since... well, she couldn't remember when. She loved Thana, but through no fault of anyone, the other girl had been constantly at their side. This morning, however, Thana had dashed off to breakfast with a hurried explanation about needing to call home for her father's birthday.

Aidan returned to his seat and began to carefully work through the tangles not smoothed out by the conditioner. The rhythm of the brush, the soft sound of the bristles, the feel of Aidan's fingers in her hair, relaxed Brina's tensed body more than her shower had.

"My older sisters," Aidan's words were soft, cadence matching his movements, "used to babysit me and they'd have me play hairdresser." Brina could hear Aidan's wistful smile. "I think they'd always wanted a little sister and I was more than willing to let them shower me with affection. Sometimes I'd wonder how close Adalayde and I would've been had she lived." He tied off the braid and laid his hands on either side of Brina's neck, gently working the muscles. Brina shivered at the touch and Aidan shifted closer. She felt his breath on the back of her neck a moment before his lips pressed against her skin.

"I love you, Brina Fine." Aidan murmured. "No matter what lies ahead, I know I'm a better person because of you and I'll willingly face an uncertain future if you're at my side."

Not for the first time, Aidan demonstrated an uncanny ability to wax eloquent. It was one of the many things about him Brina found attractive. She turned, capturing his mouth with hers. Her hand slid around his neck, pulling him closer, and his hands moved down to grip her waist. A flare of electricity, of power, washed over them and they broke apart, gasping. Brina moved and sucked in a sharp breath.

"What's wrong?" Aidan's voice was still breathless, his face flushed.

"No pain." Brina stood, stretching her arms. "I'm stiff, like I have been all week, but I'm not hurting like just a few minutes ago."

"Wow. Some kiss, right?"

Later that evening, Thana fought valiantly to suppress her laughter – and lost. Brina, face crimson, glared at her friend as Jael listened to the series of events leading up to Brina's healing.

"It seems," the Guardian spoke over Thana's incessant giggling. "Brina saving Aidan has created a link between the two. A bond with the ability to conduct energy from one to the other, depending on the need." She looked at Aidan. "I would assume you were concerned about Brina's well-being when the kiss occurred?" The question prompted another cackling outburst from Thana.

"Yes." Aidan glowered at Thana.

"And, Brina, when Aidan was injured, you were thinking about how to save him?" Brina nodded, and Jael continued. "Then I would say you two need to be careful when one of you is sick or injured. Something minor will not present a problem, but a more serious injury could have grave consequences."

Thana's laughter stopped suddenly, her expression saying she now understood the gravity of what Jael was saying. Brina and Aidan had lost all of the color their faces had acquired, leaving their skin a strange mottled shade of pink and white. Neither one had considered the long-reaching implications of what had happened between them.

"Come, Brina," Jael's voice was soft, sympathetic. "We start combat training today. Choose your weapon."

Brina took a deep breath, attempting to refocus on the issue at hand. "Shouldn't I be using the sword?"

"Eventually," Jael agreed. "I will teach you how to slay and defend with the sword, but you will also need to know what to do if you lose your weapon or are against a human."

"Like those dragon worshippers you told us about," Thana

piped up from where she was sitting.

Jael nodded again. "And this means you and Aidan will be joining Brina in training today." She motioned toward the wall. "Choose your weapons."

Less than twenty minutes later, Thana, Aidan and Brina were all sitting on the floor, their weapons of choice at Jael's feet. She looked down at them, not even out of breath, not a hair out of place.

"Again."

Brina shot Aidan a look. It was going to be a long night.

***

Metal clashed against metal, the only sound other than the ragged breathing of the pair fighting. To one side, Thana and Jael watched, their own match having ended in a draw less than ten minutes before. For such a light-hearted person, Thana had proven a fierce competitor and a quick study with a pair of short blades that seemed to erase her usual awkwardness when fighting. Aidan's favored weapon, a wicked-looking crossbow, wasn't really a close-quarter combat piece. To assist Brina, however, Aidan had become fairly proficient with a broadsword. It was this Aidan was currently wielding with such ferocity. He'd held back the first few times he'd sparred with Brina... until his girlfriend had knocked him unconscious with a surprise blow to the back of the head. When he'd woken, Jael had been standing over him with a wry smile, asking if he'd start putting forth full effort. Wincing as he'd gingerly touched the purple bump on his forehead, Aidan had agreed.

Now, Aidan was straining to meet Brina's blows, changing from offense to defense as she backed him across the room. His elbow hit the wall, inhibiting his swing. Brina twisted her blade around and Aidan's sword slipped from his fingers.

"Well, done." Jael broke the silence. "All of you." She

glanced at the wall where Aidan had been target practicing earlier. "I would like you three to take the remainder of the week off to prepare for our imminent journey."

"We're leaving?" Brina tried not to let her voice betray her nervousness.

"The time for training is over. The time for action is at hand."

Brina felt a shiver run the length of her spine. "What about school? We still have two weeks after this week off before term break. And how do we tell our families we're not coming home?"

"I will arrange for your absence from Audeamus." Jael retrieved Brina's sword and re-hung it on the wall. "As for your families, what you tell them is up to you. Though I would advise discretion rather than bold-faced honesty."

Brina immediately understood the caution. For the past three and a half weeks, the news had been filled with tales of strange deaths and disappearances. Sightings of a large, lizard-like creature were scattered throughout the news, and peppered the conversations of staff, students and strangers alike. Then, just two weeks ago, a different perspective had begun to leak out. Rather than the crazed claims ranging from aliens to space monkeys, credible witnesses had begun coming forward with explanations of dragons, and the end of the world. The first of the Draconis Churches was founded on Fatum twentieth and a new one had sprung up every few days since. Half were made up of those who believed the dragon to be Lucifyr himself, come to bring about the end of days. Their members spent most of the time crying in the churches or preaching in the streets. The other half of the institutions, however, preached the deity of the creature, proclaiming that sacrifices to it would prevent all the plagues of the world such as hunger, obesity, famine, sickness, greed and pretty much anything else with which they disagreed. Subtle threats had been made by these groups toward any who would seek to harm their new god. The kids now understood why the Guardians had gone to so much trouble to hide the dragon-slaying sword.

"What are you going to tell Headmaster Manu?" Brina asked. "He's friends with my parents, so I should probably use the same story."

"I need to take a time-sensitive research trip which requires me to leave immediately, and I've chosen the three of you to accompany me as my assistants." Jael tossed a bottle of water to each of the kids. Thana drained hers immediately while the other two took their time. "The headmaster is used to my periodic sabbaticals for 'research' purposes. Once I convince him you three are essential to my trip, he'll arrange for you to be excused from your final exams."

"And how are you going to do that?" Thana retrieved her wand and refilled her water bottle.

"Between Brina's language skills, your father's contacts, and Aidan's defensive arts grades, it shouldn't be a problem. And, if I'm not mistaken, Thana, you've traveled quite extensively yourself, which will help." Thana nodded and Jael continued, "You'll want to say all of your good-byes soon because we leave in three days."

As the trio left Jael's house, they were silent, even Thana, each consumed with their own thoughts as they trudged through the snow that had covered the grounds for weeks. Absently, Brina reached for Aidan's hand, threading her fingers through his. As soon as their skin touched, she felt a flood of reassurance and confidence in her, and their mission. The butterflies in her stomach ceased their frenzied fluttering and her muscles relaxed. From the surprised look on Aidan's face, he'd felt something similar. They didn't say anything, but kept their hands entwined until they reached Thana and Brina's room. More tranquil, but still preoccupied, Aidan brushed his lips across Brina's and went to his room.

"Thana," Brina spoke slowly, unsure if she wanted to reveal the thought that had been at the edge of her consciousness for weeks, but knowing she had to tell someone. "You know how Jael thinks me saving Aidan forged this connection?" Thana nodded. "Well, it might've started this whole energy transfer thing, but we had a connection before that. It's how I knew Aidan had gone into the dragon's cave. How I knew where he was."

Thana didn't say anything at first, strangely introspective. When she finally spoke, it was with a gravity she'd rarely shown before. "So much of you is tied up in prophecy and design. Perhaps Aidan is a part of it too. Maybe your connection is part of Elsali's plan."

Brina stared at Thana for seconds. "Do you really think so?"

Thana shrugged, moment of seriousness passing. "Or you two could just be serious lust bunnies."

A pillow sailed across the room and caught Thana's shoulder. "I'm going to take a shower. Please try to behave yourself while I'm gone."

"Who, me?" Thana gave Brina her best innocent face. "What do you think I could possibly do in such a short time?"

"Transfigure my pillow into a cat?"

"One time!" Thana gestured at the blue-and-white checkered tabby glaring at her from the foot of Brina's bed. "Besides, you love Marmalade."

Brina stroked the soft fur, and the cat closed its eyes and purred. "And do I even need to mention the time you tried to make a wolverine and a walrus become friends? I don't think Miss Waldburg has forgiven you for trying that in the dining hall."

"Point taken." Thana pouted. She suddenly brightened. "At least I managed to get rid of the cannibalistic penguins before they made too much of a mess in the library."

"True." Brina nodded, her smile tired, but genuine. She

grabbed her robe and headed for the bathroom, pausing at the door. "In case I don't tell you later, I'm glad you're coming with me." She disappeared into the bathroom, door closing behind her before Thana could reply.

When Brina exited almost a half hour later, Thana passed her without a word, knowing Aidan was waiting on the girls before cleaning himself from the sweat and grime of practice. Fortunately for them, Aidan's roommate had, like many of their classmates, been on an extended furlough since the earthquake, allowing the trio more freedom in their rooms. This had been particularly beneficial over the past few weeks when vigorous training had left them all bruised and bloody. None of them wanted to have to explain their injuries.

Brina barely slept that night despite her exhaustion. In her mind, she kept running through all of the possible scenarios of telling her parents about not coming home for term break, and how to explain her being excused from finals. Being the daughter of two educators, she knew how valuable her education was and how deeply her parents prized it, particularly in her case. She was surprised then, by their excitement over her being chosen for a research assistant to Clio Penah. Apparently, the Guardian was well-known in academic circles, a fact Brina discovered when she was woken by her parents' call early the next morning.

The melodious chimes of the mirror were quickly followed by Vani's excitement-filled voice. "Roderick just told us the news! Why didn't you tell us you were applying for an assistantship with Clio Penah?"

"I, uh," Brina sat up, shaking her head to clear the cobwebs. "I didn't want to get your hopes up."

"We're so proud of you, Brina." Vani paused, and then continued, her voice lower and more subdued. "Your father and I really are proud of all you've accomplished this year, how well you're adapting to your... handicap. It can't have been easy for you."

Brina's surprise woke her fully. Her parents refrained from mentioning her abnormality, and she'd always assumed the silence had meant they were ashamed of her. She'd gotten the impression her very existence was thought of more as a burden than blessing.

"Thank you." Brina stammered. "J-Professor Penah says my language skills will be quite valuable." Brina closed her eyes, hoping her mother hadn't noticed her slip. She needn't have worried. Her mother was still gushing over the headmaster's call. Brina climbed out of bed and began straightening her covers as her mother carried on. Movement caught Brina's attention and she turned to see Thana blinking sleepily in her direction, dumbfounded to have discovered Brina awake first. Brina mouthed 'my mother' before returning to the mirror's sightline. Vani finally paused for breath, and Brina seized the opportunity. "Well, I've got lots to do before we leave. Work to arrange with professors and all that."

"Of course!" Vani beamed at Brina. "Call us when you can, and have fun!"

"Thanks, Mom." Brina smiled back, completely stunned by the exalted expression her mother was sending her way. "I love you. And give my love to Dad."

Vani nodded. "We love you, too." The mirror went dark.

Thana crossed to Brina's side and put a hand on her friend's shoulder. For once, she didn't seem to feel the need to fill the silence with unnecessary words. She left after a moment, disappearing into the bathroom to give Brina time to compose herself. When she came out, Brina had already changed into jeans and a long-sleeved 'Nerdheart the Kareboar' t-shirt, and had begun sorting clothes for the journey.

"I'm going to the garden to talk to my dad." Thana pocketed her wand.

"Do it here." Brina grabbed her cloak as her stomach

suddenly twisted. "I'd like some fresh air."

As she slipped through the secret door into the garden, she wasn't surprised to see Aidan there already. The faint shimmer in the air in front of him indicated his *Rasha Harma* conversation had ended just moments before. Brina walked toward him, knowing he'd sensed her presence just as she'd unconsciously felt his. It seemed her heightened emotions while talking with her mother had connected with his similar state, filling Brina with a need to find him.

"How did she take the news?" Brina put her hand on Aidan's arm.

Aidan turned, bright green eyes swimming with tears. "Aside from being disappointed that I'd be gone on my birthday, she was fine." His mouth twisted into a grimace of a smile. "After all, we're only going on a research trip with a respected professor. Nothing dangerous. Nothing to be worried about." A tear escaped and he brushed at it angrily.

Brina caught his hand in both of hers and pressed it against her lips, prepared for the release of energy that would transfer feelings of comfort and calm to Aidan. "Elsali will protect us, Aidan." He nodded as he pulled his hand from hers and wrapped his arms around her. Brina rested her head against his chest, the steady beat of his heart soothing her own anxiety.

"What about your parents?" he asked.

Brina didn't ask how he'd known she'd spoke with them. "Couldn't be prouder." She hated herself for the note of bitterness creeping into her voice, but she was powerless to stop it.

"They love you, Bri." Aidan smoothed down Brina's hair with one hand, the other settling at her lower back. "They might not always know how to show it, but they love you."

Brina nodded, agreeing in her mind, but not trusting her heart not to betray how she truly felt. Aidan knew, though and kissed the top of her head. "We're gonna make them proud, Bri.

All of them."

A gust of cold wind broke the mood and Aidan released Brina. She took his hand. "We'd better head up to breakfast. I have a feeling we won't be getting many hot meals where we're going." She grinned. "Remember what happened when we tried to make dinner at Jael's a few weeks ago?" They both laughed as they recalled the disaster that had been their attempt at baked chicken, salad and a custard dessert. Unfortunately, they'd come to realize making food was not something any of them, including Jael, did well. Not even the lettuce had been edible by the time they'd finished.

Aidan groaned suddenly and Brina looked up at him, concerned. Her worry melted away when he spoke. "I don't want to be there when Thana figures that out."

***

Pectus twenty-first was cold and wet, the type of day that made people want to curl up under their warm blankets and thank Elsali they still had a day off to study for the coming weeks' finals. Brina, Thana and Aidan, however, reluctantly threw off their covers and began the last of their preparations: a quick bite to eat during which Thana attempted to consume enough food to sustain her through the upcoming journey, a final sweep for anything left behind, and dropping Marmalade at Becca and Katie's room. The girls had been more than willing to take in the furry feline until Brina's return. Marmalade had deigned to Brina's farewell head scratch and then padded off to exchange disdainful sniffs with Becca's and Katie's tabbies, Azeroth and Velma. Finally, Aidan alerted Jael that they were ready, or at least as ready as they could be for something like this.

The Guardian was waiting in the dining hall by the time the trio appeared. Only a handful of students were milling around, most grabbing breakfast, then disappearing back to the comfort of their rooms.

"I hope you've eaten." Off of the trio's nods, Jael continued. "And you've made all necessary arrangements?" They nodded again. "Then it's time."

"Brina! Wait!" Gray hurried toward them, stopping in front of Brina and ignoring the others. "I just heard you were leaving."

"We're going on a research trip with Professor Penah." Brina kept her voice polite, not seeing any need to be rude since they'd be gone for who knew how long. She felt Aidan's annoyance, though, edging toward anger.

"How long will you be gone?"

"As long as necessary, Mr. Plumb." Jael cut into the conversation. "If you don't mind, we've get a schedule to keep."

A dark flush stained Gray's cheeks. "Of course, Professor." He looked back at Brina. "I'll be waiting until you get back."

Brina took Aidan's hand, deliberately drawing attention to their intertwined fingers. "I appreciate the sentiment, Gray, but I don't think that would be in your best interest." She turned to walk away.

Gray grabbed Brina's arm. "Why don't you let me decide what's in my best interest."

"Hands off, Gray." Brina's voice was as cold as the weather. Aidan tensed, but didn't say anything, responding to the gentle pressure of Brina's hand on his. "I won't say it again."

Gray took a step closer, tightening his grip, almost daring her to react. In a quick motion, Brina released Aidan's hand and grabbed Gray's middle two fingers on his free hand, bending them backwards. She didn't stop when he let her arm go, cursing at her.

"*Grd pes!*"

Brina felt the bones in his fingers reach their limit and knew they'd snap with just the slightest additional pressure. He dropped to his knees, pain and rage warring on his face. The few people still in the dining hall stared as Brina glared down at him. "Listen well, you *arogantni kos smeti*. From now on, when someone says 'no,' you will cease and desist, or you will answer to me. Believe me when I say that is not something you want." Brina held Gray's fingers a beat longer before releasing them. Without a backwards glance at either the baffled students or Gray, who was alternating between scathing glares and pathetic whimpers while cradling his injured hand against his chest, Brina strode from the room.

After a beat, Thana spoke. "I guess that's our cue to follow." Aidan and Jael just nodded, both working to contain their smiles until they were out of the building.

Chapter Thirteen: The Countdown

Brina's jaw ached from clenching her mouth shut, but she feared if her teeth chattered any harder, they'd shatter. She and her companions had left behind the comforts of civilization three days ago, and had just abandoned Jael's car only a few hours before making camp. They'd stopped at the foot of the mountains as the sun had been setting, ready to settle in for the night. According to Jael, the mountains dampened magical abilities, negating them all over the range without any discernible pattern, making any attempt at magical transport far more dangerous than traveling on foot. Brina drew her blanket more tightly around her shoulders, and wondered again how long it would be till the sun rose. Each one of them had their own tents, and while Aidan had set Brina's up with a wave of his wand, the other three hadn't thought about how Brina would start a fire in the stove without fuel, matches or magic. Neither, she admitted, had she.

A knock on the door of the tent made Brina jump. Rather than trust her voice, she left her bed, crossed the moderately spacious living room and opened the door to let in a frosty, snow-coated Aidan. He stepped inside, shaking snow from his shaggy hair and stamping it from his boots. Without a word, he drew his wand and, a moment later, a fire roared in the stove. From under his robe, he produced a large, fluffy purple blanket covered with repeating images of a baby turtle and a kitten, arm-in-arm, skipping through a meadow filled with butterflies.

Unable to speak past her clenched teeth and numb lips, Brina settled for raising an eyebrow and giving a questioning look. She was cold, but her sense of curiosity was alive and well.

Aidan wrapped the blanket around Brina's shoulders and answered the unasked question. "My dad bought it for Adalayde when my mom told him about us." Aidan pulled Brina to him and slid his arms around her. "We both got one. I gave mine to my little brother when he was born. I'd kept it because it was from my dad, but I didn't mind giving it up. Adalayde's though... I've never been able to stop carrying it."

Brina felt her jaw unfreeze enough to speak. "I was going to tease you for having a security blanket, but now I'm torn between thinking it's adorable and wanting to cry."

"Stick with the adorable." Aidan raised a hand to brush his thumb across Brina's thawing lips. "No crying on my account."

"Duly noted." Brina tilted her head, hoping Aidan would get the hint. She wasn't disappointed. He pressed his lips to hers, warming them even as his pretty purple, slightly sad, security blanket brought feeling and heat back into Brina's body. Or, at least, that's what she told herself was causing her rise in temperature.

Aidan pulled away first, steering Brina to the kitchen table. He gently pushed Brina into a seat and began rummaging through the cupboards. Moments later, the kettle was moving toward a boil and Aidan was emptying a tin of homemade cocoa into a large white mug that declared: "Forget the Dog. Beware of Ninja Kitty."

"How'd you know?" Brina maneuvered her hands out from under the blanket in anticipation of the hot drink.

"Know what?"

"How'd you know to come here?"

Aidan paused, considering the question, then shrugged. "I'm not really sure. I just woke up and knew you were cold."

"I didn't feel any magic when we kissed, did you?"

Aidan faked an injured expression. "Are you saying our kiss wasn't magical?"

Brina made a face at Aidan. "You know what I meant, Aidan. Jael was worried this bond would cause energy transfer through," Brina's blushed, "physical contact, but it wasn't like when I was hurt before."

Aidan slid the mug over to Brina and settled into the chair

across from her. "Maybe," he spoke after a few minutes of pensive silence. "It's because I didn't feel helpless about your condition tonight. I knew that a fire, a blanket, something warm to drink, would solve the problem. Before, I wanted you to feel better, but I couldn't do anything."

"Maybe." Brina agreed, taking a sip of the cocoa. She stared down at the liquid, lost in thought.

"Brina." Aidan snapped his fingers in front of her face and she blinked. "Where'd you go?"

Brina reached out and took Aidan's hand. Her skin was still chilled, but no longer the frightening cold it had been half an hour before. "I was just wondering about the reason behind this connection. Not like the scientific explanation Jael gave us, but Elsali's reason. His plan for all of this."

"You think it's intentional, this bond? That Elsali has some design in which this plays some important role?" Aidan's fingertips played across the back of Brina's hand. Her other hand began to mimic the movement against the side of the mug.

"Everything about this seems like it's been orchestrated." Brina sighed. "Sometimes I wonder how much control we actually have, how many of our choices we really make, and how many are made for us."

Aidan knelt in front of Brina, tucking the usual strand of wayward hair behind her ear before cupping her cheek. "He gives us a choice, Bri. He always does. I have no doubt there's a plan and things far beyond our comprehension in play, but we have to decide if we're going to trust Him enough to make the choices we know are right."

Brina leaned into Aidan's palm, feeling his warmth travel through every cell. "When did you become so wise and philosophical?"

"When I realized my girlfriend was chosen to save the world." Aidan grinned. "Figured I needed to step up my game."

"Well done, Sir, well done indeed." Brina returned the smile, and bent forward for another kiss.

When the sun rose just a few hours later, Brina and Aidan were curled up on the couch, purple turtle-kitten blanket tucked snuggly around Brina and held in place by Aidan's arms. The fire had dwindled as Aidan had drifted off, but it didn't die completely, fueled by Aidan's magic. The pair didn't wake until Brina's mirror sounded for an incoming call. The shiny-happy tone identified the caller as Thana.

Brina sat up, disoriented, but warm. She stumbled across the living area to where her mirror sat. "Answer." She yawned as Thana's image appeared.

***

"This is your morning wake-up call!" Thana's excessively cheerful voice cut through the air, pulling Aidan from a bizarre dream concerning a cactus, a missing porcupine named Pablo and a score of singing mermaids. Unfortunately, Aidan's odd dream clung to him as he woke and he flailed, warding off attacking mermaids, and knocking himself off of the couch.

"Um, good morning?" Thana was smiling at Aidan's antics, but her eyes darted back to Brina, giving a look equal parts amusement and disapproval.

"I was cold last night." Brina immediately flushed. "I didn't have any way to start a fire."

Thana opened her mouth, but instead of one of her trademark snarky retorts, she simply said, "Yeah, I hadn't thought of that."

"Some help, please," Aidan called from the floor. He was so thoroughly tangled in the blanket that it took Brina several minutes to extract him. Red-faced, he stumbled to his feet. "I'm going to go change."

Brina nodded, accepting the quick kiss on her forehead without a word. He headed back to his tent, ignoring the snickers coming from the mirror.

When all four gathered in Brina's tent several minutes later, Thana was still experiencing occasional outbursts of giggling. It wasn't until Jael threatened to hex her silent that Thana's laughter finally subsided. Before passing on instructions regarding their next step, Jael apologized to Brina for the magical oversight and magicked three boxes from her tent. The risk of being stranded in a soft spot on a cold night had prompted the creation of emergency kits near areas such as where they now were, Jael explained. She'd requisitioned a few before their journey, but hadn't handed them out since magic was still an option.

Jael nodded and continued as if nothing had happened. "The passage through the mountains will be dangerous. Aside from the possibility of soft spots, any magic will be sure to draw the dragon's attention. It will make finding the beast easier once we have the sword, but to bring ourselves to the creature's attention prior to finding Lakyn would be folly. We need him to give us the sword before we can try to kill the dragon." Jael turned her focus from Brina to Thana and Aidan. "From this point on, unless we are in mortal danger, we are not to use magic."

The pair couldn't have looked more horrified if Jael had told them that lederhosen and bubblegum-pink wigs were the new required dress code. The expression on Thana's face indicated the wigs might have been preferable. Ignoring them, Jael handed each of the kids a box. "After breakfast, we head for Kripke Pass."

***

It took them longer than usual to pack up and, for the first time, Brina beat Thana and Aidan. Jael had been trained both with and without magic, but Thana and Aidan had never been forced to do things 'the hard way' except as an occasional punishment. Snow had begun falling again by the time the group started up the trail that lead through David's Valley, the first part of Kripke Pass. The trio was glad for their Fuhjyn training as their packs weighed them down, but they still found themselves tiring far faster than Jael. The *Starateli* led the way in silence, always a few feet ahead of them. She rarely spoke and only to warn them if a particular spot was treacherous. Even Thana fell into the hushed rhythm of boots cutting through snow, of inhalations and exhalations of bitter cold air, of the occasional impatient brush to clear vision as flakes clustered on eyelashes. They saw no other person and only the barest glimpse of tail or feet as wild animals scurried away from the intruders. By the time they stopped for the night, Brina was beginning to feel like she and the other three were the last people in the world.

The days blurred together as the group steadily made progress. David's Valley was left behind by Fidelis sixth and the trail faded into nothingness just a few days later. Jael, it seemed, knew where she was going as her footsteps never faltered, leading the group up winding mountain paths and across frozen rivers without error. Every so often, she'd name one of the landmarks – Easthom River, Klinger Lake, Hendrickson Hollow – but mostly kept her thoughts to herself.

Aidan's birthday provided a small break in routine as Jael presented them with three bars of chocolate she'd been saving. The kids consumed them greedily, thankful for something other than the dried fruit and nuts that usually accompanied the cured meat Jael had packed. Shortly after Aidan's birthday, the weather began to turn, the snow lessening in volume as the latter half of Fidelis began.

As the sun shone down on the travelers on one particularly warm day, Brina realized, with a start, they'd left Audeamus more than a month ago. She opened her mouth to bring the realization to the others' attention. Before she could, however, Jael stopped and held up a hand. Brina tensed, freezing where she stood. On either side of her, she saw Aidan and Thana do the same.

"Wait here," Jael ordered, dropping her pack from her shoulders. She drew a six-inch blade from her boot and vanished behind a massive *gures* tree. The trio waited in tense silence, straining to hear anything beyond the rustle of animals waking from their hibernation and the gentle ripple of a hidden creek. Minutes passed and, just as Brina had started to consider a rescue of some kind, Jael reappeared, followed closely by a man dressed in furs and hides.

He was taller than all of them, though how muscular was difficult to assess through the bulk of his wardrobe. His hair was burnt umber and long, pulled away from his strong face in a braid that disappeared down his back. Most shocking, however, were his eyes, a shade that could only be described as violet, and as close to Brina's as she'd ever seen. His eyes widened when he saw her and he cast a questioning glance at Jael.

"Yes," Jael nodded at him and then responded to the puzzled expression on the others' faces. "This is Lakyn, keeper of the sword, and distant relative to Brina."

"Wait, what?" Thana's gaze flicked from Lakyn to Brina.

"Before we became *Starateli*," Lakyn's voice was rough, as if he rarely used it. "My younger brother, Phelan, married a young woman from a non-magic tribe. They fled together during the wars. I had heard rumors they had survived, but my duty to the Guardians superseded my desire to find him." The accent that was so faint in Jael's voice was much thicker in Lakyn's.

Jael rested a hand on Lakyn's arm. "When I first saw Brina, I was struck by how much she resembled both Phelan and Brietta, and I researched her family. Her father is descended from your brother."

"So, you're, like her really, really, really old great-great something or other uncle?" Thana took a step toward Lakyn as if to more closely examine the resemblance.

"I suppose I am," Lakyn agreed. A *stoli* screeched overhead and Lakyn glanced up at the sparkling purple bird. "We should go inside." He turned his gaze back to Brina. "The *Decazmaja* have been lurking in these woods, searching for their winged master."

"The *Decazmaja*?" Aidan whispered to Brina as they followed after Jael and Lakyn.

"Children of the Dragon," Brina translated, keeping her eyes on Lakyn's back and hoping her voice didn't betray the fear she felt. She knew her hope had been in vain when Aidan took her hand. He didn't say anything, letting the gentle pressure of his fingers convey what his words could not.

Lakyn's home wasn't far from where they'd stopped, but so well-hidden they could've been standing just outside his door and never known. At one time, Brina supposed, it had been cave, but Lakyn had used the millennium he'd had to turn it into a spacious and warm place to live. The main living area was almost the size of an entire floor at Audeamus, and was packed with thousands of years of furnishings and other things. Everything spoke of a solitary life spent in this one space. Brina suspected the niche in the back, covered by a colorful hanging, lead to his sleeping quarters.

He motioned toward a pile of cushions in the center of the room. "Please, pull a seat to the fire."

Jael leaned her pack against the wall and shrugged out of her heavy cloak, hanging it on a hook by the door. She kicked off her boots and walked across the cool stone floor in her socks. As she grabbed one of the animal-skin cushions and tugged it toward the massive fireplace, the trio followed her example. By the time Lakyn joined them, divested of most of his outdoor gear, all four of the travelers were situated in front of the flames, soaking in the heat and the comfort. Lakyn sank into a cushion between Jael and Brina, his lanky frame strangely graceful.

"It seems," Lakyn studied Brina with candid scrutiny. "Elsali has not forgotten us."

"Lakyn?" Jael reached for her friend again, almost as if to reassure herself that he was still nearby.

"I have been alone for so many years." Lakyn closed his eyes for a moment. "No word from the outside world. No way of knowing how the world had changed, if people had moved on. I could not risk magic, not near the sword. And I could not leave it."

"I would have come if I could have."

Brina and her friends exchanged nearly identical looks of discomfort. The conversation was rapidly becoming too private for them to be hearing.

"I know," Lakyn continued with no trace of sarcasm or bitterness. "But the passage of time, with no word from anyone, no sign from Elsali, wore at my faith. I prayed for Him to show me I was still in His plan, that I was still doing what was right. I prayed for a message from another Guardian, for some word of my family, of my friends." Lakyn turned back to Brina. "And here, with the arrival of the Chosen, I receive confirmation that Elsali heard my prayers. He not only sent a friend and the one who would free us, but brought to me proof my brother lived, that he had a family. Despite my doubts, Elsali gave me what I had asked for."

"You were not the only one with doubts, Lakyn, not the only one who struggled," Jael confessed, her accent and speech pattern shifting as she spoke with her friend. "After you left, I was just as alone. Eventually, people came and built and lived. I lived among them, even finding those I would consider friends, but I was never one of them." She took Lakyn's hand. "We knew this would not be easy."

Lakyn turned from Brina to Jael. "The way of Elsali rarely is."

Jael nodded in agreement. For almost a full minute, they sat in silence, eyes locked, fingers entwined. Jael looked away first. "And now the time has come to finish what we started."

"Um," Thana broke the tension. "This is all well and good, but any chance of something to eat before we go all *kazhah* on the dragon?"

Lakyn chuckled. "Certainly." He stood, releasing Jael's hand. "You remind me of–"

"Casta." Jael and Lakyn spoke together, both smiling.

"Is that a good thing or a bad thing?" Thana asked.

"Good," Lakyn crossed to a series of shelves hewn into the rock. "A good thing indeed."

Jael added, "Casta was a friend of ours, a joy to be around. She kept us sane, finding humor and hope in the darkest of times."

Lakyn chuckled. "Do you remember the turkey and the missing sandal?"

Jael joined in the laughter. "Casta had to run around with the only sandal she could find, trying to catch a turkey."

Thana looked at Lakyn and then Jael before turning back to Aidan and Brina. "Okay, now I kinda want to find the dragon. Those two are freaking me out."

Brina was almost inclined to agree with her friend.

Lakyn, it turned out, was a much better cook than any of them. The meal of *birria* and wild *cazakas* was devoured before it had a chance to cool. They talked little while eating, focusing on the food Lakyn kept refilling until even Thana was satisfied. As Thana finished her fourth helping of stew, the others pushed back their chairs from the table and prepared to address the matter at hand.

"Night falls quickly here and I would not recommend initiating an attack on the dragon so close to sunset." Lakyn spoke first.

Aidan took Brina's hand, his fingers only a fraction warmer

than hers. His strength allowed Brina to speak with an unwavering voice. "Then what's the plan?"

Lakyn glanced at Jael who nodded at him to take the lead. "Tonight, we rest. Tomorrow, I will lead us to *Gleann na Tine agus Oighear*."

"Valley of Fire and Ice," Brina translated.

Lakyn nodded. "So named because the ground is covered with snow so deep it never completely melts, not even when, as legend tells it, a dragon roamed the land. This valley, in fact, is the spot where the creature first emerged and the place to which it always returns. Once there, we position ourselves with Brina at the center and cast a spell. The dragon will sense the magic and come."

"Wait a minute," Brina interrupted. "You guys can't be there when the dragon comes."

"We must be," Jael replied. "The *Decazmaja* will follow the beast. You must concentrate only on stopping the dragon." Interpreting Brina's tension correctly, Jael continued, "Thana and Aidan will be positioned on the strongest side, furthest from danger. Lakyn and I will take the weak side."

"Hey," Thana protested. "Aidan and I trained for this too."

"Indeed you did." Jael's voice was mild. "But Lakyn and I have had a bit more training."

"Only a little bit," Thana pouted. Jael raised an eyebrow. "Okay," Thana conceded. "A lot bit."

"What are their weapons?" Lakyn directed his question to Jael.

"The bow and short blades," Jael motioned to Aidan and Thana.

"Excellent," Lakyn nodded once. "We will put the boy –"

"Aidan." Brina stifled the chuckle at Aidan's expression at being referred to as 'the boy.'

"We will put Aidan," Lakyn continued. "At a high point to cover us. And," he glanced at Thana.

"Thana," she supplied her name.

"Thana will be hidden near enough to Brina to intercede should any of the *Decazmaja* make it past us." Lakyn indicated Jael with himself before turning to Brina. "You cannot allow concern for us, for any of us, cloud your mind. Your only focus is to be slaying the dragon. The fate of our world rests in your hands."

"But," Thana interjected. "No pressure."

Lakyn gave Thana a sharp look, but couldn't stop the corners of his mouth from tipping upwards. "Definitely like Casta."

Jael nodded in agreement and stood. "On that note, I think we should all turn in. Big day tomorrow."

"Brina, you will take the bed in the back. Jael, the cot. And there are enough cushions for the three–"

"No," Brina interrupted Lakyn. "I need to be with Aidan and Thana tonight. Let us have the floor." Brina struggled to articulate what she was feeling. "Things are going to be tough tomorrow. If I'm going to focus, I need this time with them."

Lakyn locked eyes with Jael for a moment before she nodded. "As you wish. Jael will take the bed," he held up a hand to stop his friend's protest. "I will take the cot." He gestured toward the back wall. "If you spread the cushions in front of the fire, the chill from the stone floor will not touch you."

A comfortable silence fell as they cleaned up and prepared to go to sleep. Once all of the preparations were complete, Jael gave them each a nod before disappearing into the back and Lakyn did the same before heading back to the cot, leaving the trio in relative privacy. Clean, warm, and comfortable for the first time in weeks, the trio stretched out on the soft make-shift mattress and pulled their individual blankets over their shoulders. They lay on their backs, Brina in the middle, less than half an inch between their bodies.

"Are you okay, Bri?" Thana broke the silence with a hesitant whisper.

"I don't know," Brina admitted. "Part of me is excited, ready to do this. Part of me is terrified, for you both and for myself. But part of me feels like this is going to be some sort of turning point for all of us. Like this is just the beginning of something even bigger than we think."

Aidan slipped his hand under the purple blanket covering Brina, searching for her hand. His fingers were cold against hers. "It's going to be okay," he said. "You'll kill the dragon and we'll go back to school. Everything will be normal."

"But what if it's not?"

"What'd you mean?" Thana asked.

Brina continued. "What if this is just the start of it?" She looked at Aidan, then Thana. "What if there's more to this than just killing a dragon? I need to know if you two are going to be willing to keep going with me if it doesn't stop here."

Aidan's answer was almost immediate. "No matter what happens, Bri, I'm with you."

"Me too." Thana chimed in. Then, unable to stop herself, she added, "though my declaration is only platonic."

The pair snickered and rolled onto their sides so they were both facing Brina. Aidan wrapped his arm around Brina's waist, turning her and tucking her back against his chest. She reached out a hand to Thana, and the trio held each other as they drifted off to sleep.

Jael found them similarly entwined when she woke them the next morning. Breakfast was a quiet affair, each as wrapped in their own thoughts and concerns for the imminent events as Brina was. There was no comfort to this silence, only a thickening tension. When Jael and Lakyn left to scout ahead, Thana excused herself to the bathroom to dress, leaving Brina and Aidan alone. Aidan drew Brina into his arms and she rested her head against his chest, the steady thrumming of his heart calming her as much as possible.

"Bri," Aidan's voice was soft, serious. "I know how important this is, but promise me, please, *amado*, that you'll be careful. I don't know if I could bear to lose you."

Brina opened her mouth to reassure Aidan and stopped. After a brief pause, she changed what she'd originally intended to say. "I'll do my best, Aidan. Our lives are in Elsali's hands now. His design, His plan, remember?" She tipped her face toward his and quickly closed the distance. Their lips met with an intensity, an almost desperation, they'd never had before. Aidan buried his fingers in Brina's hair as her arms wrapped around his neck, trying to pull himself closer. Time froze, or melted away, or lost all sense of meaning. The only thing they knew was the feel of fire and skin and heat. Aidan's teeth scraped against Brina's lower lip and her grip around his neck tightened.

"Um," Thana's voice broke through. "Bathroom's free."

Reluctantly, the couple separated, breath coming in pants, faces flushed. Without a word, Aidan disappeared through the door behind Thana.

"If you don't mind," Thana grinned at Brina. "I'll just stick with a 'good luck' and 'try not to get yourself killed.' Like I said, my declarations are only platonic."

Brina tried to glare at her friend and failed miserably. "Thanks, Thana."

"No problem," Thana cheerfully skipped across the room. "Now, what accessories go with knives?"

Two hours later, Lakyn led the group into his bedroom, through an almost invisible crevice in the wall, and into a space barely big enough for all five of them. He motioned Brina forward, motioning for the others to stay back. "Only the Chosen One may touch the blade. As it was created to destroy magic, I do not know what it would do to a magical person."

Brina knelt by the box, a hush falling over the group. A pull like she'd felt with the dragon came from inside the plain wooden container. She lifted the lid and gently turned aside the ancient cloth that had covered the blade for millennium.

It was exactly the same size as the regular sword Brina had brought with her, but the similarities ended there. It appeared, at first glance, an unremarkable piece of work. The hilt was simple, long enough for a two-hand grip, but Brina knew the weight would be perfectly balanced to allow her to use one hand if necessary. The cross-guard was simple, unadorned, unlike the elaborate and rich weapon one would imagine for a dragon slayer. The blade itself, however, fairly glowed in the dim light of the room. The metal was unlike anything any of them had ever seen. Even Lakyn and Jael didn't know what the other *Starateli* had used to forge the sword. Brina could sense, however, one thing they did know hadn't been shared: the inscription was etched in the blood of the pair who had died creating the weapon.

"*Fiat volvntas tua*,'" Brina read. "'Let Thy will be done.'" As she spoke, she reached for the hilt, her fingers fitting perfectly. She closed her eyes for a moment, silently echoing the words she'd just spoken aloud, only this time, she made them a prayer and a promise. She opened her eyes and lifted her sword from its resting place. She stood and turned toward the others. "Sheath, Lakyn."

Without a word, Lakyn handed over a plain leather sheath and Brina slid the sword into place. She strapped the belt around her waist, cinching it where she'd worn the other blade throughout the journey. She looked at the others. Jael was in her customary all-black attire, complete with a broadsword on her back and small blades on two leather straps crisscrossing her chest. Brina knew that a six-inch boot knife, though not visible, was accessible enough to be in Jael's hand in seconds. Lakyn wore leather of the same kind as Brina's sheath. Two long blades crossed his back, a hilt over each shoulder. A half-dozen throwing knives hung on each hip, a dozen more across his chest, and Brina suspected that he, too, had additional weapons concealed throughout his attire. Next to the Guardians, Thana and Aidan looked woefully under-dressed. Aidan had a short sword around his waist and a sheath of arrows on his back. His crossbow rested loosely in his right hand. Thana had her favorite knives at her waist with two back-ups in either boot. Both, like Brina, were dressed in fitted black pants and dark shirts, Aidan green and Thana blue. Brina herself wore dark purple. While the sword was her greatest weapon, she also carried back-up blades in the specially made compartments in her calf-high boots. They'd be useless against the dragon, but work well enough against humans.

Brina took a deep breath and released it, sending up a silent prayer for protection and success. "It's time."

Lakyn led the way, single file, the others following in silence. They emerged from Lakyn's home to find a beautiful day. The snow underfoot was thawing from its frozen state and many of the trees were shedding their winter coats. Fidelis was almost over and the warmth hinted at the upcoming seasonal change as the first of Lumen approached. Brina had the fleeting thought that she was a little over a month away from turning sixteen and then pushed it aside. Life outside of the moment at hand was surreal and distracting. If she wanted to reach her birthday, she knew she needed to focus.

The clearing Lakyn and Jael had found was a little over half the size of the Fuhjyn field, and raised enough to give them an advantage over any approaching *Decazmaja*. Brina drew her sword, swinging it a few times to get the feel. She needn't have bothered. The moment she raised the blade into position, she'd known it had been made for her alone to wield. It was as much a part of her as her strange eyes.

The others took their places around the clearing and readied their own weapons. After a glance around, Lakyn looked to

Jael. "Let us end this."

Jael smiled, and it held a hardness to it that carried to her eyes. "Shall I?"

Lakyn nodded, his own expression reflecting Jael's.

The Guardian slipped her wand from a side pocket and flicked the tip toward the sky. "*Vos niteo.*"

A shower of glittering sparks shot into the air and Brina felt the sword vibrate in her hand in response to the magic.

Jael's hand was moving to replace her wand when her body jerked once, twice.

The slender piece of wood fell from her fingers to the snow at her feet.

Jael opened her mouth and the tip of an arrow broke through the skin of her throat, silencing her. She fell forward, two arrows buried in her back.

There was no time to scream, to react. The *Decazmaja* had found them.

Chapter Fourteen: Battle in the Snow

A dozen hooded figures burst from the shadows of the trees, two falling before Brina had time to register that Aidan was firing. One scrambled for his sword, injured leg dragging through the snow, as Thana ran toward him. Brina took a step toward her friend and froze in her tracks, a screech overhead drawing her attention.

She felt the pressure behind her eyes and knew they'd shifted. Forcing herself to abandon her desire to help the others, she kept her gaze skyward. Barely a heartbeat had passed before she saw the silhouette that had haunted her nightmares. Her sword hummed in response to the magic the creature had absorbed and her body reacted to the weapon. She shifted her weight, balancing on the balls of her feet. Both hands settled into their places on the sword's hilt. She raised the blade, part of her mind flicking through Jael's training while the other part watched the dragon's approach. Dimly, as if at a great distance, she heard Lakyn and her friends fighting with the *Decazmaja*.

"Come on," Brina muttered through clenched teeth, adrenaline pumping through her body. "Let's finish this."

With a deafening roar, the dragon swooped toward Brina, claws outstretched. The battle cry turned to a shriek of rage and pain as Brina sliced into the dragon's leg, the sword managing to catch some flesh with the scales. She ducked to one side, escaping unscathed. Certain she now had the beast's full attention, Brina darted toward a boulder near the edge of the clearing.

She heard the flame before she felt the heat and threw herself sideways, thanking Elsali for her Fuhjyn skills. A hole appeared in the snow where she'd just been running. She scrambled to her feet and made for the rock once more. She reached it just as the dragon swung around to make another pass.

Brina narrowed her eyes, homing in on the creature's chest.

Jael's voice rang in her ears. *"There's a black spot in the center of the dragon's chest under which the heart lies. You must pierce the heart to slay the beast."* Brina tuned out everything but the darkness flying toward her.

Her breathing slowed, body tensed.

The dragon dropped, mouth open, claws extended, razor-sharp teeth and talons ready to shred flesh.

Using every ounce of strength she could muster, Brina drove the sword upwards, muscles screaming in protest at the impact of resisting scales. She jerked forward as the point pushed past sinew and scraped against bone. The dragon pulled back, screeching in pain as it beat its wings against the air. Brina drove forward, refusing to give an inch. She felt the crack of the breastbone and was suddenly airborne as the dragon fell to the ground, pulling her feet from the rock as she refused to release her grip. The beast landed on its back, legs scrabbling to regain its footing, wings uselessly churning the snow. Out of the corner of her eye, Brina saw one of the *Decazmaja* skewered by a spike on the thrashing tail. Brina steadied herself as best she could on the flailing creature and threw all of her weight onto the sword, thrusting the tip into the dragon's heart.

Brina's back arched and she opened her mouth in a silent scream as power poured up the sword and through her body. It was the shock she'd experienced touching the fountain multiplied by a thousand. It lasted for a second or for an eternity, which she couldn't say. When it began to diffuse into her body, Brina slumped against the sword, gasping for breath, dragon blood soaking into her clothes as it pooled around the wound and spilled down to the snow.

She felt familiar pressure and knew her eyes had returned to normal. Her ears, still ringing from the dragon's last roars, strained for any sound that would indicate the state of the battle. Foreign energy coursed through every cell and Brina knew she was no longer without magic. She even suspected her new

magic might be stronger than Jael had guessed. She released the
sword and slid down the dragon's side to the crimson snow,
leaving the blade in the creature's body. The sword had served
its purpose and couldn't be used again. She turned toward her
friends and her heart stopped.

Several feet away, crumpled on the ground next to a very
dead *Decazmaja*, was Thana, a wide red circle spreading around
her. To Brina's right, less than a yard from where the dragon's
head had fallen, was Aidan. He wasn't visibly injured, but was
so still and pale that Brina knew he'd been the closest magical
being to the dragon at the end. So close, in fact, that the blood
coursing down from the pierced heart was melting the snow
around him. She knew she had to go to one of them first. Brina
heard her own words echo in her ears. "*Our lives are in Elsali's
hands now. His design, His plan, remember?*"

His plan.

Brina was sprinting toward Thana before she realized she
was moving. "Elsali, please." She fell to her knees and gently
rolled Thana onto her back. The *Decazmaja* sword had pierced
Thana's heart, and the failing organ feebly pumped the blood
from the girl's body. Even as Brina watched, the flow ebbed.
She placed her hands over the wound and prayed again, "Elsali,
please." She gathered the magic inside of her. Closing her eyes,
she envisioned the power like a light, flowing down her arms,
into her hands, and pushed it into Thana's body.

Brina felt the flesh knit together under her fingers, felt Thana
take a gasp of air, felt the healing heart stutter and then begin to
throb a steady, strong beat. Brina opened her eyes. Thana was
still unconscious, but Brina knew her friend would recover. She
stood, stumbled, and fell back to her knees. She felt the magic
stir inside her, giving her strength to pull herself through the
snow to where Aidan lay. He was pale and cold to the touch.
Brina traced Aidan's cheekbones, his lips, her fingertips barely
brushing his skin. She knew she could heal him, and she knew

the cost. She could feel the toll Thana's healing had taken on her newfound magic and understood that it would take more to heal Aidan from the dragon's soon-to-be-fatal drain.

Aidan's voice played in her head. *"He gives us a choice, Bri. He always does. I have no doubt there's a plan and things far beyond our comprehension in play, but we have to decide if we're going to trust Him enough to make the choices we know are right."*

"*Fiat volvntas tua,*" Brina whispered. She placed her hands on Aidan's chest and felt the dragon's magic flow through her fingertips into Aidan's body. As it began to fade, she bent forward and pressed her lips against his, relishing the jolt shooting through her. "I love you, Aidan," she murmured against his mouth as the last of the magic slipped away and Brina let her eyes close. Her cheek came to rest against Aidan's chest, a smile touching her lips as she heard the strong beat of his heart. She felt him stir as darkness fell.

Epilogue: If the World Crashes Down

No light filtered into the small room and the swaying figure cursed the gloom as it stumbled through the chaos. Without bothering to remove its clothing, it fell onto the bed.

"*Fiat lux.*"

A ball of bluish-white light appeared in the center of the room, illuminating both the speaker and the figure on the bed. The speaker was perched on the edge of a cluttered desk, one long leg crossed over the other. She was tall, slender, with dusky skin and almost-black eyes. Her ebony-colored hair was long and streaked with silver and gold. She had studs of the same metal lining her ears, and wore a lime green t-shirt that matched her eyeshadow. Scrawled across the front in blocky letters was the song lyric "Hey you, get off my goat." Her jeans were artfully torn, and her boots had seen better days. She regarded the figure blinking blearily at her with a mixture of curiosity and disdain.

"Who're you?" Aidan slurred, struggling to sit up.

"Neysa Polyxena," the girl raised one well-sculpted eyebrow. "I'm a friend of Jael's."

"*Mine keera ennast,*" Aidan snarled, suddenly conscious that he hadn't bathed in a few days and probably smelled like the alley behind a bar. Maybe worse.

"No thank you," Neysa responded to Aidan's insult without batting an eye. She continued. "I'm not a Guardian, but I do know things."

"If you know so much, then you know that I don't want you here. I don't want anything anymore." Aidan saw her wince and knew it was because of the raw pain in his voice. Good. Maybe now she'd leave him alone.

"It's been six months, Aidan," Neysa's voice was soft as she crossed the room and knelt on the floor next to the bed.

"I don't care," Aidan reached behind his pillow and drew out a small bottle. "I just want to forget." He gulped half of the bottle's contents.

"I know it's hard–"

Aidan cut off whatever Neysa was going to say next. "Hard? You think losing Brina–" The name choked him. "You think that's just hard? It's unbearable. If I thought it wouldn't kill my mother, I'd end it."

"Brina wouldn't have wanted this."

"How do you know? You didn't know her. And we can't ask her because she's gone." Aidan downed the rest of the bottle. "There's nothing left for me."

"There are other things to live for, Aidan." Neysa put a hand on his arm.

He shook it off. "Like what?"

"I came to give you a mission." Neysa stood, voice hardening. "Your sister, Adalayde, she's alive."

PART TWO: DRAGON BLOOD

Prologue: If the World Crashes Down

The last thing he remembered before the darkness fell was whispering her name.

The first thing he knew as the darkness receded was the smell of roses and blood.

He felt the weight on his chest and realized he wasn't dead. He opened his eyes and felt a surge of relief when he recognized the bright red hair. He said her name even as he reached for her. As soon as his fingers touched her face, his relief turned to panic. He scrambled upright, catching her in his arms. His fingers scrabbled against her neck, frantically searching for a pulse he knew wasn't there.

As always, her name on his lips woke him from the dream-memory. He stared up at the ceiling, eyes sightless in the dark. It didn't matter anyway. He knew he'd only see her face. For six months, her face had been all he could see. Sometimes, he even thought he could hear her voice, smell her skin.

He sighed and sat up. He knew he would be getting to sleep only with assistance. A private establishment around the corner would supply him with what he needed. Some small part of his brain spoke up, telling him that she wouldn't have wanted this. He immediately squashed the thought. He didn't want to remember her. All he wanted was to forget.

When he stumbled back to his room two hours later, he didn't notice the shadow in the corner. His foot hit something in the dark and he swore, kicking it aside. He flopped onto his bed, not bothering to change from the sweat-and-alcohol reeking clothes he wore. When the light appeared and the multi-colored figure began to speak, Aidan was half-convinced he'd slipped into a dream. Then, the young woman with the funny name said the words that made him sure he wasn't awake. She said his sister was still alive.

Chapter One: Harder to Breathe

Aidan woke up in a strange room, in a strange bed, yet he was almost positive he'd fallen asleep – or, he admitted, more likely passed out – in his own bed the night before. He took a quick inventory. He was fully dressed, sans shoes. However, the stench of his prior night's activities, what he remembered of them, was gone. His tousled hair was still damp and, as he ran a hand through it, he suddenly remembered his visitor with the funny name. "Neysa." He bolted upright. Flashes of memory played through his mind even as his stomach roiled at the movement.

Writing a note for his parents.

A firm hand on his shoulder as they transported.

A shove pushing him under lukewarm spray.

Try as he might, Aidan couldn't remember what he'd written in the note or anything after the shower. For that matter, he didn't know how he's ended up in the clothes he was currently wearing. They appeared to be his, but were nondescript enough he couldn't be sure. The room he was in was along the same lines. Unadorned off-white walls, a single window with navy blue curtains and a matching bedspread. Nothing about this room was familiar.

A knock on the door made him jump. He opened his mouth to answer, but the door opened before he could say anything, and a figure entered. She was short, probably not even five feet tall, but athletic enough that 'tiny' couldn't be used to describe her, not like Thana. Dark brown curls framed an ordinary and intense face. Glacial gray-blue eyes regarded him with contempt and scornful interest. The slight up-tilt to her eyes and the golden tinge to her skin gave her an exotic air.

"How's the hangover?" Her voice was low, the tone sardonic.

Aidan glared at the intruder, and tried to ignore the pounding in his temples.

She smirked. "Neysa wants to talk to you. And there's food too. I'd say breakfast, but it's actually more like a late lunch." She turned to go, then tossed a final statement over her shoulder. "Kitchen's down the stairs, to the right."

Aidan sat on the edge of the bed for several seconds, evaluating if he had the ability to stand. He cautiously rose to his feet. The room wobbled a little bit, but otherwise stayed still. He followed the stranger's directions and found himself squinting against mid-afternoon sunlight flooding through a series of large windows as he entered a bright and cheery kitchen.

"Have a seat."

Aidan slid into a chair at the small kitchen table, and angled away from the windows to look at the speaker. Neysa laid a plate of buttered toast in front of him and leaned against the counter. A flick of her fingers conjured a mug of black coffee. Aidan raised an eyebrow, reluctantly impressed. Magic without a wand was difficult, and Neysa appeared to be only a few years older than he was. She had to be incredibly powerful to do something like that.

"How much do you remember from last night?"

Aidan shrugged and took a tentative sip of the coffee. It was surprisingly good. "I can't tell what I dreamed and what was real. For a while, I was sure you were part of whatever I drank last night."

Neysa tossed back her long dark hair, and Aidan saw she'd braided her silver and gold streaks. Her eyes were just as dark in the day as they had been in the night, but she'd traded in the previous night's attire for black and blue zebra-striped pants and a matching blue top with sparkles. Her eyeshadow, nails and lipstick were also metallic blue. Half of the studs in her ears had changed to hoops. He noticed, as he hadn't last night, cross tattoos on the back of each wrist. "No such luck, *ergelak mozkor.* I'm very real. And everything I said last night is true. Your sister is alive."

Thousands of questions flooded Aidan's mind even as he ignored her calling him a stupid drunk. He wasn't sure which question he wanted to have answered first. Neysa continued without waiting for a response, saving Aidan the trouble of deciding.

"The how and why are a story for a later time. Right now, here's what you need to know. I knew Jael and what she was. She didn't know about your sister, but she would've said the same thing I'm going to tell you. We're going to get her back." Neysa straightened, holding up a hand to silence the protest Aidan had been about to make. "But, first, you're in no condition, physically or mentally, to handle all of the information at once."

Aidan bristled. "Excuse me?"

"You've allowed your grief to take over." Neysa spoke gently. "I know what happened, and I know how you feel."

Aidan pushed away from the table and stood too fast. He grabbed the back of his chair for support. "You have no idea how I feel. And I think you're lying about Adalayde." He turned to storm out and tripped over his own feet, sending himself sprawling on the clean tile floor.

"Real winner you picked out, Neysa."

Aidan glared up at the familiar, but as of yet, unnamed face. The girl stepped over him, and he resisted the urge to grab her foot and make her join him. He was surprised by the thought. With the exception of Gray, he usually didn't let people get under his skin.

"Carys," Neysa chided the girl, then directed her next statement to Aidan. "I doubt she introduced herself. Aidan, this is Carys Jovan. She'll be going with you to find your sister."

Carys made a sound of disgust and snatched one of the pieces of toast Aidan hadn't eaten.

"I can do it on my own, thanks." Aidan struggled to his feet, the room starting to waver. He wanted a drink.

"Like it's my idea," Carys snapped. "You're just going to get yourself killed. Or, worse, slow me down."

"Thanks for your concern." Aidan's voice was dry. What was this girl's problem?

"You will work together." Neysa's tone left no room for argument. "Your goal's the same."

"Why does she care about my sister?" Aidan demanded.

"I don't give a *blbost* about your sister." Carys glowered at Aidan. "I want my brother back."

Aidan looked to Neysa for an explanation.

"Carys's brother, Callum, was taken by the same people who have Adalayde." Neysa poured Aidan another cup of coffee. "And getting them back will require both a clear head and teamwork."

Aidan sank back into his chair and turned his gaze toward Carys who scowled at him. He doubted teamwork was what she had in mind. She seemed to be more of the type to be plotting how to get away with his murder. A part of him suspected she probably could. He buried his head in his hands. This had to all just be some very weird dream. Why else would he just be sitting there, listening to two complete strangers? It didn't matter that something inside him told him he could trust them. He was hungover. He couldn't trust himself, and he didn't want to trust the quiet voice inside him, the voice he'd been trying so hard to ignore for the past few months. Still, he didn't leave. Something inside him was compelling him to stay, something very much like the echo of a voice saying that killing the dragon hadn't been the end of their task, but the beginning.

Neysa continued. "After you eat, I'll show you around. Tomorrow, you start training."

"Been there, done that," Aidan muttered. Shards of memories cut through him like glass. He didn't want to think about that time. What was past, was past, and couldn't be changed.

"And you've spent the last six months sleeping and drinking," Neysa's words were devoid of emotion, but Aidan felt the unspoken rebuke like a slap in the face. "Somehow I doubt you've retained the skills you learned."

Aidan defended himself. "I went back to school. I tried."

"Did you?" Again, the question was mild, but Aidan flinched.

Unbidden, the memories came to him in such clear recall that it was almost like reliving the moments.

The Fine family took up the entire first three rows, but Aidan didn't mind. He didn't want to see Brina like that. He'd blocked the journey back from his mind, only wanting to remember how she'd looked the last time he'd kissed her. The way she'd smelled like soap and roses. How her hair had been heavy and warm and soft. How her lips had felt against his. He closed his eyes with the effort and, for a moment, saw Brina's violet eyes filled with love. Then they were gone and he saw only death.

"Aidan."

He opened his eyes at the sound of Thana's voice. She slipped her hand into his, her eyes surprisingly dry. He supposed they'd both spent their grief during the three days it had taken them to return home. He knew he had nothing left to cry. He squeezed Thana's hand and tucked a wayward strand of dark hair behind her ear, swallowing the lump in his throat as he remembered the same gesture with hair the color of the sun as it slipped below the horizon.

"How've you been?" Thana's voice was low.

Aidan shrugged. They'd been back for only a few days and he hadn't left his house until that morning.

"Are you coming back to school next month?" Thana had been home as well, her father not wanting her out of his sight for long. She'd told him yesterday, however, that she'd decided

to return to Audeamus for the new term.

Aidan's throat tightened at the thought of returning to a place with so many memories. He and Thana had buried Lakyn and Jael, knowing they could only carry one back home. It had been slow going, working their way through the soft spots until they'd found a place where they were able to transport to Corakin's house with Brina's... body. He tried not to remember much of that time. Didn't want to remember. Part of him needed to go back, to be where she'd been, but another part understood the pain involved and balked at the idea. He knew his parents would want him to go back, and knew, for their sake, he'd try. He nodded once, unable to speak as his throat constricted further.

On Vir first, he showed up at Audeamus, making an effort to ignore that it would've been Brina's sixteenth birthday. Thana met him at the front doors, pointedly ignoring the inquisitive stares of the other students. No one other than Corakin knew the truth about how Jael and Brina had died. The official story, thought out by Thana and Aidan as they'd carried Brina's body out of the mountains, was that Jael's expedition had been in a valley devoid of magic when an avalanche descended on their camp. Thana and Aidan had managed to find Brina, but it had been too late to save her. The professor had been lost. Though a month had passed since their return, former classmates were still curious about the details. Like Thana, Aidan didn't respond to the questions a few brave souls sent his way. If he said anything, he knew he might start screaming.

By the time he'd finished unpacking, Aidan had begun to think that perhaps he could make it work. If he avoided places with strong connections to... his past, he might be able to remain at school. Playing Fuhjyn, of course, was out, but he had other activities he could pursue, ones that didn't remind him of what he'd lost. He was trying to keep his emotions in check as he waited for Thana to cross the room, and didn't notice the figure until it stepped in front of him.

"Should've known you wouldn't protect her, Aidan." Gray blocked Aidan's way, arms crossed over his chest, pale eyes narrowed. "Too busy saving your own skin..."

The rest of Gray's accusation was lost when Aidan's fist connected with the bigger boy's jaw. Aidan launched himself at Gray, each hit fueled by a month of rage, guilt and grief. He didn't remember Pax Ridik, his new roommate, pulling him off of Gray, or that it took both Pax and a boy named Zayne Cohen to prevent him from attacking again. Only Thana's voice cut through the haze and made him stop struggling.

Headmaster Manu signed Aidan's withdrawal papers without a word and Aidan left before Gray was released from the healing wing. Thana pleaded with him to stay, to try again, but Aidan just shook his head. It didn't matter. Nothing mattered. With a flick of his wand, he sent his luggage home and then headed off on foot, destination unknown, goal to forget.

That had been the last day, Aidan realized with a start, he'd spent entirely sober. It was now near the end of Vita, and he could remember the last five and a half months only through the haze of alcohol. He'd started by promising himself it would just be to help him sleep. Then, the pain during the day had been too much, and he'd begun to take the edge off with a nip here and there. Instead of time making things better, he'd just gotten worse. The last two weeks, he'd only left his room for more alcohol, eating only bits and pieces of the meals his mother and sisters had left outside his door. Aidan suddenly had a morbid desire to find a mirror, sure he'd be little more than skin and bones.

"All right," he forced the words out. If they were telling the truth about his sister, he needed his strength back. If he found out they were lying, he'd at least be strong enough to get away from them. At the moment, he doubted he could even take the smaller girl in a fight. "When do we start?"

"We've already begun." Neysa took Aidan's plate. "You're done drinking and laying about. Until you're dried out and have regained your strength, it's chores. And when I feel you're ready, I'll have you join Carys in official training."

Aidan raised an eyebrow. "Chores?"

"Have fun," Carys chortled. "No magic allowed."

"Carys." Neysa's voice was weary, as if reprimanding Carys was something she had to do often. Somehow Aidan wasn't surprised. The girl didn't seem very pleasant. "Don't you have work to do?"

Carys was petulant. "Doesn't he have to do schoolwork too?"

"Aidan's had four more years of schooling than you, even accounting for his recent absences." Neysa jerked her head toward the door. "Go on. I don't want you in the training room until today's lessons are complete."

Carys skulked from the room, mumbling something under her breath that sounded very much like a negative opinion of what she was being asked to do, including suggestions regarding what Carys thought should be done with her textbooks. Aidan was fairly sure two of the suggestions were illegal and at least one was physically impossible.

"I'd go change into something grubbier," Neysa suggested. "I'd recommend short sleeves and shorts. It's going to be a warm one today."

When Aidan returned to the kitchen ten minutes later, he had taken Neysa's advice and found an old t-shirt and shorts in the bag he'd discovered in his room. From the looks of it, Neysa had brought all of the clothing he owned. He wasn't sure if that made this entire thing more or less creepy.

Without a word, Neysa motioned for Aidan to follow her and led the way outside. He blinked against the bright sun, raising a hand to shield himself from the rays. As his vision adjusted,

Aidan saw a vast yard surrounded by towering trees. No other houses were in a sight, and the driveway disappeared into the woods without visual on a road. Try as he might, Aidan could hear only the chattering of birds and squirrels. He should've found it at least a little alarming that no one else was around, but he couldn't muster the energy necessary for anything other than observation.

"Where are we?" Aidan glanced over his shoulder. The house was surprisingly large for someone with Neysa's obvious skills. In fact, Aidan realized, that the inside was only as big as the outside. He didn't think he'd ever seen one of those houses before.

"Sicinfit." Neysa motioned for Aidan to follow her toward a large building at the edge of the woods.

"Never heard of it." Again, something that should've been setting off alarm bells but wasn't.

"I'm not surprised." Neysa kept talking as she walked. "We're on an island about sixty miles from the coast near Inbanco."

"An island?" Aidan was dismayed to hear how out of breath he sounded by the time he reached the other building. If someone wanted him for nefarious purposes, he wasn't going to be able to put up much of a fight. Building his strength was going to be necessary, no matter what his future held.

Neysa nodded. "Sicinfit has been in my family for generations and, since I'm the last Polyxena, it's mine now."

"The last—" Aidan started to interrupt but stopped when Neysa held up a hand.

"That's really none of your business." Neysa's voice was sharper than it had been before. "All you need to know is, we're the only people on the island, and I have protection in place to prevent transporting on or off of the island. The path you saw near the house leads to the water where my boat's docked. Should you feel the urge to head into Inbanco for a drink, don't.

Only Carys and myself can drive the boat. Once you earn my trust, you may be added to the list, but don't be counting on it."

"I wasn't planning on going anywhere." Aidan heard the peevishness in his voice, but was unable to stop himself. Did she really think he'd run off when there was the possibility she had information about his sister? What kind of a guy did she think he was?

"What you plan now and what you may be thinking by the end of the day, or the end of the week, may be two different things." The edge to Neysa's voice disappeared. She opened the double doors to what Aidan now realized was a barn. He followed Neysa inside. As his eyes adjusted to the dimness of the interior, he saw six stalls, three on either side of the barn. Five of them contained horses.

Neysa pointed to a massive beast so dark it was nearly invisible. "Abraxan." She motioned to the next stall where a small pure-white horse nearly glowed in comparison to the first. "Calais." She continued down the line. "Zetas." A palomino the color of buttermilk snorted. "Boreas." A medium-sized chestnut-and-white pinto regarded him with what Aidan suspected was derision. "And Fledge is mine." Neysa stepped over to rub the nose of a beautiful red roan. She glanced over her shoulder at Aidan. "You're not afraid of horses, are you?"

Aidan shook his head. "Just haven't had the opportunity to be around them much."

"That's going to change." Neysa stepped away from Fledge. "For the next few days, or more, you're going to be in charge of their care."

"Wait, what?" Aidan shook his head. She had to be joking, right?

Neysa continued as if Aidan hadn't spoken. "Feeding, exercise, grooming, mucking the stalls, all of that is going to be your responsibility. It'll clear your head, build your muscles and endurance again, and remind you of responsibility." She pointed at the wall where a list appeared. "Everything is there, including explanations and where to find what you need." She took a step toward Aidan and stretched out her hand. "One final thing. I need your wand."

"Why can't I use magic? It's not like we're fighting a dragon who's going to negate it." Aidan grumbled, then winced at the memory it brought forward. Fortunately, Neysa spoke, keeping him from dwelling on the past.

"Those whose magic is strong can sense spells. Using magic isn't always going to be an option where we're going. And, if you keep your wand with you, you'll be tempted to use magic, which defeats the entire purpose of what I want you to do." Neysa held out her hand again. "It'll be in the house for you when you're finished."

Neysa's dark eyes didn't waver as Aidan weighed his options. He knew he didn't stand a chance dueling with Neysa. She was too powerful. And he believed she was telling the truth about where they were and about not being able to use the boat or transport, which meant even if he did manage to leave the barn with his wand, he had nowhere to go. After a moment more of deliberation, Aidan handed over his wand.

"I'll call you for dinner." Neysa left without a look back.

Aidan stood in the center of the barn, wondering how he'd landed in such a strange situation. One of the horses nickered gently and Aidan sighed. It didn't matter how he'd gotten where he was, just what he was going to do with his current circumstances. Violet eyes swam in front of his vision and he found himself longing for a drink. "That's what got you in trouble in the first place," he muttered to himself. He crossed to where Neysa had hung the list. Work, he supposed, could make him forget too, and it looked like he didn't really have another option. He just wasn't sure it would last long.

Twelve days. Twelve days without a drink. Twelve days of hard physical labor, good food and the first nights of dreamless sleep in six months. Despite the rest, Aidan found himself still longing for the relief of intoxication. The pain of losing Brina, dulled by his prior stupor, hadn't faded. It seemed, in fact, to have increased. Aidan felt like the wound, once numb, had been re-opened without anesthetic. A part of him realized all of the poison he'd built up over the past few months needed released before he could heal, but a part of him dreaded the process. Not the pain. He could manage pain. He just didn't want to forget.

He believed Neysa and Carys were who they claimed to be, but there were still times Aidan thought he could make the argument that they'd kidnapped him because they needed someone to do the manual labor. He straightened, wiping his arm across his forehead. His shirt hung over the fence nearby, fluttering the meager breeze. He stepped into the shadow of the barn, the cool dark comforting after the blinding heat of the day. He'd burned and peeled the first day. Neysa had given him an ointment to soothe his skin that night, and had performed a protection charm each morning since.

Abraxan nickered from his stall and Aidan stopped to scratch the horse's nose. The big beast had taken a liking to him and Aidan reciprocated. Abraxan didn't ask questions or care if Aidan spoke. Most times, Aidan liked the horse better than Neysa or Carys, not that he saw much of either of them. He suspected, in fact, that Neysa had been leaving the island shortly after breakfast. Carys he only saw from a distance, running the tree line, exercising, or practicing with various weapons, some of which he couldn't even name. He was pretty sure the girl was ignoring him.

"But we don't care, do we Abraxan?" Aidan slipped into Abraxan's stall. Earlier, he'd actually seen Neysa walking down the trail leading to the shore, and had heard her threaten Carys with extra homework if a certain assignment wasn't completed by supper. Today, he had the time to do what he'd been thinking about for the past few days. He hadn't seen anyone riding any of the horses and wasn't sure it was allowed. Still, he needed to blow off some steam, and this seemed like the best way to do it.

Aidan climbed onto the stall gate and, without bothering to find a saddle, swung himself onto Abraxan's back. Surprisingly, the horse allowed Aidan to get a tight grip on his mane and lean over to open the gate. Aidan leaned over the horse's neck and spoke, "All right, let's you and me taste some freedom. What do you say?"

***

Carys watched as Abraxan and Aidan disappeared into the woods. For a brief moment, she considered contacting Neysa, but she quickly decided against it. It might be more interesting to see how things played out on their own. She still wasn't sure the type of person Aidan was, and this might give her some idea. When Neysa returned, a few hours later, Aidan hadn't yet returned. Still, Carys held her tongue until Neysa instructed her to call Aidan for dinner.

"Yeah, about that," Carys began.

"Which way did he go?" Neysa interrupted.

Carys pointed. She hesitated for a moment and added, "He took Abraxan."

"Grab your bow and knife," Neysa snapped her fingers and a six-inch hunting blade appeared. A second snap produced a longbow and quiver. "I'll take Fledge. You're going to go the opposite direction on foot."

Carys reached for her wand to summon her weapon and paused. "I didn't think he'd be gone past sundown."

"Well, he is," Neysa said, her voice harsh. "And you'd better pray to Elsali that he's all right. For your sake, if not for his. We'll never get your brother back without him."

Chapter Two: The Getaway

"*Tolol*," Aidan squinted his eyes, straining to see in the growing black. While the trees had dimmed the sunlight when he'd first set out, he hadn't realized how much more quickly the darkness would fall in the forest. He trusted Abraxan's sure-footedness, but wasn't quite as confident in the horse's ability to find its way home. And then the noises had started. A few he recognized from his recent travels: owls, bats, field mice rustling through the grass, the unique cooing sighs of woobies, and the excited chatter of a happyemo. A few sounds, however, Aidan could find no name for and he found himself wondering what lurked in these woods.

Something to his right screeched and Abraxan started. Aidan had loosened his grip on the horse's mane when it'd slowed and, as the horse reared, he scrabbled for a handhold. His fingers snagged a few hairs before he tumbled to the mossy ground. Before he could regain his footing and grab Abraxan, the horse bolted.

"I don't think this is going to end well." Aidan's gaze focused on a nearby *nainomad* bush as he sat up. He could hear twigs snapping, and leaves rustling behind it, and he started to move backwards. "Oh *blbost.*"

Aidan's eyes widened as the bush parted and a lizard-like creature emerged. He couldn't see much of it in the darkness, but knew, based on the height and the chittering warble it made, he was looking at a tatzlwurm. If he'd had a weapon and it was daylight, Aidan knew dispatching the creature would've been relatively simple. But, in the dark, with empty hands, Aidan was an easy mark.

As he scrambled to his feet, part of his brain begged him to stop, to let it be over, to let him be with Brina again. He pushed the thought away, slightly surprised that his will to live was stronger than his desire to end the pain. When had he stopped wanting to die?

Glowing yellowish-green eyes grew closer, and Aidan filed the introspective queries for future review as he began to slowly back away. Of course, that only worked if he had a future. Surviving this encounter came first. Aidan reached for his pocket before remembering Neysa had his wand. Not that it would've done much good against the tatzlwurm. Its scales prevented magical penetration. He could've created a distraction at least, and bought some time to escape. Aidan stumbled over a root and lurched backwards, shoulder colliding with a tree. His back met the rest of the trunk a second later, and he raised his hands. Consciously, he knew the gesture was futile, but the instinct to survive overrode common sense.

Aidan felt the power leave his hands moments before he heard a loud whump accompanied by a screech of pain. He cautiously opened his eyes... and gaped at the smoldering pile of ash and bone that had been a living creature seconds ago.

A strange tingling in his hands drew his attention from the remains. He shook his hands, flexed his fingers, and slowly, the feeling receded. It didn't completely dissipate, he noticed, but seemed to spread evenly until every cell in his body hummed. With a start, he realized this wasn't an entirely unfamiliar sensation. As he made the connection, a memory slammed into him hard enough to make him gasp.

The first thing to break through the darkness was the gentle brush of fingertips over his cheek. He felt the unfamiliar mattress beneath him, the ache in his body, and guessed he was in the healing wing. A whiff of roses told him who the fingers belonged to and he spoke, his voice weaker than he'd realized.

"Brina?"

She grabbed his hand. "Aidan? Can you hear me?"

He tried once, twice and then managed to open his eyes. "Brina, you're here."

"I'm here, Aidan." Tears ran, unchecked, down Brina's

cheeks. She'd never looked so beautiful.

Trying to keep his voice light, Aidan asked the question burning in his chest. "So, you forgive me for being a trottel*?"*

Her voice cracked as she answered. "You idiot." She bent over him. "Of course I forgive you for being a jerk." As soon as her lips touched his, a jolt, not entirely unpleasant, shot through him.

"Aidan!" Neysa's shout broke him from his reverie, and he suddenly heard the pounding of hooves. Neysa pulled Fledge to a stop in front of Aidan, and slid off the horse's back, drawing a blade with one hand, her wand with the other. "Are you all right?"

Mutely, Aidan pointed at the pile of ash. Neysa's eyebrows shot up, but she said nothing, rather, she whistled a series of notes and waited. After a minute where she appeared to be listening for something, she whistled again. This time, Aidan heard the horse's approach.

Abraxan thundered to a stop, snorting and puffing as Neysa ran a hand over the animal's neck. She spoke quietly, seeming to soothe the horse more with the sound of her voice than her actual words. Neysa half-turned toward Aidan. "Let's get back to the house. Then we'll talk."

Aidan nodded. He had a hunch the tatzlwurm wasn't the most dangerous thing in the woods and, despite his apparently newfound power, he had no desire to find out if it would work a second time, perhaps on something larger. He gripped Abraxan's mane and swung himself onto the horse's back. He followed Neysa through the woods, allowing Abraxan free reign rather than trusting his own imperfect eyesight. The sun had long since vanished by the time they emerged from the woods, but the overhead moon provided enough light for Aidan to now see his surroundings. When they reached the barn, he fully expected Neysa to make him rub down both horses, sans magic, before they spoke. He was surprised, then, when Neysa flicked her wand at each of the horses and then secured them in their stalls.

"Let me alert Carys that you've been found." Neysa eyed Aidan with a curious expression. "Please wait for me in the kitchen. I won't be long."

Aidan nodded and headed for the house, suddenly thirsty. By the time he'd washed up and drained his second glass of *sinu* juice, Neysa had arrived.

"Carys will be joining us shortly." She motioned for Aidan to sit.

He did so, folding his hands together tightly. He wasn't sure what he expected. A scolding for taking off. A few minutes to pack his bags before he was sent back home. A torrent of questions about what had happened, followed by disbelief. What he hadn't expected was the one question she did ask.

"Brina died because she healed you, didn't she?"

Aidan's jaw dropped. He stammered, "how... what..."

"Jael told me about what happened when the dragon was released," Neysa kept her voice soft. "How Brina kept you from dying and knocked herself out, how after that, your connection allowed you both to exchange energy, to heal each other."

Aidan swallowed hard, the memory overpowering the knowledge that Neysa had, indeed been telling the truth about having known Jael. It was the only way she could've been able to figure it out. He answered her question, "It was both of us. Brina saved Thana and me. That's what killed her."

The dragon roared again as Aidan fit another arrow into his bow. This time, he felt the rush of air as the wings pushed down. Part of his mind warned him that he should change positions, but he shoved the thought aside and released another bolt into the torso of a nearby enemy.

The scream of pain from the beast drew the attention of its followers, giving Thana enough time to dispatch the man trying to slit her throat. Aidan felt a rush of warmth behind him and fought the urge to turn to check on Brina. He took a step backwards and grabbed for his last bolt, fingers fumbling as a strange weakness passed through him. Too late, he realized he should've listened to himself about moving. The arrow dropped into the snow and Aidan saw Lakyn fall, blood spilling from a neck wound. Aidan dropped to his knees. He opened his mouth to call to Thana and saw her stagger, dispatching her opponent before crumpling to the ground. The edges of his vision began to gray as the man who'd killed Lakyn was pinned to a tree by a tail spike. "Brina," he whispered her name and let the black consume him.

The first thing he knew as the darkness receded was the smell of roses and blood.

Aidan felt the burn of tears in his eyes and pushed them back. "Can't you see it's pointless to try to help me? I'm broken. I don't know why you're even bothering to try to fix me, Neysa."

Neysa's smile was gentle. "Like Elsali, I'm drawn to the broken things of the world. I always have been. Anyone can find good in the beautiful, but it takes a special way of thinking to see possibility in something that appears beyond redemption."

He shook his head. "You don't understand. How can I have the right to do something with my life when she's gone? How can my life be worth anything when I took hers?"

Neysa reached out as if to touch Aidan and stopped. Her voice was soft, her eyes oddly fierce. "You didn't take her life, Aidan."

"You're right," Aidan interrupted, bitterness lacing every word. "Elsali did. He just used me to do it."

"Aidan, no one took her life. She gave it," Neysa's tone hardened. "To think otherwise would be to think less of an amazing, courageous woman."

Our lives are in Elsali's hands now. His design, His plan, remember? The words echoed in his mind, repeating over and over until he shook his head. "I don't want to think about this right now. Just tell me what happened, if you know so much."

"I'm afraid that's why we need to talk about Brina." Neysa didn't comment on Aidan's sharpness, or his wince at Brina's name. "When Brina used the sword to kill the dragon, all of the magic the creature had absorbed, as well as all of its own magic, was transferred to Brina."

"Yeah, Jael told us that would happen," Aidan interrupted again. He didn't want to think about any of this.

Neysa held up a hand, indicating he should allow her to finish. "It was because Brina had so much magic she was able to heal both you and Thana, bring you back from what I believe was the brink of death. In doing this, Brina passed all of that extra magic into you and Thana. It became a part of you, a part of your magic. Both you and Thana are far more powerful than either of you realize."

Aidan stared for almost a full minute before regaining his voice. "But it's been six months. Why am I just now noticing?"

"Two things," Neysa answered. "One, you haven't exactly been very observant over the last half year." She ignored Aidan's glare. "And the biggest factor, you haven't been in a situation where you'd been forced to call on so much magic."

"What about Thana?" Aidan's gaze dropped to his hands.

"I'll be going to Audeamus tomorrow to speak with her." Neysa stood. "Now, I'm going to get dinner ready. When I return tomorrow, we'll discuss how best to develop these abilities."

Aidan's rise to his feet was so abrupt that his chair nearly toppled. He was shaking his head as he spoke. "I don't want to develop anything! I just want to forget everything that happened. It's done and over! I just want to find my sister and live out a normal life." He hurried out of the room, his shoulder brushing against a picture on the wall and sending it crashing to the floor. He didn't bother to stop and fix it. He just wanted to be alone.

***

Neysa closed her eyes and flicked her fingers, repairing the shattered glass and returning the picture to its place. She opened her eyes and spoke, though she knew Aidan couldn't hear her. "A normal life might not be an option."

The battle the young man thought was over, Neysa knew, had only just begun.

Chapter Three: Day by Day

Aidan wiped the sweat out of his eyes and peered up at the rope in front of him. His arms ached more than he'd hoped they would, but less than he'd feared. Caring for the horses had built up his unused muscles enough that he'd made some progress on the obstacle course over the past few days.

"Tired already?" Carys suddenly appeared. She darted around Aidan and scurried up the rope, breathing only slightly faster than she had the previous two times she'd passed him, but she didn't look like she was going to quit any time soon.

Aidan glared as the small figure disappeared into the foliage. According to Carys, after reaching the top of the rope, the course proceeded through the treetops for another mile before the thirty-foot drop into the river. The last leg of the course was the three-mile swim down to the ocean where they could cool down for thirty minutes before starting all over again. Aidan, however, could only take the girl's word for it. He'd yet to make it to the top of the rope. Today, he was determined to at least accomplish that much. He was tired of Carys's snide remarks and snickers as she passed him time and again, tired of her anticipatory grin at dinner, waiting for Neysa to ask how he'd done. It was almost as bad as waiting for Neysa to broach the subject of his magic again. The only comment she'd made so far was to tell Aidan that Thana was indeed experiencing an increase in powers and that someone was working with her on it. While she'd added that Thana was doing well, Aidan knew Neysa wasn't sharing everything with him and Carys. He didn't press for more information though. Doing that would just open the door for Neysa to bring up the elephant in the room.

Aidan reached for the rope, wincing in anticipation as his raw hands closed on the rough rope. Neysa had used magic to heal his injuries each night, but she'd also enchanted the course with only the basest of protection spells for the actual training.

He had the bruises to prove it. She said they needed to learn how to fight through the pain.

"All right, Aidan," he muttered. "Don't be a *bailys*. You can do this." His muscles strained as he slowly made his way up the rope. Rather than think about the pain starting to make its presence known, Aidan focused on his breathing, pacing himself to the steady in-and-out of air entering and exiting his lungs. Three quarters of the way up, Aidan felt the rope begin to get slippery, and he had to force himself to keep his eyes on the next place his hands would go. The tang in the air told him what he kept his eyes from seeing: the already tender skin of his fingers and palms had begun to bleed. By the time he saw the branch to which the rope was attached, he felt no relief, only grim determination to make it. He threw one arm over the branch and pulled himself up, biting his lip to keep from screaming as his arms rebelled against the strain. He balanced his body on the branch, cheek resting on the rough bark as he breathed in the sharp, clean smell of trees and fading sunlight. It would be dusk soon and Aidan forced himself to maneuver into a sitting position. He didn't want to be in the woods at dark again, and he didn't want to give up.

The closest tree was an ancient hickory, towering above the elm in which he currently sat. Now that he was in the tree, he realized he'd never thought about how to get from one to another. He scoured the hickory tree for the most promising branch and carefully judged the distance between the two trees. Slowly, he stood, balanced precariously on the narrow piece of wood under his feet. He edged his way down the branch until he felt it bowing beneath his weight. He took a step backwards, closed his eyes, took a deep breath, and leaped.

He opened his eyes as soon as his feet left the branch, and stretched his arms out to catch himself a moment later. As he clung to the trunk, he remembered a tree-fact he'd forgotten. Hickory bark peeled upwards, and was almost as hard as the tree itself. He shifted, trying to maneuver himself into a less painful position. A branch stuck out less than a foot to his right and another foot down. At the moment, reaching a lower branch seemed more feasible than trying to climb up for a higher branch. Aidan loosened his grip on the trunk and let himself slide. He bit back a groan as the rough bark broke beneath his descent. He couldn't bring himself to slide any further and made a desperate lunge for the branch.

As he fell, Aidan heard the release of the netting enchanted to catch anyone before they reached the ground. Before he could be ensnared in the webbing, Aidan's arm caught on a branch, the impact snapping his forearm even as his weight and momentum pulled him downward. He heard the crack, the tear of skin as bone ripped through, and then a loud pop as his shoulder dislocated. The pain was immediate, fierce, and followed him from momentary clarity to the waiting darkness.

The next time he opened his eyes, he had to blink twice at the concerned face peering down at him. When she realized he was awake, Carys's eyes quickly clouded over and the more familiar expression of amusement and derision took its place. "I sent for Neysa. I left my wand back at the house so I can't do any healing spells."

"Who'd you send?" Aidan asked the question as much to distract himself from what felt like white-hot spears jabbing his entire right side.

"None of your business." Carys's chin jutted out rebelliously. "You're just lucky I decided to go through an extra time rather than heading back without you." With detached interest, she motioned to his arm. "Does it hurt?"

"No, it tickles." Aidan surprised himself with the amount of venom he was able to put into the words.

"Carys." Neysa's voice cut through the silence that had fallen after Aidan's statement. "I'll take it from here."

"Suit yourself," Carys shrugged and headed back toward the

house, easily picking her way through the tangled underbrush.

Neysa knelt next to Aidan and he followed her gaze down to his arm. Immediately, he wished he hadn't. His forearm wasn't just broken. A jagged shard of bone poked through his skin, stained crimson with the blood soaking his clothes.

"Shoulder dislocation," Neysa murmured, hands hovering, but not touching. "Compound fracture through the skin." She raised her eyes to meet his. "I'm going to set the bone and put your shoulder back before we go back to the house. I can take some of your pain, but it won't be pleasant."

"Unpleasant? That'll be a change," Aidan's lips were white and his face was rapidly losing color, either from the pain or the blood loss, perhaps both.

Neysa gave Aidan a grim smile that didn't quite reach her eyes. She laid her hands on Aidan's shoulder, her gentle touch causing him to suck in a sharp breath. "Close your eyes."

Aidan did as she asked, desperately searching through his mind for a memory, searching for a pair of violet eyes. Before he could grasp the thought, he heard the pop and bit back a scream as his shoulder slid back into place. He kept his eyes clenched shut as he felt Neysa's fingers skim down his arm.

"*Brina*," he thought, frantic for anything to distract him from the pain he knew was coming. This time, he couldn't hold back the scream, but, mercifully, it cut off as darkness overtook him.

A flash of bright red caught his attention; the girl it belonged to kept it. He was already partway up the hill when he noticed Belladonna Juniper jab her wand toward the tree containing the new girl he'd been watching. He increased his pace, praying this girl he didn't know wouldn't be hurt.

Months had passed, but his interest in the red-headed girl hadn't waned. His blood boiled when he saw Gray Plumb grabbing Brina's chin. Before he could intervene, Brina's fist conveyed her feelings. Then, when he finally touched her, taking her injured hand in his, he was nearly overwhelmed by the

desire to protect her. When his fingers skimmed her skin, he
fought against the urge to take her into his arms. When she
confessed her secret, he couldn't stop himself from moving
closer, wanting nothing more than to touch his lips to hers, even
if it earned him a punch to the jaw. When she closed the
distance between them, his heart sang. He never wanted to let
her go.

Raised voices pulled him from his pleasant dream-memory.
He kept his eyes closed, but listened to Neysa and Carys.

"You can't be serious." Carys's voice sounded strained with
the effort of keeping her volume down.

"There are more of them and they have less training. I'll
leave in a few days, but I'll need to spend that time researching.
I need you to work with Aidan." Neysa's tone left no room for
argument, yet Carys persisted.

"But if you're right about when–"

"I am well aware of the timetable," Neysa snapped. "But
with Jael gone, resources are limited. This isn't a guaranteed
rescue mission, Carys."

"I know." Carys's voice softened so much Aidan had to
strain to hear her next words. "But I have to hope, Neysa. I have
to believe Callum can be saved." She paused, and when she
continued, her voice was so raw Aidan could almost taste her
pain. "He's all I have to live for."

Before Aidan could hear Neysa's response, reality faded
away and he knew nothing else until the next evening. When he
first opened his eyes, Aidan couldn't remember where he was or
why his arm was bound to his side. He sat up, head pounding
and stomach rumbling from lack of food. As he looked around
what he now recognized as his room, he realized that what little
light he could see by came from the flow of a setting sun. He
swung his legs over the side of the bed and paused, waiting for
the room to stop spinning. It took him fifteen minutes to get the
kitchen, but he did it on his own.

Surprisingly, he found a plate of cold chicken on the table next to his wand. He ate without thought, summoning a drink without leaving his chair. He felt the strength returning to his body as it absorbed the nutrients and he was suddenly ravenous. After finishing the chicken, Aidan began rummaging through the cupboards, eating as he went. By the time he heard Carys's footsteps, he'd consumed half a dozen apples, a small loaf of bread, sixteen carrots, another three drumsticks and half an apple crisp. He had a fleeting memory of laughing at Thana for eating so much, and then it vanished as Carys entered the room.

"Neysa's off doing save-the-world stuff." Carys looked everywhere but at him and Aidan realized, with a start, he wore only a pair of black sweatpants. "Which means I'm in charge of your training. Neysa said you'd need two days to recover enough to start again—"

"I feel fine," Aidan interrupted.

"What?" Now Carys looked at him.

"My arm and shoulder were aching a bit when I woke up, but they feel fine now."

Carys crossed the room and reached for the bandages, ignoring Aidan's flinch when her cold fingers brushed his skin. When her initial pressure on his wounds caused no reaction, Carys pressed harder. Without waiting for permission, Carys began removing Aidan's bandages. When he jumped again at the feel of Carys's icy touch, she scowled. "What's your issue?"

"Your hands are like ice." Aidan stepped back and finished unwinding his wounds, oblivious to Carys's glare.

All animosity fell away as Carys gaped at Aidan's unblemished arm. He had no scar, no discoloration, no indication he'd had a bone poking through the skin less than twenty-four hours before. Tentatively, Aidan rotated his arm, bending and flexing the muscles even as he readied himself for the first twinge of pain. It never came.

"What did Neysa give me?" Aidan stared at his arm in

shock. Even Jacen Raphael at Audeamus, a gifted Healer in his own right, couldn't have provided such excellent results in such a short time, not with multiple injuries like he'd had.

"A basic bone knitting potion and a pain-reduction charm. It should've taken at least forty-eight hours to completely take effect," Carys stepped forward again, stretching out her hand as if to touch Aidan. After just an inch or so, she stopped, and dropped her hand back to her side. Aidan didn't notice. "How'd you do it?" Carys demanded.

"Me?" Aidan tore his eyes from his arm, startled. "I didn't do anything." The anger in Carys's eyes made him take a step back. "I don't know how it happened, honestly, Carys." He held up both hands.

Carys blinked, face blank once more. "No, I don't suppose you would have the power to heal like that. If you'd been that extraordinary, your girlfriend would still be alive."

Aidan felt the air rush from his lungs. Carys bolted before Aidan could recover. He staggered to the nearest chair and collapsed in it. Even as the pain of Carys's accusation made its way throughout his body, Aidan found images flashing through his mind.

Brina waking him in the healing wing.

Brina's shoulders and back healed by a kiss.

Seeing the hole in Thana's blood-soaked clothes where she'd been stabbed.

The pile of ash he'd created.

Neysa's voice. "Both you and Thana are far more powerful than either of you realize."

Aidan's heart began to pound. Neysa had been right. Carys had been right. He'd done this himself with the power he'd stolen from Brina and from the dragon. Aidan ran his fingers down the length of his arm and asked, "what's happening to me?"

Chapter Four: Fighter

Carys was barely aware of the floor beneath her feet as she fled. She was through the door and halfway across the lawn before she realized the dew had fallen. Not that she felt it, or anything else for that matter. She'd simply seen the wet glistening in the moonlight and knew that her bare feet were making their way across damp grass.

By the time Carys had scrambled up the *nosidam* tree and pulled herself into the treehouse, she knew her feet were bleeding, and she was fairly sure she had tears on her cheeks. With trembling hands, Carys flicked her wand toward her injured feet, muttering the correct incantations to stop the bleeding, stave off infection and close the wounds. The final flourish was steadier than the first, and Carys wiped her face with her free hand as she pocketed her wand. She cursed herself silently, furious with her reaction to Aidan's sudden self-healing. He had nothing to do with her own issues. While she still didn't want to like him, this extreme negative reaction was uncalled for.

"It just isn't fair," she whispered, tucking her legs up to her chest. As she wrapped her arms around her knees, she heard the echo of her Aunt Sun's voice. *"Life's not fair,* mos-saeng-gin gae. *And I aim to make sure you're well aware of it."*

Carys had learned her lesson well.

Her teeth began to chatter in response to the chill in the air and she instinctively pulled her legs tighter. She'd spent the last nine years reacting to outward signals to prevent her body from harm and didn't even think about the gestures anymore. Her mind was filled with the past, eyes glazed over as she re-lived insults and injuries until she curled onto her side, pressing her lips together to keep back the whimpers. Only as the moon began to sink back down toward the horizon did Carys slip into unconsciousness.

Despite the lateness of when she'd finally fallen asleep, Carys woke as soon as the first rays of daylight appeared. A quick once-over showed her prior night's minor scrapes to be healed and she wasted no time dashing back to the house, more carefully this time, hoping to avoid Aidan until absolutely necessary. In this, she both succeeded and failed. She found Aidan in the kitchen.

Based on his disheveled appearance, he'd come back to the kitchen after being outside for some insane reason – she refused to think it might have been to look for her – then, apparently, he'd fallen asleep, head resting on folded arms. Carys reached out, intending to wake him, and then hesitated. After a moment, she turned and left, heading for her bathroom for a long, supposedly hot, shower.

Aidan was still sleeping when Carys descended the stairs half an hour later, much cleaner and with all her emotional shields in place. She stood behind Aidan for almost a full minute, studying the sleeping figure, before she grabbed his shoulder, making sure to dig in her fingers when she realized it was the injured one. Just to test how well he'd healed, of course.

Aidan woke with a start, jerking from his chair hard enough to almost send him tumbling to the floor. Carys chuckled. "You'll wanna wash-up before breakfast. You're filthy." She turned from Aidan and began to rummage through the cupboards for something to eat.

"What... where..." Aidan stammered. "What happened last night?"

"Nothing," Carys kept her voice cool. "Just suddenly didn't want be around you anymore." She shot a look of disdain over her shoulder, hating herself for it, but knowing it was necessary. She wasn't going to let him see her weak. "Looking and smelling like that, can you blame me?"

***

Aidan flushed at Carys's words, opening his mouth to retort that his present state was due to searching for Carys half of night, then closing it. He shrugged. It wasn't worth it. Before she could send any more insults his way, he headed for his room to shower. He didn't understand Carys, and he wasn't entirely sure if he wanted to. Something about her was off. When she'd say cruel things, he could sense she was almost forcing them out. She acted like nothing phased her, but he'd seen the flash of vulnerability in her eyes right before she'd run off the previous night. And he'd seen Neysa with her. He had a hard time believing Neysa would put up with someone so harsh without a good reason and he had a suspicion as to what Neysa's reason might be. When Carys had been at the cupboards in the kitchen, he'd seen her shoulders, and a strip of skin at her lower back. The scar tissue was knotted and twisted, running under the cloth of her black tank top in such a way it made Aidan think her entire back was covered. It may have been from some sort of accident, but he suspected a darker reason.

Throughout his shower and until he went back into the kitchen, Aidan found his thoughts circling back to Carys's strange behavior, turning actions, words and expressions over in his mind, matching them with what he'd seen, searching for answers to the way the girl behaved, until he was certain his suspicions were correct. If Carys had been abused, it would explain a lot about how she acted. Her snarky remarks and tough-girl attitude may have been part of her personality, but they were also a defense mechanism.

As he walked back downstairs, he resolved to try to be more tolerant. After all, he of all people could understand how life's circumstances could make a person behave in ways that weren't entirely pleasant. However, as he stepped into the kitchen, he saw Carys was gone. A note sat on the table: *Be at the beach in twenty minutes. We're starting your training.*

Aidan flipped over the paper then snorted in annoyance. "Would it've killed her to say when she'd written it?" He crumbled the note and tossed it into the trash. "She can wait. I'm starving." Understanding was one thing. Falling in line was something else.

***

Carys pushed sweat-dampened curls off her forehead and squinted against the morning sun. She put her hands on her knees, focusing on drawing in deep breaths of salty sea air. The physical exertion had cleared her head and dispelled much of her previous bleakness and anger. To her supreme irritation, however, Carys found Aidan still hovering at the edge of her mind. She straightened, fully intending to go through the course one more time, but the crunch of sand and rock alerted her to Aidan's presence. She turned toward the sound, suddenly conscious of her red face and sweaty clothes, and angry at herself for noticing. Carys snapped at Aidan, "nice of you to finally show up."

"Sorry," Aidan's voice was dry. "I had a bit of a late night."

Carys felt her face flush a deeper red. "I never asked you to come looking for me." She waived a hand dismissively, uncomfortable with the conversation heading in the direction of anything resembling personal. "It's a moot point anyway. We have work to do. And, based on your past performance, you need all the extra time you can get."

Aidan gritted his teeth and took a sharp breath through his nose. "Then I guess we'd better get started."

Carys put her hands on her hips. "Why don't you do a lap to warm up?"

"*Rydych yn ormod o geffyl blaen a byr,*" he growled.

Had he seriously just called her bossy and short? Carys grinned. She knew he could get up the rope now, but that he still wasn't sure how to get from one tree to another, and he clearly didn't want to ask her.

"Scared of falling again?" Carys taunted.

"I'm not a monkey. How am I supposed to get from the tree with the rope to the next branch?"

Carys rolled her eyes. "Follow, *kumozaru.*" Without waiting to see if Aidan was following, Carys darted up the beach. Hopefully a good, hard run would clear her mind of this preoccupation permanently. She didn't like the idea of letting anyone close. It had taken a while before she'd let Neysa in and even doing that was still hard sometimes, but something deep inside of her said letting Aidan close was going to have some serious and drastic consequences. She wasn't sure she could handle those.

***

Aidan started after her, surprising himself with how quickly he caught up. Carys looked over her shoulder and almost stumbled as Aidan passed her. Even accounting for his longer legs, just yesterday he would've been lucky to only be a step or two behind before they reached their goal. When he skidded to a stop next to the rope, his breathing was still even, and barely faster than it had been when he'd started. He didn't have time to think on it, as Carys appeared. Without pausing, she grabbed the rope and began climbing. When she was a quarter of the way up, Aidan began to climb. Carys paused at the top and glanced down. Aidan kept his face carefully blank as Carys wrapped her arms around the branch the rope was bound to. She released her feet from the rope and swung upwards, wrapping her legs around the same branch. She inched along, hand over hand, until she was directly over a branch from the next tree. Aidan made an involuntary noise as Carys let go with her hands, leaving her hanging by her legs as she used her now free hands to grab the branch below her. She unlocked her legs and let her weight swing her around until her feet were able to find the lower branch. As she walked to the trunk of the tree, she shot Aidan a smug smile, and disappeared, leaping lightly from tree to tree with virtually no noise.

"You've got to be kidding me," Aidan muttered. He glanced up at the branch above and then back to where Carys had disappeared. Aidan's lips flattened into a line as he grabbed for the branch and then swung his legs up to lock around it. He had a grim feeling it was going to be a long day.

Two hours passed before the pair paused for water, and only then because Carys decided it was time to begin actual training. Aidan was surprised at how little his body was protesting the work-out, especially the arm he'd injured. He started to wonder if this was another byproduct of his being healed, but before he could get very far, Carys interrupted the thought.

"I've heard you're a fair shot," Carys vanished her water bottle with a flick of her wand. Another wave conjured a crossbow and a long bow, each with a quiver full of arrows. "Let's test that rumor." She motioned at the weapons lying on the grass at the edge of the beach. "Choose your poison."

A brief flash of deja vu swept over him as he remembered hearing Jael asking them to choose a weapon. The corner of his mouth twitched at the memory of Thana that followed, this tiny thing who made Carys look big by comparison, running for a pair of nun-chucks. He bent to automatically take up the crossbow, and a surreal wave of emotion washed over him. He knew this bow.

"Aye," Carys flushed, cleared her throat, and spoke again. "Yes, it's yours. Neysa retrieved it from Lakyn's home shortly after you returned."

"How did she know where to go?" Aidan kept his eyes on the crossbow, running his fingers over the smooth metal.

"Jael, had left instructions in case anything happened to

her."

"What are we shooting at?" Aidan's voice was rough and he refused to look at Carys as he struggled to get things under control. He could feel her eyes on him, studying him as his emotions played across his face. For the first time in days, he craved the solace of a drink.

"Let's start with something simple." Carys retrieved the longbow from the ground. She pointed at a driftwood log about twenty yards up the beach.

Aidan nodded and fit a bolt into his crossbow. His first shot went wide.

Carys's did not.

Aidan flushed as Carys hit the center of the log with a solid thud. To his surprise, the girl nodded and motioned for Aidan to fire again without making one of her usual disparaging comments. Aidan raised his bow again, slowing his breathing, emptying his mind as Jael had taught him. This time, he was only inches from Carys's bulls-eye. He allowed himself a partial smile as he waited for Carys to take her second shot.

The sun was well overhead by the time the pair stopped for lunch. They sat under a large oak tree, the grass soft and cool after hours on the sand. Aidan and Carys each summoned their own meal and ate in silence. After vanishing his leftovers, Aidan turned to Carys. "What's next?"

Carys grinned. "How are you at hand-to-hand?"

***

Aidan stared up at the cobalt sky where the stars were just beginning to break through. With a growl, he pushed himself to his feet. "Again."

Carys sighed. "You're a glutton for punishment. Or," she added, "a masochist." She glanced up at the new moon. They needed to quit. "No more tonight. We'll pick up again tomorrow."

Aidan shook his head, the set of his jaw stubborn. "Again." He took a step toward Carys, his expression determined.

"No," Carys repeated. She was tired and could see Aidan was worse off. She'd thrown him more times than she could remember and landed more blows than he'd deflected. She'd tried to pull her punches as often as she could, but she'd still made contact on more than one occasion, resulting in scraped fingers and knuckles. Aidan's right eye was swollen shut, his lips bloody. She suspected his torso would be a mass of purple and black if he wasn't healed soon. Her cheek was swollen where she'd struck a tree after Aidan had managed to shake one of her holds, and she suspected it would be bruised by the time they got back to the house, if it wasn't already. She was going to need Neysa to help her heal herself. "Tomorrow."

Carys turned to go and Aidan grabbed her arm, pulling her to a stop.

The instincts that made her a superb fighter kicked in, and she twisted away from Aidan's grip, bringing her leg sweeping behind his and knocking him back to the ground. Carys knelt on Aidan's shoulders, pressing her heels into his sides. She leaned down, far enough to be in his face, but not so low that her balance would be off. "I said, we'll pick this up tomorrow. You need healing and rest."

"Don't tell me what I need." Aidan twisted under Carys, trying to knock her off, something almost manic about him. "You don't know me."

Carys shifted, digging her knee into the soft tissue and nerves between Aidan's shoulder and collarbone. Aidan stopped squirming, face grimacing in pain. "You're right," Carys snapped back. "I don't know you. And you know what, I don't actually care to. What I do care about is getting my brother back and I can't do it with a screw-up like you watching my back." Carys pushed off of Aidan's shoulders to get to her feet. "Do whatever you need to do to get your head where it belongs, or I'll tell Neysa to toss you back in whatever bar alley she found you in."

Carys was a yard away before Aidan scrambled to his feet. "Fine!" He shouted after her. "See if I care! Adalayde's probably dead anyway, just like your brother!"

Carys spun around, eyes flashing. "Take that back!"

"Why?" Aidan asked. "What proof has Neysa given you? How do you know Neysa isn't training us to do something for her? Why should either of us think that cares about us at all?"

Carys darted back across the sand, expression twisted in fury. "You have no idea what you're talking about. You don't know anything about me or Neysa. My brother's alive. I know it."

"So what if he is?" Aidan glared down at Carys. "He's not looking for you, is he? Not that I could blame him."

Carys's hand shot out and met Aidan's face with a sharp crack. She almost imagined she could feel the sting. Her lips were white, trembling as she spoke. "Maybe if you hadn't been out getting your girlfriend killed, my brother and your sister might've been found by now." Carys ran back up the beach before Aidan could see the tears shining in her eyes.

***

Aidan stared after Carys for a full thirty seconds before moving. His remaining energy had left him when his anger had drained away, and he couldn't bring himself to run after Carys. Besides, he wasn't sure if he wanted to apologize or retaliate. He trudged back toward the house, weariness growing with each step. The house was quiet by the time Aidan reached it, with no sign of either Carys or Neysa. He showered and promptly fell into bed, not even bothering to attempt healing himself.

When he woke the next morning, he severely regretted his

decision to get into bed as quickly as possible. Aidan winced as he gingerly climbed out of bed. Clad in only his boxer shorts, Aidan opened the closet door and peered at himself in the full-length mirror. The flesh around his right eye was the deep purple-black of a ripe plum and puffed up so his eye was only a bright slit in the discoloration. His bottom lip was swollen, cracked. Multiple bruises decorated his torso, a mottled array of blue, purple, black, green and yellow.

There was a light knock on the door and Carys entered without waiting for a response, already talking, "So, if you're not still being a jerk about last night..." Carys's voice trailed off as she saw him.

Her face flushed, but she refused to acknowledge what Aidan assumed was her embarrassment at his state of undress. Then her eyes widened as she saw the full extent of his injuries. She covered her surprise, but not before Aidan jumped at the opportunity to be snarky, unable to resist. "Want to give me a hand or are you just going to stand there ogling me?"

Carys's blush deepened, and Aidan could see anger mixed with her embarrassment. She pulled her wand from her pocket. "*Arua.*" A small jar appeared in her hand. She set it on Aidan's dresser. "Use this on the bruises and you'll be good in an hour. Fix your eye and lip on your own." She disappeared out of the door without a backward glance.

Aidan stared to smile at Carys's reaction, but the movement made his split lip bleed. "Ow." He reached for his wand and sighed. Healing spells had never been his specialty and, apparently, his newfound self-healing power didn't work all of the time. Pointing the tip of his wand at his lip, he muttered, "*kinderdost.*" Within seconds, only the slightest bit of swelling could be seen. Satisfied with the results, he repeated the spell on his eye, returning his sight to normal and reducing the size and color of the bruise to near invisibility. Once done, he retrieved the bottle from his dresser and eyed it speculatively. After a moment, he sighed. "Oh well," he murmured, "at least no one's around to see if it turns me green."

When Aidan appeared in the kitchen fifteen minutes later, his skin was still a light tan and his bruises were on their way to being healed. He did, however, smell like peppermint, but he considered it a small price to pay for feeling better. Carys was bolting down a bowl of cereal when he arrived, and didn't look up when he spoke. "Thank you for the lotion. I really appreciate it."

Carys bobbed her head in response, but still didn't look at him, though the corner of her mouth did twitch minutely when he passed, probably in response to the scent of peppermint Aidan ignored the amusement and turned his attention to finding food. Between their fight and her then giving him the ointment to help him feel better, he felt like he was beginning to get how she thought. After all, he could understand lashing out from a place of fear and hurt. He didn't even want to think about some of the things he'd said to his family members over the last six months. He caught Carys out of the corner of his eye, watching him with puzzled eyes and suddenly realized that she found his behavior just as odd as he found hers. He sat a plate at his usual seat, but didn't start eating. He needed to do something first. He held a hand out to Carys. "Truce?"

Carys eyed his hand, her voice suspicious. "What're ye playin' at?"

Aidan raised an eyebrow. This was the second time he'd heard Carys slip into the accent of the north. He didn't comment, though, and continued on his original train of thought. "I know you don't really like me, but it doesn't matter. We don't have to like each other. We do need to work together though. So, let's agree to stop tormenting each other, and start getting ready to do some damage."

"What changed?" Carys slipped her hand into Aidan's and gave it a firm shake, before quickly releasing it. Suspicion hadn't entirely left her eyes. "You hated me last night."

Aidan shook his head. "Not really. I'm just angry at pretty much everyone anymore." He shrugged. "It wasn't personal."

Carys snickered and Aidan looked up at her, surprised. "I've been angry at everyone for years." Her eyes sparkled when she smiled. "But sometimes it is personal."

Aidan snorted in amusement, nearly spitting out the mouthful of milk he'd just drank. He swallowed and coughed, eyes watering and face red. "Good to know," he said when he could finally speak.

Carys shoved her last spoonful of cereal into her mouth and stood. "Meet you on the course. Two times through to warm up and then I'm going to humiliate you again." She was still smirking when she hurried out the door. Aidan would've grinned in return, but instead busied himself with bolting down his meal before he took off for the obstacle course.

Four hours later, he found himself gloating over two perfectly placed arrows. Ten seconds later, he was tumbling, head over heels, down the hill toward the beach as Carys laughed. He scrambled to his feet faster than he'd anticipated, and almost lost his balance again, eliciting another burst of laughter from Carys. He took two steps back up the hill and, suddenly, he was running. Judging by the gasp that escaped from Carys before he slammed into her, his speed shocked her as much as it had him. They tumbled to the ground together, Aidan landing on top of her. Without a conscious thought, his body shifted as they came to a stop so his knees took his full weight, sinking into the mossy earth on either side of Carys's waist. He didn't want to hurt her, not really. His hands had released Carys's upper arms, and now rested on the ground, his face inches from hers, breath mingling as they panted for air. He wondered if his eyes were as wide as hers.

"How did you do that?" Carys asked, still breathless.

Aidan shook his head, unsure how to answer. He wasn't sure

if he was ready to tell the truth, or even if he understood it. His gaze locked with hers and he swallowed hard. He'd never realized her eyes were the exact shade of the sky over a stormy sea, a gray-blue that could haunt a man. Under the sweat, he caught a whiff of lilies, subtle and not at all unpleasant.

***

Carys couldn't look away, caught by Aidan's gaze. His bright green eyes held flecks of gold that shifted and shimmered as she watched. She was suddenly very aware of Aidan's body against hers though she couldn't feel it. Without realizing what she was doing, Carys pushed herself up and pressed her lips to Aidan's. It was impossible to say who jumped back faster or further, both staring at the other, eyes wide.

"I..." Aidan stammered as heat flooded his face.

Carys put a hand to her mouth, not speaking.

"I have to go." Aidan stumbled to his feet and ran.

Carys didn't move for several minutes, thoughts and questions jumbled together as she ran her fingers over her lips. She stood slowly, moving as if in a trance, and made her way back toward the house. She went immediately to her room, suspecting Aidan had sequestered himself in his own room, but not wanting to risk seeing him.

It wasn't until Carys was in the shower, sloughing off the day's grime, that she felt her stomach clench. What had she been thinking? She didn't even like Aidan... did she? She watched the steam billow around her, tempted to crank up the heat and scald her skin, just to see if anything had changed. She used the tip of her index finger to trace her bottom lip. For the brief moment when she'd been kissing Aidan, she actually felt the brush of skin against skin, the warmth of Aidan's mouth, lips parted in surprise. It had faded after just a few minutes and now she was beginning to doubt it had even happened.

"But it did happen," she insisted. "But why? Why now? Why him?"

Are you sure you want the answers?

Carys froze. She hadn't been praying, at least not consciously. She hadn't prayed since leaving Aunt Sun's and voluntary prayer had ceased long before that.

You may have stopped talking, but I never stopped listening.

Carys swallowed hard around the lump in her throat. "I don't understand."

You never truly left me, Daughter. Your heart has always been with Me.

"You left me, Elsali." Carys heard the accusation in her voice. "Abandoned me to Aunt Sun. Let me curse myself."

All things are part of My plan. You are here for a reason, as is Aidan. I am working in his heart, as I am in Yours. Listen to My voice. Listen and obey. I'm here. You're never alone.

***

In his bathroom, Aidan stood under the hot water, head bowed under the stream, water mingling with his tears. He knew he felt for Carys, wondered what had happened to make her so cold, but it was nothing like what he'd felt for Brina... was it? The pain of losing Brina had faded to a dull ache without him being aware of it and he clung to the ache, poking at it like a bruise, using the resulting pain to remind him of what he'd lost. He tried to recall what Brina looked like, and felt a moment of panic when all he could remember was her eyes and the scent of roses. A rush of relief flowed over him as Brina's face floated into his mind. The details were blurred a bit, but fresh tears spilled over when she smiled. "Brina, *amado*," he whispered. "I miss you so much." He slumped to his knees as he heard her voice echo, *I'll always love you, Aidan. No matter what the future holds.*

"Elsali," for the first time in months, Aidan addressed his Creator. "Why? Why did You take her from me? Why did You put me here with Carys? I don't understand. Please, Father. Please."

Peace, child.

Aidan let out a shuddering breath.

I'm here. I've never left. You're in My hands, as is Brina. She finished the mission I had for her. Her part of your world is complete and she is home.

Aidan closed his eyes.

Be at peace. Follow My plan. No guilt. No fear. I will speak to your spirit. Listen and obey.

Aidan nodded, unable to speak. A tranquility he knew could only come from Elsali flooded over him, washing away his pain and confusion as clearly as the water washed the first from his body. For the first time in six months, he felt as if his life could have meaning again.

Both he and Carys were quiet as they joined Neysa for dinner an hour later. If their mentor noticed their silence or their red-rimmed eyes, she chose not to comment, asking instead about the training.

"It's going well," Aidan said, gaze never leaving his plate. "Thank you for my bow."

"You're welcome." Neysa took another ear of corn.

"Any word on when we'll be heading out?" Carys's voice was soft.

"Another week or so," Neysa answered. "Thana's group still needs some time to train. I'll be spending most days with them, unless you two think you'll need me."

Aidan looked towards Carys, then quickly looked away again when he saw her glancing his way. He said, "We'll be fine."

Neysa nodded. "Then I'll return to Audeamus in the morning to stay for a while, and I'll send word as soon as I've determined that we're ready to go."

The pair nodded their agreement without saying a word. Aidan's thoughts bounced around from place to place and he spared a moment to consider how the staff and students of Audeamus must've reacted to their introduction to Neysa. The thought of Headmaster Manu meeting Neysa dressed as she was today – gold and silver-streaked hair in rows of waist-length braids, blue make-up, piercings, shiny silver leggings under a blue-and-gray camouflage shirt/dress and scuffed black knee-high boots – made him smile. Then he remembered why Neysa was going to Audeamus in the first place and his smile vanished. He returned to his meal in pensive silence. Finally, Carys excused herself, leaving Aidan and Neysa alone.

"Is Thana learning to control her extra power?" Aidan didn't take his eyes from his plate. His fork scratched patterns against the ceramic.

"Yes." Neysa's tone was cautiously flat.

"How?"

"She practices simple spells, starting with small ones like summoning, increasing the size of the object or its distance. Ones like *ignis fatuus* or *thalaca*, she has to practice away from people and under supervision in case something gets out of hand."

"Good to know." Aidan slid back his chair. He deposited his dishes in the sink and left with a barely audible good-night. He just wanted to make sure his friend was all right. He wasn't interested in experimenting with whatever new powers he had. Not when he considered the price they'd taken.

***

Neysa sighed and took her own dishes to the sink. With a wave of her hand, she started them washing. She really didn't feel like doing it by hand at the moment. She stood there for a moment, watching the first plate being scrubbed clean.

"Neysa?"

Carys's voice was small. Neysa turned, hoping this wasn't going to be one of the times the younger girl was going to be difficult.

Never one for preamble, Carys immediately said what was on her mind. "I kissed Aidan."

Neysa's jaw dropped. She would've been prepared for Carys to say she'd punched Aidan, not kissed him. Neysa blurted out the first question that popped into her mind, "Why?"

Carys flushed. "It seemed like a good idea at the time."

"Oh, Carys." Neysa shook her head. Based on how Aidan had taken Brina's death, he couldn't have reacted well to the kiss. "What were you thinking?"

Carys waved a hand impatiently. "Doesn't matter. That's not what I needed to talk to you about."

Neysa's eyebrows shot up. What else could have happened? "It's not?"

"No." Carys took a deep breath. "I felt it."

"Felt what?" Neysa was confused.

Carys's face turned bright red. "The kiss."

Neysa's eyes widened. "You mean 'felt it' as in..."

"Yes, as in I could feel his lips on mine," Carys's face flamed brighter, but she stubbornly continued. "After he... left, I could still feel for almost five whole minutes, but just my mouth." Carys's tone turned pleading. "What's happening?"

"I have a theory," Neysa admitted slowly. She hadn't expected it to come out like this, but Elsali's timing was always better than her own. "But it's going to require you and Aidan to be honest about some things in both your pasts."

Carys blanched, color draining from her face as quickly as it had come. She drew in a shuddering breath, her mouth flattening into a grim line. "All right."

Neysa regarded the young woman, searching for hesitation.

If Aidan shared and Carys balked, their fragile connection would be shattered and, she feared, all would be lost. Both of them were so scarred by their past, both physically and emotionally, that they couldn't see how much they needed each other. What Neysa read in Carys's eyes was encouraging. They were troubled, frightened, but not deceitful. Neysa nodded. "Go to the living room. I'll get Aidan."

Fifteen minutes later, the trio was seated in the cozy sitting room, the two younger ones looking to Neysa for answers. It was hard, sometimes, to remember they weren't so much younger than she was since they always deferred to her. Though, she had to admit, she often felt much older than her years. She tucked her feet up under her, arranging herself into the most comfortable position the plush dove-gray recliner had to offer. Opposite her, Aidan and Carys sat on the matching couch, one on either end with a cushion between them.

"Each of you has a story the other doesn't know. As I am privy to both, I can speculate at what's happening, but I can't say anything without you each agreeing to share." Neysa turned toward Carys. "You have to go first."

"Where do I start?" Carys kept her eyes on Neysa, her fingers twisting together so tightly that her knuckles were white.

"At the beginning." Neysa's voice was gentle, but firm.

Carys closed her eyes, and Neysa knew she was fighting down the panic that surfaced whenever she recalled her early years. "I am a *teleia mnimi*. Everything I see, everything I hear, I remember. My first memory is of lying in the hospital nursery, watching two men steal my brother..."

Chapter Five: Times Like These

Carys heard the sound of her flesh tearing above her aunt's labored breathing. Whatever Sun Wywryd was using this time sent white hot flashes of pain with each strike, leaving a dull throb until the next blow turned the previous injury into agony once more. Blood ran down her back in rivulets, staining the carpet and bringing a new bout of lashes. Carys fought against the gray threatening to take her, sure that if she allowed herself to lose consciousness, this would be the time she didn't wake up.

It wasn't the first time the ten year-old had had such thoughts. Very rarely did a day go by without some form of Aunt Sun's 'discipline.' More often, Carys received small blows and jabs throughout the day as her aunt found reasons. The more vicious abuse occurred when Carys disobeyed a specific edict, even if unintentionally. This time, however, Carys had gone against her aunt's wishes purposefully. In the long run, she supposed, it would be worth it. Chopping off fourteen inches of heavy curls would make dodging her aunt's grasping hands easier. Aunt Sun had forced Carys to wear her long hair in a braid, and often used it to yank the girl back from whatever she was doing. The new, almost boy-short cut would take a long time to grow long enough to braid again. The haircut alone hadn't done it though; it had just been the final straw. As always, Aunt Sun had grabbed for Carys's hair when the girl had mentioned her missing brother. When she'd found the convenient handle gone, she'd exploded.

"I will not have ye makin' wild stories," Aunt Sun's breathing was ragged. "Ye have no brother. No one else to blame for me sister's death. That be all yer fault."

Carys was sure there was more to the tirade, but it faded out as she lost consciousness. Her final thought was that this time, maybe this time, she would finally have some peace. The thought wasn't as unappealing as it might have once been.

When the pain woke her hours later, Carys had a momentary wish that she'd stayed in the dark. Then, as always, the image of a dark-haired baby, blue-gray eyes wide with fright as he disappeared through a hospital door, brought Carys back to herself. It was always the same. No matter how often Carys was tempted to end her life, whether proactively or passively by provoking Aunt Sun, the one thing keeping her alive was the memory of her brother and the hope of finding him someday. She focused on those gray-blue eyes, using them to anchor herself, to give her brain time to start processing through the pain. Then, she began to take inventory of her injuries.

Based on the pool of sticky, cooled blood surrounding her, Carys estimated she'd been unconscious for at least two hours, if not three. She risked opening her eyes. Aunt Sun was gone, most likely to the Pingkeu Kokkili for her ritual after-beating drink. It was always a good idea for Carys to be gone before Aunt Sun returned. Usually, Carys cleaned up any mess in an effort to postpone additional fury, but this time, she suspected she'd be lucky to be able to get out of her aunt's sight. She shifted and had to bite back a scream. She couldn't stop the whimper and hated herself for it. The world began to gray out again as she pushed herself to her hands and knees.

Inch by agonizing inch, Cary crawled toward her room, leaving a trail of her own blood smeared dark against Aunt Sun's white floors. After what seemed like hours, Carys flattened herself against the rough wooden planks of her bedroom floor and pulled herself under her bed, hoping it would be enough. Before she let the darkness take her once more, she waved her wand toward the hallway, only having the strength to glamour the blood, disguising rather than removing. As she slipped back into the unknown, she prayed to One she told herself she no longer believed in. "Please, don't let her find me."

Seven years later, the memory still made Carys shiver. She

hugged herself and continued the story, eyes never leaving a spot on the floor in front of her. "I stayed under my bed for three days before I could heal myself enough to move. I couldn't do anything about the scars. By the time I saw my aunt again, she'd calmed enough to have cleaned my blood – I still don't know when the glamour faded – and I no longer feared for my life. But I knew it was only a matter of time before she did it again, and I never wanted to be hurt like that again. Less than a week later, I found the spell I wanted, one that would keep me from feeling pain. I was young; I didn't know what I was doing." A tear slipped from Carys's eye. "I haven't felt anything since." She looked up, cheeks stained red. "Until this afternoon."

"This afternoon?" Aidan started to ask, then stopped. "Oh." His cheeks flushed as everything clicked into place. "Oh!"

Neysa stood and crossed the short distance to the couch. "And now Aidan understands." She placed a gentle hand on Aidan's shoulder. "Aidan, please share your story so Carys will know as well."

Aidan hesitated. "May I ask Carys a question first?"

Carys nodded, fighting back her instinct to shield herself again after being so vulnerable.

"How did you get out?"

Carys swallowed hard. "Not much later, I ran away to Vosescrus. Two years ago, Neysa found me and brought me here. She was seventeen at the time, but was more of a mother to me than my aunt ever was."

***

Aidan started to reach for Carys and then thought better of it. He'd wait to consider what all of this meant to him. He stood and crossed to the window. The memory of Jael doing the same thing when she told her story flitted through the back of his mind. "After the earthquake at Audeamus, the deaths of my schoolmates, Zoe and Asha, ate at me, and not just because I'd known them. In the following weeks, I found myself drawn to the Fuhjyn field only to turn back when I saw the investigators who'd been sent to find cause of death. Eventually, they left, but I still ignored the pull. Then, one day in the middle of Fatum, I couldn't hold out any longer..."

The tug toward the field was stronger than ever. Aidan had been resisting for weeks and he was getting tired. Part of him knew it would almost certainly end badly for him, like it had for Zoe and Asha, and part didn't care. He was more than halfway to the field before he realized where he was going and, by then, the pull was too strong to break.

The field was a disaster, most of the landmarks destroyed or moved. Still, Aidan made his way to the ancient oak Brina had used in their first Fuhjyn scrimmage. It lay on its side, twisted roots half out of the dirt, revealing a gaping hole. Without hesitating, or questioning why he wasn't hesitating, Aidan jumped into the hole. As he traveled deeper into the earth, a sleepy sort of tranquility came over him. The stench – which reminded him of a cross between the defensive odor of a skunk and a dead vorbyd *that had been lying under a summer sun for a few hours – seemed inconsequential. His growing weakness was of no concern. Even when he stumbled and found himself without the strength to stand, he felt no panic. Then the darkness came...*

"I woke, well, half-woke really, when Brina said my name. I don't remember much of the journey out except the smell and the heat, and Brina at my side. The next thing I knew was the touch of Brina's fingers on my cheek, her hand in mine." Aidan swallowed hard and continued, knowing the pain of the memory was written on his face. "According to Healer Jacen, I shouldn't have woken up. Ever."

He returned to his seat, determined to finish the story.

"Later, Jael told me that the dragon had drained nearly all of my magic. She speculated that Brina had healed me, transferring enough of her own energy into me that my body had enough time to recover. I never healed myself, only Brina, and only once. I figured it was some residual thing from her healing me. Then, I healed myself last night." He glanced at Neysa who nodded once. "But that isn't the only recent change in my powers." He quickly recounted what had happened the night he'd ridden off on Abraxan.

"All this came from Brina healing you one time?" Carys asked.

Aidan shook his head. He'd saved this part for the end, dreading the telling and the pain that would come with it. "None of us realized how fast everything was going to happen." He struggled to keep his voice even as he recounted the battle that had taken Brina from him. He couldn't stop the crack in his voice when he told of waking and finding her dead, but he pushed on, ending with he and Thana's realization of how they'd survived.

"And you think what Brina did, it changed your magic?" Carys directed the question to Aidan.

Neysa, however, was the one who answered. "I know it did. Aidan's other companion, Thana Decker, was also healed by Brina, brought back from the brink of death. She's also showing an increase in power, strength and speed."

"Which is why we'll need her to come with us to get my brother," Carys said.

Neysa nodded. "The only chance we have is if Aidan and Thana fight with us. I'll be leaving at first light to return to Audeamus and I'll contact you as soon as I get a better idea of when Thana and the others are ready."

"Neysa," Aidan looked up at the young woman. "What exactly are they, are we, getting ready for?"

"To fight the Children of the Dragon."

He felt the color drain from his face, the nightmare cold that haunted his sleep stealing over him. He shivered as he spoke, his voice barely above a whisper. "I didn't realize any had survived."

"Not all of them were in the mountains that day." Neysa's voice was calm, but Aidan could see the tension in her body. "Another group was preparing for something else. They're a fringe group. Fanatics of a different sort. Ones who had some sort of plan in place for after the Chosen One killed the dragon."

"I'm lost." Aidan appeared relieved to see that this was new information to Carys as well.

"Details are vague. All my family has been able to collect over the years are fragments. Most sent to spy never return. Or they're followed home." Neysa's lips pressed together in a thin line and Aidan could see the struggle for control over her emotions. "We do know it was this group who took Adalayde and Callum, and that those two were chosen very specifically."

"Why them?" Aidan asked. He had a feeling he was missing some sort of personal connection to Neysa, but didn't feel comfortable asking her about it. Better to focus on the matter at hand.

"From what we can tell, the *Decazmaja* needed several things for a spell of some kind. Dragon blood, dragon heart, and two very specific people. A male and a female twin, but not related, born to a dead hero, on the same day, in the month of Fidelis."

"Wow, that's specific," Aidan raked his hand through his hair.

"They waited thousands of years for those exact requirements to be met." Neysa's tone was serious. "Their dedication is unmatched."

"What do the *Decazmaja* want with my brother... and Aidan's sister?"

Carys tacked on the last almost as an afterthought, but Aidan didn't blame her. She'd known her whole life that someone had stolen her brother. He was still trying to wrap his head around the fact that his sister was alive.

"I'm not sure. That's one thing we've never been able to discover. But if they're needed for a spell, and dragon's blood and heart are other ingredients, it can't be anything good." Neysa didn't make eye contact.

Aidan understood almost immediately, though he wished he didn't. "They're a sacrifice."

Neysa nodded, eyes still on her hands. "I believe so."

"A sacrifice for what?" Carys's voice sounded years younger than her age.

Now Neysa looked at them. "Understand this is only a theory. I have no real proof to back it up." She took a deep breath. "I believe it's a binding spell. I think the *Decazmaja* are trying to resurrect the dragon and control it."

Chapter Six: Full of Grace

Aidan couldn't sleep. It was three in the morning and he'd been staring at his ceiling for over four hours. Not that the pale gray color was anything interesting. Now if it had been covered with frolicking chinchillas... his sister Zoe'd had a chinchilla named Elliot who used to scare the woobies he'd had as a child, which now that he thought of it were... Aidan growled in frustration and punched his pillow. His brain had been chasing these crazy thoughts all night, trying to avoid thinking about Adalayde, what had been done to her, what was going to be done. And then, there was Carys.

He couldn't stop thinking about her either and about the story she'd told about her aunt. Every complaint he'd ever made about his life paled in comparison to what she'd been through. When he'd first met Brina, he'd thought of how she'd had a tougher life than he'd had and how she'd never complained. Now, he knew he'd never really understood what a troubled life was like. He'd always had enough food, a roof over his head, a place where he felt safe. He couldn't imagine being a child and never knowing if today was the day you'd be beaten to death by someone who was supposed to love you.

"No more," he said out loud. "No more pity parties. I'm going to be thankful for what I have and what I've had, and I'm going to move forward."

Now, if he could just figure out what that meant in relation to Carys...

***

Carys had given up the whole lying-in-bed-when-you-can't sleep thing years ago. She and insomnia were old nemesisis... nemesi? She shook her head and resumed her 'sleepless night' workout routine: one hundred sit-ups, seventy-five push-ups (and not those wimpy 'girl' ones), and thirty-five pull-ups. She was trying to increase her pull-up number to forty. It seemed like the easiest way to distract her mind from the chaos inside. She'd been begging Neysa to tell her more about the people who held Callum, and now she realized why Neysa had held off. Before, she would've left the instant Neysa had turned her back, bent on rescuing her brother despite the odds. But that had been before Aidan.

An hour later, a showered and still unable to sleep Carys, clad in her favorite Hoban the Hedgehog pajamas – the kind she usually only wore in the privacy of her own room – made her way to the kitchen for a light midnight snack. She was half-way to the refrigerator, singing the new Nomad song as she went. "Lonely wanderer, won't you please come home..." She did a little half-step... and realized she wasn't alone. She let out an undignified squawk – which she would later vehemently deny and threaten Aidan with disembowelment if he ever mentioned – and slipped, her fuzzy squirrel slippers not offering much traction on the tile floor.

***

Aidan stared in wide-eyed shock, fork still in his mouth, as Carys ended her startling performance in a heap next to the table. A full thirty seconds of silence followed. As Carys scrambled to her feet, face bright red under her tan, she pointed a finger at Aidan. "Not a sound. No words, no laughter. Nothing."

Aidan held up his hands, having managed to remove the fork from his mouth. He shook his head, pressing his lips together to show his intent, though for a moment, he wasn't sure he was going to be able to restrain himself.

"What're ye doing down here?" Carys sputtered, northern accent thickening her words.

Catching butterflies with marzipan popped into Aidan's head, but he restrained himself and went with honesty. "Couldn't sleep." He gestured toward the pie plate in front of him. "Want some?"

Carys opened her mouth to give a snarky reply, then shrugged and took a seat. Aidan didn't blame her. Neysa's apple pie was awesome. She was a much better cook than Jael had been. He was surprised to find that the thought of his former teacher didn't bring nearly as much pain as it had before.

The pair sat in fairly comfortable silence, enjoying their snack, until Aidan spoke. "Do you mind if I ask a personal question?"

Carys stiffened. Her nod was terse, but it was an agreement nonetheless.

"The scars on your back. If they're not from a curse, why hasn't Neysa healed them?"

"I won't let her." Carys put down her fork, appetite apparently gone. "They remind me that I'm a survivor. That I'm stronger than I think." After a moment, she surprised Aidan by asking him a question. Sort of.

"Tell me what it's like." She didn't meet his eyes. "Having a family."

Aidan weighed his words. He wanted to be honest and to give Carys's request the consideration it deserved. He'd also never really thought about it before. "It's crazy, and frustrating, and wonderful and everything all mixed up into one. You'd do anything for them, but sometimes you want to kill them yourself." He smiled at a memory. "When I was just a year old, my mom remarried and I was adopted by my step-dad. He already had three daughters of his own. Elena was four. Zoe and Zahra were two. They adored me and I hero-worshiped them. I used to follow them everywhere and they never complained. Then they'd dressed me up in their old Halloween costumes and I decided having sisters wasn't as fun as I'd thought. Myrtle the

Mighty Turtle and Princess Everbright Starlight weren't exactly my style."

Carys snickered and quickly glanced at Aidan, as if waiting for a reproach. He was chuckling too. Her amusements, however, ended abruptly when Aidan asked, "what about Neysa? Doesn't she talk about her family?"

Carys turned her head so she was facing away from Aidan. She couldn't, however, hide the pain in her voice as she relayed the story. "Neysa grew up here with her parents and two sisters, her paternal grandparents, her aunt, uncle and their six girls. When Neysa was fifteen, her father and his sister were coming back from scouting a group of Decazmaja who'd been involved in the kidnapping of two children thirteen years before."

Aidan swallowed hard. He didn't need Carys to tell him who those children had been. Neysa had been connected to his family for longer than he'd realized.

Carys continued, "She was out picking flowers to decorate the tables for their homecoming when she saw the smoke. By the time she got back to the houses, it was all over. All three houses were burning."

When she paused, her face growing pale, Aidan wasn't sure he wanted to know what happened next, not if it could make tough Carys look nauseous.

"She realized that she couldn't hear anyone, so she ran for the beach, thinking maybe her family had survived and had headed for their rendezvous point. Instead, she found fourteen bodies. No heads." She turned so that she was looking directly at him. "The Decazmaja had followed her father and aunt back to the island. She knew it was them because she found one of their blades lodged in her thirteen year-old sister's stomach. They don't use magic to kill."

"They killed her whole family?" Aidan involuntarily glanced toward the stairs. His heart gave a painful twist and his stomach churned. He was starting to regret the three pieces of pie he'd eaten.

Carys nodded. "I never asked about them again. She's told me other bits and pieces over the last two years, but I never wanted to press."

"Well, you can ask me anything you want about my family." He smiled at the delighted expression on Carys's face, bleak cloud vanishing as the subject changed.

"Tell me your favorite memories." She didn't try to hide the eagerness in her voice.

Aidan's smile widened as he let thoughts of his family come forward. "Well, this one time, my little brother, Alaric, decided to try to sneak his guinea pig into church by putting it in his pocket. That didn't go over very well..."

Chapter Seven: Love Heals

The rotating blade flashed in the afternoon sun. Carys twisted and the knife thudded harmlessly into the wood behind her.

"How did you do that?" Aidan plopped down on the grass.

Carys removed her blindfold and glanced at the barn wall behind her. All six of Aidan's daggers were buried in the wood at least an inch. She stretched out on the cool grass at Aidan's side. "When I left Aunt Sun's, I was too young to get a real job, and I didn't really have many options. On my second night, I stole some fruit from a stand downtown. As I was running away, the owner threw a halibut at me."

"A halibut?" Aidan interrupted. "Like the fish?"

Carys nodded. "At the last moment, I dodged it. Somehow, I knew it was coming. The fish hit an old woman named Eddison Pennybanks. Her driver went after the shop owner and I got away." Carys crossed her arms and stared up at the sky. "A teenager named Parker Faeggin spotted me and sent one of his crew to bring me in for a 'talk.' Turned out that area of downtown was his territory. When he saw I'd given his man a black eye, cracked ribs and more bites than he could count, he offered me a place on his crew. He had me practice dodging until nothing could touch me, but I've had a knack for it as long as I can remember." She glanced sideways at Aidan, an almost shy expression on her face. "I never did show Faeggin my other gift."

Aidan raised an eyebrow. Carys whistled two high notes, then two long low notes. A few seconds later, a small flash of red and a little bird sat on Carys's outstretched hand.

"Is that a–"

"A mimic bird." Carys completed the thought. She whistled a low note, then spoke quickly and clearly. "Lunch will be in ten minutes." She whistled another series of notes.

The bird hovered for a moment, then fluttered over to Aidan. One beady, intelligent eye regarded him for a moment, then the mimic chirped back Carys's message in its entirety.

"How'd it know who to give the message to?"

Carys shrugged. "Don't know. Whoever I'm thinking of when I give the message gets it. I don't know how the mimics know where to go for that matter. Or even how I can call them. I've just always been able to."

A memory clicked into place. "That's how you told Neysa I'd broken my arm when you didn't have your wand."

Carys nodded. "Aye. I admit, it's been a handy little talent." She rolled onto her side, propping her head on her hand. "It's no healing ability–"

"But it's all you," Aidan countered. "You have these powers and you didn't get them from anyone. You were born special."

Carys's cheeks turned red. "We both were, Aidan. I don't think it was Brina who had the healing ability. I think it was you all along. I think she got some of that from you, not the other way around." She sat up, looking away from him. "After what Neysa told us last night, I think it's not just you and me who're special. There's something about us and our siblings, something the *Decazmaja* need. It's why we were chosen, why we fulfill the prophecy."

Aidan sat up as well. He'd never thought of it like that before, but it made perfect sense. "I think you're right. I think there's something much bigger at work here." Suddenly, he remembered what Brina had said about how she didn't think going after the dragon was going to be the end, and how he and Thana had promised to see it through. "It's gotta be more than just a single dragon."

Silence fell for a moment, then Carys bounced to her feet. "No use trying to figure it out on an empty stomach. Lunchtime." She held out a hand.

Aidan slid his hand into hers, using the leverage to pull

himself into a standing position. As soon as his feet were steady, he started to loosen his grip, and then started, jaw hanging open as a jolt passed from his hand to hers. Carys's eyes went wide as she stared at their linked hands.

"You felt that?" he asked.

Carys nodded. "And I can feel your hand." Her voice was little more than a whisper.

Aidan kept his fingers wrapped around Carys's as he took a step forward. "What you said, about the healing, I think you might be right. I spent a lot of last night thinking about this, wondering if I could heal you." He looked down at Carys. The raw emotion in her eyes made him wince. He'd never seen anyone look so terrified and vulnerable at the same time, as if every protective wall had been torn away. "I'm willing to try, Carys, but are you sure you want this before we go after our siblings? We're going to be fighting, probably injured. If this works, are you sure you want to be able to feel before that happens?"

Her voice was soft. "Do you know what it's like, to fight without being able to feel anything? I could be wounded, dying, and never know until it was too late. And, practicalities aside, after nearly ten years, even pain would be welcome."

He could tell she was forcing herself to keep meeting his gaze, to not put up her guard. Aidan shifted his hand, threading his fingers through hers. He nodded and ignored the pang that went through him as he realized how natural it felt to be holding her hand. "Okay then. After lunch, I'll try."

***

Carys smiled, hoping Aidan would mistake the blush in her cheeks for a delayed reaction to their recent activities. She walked silently at his side, relishing the first contact she'd felt in years. Aidan's hand was warm, his calloused fingers rough against her skin. She almost protested when they broke apart, but held her tongue and followed him into the house. Neither one spoke as they moved about the kitchen, each stealing glances when they thought the other's back was turned. They ate and cleaned up without a word, tension growing as their meal neared its end.

When they had nothing left to do in the kitchen, Aidan led Carys into the living room. He sat on the couch and motioned for her to take a seat next to him. She'd never been so nervous before and had a feeling her palms were sweating as she sat down on the couch. Part of her kept telling her over and over not to get her hopes up, that it probably wouldn't work. Another part of her was just thinking about how at least she'd be able to feel it when he tried. That alone should be enough, even though she knew it wouldn't.

"I don't really know how this works," Aidan confessed. "I've never done it intentionally before."

Carys nodded mutely, holding her breath as she prayed Aidan wasn't trying to talk himself out of helping her. It would be one thing for him to try and fail; another to decide he didn't want to try at all.

Aidan extended his hand and ran his fingertips over Carys's cheek. She gasped at the sensation, then her eyes filled with tears as he took his hand away. It didn't last. As soon as they broke contact, the numbness started to return, just as it had before. A sharp pain went through her chest and she almost wished her inability to feel had included emotions. This was why she tried not to hope, because hope was always destroyed. At least it had always been that way in her life. Apparently, this wasn't going to be any different.

***

"It's going to take more magic than that." Aidan shifted so

that one denim-clad knee pressed against Carys's leg. His heart was pounding so loudly that he was sure she could hear it. Half of his brain said it was anxiety about what he was trying to do, while the other half countered that it was anticipation about what he needed to do. He tried to ignore both. He took a deep breath, letting his lungs fill with the scent of lilies that always hovered around Carys.

His hand trembled as he reached for her face again. This time, he didn't brush her cheek, he cupped it, palm pressing against her skin. He let his mind fill with his desire for Carys to be healed and, with a guilty twist to his gut, allowed his growing feelings for her to come forward. He didn't love her, not like that, but he knew the potential for something more existed. He only hoped what he did feel would be enough.

He bent his head, hesitated for a fraction of a second, then closed the distance to press his lips against Carys's. He expected the jolt this time and moved his hand to the back of her head to prevent her from unintentionally breaking the connection. This time, he felt the magic pass from him to her, and still he lingered a moment more, enjoying the feel of her mouth against his. Then, he pulled back, keeping his fingers in the thick tangle of her curls as he met her eyes. He was breathing hard, partly from the energy transfer, partly from the kiss. He dropped his hand. Still, it felt like they were connected, as if he could each sense everything she was thinking and feeling.

"Did it work?" He almost didn't want to ask the question, but he had to know the answer.

She nodded slowly, an expression of pure wonderment on her face as she opened her eyes.

"I can't promise it'll be permanent." He made himself say the words, loathe at having to caution her when she was so obviously happy, but knowing she needed to understand.

She put her hand on top of his. "It's more than I could've hoped for." Her expression was almost shy.

Aidan stood abruptly, face flushed. "Um, I have to go." Without a second glance, he hurried from the room. He hated himself even as he fled, but couldn't seem to stop his legs from carrying him further away. His room didn't have enough distance from Carys, so he headed for the barn. The horses regarded his entrance with mild interest. Abraxan snorted in greeting as Aidan slipped into the animal's stall.

"Hey there, boy." Aidan wasn't even out of breath, but he couldn't bring himself to marvel at that, not now. He ran his shaking hand down the horse's neck. "Must be nice, not have all the drama that comes with being human."

Abraxan's tail twitched and Aidan rested his head on the beast's side. "I don't know what to do." He was no longer sure who he was addressing: the horse, himself or Elsali. "I love Brina... or loved her? I don't know anymore. And now there's Carys and I think I'm falling for her. Is that betraying Brina's memory? Is it unfair to Carys to see if she feels the same way when I'm not sure if I'm over Brina?" Aidan fell silent, waiting for an answer, waiting for the solution to all of his problems.

As minutes passed into an hour, nothing came. Afternoon heat faded to evening cool and still Aidan waited. He'd never felt so alone.

***

Carys took a deep breath, trying to steady her thudding heart. She could feel Aidan's magic surging through every cell in her body. The sensations were overwhelming and she shut her eyes again. Even though Aidan was no longer touching her, she felt his presence lingering, a phantom caress flooding her body with heat. Her lungs filled with the scent of cedar and Spanish moss that she immediately recognized as him. She turned her head from side to side, the feel of her hair brushing against her forehead making her smile. It was the small things most people took for granted that she reveled in. The couch beneath her. The light pressure of her clothes, of her shoes. The heat from the sunlight streaming through the window. The ache of well-worked muscles.

She heard the door slam before her brain had fully comprehended what had happened. When it caught up, the term 'blindsided' took on a whole new, and more real, meaning. For the first time in nine years, she felt the heat of her tears as they ran down her cheeks, dripped from her chin. She stumbled to her feet, vision clouded as she headed for her refuge. Ignoring the scrapes and scratches burning across her bare arms and legs, Carys ran through the woods and pulled herself into the treehouse.

"What was the whole point of this, Elsali?" Carys didn't curb her tone or her volume. "Why make me care about Aidan, only to have him run away? It's not fair!" She waited for the inevitable rebuttal that life wasn't fair, but nothing came except silence.

As she lay on the rough wooden floor, waiting for some answer, some confirmation, lyrics from a favorite Nomad song drifted into her mind. *When I need You and You don't answer, when silence is Your only reply, I may feel alone and scared, not understanding why. What I forget and must recall, is You've told me before, no matter what I feel, I'm not alone at all.* She pushed the words away, stubbornly clinging to her anger, but they floated back, repeating in her mind over and over again.

When she woke, hours later, the treehouse was dark, with only the barest sliver of moonlight entering between the slats. She didn't exactly feel better, but the memory of the lyrics remained and she clung to them as she slowly walked back to the house. She hadn't realized until recently just how much she'd missed Elsali. She might not understand what was happening, but she was determined not to give up on Him again, no matter how angry she was. Aidan's door was closed when she passed and she hurried by, not wanting an awkward confrontation. Morning seemed like a better time to deal, if only because it meant she wouldn't have to deal right now.

***

Dawn finally broke with no sleep or answers to be found. Aidan reached the kitchen first, every muscle tensed, ears straining for the first hint that Carys had entered the room. Not that he had any idea what he was going to say to her when she did. He barely registered pouring himself something to eat, his entire body straining for the first sounds of her approach. When she finally did come down, almost an hour later, he'd managed to eat only a few spoonfuls of soggy cereal. Now he was regretting even those bites as his stomach churned and he tried to gather the courage to say something.

Carys, however, spoke before Aidan had the chance. "I just want to thank you for what you did. I know it couldn't have been easy." She kept her eyes fixed on the contents of the refrigerator.

"You're welcome." Aidan cleared his throat. This was far more awkward than he'd imagined. "So, um, you can still–"

"Feel?" Carys finished his thought. "Yes. Doesn't look like a repeat will be necessary."

"Oh," Aidan fought to keep his voice neutral even though he felt like he'd been punched in the stomach. "That's good then." Mentally, he kicked himself. No wonder he hadn't gotten answers to his questions last night. No conflict existed between his feelings for Brina and a relationship with Carys. She obviously felt nothing for him but gratitude and friendship. The first kiss had been a fluke, or a defensive strategy intended to distract him. Everything else had been him reading too much into innocent words and gestures. Like the sheen in her eyes right now. He might've thought they were tears, but now realized that her eyes were probably just watering because she hadn't been awake very long.

She set her bowl of peaches on the table but didn't look at him. "When we're done with breakfast, I'll take you to the weapons' room. It's time you picked out what you'll be taking."

"Okay," Aidan took a deep breath and tried to clear his head. "But there is something I need to show you before we do anything. Another... weapon, I guess you could call it." He threw away the rest of his food and went to the sink to wash out the bowl. "Meet me in the stables when you're done eating."

By the time she joined him, he'd managed to regain his composure. He took out his wand and set it aside. "Remember how Neysa and I said that what Brina did changed me and Thana?" He surprised himself by being able to say her name without wincing, but he ignored that for the time being. This was more important. "Well, if we're going to be fighting together, you should probably see this."

He held out his right hand toward a bale of hay stacked against one wall. Summoning up the energy that seemed to always be lurking about inside him, he focused on the object and thought "*Aicilef.*" Slowly, the bale rose in the air. He gestured with his hand, intending to move the hay to the other end of the stable.

Carys ducked as the bale flew across the stable, nearly hitting her as it careened into the walls. It bounced around, never quite making it past the middle of the room as it knocked bridles and pitchforks off of the walls. She turned and glared at Aidan. "You wanted me to see that you can take my head off with some hay?" The words were barely out of her mouth when she saw he wasn't holding his wand. Her eyes widened.

"Sorry," Aidan said. He lowered his hand, and the hay dropped to the floor. He crossed over to it and sat down, an expression of pure frustration on his face. "Do you remember what it was like when you first got your wand? The first time you managed to cast a powerful spell? One with real, visible results?"

Carys nodded, her annoyed expression fading as she listened.

"Well, it's like that, only a hundred times more intense." Aidan looked down at his hands. "And it's not channeling down a wand designed to help control and focus the magic. It's exploding out of your hand. It's wild and unpredictable."

"A little bit like a dragon?" Carys's voice was soft as she took a step toward him.

Aidan nodded. He had to tell her, even if their relationship was difficult at best. He meant what he'd said. If they were going to be fighting together, she deserved to know what he had to offer, and what the short-comings were. The words were coming out of his mouth before he could stop them. "It scares me sometimes." He glanced up at Carys and she moved closer, as if to comfort him, and he froze. She stopped, apparently thinking better of it, and he relaxed slightly. He wasn't sure if he'd wanted her to keep going or if he was grateful she hadn't. All he knew was that he had a hard time thinking straight when she was around.

"We're born with magic, Aidan," she said. "And we all have to be taught the proper way to use it, how to control it. It's like a muscle. When you played Fuhjyn, you practiced, right? It didn't matter if you were playing the hardest or the easiest team, you ran plays, conditioned, right? You had to train your body. Magic is like that. You just need to keep at it."

Aidan sighed. He knew what Carys was saying was right. This magic was a part of him, even if he hated it. He blinked, a thought occurring to him. Maybe that was it. Maybe he was having a hard time controlling it because of how he felt about it. He hated it because of what it represented to him, because he felt as if it was the magic that had caused Brina's death. And, if he was completely honest, he was scared of it. Not physically scared, but more scared of what would happen if he tried something and completely lost control, if he became responsible for yet another person's death. That fear fed his hate. He viewed the magic as if it were some foreign substance, an illness or infection, not a part of him. Maybe all he needed to do was accept it and let himself admit that it was his.

Easier said than done, he knew.

Chapter Eight: Dreams of a Journey

Days passed without a word from Neysa, and Aidan and Carys had settled into an awkward, yet cordial, routine. They ate their meals together, ran, trained, and carefully avoided all physical contact, and all but the briefest of eye contact. While Carys continued to push herself toward excellence in every form of weaponry, Aidan spent hours working on controlling his new magic. Slowly, as he began to focus on what he wanted rather than let his emotions guide him, his body became used to the magic. He forced himself to quit thinking of it as something apart from himself and intentionally referred to it as a part of who he was, even in his thoughts. The first time he was able to move a bale of hay from one place to another without the slightest bobble, he knew he could do this.

Once the first obstacle had been cleared, everything came together. Everything he had once used his wand for, he now tried without it to great success. Not counting, of course, the time he accidentally spilled juice all over the weapons Carys was cleaning on the kitchen table. She'd insisted he clean up without magic at all and he'd known better than to try an argue. He'd learned his lesson, and all magic around Carys was done with a wand, especially when liquid was involved.

Then, on the last night of Otium, everything came to a head. He and Carys both collapsed into their respective beds, exhausted enough to fall asleep without the usual mental cacophony that usually kept them up for at least an additional hour or so. Only an hour or two had passed when it happened.

The dream came to Aidan first, Carys only seconds later.

The setting sun turned the snow-capped mountain peaks a blood-red that matched the crimson rivulets flowing from a metal chest. The streams ran down into a small dip in the ground, forming a pool of blood. A man and a woman stood on either side of the chest, each holding an ancient golden goblet.

They took turns pouring a thick, dark liquid into a hole on the top of the container. As they poured, they chanted in an unknown tongue. "Raktadalli snana dryagan hrdaya jiva mattu savu mattu maya tumbisalpaṭṭa prani mattu manuṣyana rakta, yogya eradu marpadu." *Their words faltered as two figures came toward them.*

The girl was tall and thin. She had straight, waist-length brown hair with a thin streak of dark green on the right side. Her eyes were icy green, the cold of a frozen sea. The boy was shorter than his companion by several inches, stocky and muscular. His dark brown curls tossed in the breeze, his pale gray-blue eyes narrowed with some unknown emotion. Both appeared to be in their late teens, but something about their presence broke the chanters' rhythm.

A woman, her light hair streaked with barely noticeable gray, came up behind them. Without looking her way, or even indicating that they knew she was there, the girl spoke, "How much longer?"

The woman glanced at the sun, now barely a sliver on the horizon. "Soon, Adalayde, soon."

"You say soon every time we ask." The young man sounded more exasperated than his counterpart.

"It is the seventh of Fatum, my son." The woman brushed aside the boy's impatience. "And tonight, as the full moon reaches its zenith, you will both be transformed."

Adalayde smiled and looked at the young man beside her. "It's almost time, Callum. We'll finally be able to avenge the deaths of our family and bring peace to our world, as it should have been under our mother's hand."

Neither one saw the cold gleam in the woman's pale brown eyes, but the two dreamers saw and understood.

Aidan bolted upright, eyes wide, body thrumming with adrenaline. Based on the angle of the light coming through the window, he guessed it was mid-afternoon, far later than he'd slept in months. Something about the dream had kept him asleep longer than usual even though the dream itself hadn't felt very long. He was out of his bed and into the hallway before he'd fully processed where he was going... or the fact that he was wearing only florescent rainbow boxers and mismatched socks.

Carys opened her door just as Aidan raised his hand to knock. Her eyes held a similar note of panic, her skin pale under her normal golden glow. Immediately, he knew what had happened.

"You saw it, too?" Carys's voice was low, strained.

Aidan nodded. "I don't think it was a dream, at least, not completely."

"We need to go. We can't wait for Neysa."

He heard his own urgency in her voice. "Do you know where they are?"

"I recognized one of the mountain peaks. It's a range near where I was raised, the village of Euran." Carys ran a hand through her curls. "Most of the people call them the Red Range because of the way the sun makes them look, but locals call them the Blood Hills. They're extremely dangerous. People who go in to those hills don't come out. There's stories of all kinds of creatures making their homes in caves and valleys."

"I guess we know the real story now." Aidan put a hand on Carys's shoulder without thinking about it. "We'll get our family away from that woman, Carys. I promise."

Carys's lips trembled. "They think she's their mother, Aidan. That she's a good person."

The sight of tough-as-nails Carys nearly shaking broke Aidan's heart, and shattered his defenses. He drew Carys into his arms and she rested her cheek against his chest, arms circling his waist. The thought that they fit well together came into his mind, but he pushed it out, knowing he had more important things to focus on. "We can do this. Together, you and I will show them the truth, and we'll bring our family home."

Carys sniffled. "Thank you," she whispered.

Aidan tensed as Carys pulled back, as if unsure how she was going to react to their contact, and said the first thing that came into his mind. "I think we should get dressed first."

"You mean you don't want to go fight in rainbow boxers?" Carys raised an eyebrow.

Aidan flushed as he suddenly remembered what he was wearing.

"Meet you downstairs in ten minutes." She gave him a shy half-smile as she closed the door.

"Note to self." Aidan closed his eyes. "Buy more manly boxers."

***

They ended up having to put off leaving until the next morning. By the time they'd dressed, eaten and discussed their options, it was clear they wouldn't be ready before dark and Carys wasn't sure she could steer the boat at night.

"Wait, is the boat even here?" Aidan was struck by a horrible thought. "Didn't Neysa take it when she went to Audeamus?"

"She did, but it has an enchantment that allows her to send it back to the island until she needs it again." Carys paused in front of the pantry. "How much food do you think we should take?"

Aidan shrugged. "I'm more concerned with how well we'll be able to transport with so many weapons." He'd been practicing with his magic, but he knew there was a good chance they'd been fighting in a soft spot where even his magic wouldn't work.

The table was covered with blades, bows, and some intricate

devices Aidan had never seen before. Some of the knives were enchanted and emitted an ethereal glow. Others weren't as shiny, but he knew they were just as sharp and just as deadly.

"I don't think we should risk transporting." Carys sighed. "I barely passed my test when it was just me. Trying to transport with anything else will be difficult at best, dangerous most likely, considering the weapons we're taking."

"If we walk, we won't make it in time."

Carys gave him a sheepish smile. "I was thinking more along the lines of driving."

"Uh-huh," Aidan said slowly. "And how were you planning on us procuring a car?"

"Desperate times and all." Carys wiggled her fingers at Aidan. "I wasn't just a good pickpocket."

In the end, with no other option, Aidan agreed. Both hoped Neysa would contact them before theft became a necessity, but they hadn't heard from her since she'd left. The pair had tried several spells and contacts, even reaching out to Audeamus with no luck. No one knew where Neysa was, and those who were supposed to be with her had apparently suffered the same fate. Headmaster Manu had reassured Aidan that all was well and he'd pass along a message to Thana and Corakin as soon as he saw them. The headmaster didn't seem overly concerned with the lack of communication and Aidan didn't want to raise any alarm, so he didn't let on the importance of speaking with Neysa or any of the others.

Only one other option remained. Just before they went to bed, Carys agreed to try her unique form of communication if they hadn't heard back from Neysa by morning.

"I'm not sure if it'll work," she warned Aidan. "I don't know how far a mimic bird can fly without rest, or if they'll even try to get to the mainland."

"What about calling one once we get ashore?" Aidan paused in the hallway, hand on the door to his room.

"I can try," Carys agreed. "But mimic birds are rare in the city. It could be days before I find one."

Aidan nodded. "Trying's better than nothing." He turned toward his room, paused, and added softly, "it's going to work out, Carys. We'll find our siblings. Neysa will find us. You'll see." He repeated. "It'll all work out."

"Thanks." Carys was facing her own room. "And, Aidan." The words rushed out, as if she thought she'd stop if she thought about them too long. "Just because Elsali doesn't answer, doesn't mean He's not there. Whether we feel it or not, we're never alone." Her face bloomed red and she hurried inside.

Aidan opened his mouth, unsure what he was going to say, knowing only that it should be something. The door clicked softly closed before he could get out a word. He was far more introspective than usual as he lay in bed, waiting for sleep to claim him. He realized, with a touch of wry humor, that Brina might've mockingly called his mood pensive while Thana would've stuck with moody, and he had a feeling Carys would be more inclined to agree with Thana. Both of the other girls, however, he knew would agree with what Carys had told him. Just as he felt the heaviness of sleep come over him, he whispered, "Message received."

Chapter Nine: Family

The sunrise was till fading on the horizon as Aidan and Carys walked down the path toward the beach. Each carried a shoulder bag with a change of clothes, food and weapons. Lots of weapons. Much to Aidan's relief, Carys's enlargement charm had given them enough room for a blanket as well. He'd never gone anywhere without Adalayde's blanket and heading off to find her without it just seemed wrong somehow.

Carys stared straight ahead as she walked, apparently determined not to show how much it hurt to leave the only real home she'd ever had. Her spells had been strong, voice unwavering, as she locked down the house, put the animals into an enchanted sleep that would keep them safe and, finally, cast a protection spell to prevent anyone else from finding the island.

Only a few days ago, Aidan doubted he would've noticed anything wrong. Today, he saw the sadness in the set of Carys's jaw, the anxiety in the tension of her shoulders, the determination in each step. Still, he didn't know what to say, how to reassure her. In the end, he settled for silence. No words seemed preferable to the wrong words.

The ride to the mainland was a quiet one, broken only by the gentle lapping of water against the boat and the occasional cry of a white gull. Aidan kept an eye out for the mimic bird Carys had called before leaving, but saw nothing. The little bird hadn't seemed discouraged by its mission, flitting off as soon as Carys completed her request. Aidan had taken that as a positive sign.

Inbanco was noisy and crowded after weeks of isolation on Sicinfit. Aidan saw his own distaste on Carys's face, though hers was stronger. He'd grown up in Aliquantulus, a city almost twice the size of Inbanco, and over three times the size of Carys's home of Euran. He'd never before minded the hustle and bustle, and yet he found himself longing for the relative tranquility of training on the beach or taking Abraxan for a ride through the woods.

Once Carys had sent the boat back to Sicinfit, the pair set off on their less-than-legal task. After ten minutes of searching through rows of vehicles parked outside Excelsior Mall, they finally found one without alarm enchantments, and it was fairly easy to see why. At some point in the distant past, the car had been a beauty, but time and lack of care had dulled the black finish and rust covered most of the car's body. If the owner had good insurance, Aidan supposed, they'd actually be doing him or her a favor.

It took Carys only a few seconds to hot-wire the vehicle, no wand required, and the pair started to make their way out of the city. The light glamour Aidan cast was strong enough to hold until they passed the city limits. They would, Carys explained, need to change license plates before too long, but they shouldn't need to worry once they were further north. This wasn't the type of car that caused too much of a commotion when it went missing.

"Now, the '67 Fecit Lupus, those are good for a high-speed chase through three districts if you're spotted." She grinned at the expression on Aidan's face. "Or so I've heard."

"Never stolen one?" Aidan tried, successfully, to keep his voice light.

"Never got caught," Carys corrected him. She sobered. "I haven't done anything like this since Neysa found me."

"And you wouldn't have done it today if it hadn't been necessary." Aidan assured her, immediately catching the guilt she was feeling. He still found it a bit disconcerting how much in tune with her emotions he'd been recently. "There's no other way for us to get to our siblings in time. And, if the dream was as accurate as I think it was, it's not just Adalayde and Callum who're in danger."

Carys nodded, her expression grim.

Nothing more was said until the pair stopped for gas, just

outside of Inbanco, and then it was just confirmation that they would switch driving throughout the day and night until they reached Euran. The weather was unseasonably warm and sunny. Not a trace of snow, even as they traveled further north. Neither felt the need to speak, to do more than watch the scenery passing by or pay attention to the sparse traffic on the road. Occasionally, when they thought the other wasn't looking, they stole glances, but nothing more. Monotony gave way to monotony and four days stretched into what seemed like years. By the time they reached the outskirts of Euran, their surreptitious looks and the time spent in their heads had brought a subtle tension into the car, but it wasn't anything they felt compelled to address. They had more important things on their minds.

"Tomorrow's the seventh." Carys broke the silence. "The Blood Hills are a one to two hour walk outside the northeast side of town, and we have until sundown to find our siblings."

"We need to stop for the night. Get a real meal and more than just a few hours of sleep," he said. "Where's the best place in town–"

She cut him off. "I don't want to go into Euran."

"You think your aunt will see you?"

She shook her head. "Aunt Sun died last year."

He opened his mouth, then closed it, unsure as to what he should say.

She stared out the window at the town in the distance. "Running away wasn't my first choice, you know. I'd tried other things. I tried reasoning with her. Tried avoiding her. When that didn't work, I tried talking to the other adults in my life. Professors, a pastor; I even called the police. No one believed me. Aunt Sun was a respected member of the community. Her vices were hidden behind glamours, healing spells, and the reluctance of people to see her for who she truly was. I don't think I could go into Euran, see the people who were supposed to help me, and not want to bring the *Decazmaja* into town."

"We can sleep in the car, Carys. We don't need to go anywhere." Aidan kept his voice gentle as he parked the car between a pair of trees capable of keeping them hidden while they slept.

"You're taller," was her only reply. "You should get the backseat."

The pair situated themselves in silence. As Aidan pulled his blanket – lightly glamoured to appear more blandly masculine – up to his chin, so soft he might've imagined it, he heard Carys whisper, "thank you." Then sleep dragged him under.

The morning sun woke him hours later and, for a moment, he couldn't figure out why the car wasn't moving. He blinked a few times and then remembered they'd reached their destination. He sat up, quickly grabbing his blanket as it fell. His breath blew out in plumes as he secured his blanket more tightly around him. It was the first cold morning of the season. He leaned forward, fully intending to wake Carys, and paused.

She'd curled onto her side, her own blanket covering all but a small section of her face. The tip of her nose, her closed eyes and her tousled curls were the only things visible. In her sleep, her features softened, making her look younger and more vulnerable than Aidan had thought possible. He felt a tug at his heart.

He sat back, not quite ready to disturb Carys's peaceful slumber. "Elsali?" Aidan rested his head on the seat as he silently prayed. "Carys said I should remember that even if You didn't answer, You're here. I'm going to step out in faith and believe she's right. Believe that You care, that You have some reason for staying silent when I've asked questions."

Aidan waited, closing his eyes again. He would listen and wait, even if his answer never came. As he felt himself drifting off to sleep again, he heard the quietest of whispers.

Well, done.

When Aidan woke again a couple of hours later, his mind was clear, focused on the mission ahead. He hadn't heard an actual answer from Elsali, but the peace he felt about the upcoming task was more than enough. It took him a moment to realize Carys was up. It had been her opening the door that had pulled Aidan from a strange dream about attending a wedding where a slightly overweight and overly coiffed minister wearing a sequined white suit stood in front of an attractive couple. He'd been standing next to his sister, making some sort of snide remark while the pair being married gazed at each other with the kind of intensity he was starting to feel toward Carys.

He carefully folded his blanket and, after a moment's hesitation, put it back into his bag. He'd considered leaving it in the car. After all, one typically didn't combat crazy cult people with purple fleece, but something in his spirit hinted that he could have reason to need the blanket soon. What the reason could be, he had no idea, but he wasn't about to discount something that could be a message from Elsali.

Steeling himself to leave the warm comfort of the backseat, Aidan clambered out. It wasn't nearly as cold as he'd feared, but the bite in the air had been absent only the day before. He suspected they'd see snow before the end of the week, if not the end of the day. The thought of snow in the hills brought back memories that didn't have as much pain to them as they once had.

"Morning." He nodded at Carys and yawned. "How'd you sleep?"

"Fine, and you?" Carys was stretching, warming her muscles for the activity ahead.

"Better than I expected." Aidan grabbed his toothbrush. Yes, they'd stolen a car, driven across the country, and now planned to fight hordes of crazies that greatly outnumbered them, but he didn't see the need to have morning breath while doing it.

"There's a stream about a quarter of a mile that way." Carys pointed. Aidan saw now that Carys's curls were damp. "Sometimes a cleaning charm just isn't enough."

Aidan nodded in agreement, and went off in the direction Carys had indicated. The stream was cold, and finished waking him. By the time he dressed and returned to the car, he felt ready for what they were going to face. Or, at least, as ready as he could be.

Carys was already strapping on weapons when Aidan reached the clearing. A short sword, blade easily as long as her forearm, sat in a custom-made sheath along her spine. She had a dozen crossbow bolts on each hip and throwing blades tucked into each boot. She fastened her right wrist-sheath as Aidan retrieved his bag from the backseat. Her crossbow was on the ground next to her. It would be the last thing she'd pick up.

He stuck with his strengths. He had back-ups blades in each boot, but pulled his crossbow from his bag, a smile on his face. A longbow followed. Two enchanted straps went over his shoulders. The left side provided never-ending bolts; the right, the more traditional arrows. He had a regular stash in his bag just in case, but he definitely preferred the magical supply. No risk of running out. Carys wasn't sure if the Blood Hills had dead spots, so while they were both relying on Aidan's increased abilities, weapons were smart to have just in case. Once everything he needed for a fight was in place, he shrunk his bag and slid it into an outside pocket.

"Are you going be okay carrying all that for a couple miles and then fighting?"

Carys's glare in response to his question brought up Aidan's hands in a gesture of surrender.

"All right, all right. Just trying to be chivalrous."

Carys gave a grim grin. "Screw chivalry. Let's get to work."

Aidan nodded, and followed Carys toward the hills.

The scattering of trees they'd started in thickened, gradually turning into the forest they'd seen in their dream. The ground began to slope upwards as the sun climbed in the sky. After three quarters of an hour, they reached an elevated clearing and paused. Aidan recognized a pair of peaks to the northwest.

"Based on where those hills were in our dream." Carys leaned against a boulder. "We're going in that direction." She pointed.

"Another thirty minutes or so, you think?" Aidan sat on a fallen tree, more out of habit than any actual need to do so on his part.

Carys nodded absently. Her mouth flattened into a straight line, and her normally clear eyes clouded. "What if..." Her throat clicked when she swallowed. "What if they won't come with us? If they fight with the *Decazmaja*? I mean, on their side instead of ours."

Aida considered her question carefully. Carys had been waiting for her twin her whole life. Finding him had been the only thing keeping her going most days. To lose him, not to death, but to choice, would destroy her. Aidan knew what he needed to say. "Then we capture them and taken them back to Neysa. Together, we can deprogram them, and show them the truth."

"I won't be able to kill him, Aidan." Carys stared at the hills. "Not to save you or the world or even myself."

"I know." Aidan stood. "Let's not let it come to that."

"Chameleon charm?" Carys straightened.

Aidan nodded. He waited for her to take out her wand. While he had his with him, he didn't really need it anymore. Both muttered the spell at the same time. When they looked up, the other had disappeared, blending into their background with the faintest shimmer.

"We might want to add a tracking spell," Aidan suggested. "Otherwise we're going to run into each other."

"Good idea."

"*Jowklac.*" The pair cast their spells toward the last place they had seen the other one. A faint tingling flowed over them, and then they could sense where the other was standing.

"I'll lead," Carys said. Aidan didn't need to see her to catch her anxiety. He waited until he knew she was several steps ahead of him, then fell into place behind her. The end was coming. He could feel it.

They'd been walking for twenty minutes when they heard voices ahead of them. Aidan knew Carys was settling her crossbow into position, her first bolt in place, and he readied his own weapon. He didn't want to risk alerting anyone strong enough to sense a spell.

Through a break in the trees, the owners of the voices became visible. Two were almost certainly *Decazmaja*, dressed in similar dark clothes, swords buckled around their waists. One was male, the other female, both with dark short-cropped hair. The woman's features were harsh, cruel-looking while the man had a youthful face that seemed out of place in the situation. The other two figures stood between the two *Decazmaja*. A sharp hiss from Aidan's right told him that Carys had seen her brother.

None of the four seemed to be aware of their observers, more concerned with the growing intensity of their conversation. Aidan and Carys paused to listen. Best to know what they were getting themselves into, no matter how much self-control it took.

"Our mother knows we will not miss the ceremony." Callum's light gray-blue eyes flashed, their similarity to Carys's uncanny.

"We have been there every night this month." Adalayde continued the thought easily, as if she and Callum often spoke as one. "It is an insult to follow us as if we would shirk our duty."

"Though I do wonder why you've chosen today to be overly attentive to us." Callum glanced at Adalayde. "Does our mother know something about today that we don't?"

"Ye would needs be to ask her." The male *Decazmaja*'s accent marked him as local.

"But we be havin' our orders, and I dinna intend to be crossin' yer mam." The woman's brogue was thicker, giving her birthplace as being closer to Eimhir than Euran.

"And if Callum and I don't want you here?" Adalayde put her hand on the hilt of her sword, the threat anything but subtle.

"Ye dinna have a choice in the matter." The man's pale eyes showed no emotion.

Adalayde's eyes darkened and a scowl formed on her face. She took a step forward, half-drawing her weapon. Callum put a hand on her arm. "Peace, Adalayde."

Aidan saw the slight shift in his sister's eyes and knew what was coming. He took a step forward and sensed Carys do the same.

In a move so fast Aidan and Carys barely saw it, Callum spun to the right, his fist connecting with the male *Decazmaja*'s jaw. The man stumbled backwards, dazed but not down. Adalayde's sword flashed and the woman glared at her from the other end of the point.

The confrontation may have ended differently if a voice hadn't called from the far side of the clearing. "Gilroy! Senga!"

"Yer mam be callin' fer us." Senga smirked. "I'm sure ye dinna wanna explain this ta her."

The tip of Adalayde's sword wavered, then fell. Her shoulders slumped in defeat. Callum's hands dropped to his sides, but stayed in fists. The fight in them went out as quickly as it had started.

Carys's arrow found its mark first with a meaty thud as the bolt struck Gilroy's chest. Aidan shot twice, the first arrow passing through Senga's throat even as she opened her mouth to call out. The second shot went through her left eye and into her brain, dropping her before her hands finished grabbing the arrow in her throat.

Only a few seconds had passed since the first bolt was loosed. Callum and Adalayde spun around toward the direction the shots had come from. Carys and Aidan's chameleon charms faded as they stepped forward, bows pointed toward the sky, their free hands up, palms out.

"We just want to help." Aidan found his eyes drawn to his sister. "Please, talk to us."

"Senga! Gilroy!" The voice was closer.

Adalayde glanced at Callum and silent communication passed between them. For one heart-stopping second, Aidan was sure he and Carys were about to be killed by their twins. Then, he saw something flash across Callum's face and Adalayde nodded with an almost weary resignation.

"We're going to move, nice and easy," Callum spoke.

"That way." Adalayde motioned with the sword.

Carys and Aidan kept their gazes on their twins as they walked. Once they passed through a grove of pine trees, they stopped. Callum quickly cast protection and shielding charms while Adalayde watched Carys and Aidan.

"Now, speak." Adalayde's voice held the ring of authority associated with those who are used to giving orders and having them obeyed. "Callum seems to believe that you have some importance to us. I don't. Prove one of us right."

Aidan and Carys looked at each other, at a loss for words. In all their planning, neither one had thought about how to explain who they were or why they were here.

"My name," Carys started, "is Carys Jovan." She looked straight at Callum. "I'm your sister." Callum's eyes widened even as Adalayde's narrowed in suspicion. Carys continued, never taking her gaze from her twin. "That woman who you think is your mother, she's not."

Adalayde interrupted. "She may not have birthed us, but she raised us after the *Custos Morum* killed our families and cast her out."

"I don't know what that woman told you." Aidan kept his voice gentle. "But it's not true, at least, not all of it. My name's Aidan Preston and, Adalayde, you're my sister. My twin, who I was told died at birth."

"You're lying," Adalayde growled, shaking her head.

Carys shook her head. "He's not. That woman stole you, Adalayde. You and Callum. My mother died and I was sent to live with her sister, but I never forgot seeing my brother being taken from his crib by two men."

"You're a *teleia mnimi*." Callum took a step toward Carys and she nodded, tears shining in her eyes.

"Callum, don't," Adalayde warned.

"I have a..." Callum glanced at Adalayde who shook her head. He returned his gaze to Carys, a determined expression on his face. "I guess you could call it a gift. If I'm touching you when you speak, I can sense if you're telling the truth."

Without a moment's hesitation, Carys held out her hand and Callum took it. Adalayde shifted behind him, but he only had eyes for the young woman in front of him. Instinctively, Aidan took a step closer to Carys as if to protect her, though if his sister moved against his... friend, he wasn't entirely sure what he would do.

"Tell your tale," Callum instructed.

Carys repeated what she and Aidan had already said, and then continued with her own story, including all the relevant facts and finishing with she and Aidan leaving Sicinfit. Callum kept his face blank throughout Carys's telling, but he couldn't prevent the flash of joy lighting up his eyes when Carys repeated that she was his twin. Adalayde saw the reaction as well and sheathed her sword as if she couldn't, or wouldn't, fight against Callum.

"What about him?" Adalayde pointed at Aidan as soon as Carys had finished speaking.

"I have nothing to hide." Aidan stretched out his hand.

"I don't think so," Adalayde shook her head. "Callum can sense the truth, but it's based on if you believe what you're saying is true. All she has to do is believe she's his sister, doesn't mean she actually is. My ability is a little more, shall we say, thorough."

"Adalayde can see into a person's history through something they own." Callum had apparently lost any reluctance toward helping Aidan and Carys. He clearly believed Carys's recounting as truth. He was still holding Carys's hand.

"Only things as far back as the item has been with them." Adalayde glared at Callum, annoyed with his acceptance. "So, your oldest, most important item, please." She held out a hand.

"Yeah, because I'm sure he carries something valuable like that with him." Tension was evident in every word Carys spoke.

Aidan chuckled and three pairs of eyes turned his way. "I actually do have something." He pulled his bag from his pocket, unshrunk it with a quick burst of magic from his fingers, and opened it, ignoring the sharp intakes of air from both Adalayde and Callum at his wandless magic. He reached into the bag, snapped his fingers and caught the edge of his purple blanket. He kept his gaze firmly focused on his sister as he stepped forward, arm outstretched.

"Is this a joke?" Adalayde eyed the cavorting creatures.

"If you're not going to believe me based on what I say." Aidan's voice was mild. "Why don't you see for yourself?"

Chapter Ten: Eyes Open

A young woman, heavily pregnant, mahogany hair gleaming in the setting sun, opens a box and takes out two fuzzy blankets. One is green with kites. The other is purple with skipping turtles and kittens and floating butterflies. A tear slides down her cheek.

A tiny baby sleeps in an enchanted crib, healing and strengthening charms working on his too-soon-born body. The red-haired woman finally wakes from her long sleep and cries, clutching the purple blanket to her chest as she looks at her son.

A baby boy, fine blond hair peeking out from under the purple blanket, watches his mother exchange rings with a tall, dark-haired man. The man's face shines with love as three smiling girls look on.

The boy is a toddler now, holding the purple blanket close as his mother tells him the story of his lost twin. His green eyes fill with tears, his heart understanding the words his mind could not.

On the first day of school, he sneaks the blanket into his Star Riders book-bag. When another boy finds it, the green-eyed boy says it belongs to his sister. He doesn't say that she is dead.

A new baby, a boy, reaches for the purple blanket. The blond boy gives his half-brother the green blanket. He will keep the purple one.

The green-eyed child is older now, trying to convince the red-haired woman that he's old enough to go to camp. She mentions his sister and he knows it will not be this year his mother will let him go.

The baby is no more; a teenager has taken his place. He is leaving for grown-up school and his mother cries. He does not tell her of the purple blanket going with him.

A red-haired girl captures his attention and he wants to know her better. Months later, he will tell her why his mother cries in the healing wing and of the name spoken there. More time will pass before he shows her the blanket though. When he does, her love for him shines in her violet eyes.

He cradles the girl with the violet eyes, sobs ripping through his body. He doesn't understand why he's lost her too. He feels that the hole in his chest will never heal.

Oblivion. Darkness and dim images fill his time. Pain seeps through and he drowns it, ending his night like the others before, purple blanket soft against his cheek. A new face appears in the darkness with a promise of purpose. The boy's sister is alive.

The young man's broken heart is mending and he fears what it means. A girl with dark curls is on his mind, but he doesn't want her there. Her light gray-blue eyes haunt him anyway.

He's frightened by the changes his body has gone through. His magic is stronger, wilder, and he can heal himself. He doesn't want this.

The first kiss surprises him. The second unnerves. His feelings for the girl with the gray-blue eyes are growing and he's not sure what they mean. He runs his hand over the purple blanket as he thinks, wishing he could talk to his sister.

It's time to leave and he holds the blanket, unsure if he should take it with him. It goes into the bag and he leaves his room. Part of him thinks that, maybe, he will give it to his sister at last.

Adalayde slowly raised her head, her fingers clenching the blanket. Her face was tight and pale, ice green eyes burning. Aidan took an instinctive step back, wanting distance between himself and the anger in those eyes. He still had a hold of one edge of the blanket and stopped when Adalayde didn't let go.

"Dooriya will answer our questions now, Callum. And she will do so holding your hand. She will allow me to use my ability on one of her possessions as well. No more lies." Adalayde's voice was quiet, deadly, and Aidan understood that the anger was not directed at him. She looked directly at Aidan now, her tone softening as she asked, "our mother?"

Aidan moved closer to his sister, gently pressing the blanket into her hands. "She's alive and she's never forgotten you."

Adalayde drew in a breath that sounded like a sob. "Does she know?"

"About you?" Aidan shook his head. "I didn't want to get her hopes up. I wasn't sure if we would find you."

The young woman glanced at Carys and then back to Aidan, a question in her eyes. His ears burned as he realized Adalayde had seen everything. He cleared his throat and changed the subject, not ready to address that issue just yet. "I'm sure both of you have questions, but there's actually more pressing matters at hand."

"The ceremony," Callum spoke up. "If our... if Dooriya lied about where Adalayde and I came from, it's likely she lied about other things."

"We believe she is trying to raise a dragon," Carys said bluntly. They didn't have the time to ease their siblings into it.

"The one murd... killed last year?" Adalayde carefully folded her blanket. "We buried it and mourned, taking the blood and the heart for this ceremony. Without it to help us, Dooriya said that Callum and I were to receive the creature's magic, strength and wisdom through a spell. With our new powers, we would defeat the Ortus army and reclaim her throne."

"Adalayde and I vowed to avenge its death," Callum added.

"That might be difficult." Aidan fought to keep his voice level. "The girl who killed it died healing my friend and I."

"The girl with the violet eyes." Adalayde must've made the connection from her vision.

Aidan nodded, not trusting himself to speak, not when his emotions were already so close to the surface.

"You loved her." It wasn't a question.

"Yes."

"And now...?" Adalayde kept her eyes on Aidan, but he knew where her thoughts had headed.

Aidan opened his mouth, feeling the weight of Carys's gaze. This wasn't how he'd wanted to go about analyzing his feelings for Carys. Too much was going on, too many differing thoughts and emotions. No matter what he said now, it wouldn't ring true.

"Aidan!" A familiar female voice echoed through the protective shield, saving Aidan from having to decide what he was going to do.

"Thana?" Aidan turned, instantly recognizing the voice, though scarcely able to believe that he wasn't hearing things.

"Who?" Callum tensed. Carys put a hand on her brother's arm.

"She shouldn't be able to do that." Adalayde retrieved her sword, tossing her blanket back to Aidan.

"Thana and I gained additional power when Brina healed us." Aidan tucked the blanket back into his bag with one hand and held his other hand out toward Adalayde. "Our magic is a bit stronger than the average person." He glanced at Callum. "Can you lower the shield for them?"

"'Them?'" Callum and Adalayde echoed Aidan's word choice in unison.

"Reinforcements." Carys grinned.

Callum muttered the spell's counter-charm at the spot Aidan indicated. A slight shimmer shook the air and outside noises began to seep through. At first, they could see nothing but the trees. Then, a tall, slender figure appeared from between two pines. Her long hair was pulled back in complicated, multi-colored braids and, for once, her clothes were plain, a dark green that blended well with the forest.

"Neysa!" Carys ran to her mentor and threw her arms around the startled-looking young woman.

"Aidan!" A dark-haired blur darted around Neysa and slammed into Aidan.

"Hey, Thana." Aidan chuckled as he hugged the tiny girl. He hadn't realized just how much he'd missed her until now. It was like a missing part of him had been found again. He briefly wondered if the magic inside him was connected to the magic inside her, then she stepped back and peered up at her friend, dark blue eyes shining.

"I like the haircut." Aidan ruffled the short locks. "How long till Neysa's got you pierced and dyed?"

A grin split Thana's face as she bounced on the balls of her feet. "Wait till you meet the guys."

Aidan looked up, startled. He'd only been expecting Neysa and Thana, even though he now recalled Neysa referring to Thana's group. He'd never given it a second thought, too caught up in his own drama. Now, he turned toward Neysa. Standing just behind her were five young men. One came forward to take Thana's hand and the girl opened her mouth, mostly likely to launch into a thorough explanation.

"Introductions will have to wait," Neysa interrupted before Thana could get started. "We need to move into a more private place. There's some new information I need to share before we go any further and I'm afraid that an area this open, even with its charms, isn't safe enough."

"Follow me." Callum led the way, Carys and Neysa directly behind him. Four of the new additions brought up the rear. Callum stopped at a pile of boulders, waited for everyone to catch up, and then stepped through a nearly invisible space.

Aidan followed Neysa, not looking around until everyone else was already inside. The area was a near-perfect circle, and just large enough for all eleven to crowd in, even the big guy who towered over everyone else.

"Adalayde and I use this when we need to speak without fear of Dooriya overhearing. We carved protection charms into the surrounding rocks." Callum settled himself on a nearby boulder and gestured for Neysa to begin.

Neysa snapped her fingers and an ancient-looking scroll appeared. She unfurled it, taking great care not to damage the delicate paper. "Corakin translated this. What the *Decazmaja* are planning, it's not what we thought at all. It's worse."

Epilogue: Waiting for the World to Fall

Aidan stretched his legs out alongside Thana's. Carys and Callum sat on Thana's other side, looking at each other like they couldn't quite believe the other one was there. Adalayde was perched on a small rock to Aidan's right. On the opposite side of the circle were Neysa and the five strangers, apparently discussing their part in the upcoming strategy. The sun was directly overhead; they had until sunset.

"Thana." Aidan looked down at his friend. His head was still spinning with everything Neysa had just told them. "What happened?"

Thana shrugged. "I'm not sure where to start."

"Last time I saw you, you were watching me get kicked out of school. You said you were going to be normal, move on with your life." Aidan still couldn't believe she was here. "You could start there."

A sad smile, out of place on her normally cheerful face, curved Thana's lips. "I don't think normal's really in the realm of possibilities for any of us anymore."

"Who are they?" Carys motioned toward the group of guys, one of whom kept stealing glances at Thana. "Aidan never mentioned any other friends from Audeamus."

"That's because they weren't at Audeamus last year," Thana explained. "Four of them came because their aunt replaced Jael." An expression of pain crossed Thana's face. "As history professor, I mean. And things were all right for a while." She paused, as if gathering her thoughts. "And then they weren't. Strange things were happening to me and I didn't know what to do. Even then, I thought there might be a chance at a normal life. Boy was I wrong."

PART THREE: DRAGON HEART

Prologue: Waiting for the World to Fall

She hadn't seen Aidan in seven months, but it didn't really feel as if any time had passed. She knew part of it was because they'd been through so much together, but it was much more than that. She knew her magic – her new magic – was bound to Aidan's. With her healing and her death, Brina had bound the two people she loved to each other more tightly than any magical bond known to man, but when Aidan asked her what had happened to change her outlook, she was at a loss how to explain it. Then Carys – at least, that's who Thana assumed the dark-haired girl to be – asked about the guys and Thana knew where to start.

"...I thought there might be a chance at a normal life. Boy was I wrong..."

Chapter One: Breathe Again

Thana stood outside the front doors, hesitating for just a moment before taking the last step that caused the doors to swing open. The lobby was dark, lit by only the basest of candlelight. A shadow moved and a familiar figure stepped forward.

"Corakin." Thana rushed forward, throwing her arms around the startled professor's waist. She'd asked Headmaster Manu not to meet her when she'd inquired about arriving early. She was glad, though, that Corakin had come.

"*Zatishie*, Thana, *zatishie*," Corakin smoothed down the girl's hair. "Welcome home, *salah sedikit*."

Thana pulled back, sniffling and wiping the back of her hand across her cheeks. This was the first time she'd heard someone refer to her as 'little one' and she hadn't minded. She was just so glad to see someone who wasn't treating her like a freak. The cat she'd inherited from Brina wound around her ankles, peering up anxiously at her, as if sensing her emotions. She reached down and scratched behind its ears before flicking her wand at the luggage behind her. "Did the headmaster agree to me getting my old room back?"

Corakin nodded, following Thana up the stairs. "He's trying to arrange it so you and Aidan don't have roommates, but–"

"Aidan's definitely coming back?" Thana asked sharply. He'd still been debating the last time they'd spoken, and she'd assumed his silence since the funeral had meant he'd decided against returning. "You've talked to him?"

Corakin shook his head. "Not personally. Headmaster Manu just told me Mrs. Preston called yesterday to say that Aidan would be returning to Audeamus."

Thana's expression grew serious, something that had been happening far too often in her opinion. Sometimes she really missed how carefree and happy she used to be. "I'll be glad to see him, but something about him returning feels... off." She walked through the dining hall and tried not to notice how eerie it was, how deserted and quiet. Arriving at school before anyone else had arrived wasn't something new for her, but after everything she'd been through, the shadows seemed more menacing than mysterious, the emptiness more sad than promising. Yet another way she'd changed, she supposed.

"What do you mean it feels 'off'?" Corakin opened the door to Thana's room and followed her inside.

Thana shook her head. "I'm not entirely sure. I just have this feeling that he's not quite right."

"After losing Professor Penah and Brina, are either you actually *bene*?" Corakin's voice was soft.

"Point taken," Thana conceded. 'Good' wasn't a word she'd been able to use to describe herself in a while. She let her trunk settle at the base of her bed. Marmalade immediately began stalking about the familiar territory. Thana sighed. "I suppose it's nothing, just me projecting my own feelings about being back." She looked around the bare room. Her father had come to get her things after the last year ended. She supposed someone had done the same for Brina's belongings. She hadn't thought to ask.

"The headmaster had Sophie Landers pack up Brina's things... after," Corakin answered Thana's unasked question.

"How much does everyone know?" Thana tried to keep her tone casual, but Corakin wasn't fooled.

"You three were with Professor Penah in the mountains. There was an avalanche. You and Aidan found Brina, but it was too late to save her. Clio was never found."

It took Thana a moment to realize that Corakin was referring to Jael. With a start, she remembered that while Corakin knew about their true mission, he hadn't known the truth about his colleague. Jael had originally asked the kids to keep her true identity a secret, even from Corakin, and Thana didn't know if

Jael's death made the silence more or less important, but she wasn't going to betray what she did know of Jael's wishes. It saddened her, though, to know she had to hide things, even from Corakin.

"That's not what happened, is it?" Corakin's normally bubbly attitude was subdued, the expression on his face saying that he wasn't entirely sure he wanted his question answered.

Thana shook her head.

"It was the dragon, wasn't it? It killed Brina and Clio."

"Not exactly," Thana's voice was soft. She didn't want to have to explain, to relive those awful moments, but if anyone deserved the truth, it was Professor Gibberish, especially since she had so much she couldn't tell him. She took a deep breath, closed her eyes, and released the air in one exhalation. She began to speak, slow at first, then faster, as if the telling were releasing some poison she hadn't even known was in her.

Thana heard the duel impacts before her eyes processed what was happening. She opened her mouth to scream as a third arrow found its mark and the body crumpled to the ground. A hurt sound managed to squeeze past the tightness in her throat and then chaos descended.

Out of the corner of her eye, Thana saw two of the Decazmaja *fall, Aidan's arrows in their chests. One was merely wounded and was even now trying to reach his lost sword. The sight of the weapon, lying in the snow, broke through Thana's shock. Her blades were in her hands, her feet moving, even as she heard the dragon scream from the sky. Thana let everything drain away until all that remained was the enemy and the fight. The injured* Decazmaja's *throat was slit before Thana realized that it was finished and the blood melted the snow everywhere it fell. Hearing someone behind her, she spun and released one of her knives as she went. It found its mark easily, dropping the man in black who was heading for Lakyn's unprotected back.*

A blow from behind staggered her and she stumbled

forward, narrowly avoiding the follow-up swing from the business end of a sword. Thana turned to face her attacker, off balance and struggling to keep her feet. Her remaining knife was in her left hand and while she was fair with that hand, it wasn't her strongest. The tip of the woman's blade hovered at Thana's throat. One step forward and a flick of the wrist and it would be all over.

An ear-splitting scream caught the attention of every Decazmaja *in the clearing and Thana took advantage of the lapse. Her left hand struck out, burying her dagger in the woman warrior's chest as she pushed the* Decazmaja *back. She left the weapon where it was, and bent to snag her back-ups from her boots before running toward Lakyn who was battling three men at once. A burst of flame distracted her and she saw Aidan standing far too close to where Brina struggled with the dying creature. Instinctively, she turned to go to him and felt a shard of cold pierce her chest. The pain that followed was intense, nearly driving her to her knees.*

"Elsali, help me," Thana whispered as she jerked her body forward, pulling it off of the sword that had run through her. She knew the wound was fatal, could feel her torn heart struggling to beat. Using the last of her strength, she twisted toward her attacker, and let her falling body be the force that drove her knives through the man's torso, tearing him open from ribcage to waist.

The snow underneath her warmed as her blood spilled from her and the pain dulled as her eyelids grew heavy. She knew she should try to stay awake, that she had a fight to finish, but a weariness had soaked into her bones and she couldn't resist any longer.

"The next thing I remember is opening my eyes and seeing Aidan holding Brina's body. She was covered in blood, too much to be from any of her minor wounds, and there were footprints from where I'd fallen to Aidan," Thana looked down at her hands. "There was no physical reason for her to be dead. We knew what happened. She'd used the magic she'd gotten from the dragon to heal me and Aidan. We killed her."

"*Das ist nicht wahr.*" Corakin shook his head. He repeated the sentiment with an unusual amount of intensity. "That's not true."

Thana looked up, her cheeks damp with tears. Corakin was also weeping, but his gaze was solid. He wasn't just saying the words because they were what he was supposed to say. He truly believed them, and that alone was what made the tightness in Thana's chest ease. Corakin pulled a dark green handkerchief from his pocket and blew his nose with a loud honk.

"Thank you for sharing the truth with me." His voice sounded stuffy. "I'll leave you to your unpacking." He turned to go, then paused by the door. "If you ever need anything, Thana, anything at all, don't hesitate to ask."

"Thank you." Thana didn't trust her voice enough to speak above a whisper. Once the professor left, Thana looked around the room, feeling the emptiness closing in around her. She'd never like being alone, even as a small child. Despite not having any siblings, she'd rarely spent time by herself. Once she'd met Brina and Aidan, she'd felt more comfortable in silence, but had never really gotten over her aversion to solitude. After losing Brina and, for all intents and purposes, Aidan as well, Thana wasn't sure if she'd ever not feel alone again.

A loud meow from the floor pulled Thana from her maudlin mood. She bent and gathered Marmalade into her arms. The blue-and-white checkered feline purred loudly, blinking its large blue eyes at its new owner. Thana stroked the animal's fur as she sat on the edge of her bed, letting the creature comfort her as best it could.

Being still had never been Thana's strong suit and that much hadn't changed. It apparently wasn't one of Marmalade's virtues either. The cat leaped off of Thana's lap and made its way over to the other bed, the one that had been Brina's. It curled up at her previous spot at the foot of the bed and watched as Thana began pacing. Almost unconsciously, she drew her wand and began to unpack. Her clothes and personal items found their proper place, settling back into the same spots they'd inhabited a year before. When she finished, she looked around the half-furnished room and a wave of deja vu washed over her. Aside from the cat, her room was now identical to how it had been a year ago before Brina had moved in. Now all she had to do was try and pick up where she'd left off. Somehow, she didn't think it was it was going to be as easy to do as it sounded in her head.

Chapter Two: The Awkward Good-Bye

Thana woke at dawn and silently went through her morning routine, which now included feeding Marmalade before her shower. When she'd first retrieved the cat from Becca Davenport, she'd tried waiting until after she'd bathed and dressed before giving the creature its breakfast. That had ended badly for all involved, not the least of which was the very wet and very angry cat. Thana now made sure her bathroom door was locked when she showered, not wanting a repeat of what her father jokingly referred to as the attack of the psycho cat.

By the time Thana was ready for breakfast, she could hear other students beginning to arrive. She tied back her long hair and gave herself a once-over in the mirror. For the first time in her life, she was nervous about being around people. The deaths of an Audeamus professor and student – one of the Fines, no less – had been covered by every media outlet in all of Ortus. By the time Brina's funeral had been held, Thana's and Aidan's faces had been plastered on every front page and breaking news segment in the world. Thana hoped things had calmed down now that school was ready to begin, but she still wasn't sure how her classmates would react to her being back. She took a deep breath and let it out slowly.

"Elsali be with me," Thana whispered as she opened her door and stepped into the hallway. To her relief, she didn't see another person until she was seated in the dining hall.

"Welcome back, Thana." Sophie Landers slipped into a seat nearby. "It's good to see you."

"Thanks." Thana managed a smile. Sophie returned it, and then turned her attention back to her pancakes. At least one person wasn't going to be acting weird around her, Thana thought.

Then, the Juniper sisters entered the dining hall with their parents. As soon as the girls spotted Thana, their mindless prattle changed into hushed tones that weren't quite lost in the semi-emptiness of the room.

"That's Thana Decker." Damiana attempted to discreetly point at Thana and failed. "She was with Professor Penah and Brina Fine when they died."

"Poor girl," Mrs. Juniper whispered.

"I wouldn't feel sorry for her, Mom," BD sneered. "I wouldn't be surprised if she played up the whole thing for the attention."

"Belladonna." Mr. Juniper's voice was faintly chiding, but held no real reprimand.

"Trust me, Daddy," BD continued. "Thana is a real drama queen."

Thana took another bite of her pancake to prevent her from saying something she'd regret. Well, she'd regret the consequences anyway. The action itself might make her feel better, even if just for a short while. A group of giggling first years passed behind her, and she felt her cheeks suffuse with heat when she heard snatches of their conversation.

"...saw her on the news..."

"...ragged and bloody I heard..."

"...wonder what really happened..."

Thana put down her fork and tapped her wand on the table. Her half-full plate vanished. She suddenly didn't have much of an appetite. She pushed past second years Amira Woody and Sadie Matthews who stared after her with curious eyes and hurried toward her room. She entered, one foot ready to take her a step closer to the comfort of her bed when she saw them.

Two young women stood by the previously vacant bed.

"Hi." A tall brunette stepped forward, hand outstretched. "I'm Elle Monroe, final year." Thana forced a smile and shook the new girl's hand. "This is my sister Andrea." Elle motioned to the blond. "She's just helping me move. She graduated last year from the Evestigo school."

"Nice to meet you both," Thana's voice was stiff. Elle seemed nice enough, but Thana hoped the new roommate would be preoccupied enough with her focus to not want to be overly sociable. Thana didn't think she could manage an entire school year of having to feign interest in conversation. She wanted distraction, not interaction.

Just then, as if in answer to her unspoken plea for a way to avoid participating in banal small talk, Thana's wand vibrated, signaling a message. She excused herself and crossed over to her side of the room, as much for something to do as anything else. A quick flick of her wrist caused a silver ribbon to shoot out of the end of her wand. It hung in the air as Thana read the brief message from Aidan.

"If you'll excuse me." Thana addressed the Monroe sisters. "I have to meet a friend downstairs."

Elle and Andrea nodded and then turned to continue unpacking Elle's belongings. To Thana's relief, neither one seemed inclined to ask her about what had happened, or appeared annoyed by her abrupt behavior. She only hoped the attitude would persist. If it didn't, well, she'd worry about that at a later time.

Thana made use of her usual shortcuts and made it to the lobby without encountering anyone. As soon as she stepped through the hidden panel, however, she saw the area teeming with students and their families. She hurried toward the front doors, keeping her eyes focused on where she was going while doing her best to ignore the stares of those around her.

Aidan stood in the doorway, luggage hovering behind him. Thana almost stopped and stared along with everyone else. She barely recognized him. He hadn't cut his hair since Brina's funeral and, judging by the scruffy stubble across the lower half of his face, hadn't shaved in at least a few days. He'd lost weight, leaving his already lean frame little more than skin and bones. His fair skin was paler than usual, with the exception of the dark circles under his eyes. Thana suspected he'd grabbed clothes from his floor, and she wondered if they were even clean. Despite all of this, Thana went forward and hugged her friend, grateful for his presence.

"We're in our old rooms." Thana pointedly ignored the growing whispers around them and led the way back to the Thirteenth Floor. They didn't speak as they walked, but this silence wasn't uncomfortable for her. She and Aidan had an understanding strengthened by all they'd been through. They didn't need to talk about it. As soon as they entered his room, she made herself comfortable on Aidan's desk chair as he started unpacking. Or at least what she assumed was supposed to be unpacking and not poking at random items with his wand.

"I haven't seen you since..." Thana let her voice trail off, then changed the subject. "How are you doing?" The dark look that Aidan shot over his shoulder answered her question well enough. "I miss her, too, Aidan."

"I don't want to talk about B... about her." Aidan cut Thana off, turning his back to her completely.

"Okay," Thana hopped off the chair. "How can I help?"

"I'm good," he snapped and she immediately stilled. His voice immediately softened and his shoulders slumped. "I just need some time alone. Meet you at lunch?"

"Of course." Thana slipped out of the room, but not before she saw Aidan sink to his knees next to his bed. Suddenly, Thana needed privacy, and she knew of one place that would most likely be empty. She kept her head down, avoiding eye contact as she went.

As soon as she stepped out of the corridor and into the garden, all the strength ran out of her legs and she dropped to the ground, unable to accept what her eyes were seeing. The hedges that had once provided a natural barrier between the garden and the rest of the grounds had turned wild far faster than they should have been able to do. Growing inward, branches and vines twined with the tall grass and wildflowers springing up from the once-manicured space. But the most drastic change was at the center, and it was this that sent Thana to her knees. The ancient fountain, sealed with the blood of the *Starateli*, had stood since nearly the beginning of time. Now, it lay in a pile of rubble that hinted at none of its original shape.

"Brina," Thana whispered, feeling hot tears slide down her cheeks. She knew the fountain had crumbled the moment her friend had poured the last of her energy into Aidan, though she couldn't say how she knew it. The realization of what she'd lost flowed over Thana, and she wrapped her arms around her knees, buried her head in her arms and sobbed.

Every memory she had of her time with Brina came flooding back, bringing with it fresh pain, clean and sharp. It wasn't just the ache of missing a friend, but the almost physical pain of a missing limb. She could still feel it there, hurting, but had no way to ease it. The part of her that had experienced the instant connection with Brina, that had made the two of them more like sisters than just friends, had been ripped in two and, despite time passing, the injury was still raw.

When her tears finally subsided, her entire body ached, as if she'd spent the day doing hard, physical labor, but the pain in her chest had eased the slightest bit. She could at least breathe and function again. Anything more than that, she wasn't sure she could handle.

The heat of the sun on the back of her neck told her it was mid-day. She'd spent more time in the garden than she'd intended. She stood, stretching her stiff muscles and swiping the back of her hand across her cheeks. She took out her wand and muttered an anti-red-eye spell before heading back up to lunch. The last thing she needed to do was give people more reasons to stare.

Aidan was waiting for her in the dining hall, the only indication of his frayed emotions the twisting of the edge of his shirt. His face was still drawn, but he at least met Thana's eyes as she came forward. A shadow fell across them and Thana looked up to see the one person she despised more than the Juniper sisters, and the last person Aidan needed to see. Unfortunately, she couldn't do anything to stop what was coming.

"Should've known you wouldn't protect her, Aidan. Too busy saving your own skin–" Gray's next words were lost in the sound of Aidan's fist connecting with the young man's face.

Thana gasped as Aidan followed his punch and launched himself at Gray, an expression of fury on Aidan's face like nothing Thana had ever seen. Sixteen year-old Pax Ridik dropped his tray on a nearby table and made a grab for Aidan. Fifth year Zayne Cohen joined his friend as Aidan struggled to get free.

"Aidan, please." Thana found her voice. "Stop."

As quickly as his temper had flared, the fight went out of him and he sagged in his classmate's arms. They hesitantly released him, their wary expression saying they'd be ready to restrain Aidan again if he made another move toward Gray. Instead, Aidan turned toward Thana.

"I'm done."

Without waiting for a response, he left the hall. Any of the students who hadn't been staring before were all staring now, even the ones who'd been so polite to Thana earlier that day.

"Sbwriel isel-dosbarth," Gray spat out the insult, holding his jaw. He shook off Zayne's helping hand. "I'd sue him if he had anything worth taking."

"Shut up, Gray," Thana snapped, her voice shaking with anger. How dare he call Aidan low-class trash!

"Brina–" Gray began.

Thana turned on him, eyes flashing. "You know nothing about Brina or what happened! If you so much as speak her name in my presence again, I will curse you so badly even your own mother won't recognize you." She stomped off, heedless of the students who scrambled to get out of her way.

The room was empty when she got there and Thana sank to the floor next to her bed. Her hands were shaking as she covered her face, struggling to calm her emotions. Now that her initial anger at Gray was fading, the impact of Aidan's departure hit her. She was alone.

"Elsali," Thana's voice broke. "Elsali, I..." She faltered, unable to find the words to express the turmoil within her heart. For the second time that day, Thana burst into tears. She'd cried when she'd seen Brina's body, shed tears at the funeral, but she hadn't really grieved. If she was fully honest with herself, part of her had held onto the childish notion that being back at Audeamus would make everything all right, that somehow, Brina and Jael would be waiting and everything would be the way it had been before Brina had discovered her destiny or fate or whatever it was. Thana's head had never acknowledged her hope, but her heart had clung to it, stubborn as could be.

"Thana?" The voice was soft, mostly unfamiliar. Footsteps brought the owner closer and still Thana didn't look up. "Is there anything I can do?"

Thana lifted her head enough to peer at her visitor through a fall of dark hair. It was her new roommate. Elle knelt next to her, compassion rather than pity written on her face. Though she appreciated the gesture, Thana shook her head. No one could do anything. "Thank you."

Elle nodded and stood. "If you need anything, please ask."

"I will," Thana's voice was muffled as she wiped her hands across her face. She was pretty sure she wouldn't be taking Elle up on her offer, but she was grateful for it.

Headmaster Manu's voice boomed into the room suddenly. "All students please report to the main auditorium for the welcome assembly." After a brief moment, he repeated the message.

"Do you want me to save you a seat?" Elle asked.

Thana shook her head.

"I'll see you later, then," Elle gave Thana a final concerned glance and left.

Thana sighed and got to her feet. From its perch on the foot of the bed, Marmalade raised a paw and meowed. She scratched the cat's head as she took a minute to regain her composure. Once she'd done so, she headed for the bathroom and splashed some cold water on her face. She looked at herself in the mirror and tried for her best serious voice. "You can do this, Thana. You've fought the Children of the Dragon. School should be easy." She made a fierce expression at herself, the illusion of strength failing as her bottom lip trembled. She prayed, calling to mind verses from her childhood, "Elsali, please hear me, *vox clamantis in deserto.* Hear me crying in the desert. *Fiat volvntas tua.* Your will, not mine." After a moment of silence, she set her jaw, turned and walked out of the room.

Chapter Three: Day Late Friend

Voices from the dining hall drew Thana's attention and she decided to detour from her original course. It wasn't like she hadn't heard the welcome speech before. Besides, she was interested in any excuse not to be surrounded by other students.

"I told you we were going to be late." The largest man Thana had ever seen stood with three young men in the center of the room. His deep voice rumbled as he talked, making him sound harsher than she believed he was. If she had to bet, she'd bet he was just a big teddy bear. Kind of like her dad, but younger.

"Where is everyone?" A sleepy-eyed young man with brown hair spoke up.

"The main auditorium." Thana entered the room as she answered. All four turned toward her. "I'm Thana Decker, second year."

"I'm Robb Durand, fifth year." He smiled, teeth shining white against his dark skin. "These are my brothers."

"I'm Jozy, fourth year." The grinning young man bounced on the balls of his feet, apparently unable to stand still, something Thana could understand. His light green eyes sparkled merrily.

"Jaiseyn." The second young man who'd spoken nodded at Thana. "I'm a third year."

"Me nombre es Henry." The shortest of the four waved. *"Encantado de conocerte."*

Thana gave him a puzzled look. Insults in other languages, she was fluent in. Practical, conversational skills, however, she was sorely lacking.

"He said it's nice to meet you," Jozy translated.

Henry nodded and smiled.

"Would you mind showing us the way to the auditorium?" Robb asked.

"No problem." Thana motioned for the group to follow her.

"Nice hair, by the way." She grinned at Jozy as she led the group down the stairs. His jet-black hair stood straight up in an impossibly long mohawk, large sections of which were a dark purple. Thana loved it. She'd tried coloring her hair once. Never again.

"*Gracias.*" The piercings in Jozy's bottom lip flashed as he spoke.

"Don't encourage him," Robb commented.

"Robbson Weylin Durand!" A woman's sharp voice cut through the otherwise empty main lobby.

"Ma?" Robb straightened. He towered over the shorter woman, but still quelled under her gaze.

"Didn't I tell you to get everything from the car before you came in?" She reached up, higher than Thana would've thought possible for her height, and smacked the back of Robb's head. Jozy snickered and received a slap of his own. "And you too, Josue Ximen Durand!" She turned towards Thana, and graced the girl with a smile. "Hello, dear. I'm Marcile Durand, mother to these four."

"And ten others," Jaiseyn interjected. A sharp look from Marcile stopped wherever his thought had been going, and turned his next statement into an apology. "Sorry for interrupting, Ma."

"Nice to meet you, ma'am. I'm Thana Decker." Thana held out a hand and Marcile shook it.

Jozy sniffled, "why'd you have to hit me?"

"Where's Pepino?" Marcile raised one eyebrow.

Jozy's eyes grew wide as he began frantically looking around. "Pepino? Pepino?" He turned to his mother and wailed, "I lost him!"

Thana put her hand over her mouth to hold back a giggle she was helpless to stop.

"Seriously?" Robb punched Jozy's arm. "Man up."

Robb flinched as his mother slapped the back of his head

again. "Don't hit your brother."

"Sorry, Ma." He looked at his feet.

Marcile whistled and a ball of black and purple fur bounced into the room.

"Pepino!" Jozy ran toward the creature and scooped it up in his arms.

"Is that a happyemo?" Thana asked the young man next to her.

Henry smiled. "*Sí.*"

"I didn't think they made good pets." Thana watched Jozy hug the creature, all the while chattering away at it. "Like they're too high strung or something."

"Yeah, most are." It was Jaiseyn who answered. "But, then again, so's Jozy."

"If he forgot Pepino, why'd I get slapped?" Robb cringed away as he spoke, as if he wasn't sure what side of the 'talking back' line he was on.

"Because you forgot Maurice." Marcile held up a fluffy, stuffed pink unicorn.

"Ma!" Robb grabbed for the unicorn, darting a quick glance at Thana.

"Robb brought Maurice. Robb brought Maurice." Jozy began dancing around, his happyemo capering about his feet with equal enthusiasm.

Without a word, Robb swung the unicorn at Pepino. As the happyemo flew through the air, it hooted excitedly. It wasn't until it hit the wall that it started its sad cry, turning a bright teal as it did so. To Thana's surprise, Jozy's mohawk changed to match. She was impressed. It took a complex coloring charm to accomplish that.

"Mama, Robb hit Pepino!"

Marcile reached up and grabbed her sons by their ears. Thana stifled another giggle. "You listen, and you listen good. Robbson, you're the oldest and I expect you to take care of your brothers, to make sure they don't cause any trouble. And you," she directed her next statement at Jozy, "need to make your brother's job easier. Stop behaving like a fool. If your Aunt Morcades has to discipline you, you'll get it twice as bad when you come home." She released her sons' ears and they straightened, ruefully rubbing their injured appendages. "Now, say, 'yes, Mama.'"

"Yes, Mama," all four faithfully chorused.

"Much better," Marcile said as she turned her attention to Thana with a smile. "It was nice to meet you, Thana. Do me a favor and keep my boys in line, would you? They need a firm hand."

"I'll do my best, ma'am." Thana's smile was tight, forced, and had nothing to do with her feelings toward any of the Durands. In fact, she liked Mrs. Durand, but Marcile's request had made Thana think of what Aidan and Brina would've said about Thana's own inability to behave herself.

Fortunately, Marcile didn't seem to notice. She turned her attention back to her sons. "Now, come give your mama a hug."

Without the least bit of hesitation or embarrassment, the young men each embraced their mother. Then, as she walked away, Robb picked up the unicorn and dusted it off. He glanced at Thana. "You aren't going to say anything about Maurice, are you?"

Thana mimed locking her lips and throwing away the key. Robb nodded, waved his wand over the unicorn and it vanished.

"Ready to go?" Thana asked. The boys nodded and the group walked on. "So, there are ten more of you?"

Jozy answered. "All girls. Julie and Janet are fifteen; Alexis and Sarah are thirteen; Cheri and Amber are ten; Dede and Monica are eight, and Lawanda and Lacilla are the youngest. They're six. Julie and Janet will be coming to Audeamus next year. They missed the cut off age by a few weeks. Us boys are the only ones who aren't twins and Ma says all the time she's glad for that, especially for me because she says it'd take a stronger woman to have double of me–"

"Jozy." Robb cut through his brother's babble. "Really? You need to calm down."

Thana laughed. She couldn't help it. She was so used to being the most hyper person in the room that she'd never been able to fully appreciate the humor of the situation. It was surprising how good it felt to laugh again. Robb shot her a dirty look and she grinned up at the large man.

She stopped in front of the auditorium entrance and took a moment to compose herself. She saw Jozy attempting to do the same, but wasn't sure if he succeeded before she slipped through the magic-canceling barrier. She frowned, rubbing at her arms. The magic-canceling charm had left an odd, clammy feeling on her, like the touch of something cold and slimy. She wondered if it had been redone over the break on account of the previous year's events. While the public didn't know the actual truth, enough rumors had gone around to warrant an upgrade in security.

"Are you okay?" Robb settled into the seat next to her.

"Yeah, fine," Thana answered absently.

The headmaster was in the middle of his welcome speech and the boys turned their attention forward, seeming to be paying attention. Thana, however, let Headmaster Manu's voice wash over her, lost in her own musings. The sensation of having her magic neutralized had been different than before. Not stronger, exactly, but more like what she'd felt around the dragon – and the thought was enough to frighten her. Who could cast a spell that powerful? Then again, the thought tickled at the back of her mind, maybe it wasn't the magic. Maybe it was her. Something hadn't been right with her since Brina had healed her and she hadn't been able to put her finger on it...

"Thana." Robb touched her shoulder.

She jumped and looked around. Students were out of their

seats and leaving the auditorium. She shook her head, trying to clear it. She'd heard nothing of the headmaster's speech. Hopefully there hadn't been anything important in it.

"Robbson," a cool, low voice cut through the cacophony. "Josue, Jaiseyn, Henry."

"Aunt Morcades," all four boys answered as one.

Thana stared. The tall, slender woman was the most beautiful person Thana had ever seen. Pale blond hair fell to her waist, pulled back from her perfect face with a simple rose-colored ribbon. Her eyes were a silvery gray, pale against equally fair skin.

She spoke again. "You were late."

"Sorry, Aunt Morcades," the boys chorused again.

Her eyes traveled over her nephews and landed on Thana, lighting up in recognition. "Miss Decker." She held out a hand. "It's a pleasure to meet you. I am Professor Durand, the new history professor."

Thana blanched. Morcades Durand was Jael's replacement. Of course the school would have needed to hire a new professor, she realized, but it hadn't been something she'd really thought much about. Morcades released Thana's hand, a sympathetic expression on her face.

"Clio Penah was an exemplary history and professor, as well as a truly wonderful person. She will be missed." Morcades's voice was stiff, but Thana sensed that it was more due to the professor's inability to express herself rather than any false feeling. She could see a loss in Professor Durand's eyes that spoke of more than professional admiration. Thana was certain that the new professor had known Jael, how well was hard to say, but a personal relationship had definitely been there.

"She was," Thana managed to get two words around the lump in her throat.

Morcades looked sharply at her nephews. "You'd best go unpack. Don't want to leave off till tomorrow what would be best done today."

As the stately woman walked away, Robb spoke softly. "She's our father's sister. Means well, but is as tough as a cornered *hipogloso* and about as nice when she's pushed."

"Mm-hm," Thana murmured, watching the professor go. How well had the woman known Jael? Was it possible she knew the truth of what had happened to the Guardian whose teaching position she now filled? Without a word, Thana followed the Durand boys back up to the Thirteenth Floor, mind preoccupied with possibilities. She said a distracted good-bye and went into her room.

Elle nodded at her, allowing the younger girl her space. A part of Thana's mind appreciated the gesture, and she made a mental note to thank Elle at a later point in time. She had too much on her mind at the moment to consider anything else.

Sleep was a long time coming for Thana that night. Thoughts and images merged into half-dreams, keeping her on the edge of sleep, not letting her wake enough to reason through the issues, but not allowing her true rest either.

A bang from the shared bathroom woke her less than thirty minutes after she finally drifted off into a light and troubled sleep. Startled, Thana bolted upright, wand in hand before she even realized she'd reached for it. A small ball of silver-blue light appeared in front of her though she hadn't remembered conjuring it. Wand held in front of her like a weapon, Thana climbed out of bed and padded across the room, almost as silently as the cat by her side. She placed a hand on the partially opened door, and hesitated for the briefest of moments to wish for one of her blades. Tensing her muscles, she pushed open the door.

The startled young man on the other side stopped, fortunately, in the process of removing his pants, and stared at Thana. His light brown curls were in disarray, as if he'd just pulled off his shirt. He wasn't very tall, not like the oldest of the

Durands, but still managed to be almost a foot taller than Thana, not that it was much to brag about. He had an athletic build, not too thin or too broad, lean, hard muscles under tanned skin... and Thana's face grew hot as she realized she'd been staring at his bare chest.

"Who are you?" Thana was proud at how fierce her whisper sounded.

The young man raised an eyebrow, otherwise keeping his face expressionless. "Kase Thorne. Fourth year transfer from Aliquantulus."

Thana cautiously lowered her wand. "Why are you in Aid – Pax's room?"

Kase's hazel eyes studied Thana with a scrutiny that would've made her squirm if she hadn't been annoyed at being woken in the middle of the night by a stranger.

"I'm Pax's new roommate. Headmaster Manu contacted me this afternoon and said a spot at Audeamus had opened, and it was mine if I wanted it." The bathroom's candlelight gave his irises gold streaks.

"That didn't take him long," Thana muttered angrily.

"Excuse me?"

"Don't worry about it," Thana sighed, anger disappearing as quickly as it came. She reminded herself it wasn't the headmaster's fault Aidan had lost his temper, and decided to leave. "I'm sorry I bothered you." She turned to go.

"Good night." Kase's voice was quiet. "May you sleep well." The door shut before Thana could respond, but she didn't feel any animosity or rejection, just the weariness that came with a long day.

Whether Kase had worked some magic, or Thana was just finally exhausted enough to overcome her insomnia, she didn't know, but she managed to sleep dreamlessly until Marmalade woke her in time to shower before breakfast.

Chapter Four: Outcast

Thana scowled down at her schedule as she walked to the dining hall. She loved Professor Gibberish, but had no desire to start the day with a language class. With a groan, she remembered her constant misspeaks in the previous year's class, including one occasion where she apparently told the class that her family died before she was born and her deepest desire was to ride a goat through the school. Aidan had attempted to sketch a picture of the image, resulting in hours of mocking from Brina and Thana when the picture came out looking more like a stick figure standing on a very abnormal-looking dog. The memory left her torn between a desire to laugh and a desire to cry. She supposed it was progress that she wanted to laugh at all, but she couldn't find the joy in the fact. Apparently, she wasn't quite there yet.

So engrossed in her schedule was she that Thana walked into a very large, very solid, human wall. Startled, she looked up at a smiling Robb Durand. Other students gave he and Thana a wide berth. It was impossible to tell which of the pair was being avoided, though Thana suspected two very different reasons existed behind their classmates' behavior. Robb did look kind of scary.

"Waiting for your brothers?" Thana guessed.

Robb answered. "Just one. Jaiseyn and Henry went to breakfast already. They're meeting us before class. Jozy's not really a morning person, so I sometimes have to resort to drastic measures to get him out of bed."

"Drastic measures?"

The door opened and a disgruntled Jozy stood in the doorway, mohawk a bright lime green. Behind him, Thana could see the happyemo bouncing on the bed, chattering and hooting as it went higher and higher.

Robb grinned. "I gave Pepino caffeine."

"Not funny," Jozy shut the door, cutting off Pepino's sounds of joy. "Jerk."

Robb responded to the comment by reaching around Thana and punching Jozy's arm. The young man scowled, but the expression contained no animosity. Still bickering, the pair followed Thana into the dining hall.

Thana chuckled at the interaction as she headed for her old table. With Robb and Jozy flanking her, she could ignore the stares and whispers all around her. She felt a brief wave of sadness when Robb took Brina's place and Jozy slid into Aidan's seat, but it didn't last and Thana began eating with her usual gusto, her appetite finally seeming to have returned.

"Can I see your schedules?" she asked around a mouthful of toast. The boys handed over their papers without a word, intent on consuming as much of Chef Dobbs's fine strawberry pancakes as they could manage. Thana had no compunctions about eating and talking, and so finished her second slice of cinnamon toast while commenting on the classes they shared. "Why're you both taking Final Year History? Didn't you take it as second years at your old school?"

Jozy paused from his meal to answer. "I hadn't taken it yet, but Aunt Morcades got so angry at Robb's professor back home, she told our parents that the rest of us should wait so we could take it here. Then she got hired here and we didn't really have much of a choice in the matter."

"Is that why you're taking Basic Languages II?"

Robb grinned, teeth flashing white against his dark skin. "That's just because we're stubborn. Our whole family speaks four languages and we kept protesting having to take the class."

"Then Mama found out." Jozy ruefully rubbed the back of his head and Thana didn't have to ask why. "We tested out of the first one, but were told we didn't have enough of a grasp on the grammar to go to the advanced classes," he paused, then added. "Except Henry, but he didn't want to go alone."

Out of habit, Thana glanced up at the clock to see how much longer she had until she had to head to class... and her stomach turned to ice. Last year, a large clock had hung on the wall above the entrance to the hall, an ornate number thirteen in the center of its face. Now, in its place, was a plain, silver-rimmed clock with somber black numbers. In its center was a smiling picture of Brina. Thana swallowed hard, throat and mouth dryly working to down a slice of orange. She pushed back her plate, appetite gone. Tears pricked at her eyes even as she thanked Elsali that Aidan hadn't seen the school's well-meant memorial. She had a feeling it wouldn't have been very appreciated.

"Thana," Robb repeated her name.

"Sorry, what were you saying?" Thana tore her attention from the clock.

"That guy's been staring at you." He pointed discreetly toward the table behind them.

Thana glanced over her shoulder, fully intending to yell at whichever of her floor mates was being rude. Instead, her eyes locked with the green-gold ones of her new suite mate. Kase returned the stare unabashedly, seeming no more embarrassed at being caught than he had been the night before. The strange thing was, unlike most of other guys who might react the same way, he didn't have the slightest trace of arrogance.

The moment between them was broken when the Juniper sisters, clearly eyeing Kase, situated themselves between Thana and the young man. Apparently, Aidan's absence hadn't served to make BD's heart grow fonder, Thana observed. Though judging by Gray's face when he walked by and glanced up at the clock, his feelings hadn't changed. Thana felt a pang of guilt as she remembered how harshly she'd treated the young man. Then she recalled Gray's possessive behavior before they'd left last year, followed closely by the memory of his fight with Aidan the previous day. Thana's guilt evaporated and she turned back to the Durands, ready to leave. "Let's go get your brothers. It's almost time for language class."

"No need," Jaiseyn spoke up from where he and Henry were standing behind Robb. "Lead the way."

When they reached the classroom, Corakin greeted them with his usual enthusiasm, but Thana saw the shadow cross his face as the two seats next to her were filled. She wasn't the only one saddened by the absence of her friends. As Professor Gibberish opened his mouth to begin his introduction to the class, he paused, thrown off by a commotion at the back of the room. All eyes turned to see a slightly disheveled Paschal Kuryakin slowly making his way up between the seats.

"Mr. Kuryakin, what happened?"

"Sorry, I'm late, Professor." Paschal nearly stumbled. "I was walking by a room when, suddenly, a door flew open and a bright green ball of fur leaped out. It jumped on my head and knocked me down before bouncing down the hallway."

Jozy's eyes went wide and he looked up at his older brother. "Go," Robb whispered urgently. "If Aunt Morcades finds out Pepino got loose..." He let the unspoken threat hang in the air.

"Professor?" Jozy shot up from his chair. "I need to go."

"What was that?" Corakin switched his gaze from Paschal to Jozy.

"Um," Jozy searched for a convincing lie for a moment before giving up and blurting out the truth. "It was Pepino."

"A cucumber?" Professor Gibberish furrowed his brow in confusion. "*No la entiendo.*"

"Pepino's my happyemo and I think he got loose. Someone," he glared at Robb, "gave him caffeine this morning, which is why he's green, and he was bouncing around in my room when I left. He must've gotten out somehow and I need to go get him before–"

"Go. *Vite, vite.*" Professor Gibberish cut off whatever Jozy was going to say next. Amid the laughter of his classmates, Jozy hurried from the room.

"Psst, Thana." An annoyingly familiar voice beckoned from Thana's right.

Thana kept her eyes straight ahead, the only acknowledgement of what she'd heard being the tightening of her mouth. Unfortunately, deterring BD required more decisive action than just ignoring her.

"When are you going to tell us what really happened out there?" BD's comments were still hidden under the class's mirth. "We all know you're just dying to share." She snickered. "Sorry, poor choice of words."

Thana's hand was on her wand before she'd even realized she was moving. She'd already half-turned in her seat, fully intending to turn BD into a rat, or maybe a turnip, when a hand closed over her wrist. She looked up, expecting Robb, but he hadn't moved. Instead, she found herself staring into Kase's eyes, flecks of gold shimmering amid the green and brown.

"Take your hand off of me." Thana spoke through gritted teeth.

"I don't think so." Kase's voice was mild, expression calm. "If I let go, you're going to do something you regret."

"Trust me," Thana growled. "I won't regret it."

"Yes, you will." Kase kept his tone soft, chipping away at Thana's anger with every word. "You're a good person, Thana."

"How do you know?" Unable to sustain her rage at BD, Thana lashed out at Kase. "You don't know me. You think because you see some article or news piece about the survivors of some avalanche, you know me?" Thana stood, wrenching her arm away from Kase. She continued, oblivious to now being the center of attention. All of the anger she'd been feeling bubbled up now, eager for a chance at release. "You don't have any idea who I am or what type of person I am. Mind your own business and stay away from me." She glanced at Corakin. "I'm sorry, Professor, I can't be here right now." Without waiting for permission, she ran from the room.

She didn't see the Durands or Kase again until lunchtime. Jozy and Robb sat in the seats they'd been in for breakfast while Jaiseyn and Henry filled in two empty spaces across from them. Kase watched Thana as he slid into a seat at the end of the same table. He didn't say a word as he filled his plate, eyes flicking back up to Thana every few seconds. She glared at him, trying to muster the same anger she'd had earlier, but failing. The most she could manage was annoyance at his interference and curiosity about who Kase was. She didn't like it. If she wanted to be mad at someone, she wanted to be mad. She didn't want some weird thing – she didn't want to use the word 'attraction' – to make her all forgiving. She shook her head, turning to Jozy.

"Did you find Pepino?"

He nodded. "He was in the kitchen, looking for mangos."

"Mangos?"

"Thana," Robb interjected. "You don't want to–"

Jozy told the story with barely a pause. "We used to have a goat name Chivo and that goat loved him some mango leaves. We'd try to give him other types of leaves, but he'd just keep jumping up and grabbing onto the mango leaves and we'd tell him, 'Chivo, if you don't quit eating those mango leaves, Grandma's going to kill you.' And she did and made him into stew and we ate him. Well, I didn't, because it was Chivo and I was sad."

Thana could feel the horrified expression on her face.

Jozy didn't seem to notice. "So, Mama bought me Pepino and he never eats the mango leaves, but I buy him mangos for treats and he really likes them." He grinned as he finished.

"Was all that really necessary?" Robb asked.

"*No me grites*," Jozy pouted.

"I'm not yelling at you," Robb countered. "But if you keep yapping, I'm going to hit you."

"Mama told you to be nice to me," Jozy retorted.

"And who's going to tell her?"

Jozy looked over at his other brothers and frowned. Both Henry and Jaiseyn were resting their heads on their folded arms, apparently sleeping. "I'll tell Aunt Morcades."

Thana chuckled, her dark mood lifting as the boys bantered. She could do this. She'd dealt with girls like BD before and she'd never let them get the best of her. She wasn't going to start now. As for Kase, well, she'd avoid talking to him, even looking at him, and, eventually, he'd leave her alone. Whatever this weirdness was between them would go away and she'd be able to focus on normal stuff like school and eating.

Right?

***

"Thana!" Becca Davenport called across the library, earning a mildly disapproving look from the librarian, a sweet woman named Vanya Beatus. "Sorry," Becca whispered as she crossed the room and slid into the unoccupied seat across from Thana.

Jaiseyn and Henry, sleeping in the other two seats, didn't move. Robb glanced up and nodded at Becca. Jozy waved enthusiastically, but didn't speak. It may have been due to the ten previous warnings he'd received from the librarian's assistant, Sophie, or, more likely, he'd mastered the silence charm he was supposed to be casting on Thana, but had accidentally cast it on himself. Thana suspected the latter.

"Hi, Becca," Thana said uneasily. It had been six days since her outburst in language class, and the whispers were still rampant. The gossip she'd been subject to the first day was nothing compared to what had been happening over the past week. She'd been relieved that morning when her fourth period biology class had been canceled due to Professor Karan's ear infection, leaving her free to join the Durands in the library during their free period. When she was with them, she found it easier to ignore everyone else.

"I just wanted to personally remind you about the Fuhjyn tryouts coming up." Becca smiled, blue eyes sparkling. "I'm the new captain."

"Congratulations!" Thana put as much enthusiasm into the whisper as she could.

"Thanks." The nineteen year-old glanced at the librarian, then continued in a low voice. "We need you back on the team."

"I'll think about it," Thana promised. "That's about all I can give right now."

A pair of new first years walked by, whispering furtively behind their hands as they gawked at Thana.

"Don't you have something better to do?" Becca snapped at the girls, earning a severe look from Ms. Beatus. She turned back to Thana. "Don't let these *idyjoty* keep you from having a good year."

"Thanks," Thana smiled.

"Third day of our off week, down at the field." Becca stood. "And if any of the rest of you are interested in playing for the Thirteenth Floor, I'll see you then too."

"What position did you play?" Robb asked, keeping his voice low enough to avoid the librarian's attention.

"Praelia." Thana bent her head over her book, pretending to study. She wasn't sure she wanted to talk about it.

"And you don't like playing anymore?" It seemed Jozy had finally mastered the counter-spell and could speak again.

Thana wasn't sure how to answer the question. She did miss the game, but every time she thought of playing, her mind would flash back to the hours she and Brina had spent running through the field, the games they'd won, the expression of triumph on Aidan's face when Gray lost the captaincy. Each one brought a stab of joy and sadness strong enough to make Thana's heart hurt. She stuck to the truth. "I do. I love it," she paused. "There's just too many memories."

"Your friends, they were on the team, too?" Robb asked

carefully. None of the Durands had pressed for information about Brina and Aidan, even when Thana could see the questions in their eyes.

Thana nodded. "Aidan won the captain's spot from Gray."

"I thought once a captain was appointed, unless something pretty bad happened, they kept their spot until they graduated or gave it up." Robb half-turned toward Thana.

"It's a long story." Thana stood.

"I love stories!" Jozy exclaimed. He clapped his hands over his mouth and looked over at Ms. Beatus. She raised both eyebrows and motioned toward the doors with her wand. Jozy nodded, both hands still on his mouth, as if he could hold back the words that wanted to explode out of him.

"Come on, I'll tell you all about it at lunch." Thana led the group from the library.

Less than twenty minutes later, she found herself laughing through her retelling slash re-enactment of the match between the two Thirteenth Floor teams. Even her sadness at the memory couldn't detract from her amusement at the recollection of Gray's defeat. It truly had been one of the high points of the previous year, before all of the insanity had taken over.

"Kase is staring at you again." Robb pitched his voice under the laughter of his brothers and the other students who'd stopped by to listen to the story.

Thana's cheeks tinged pink, but she refused to look. Over the past few days, she'd felt Kase's eyes on her while walking through the hallway, sitting in class; if he was there, she felt him watching her. And, loathe as she was to admit it, she'd found herself thinking about him, wanting to meet his gaze, to find out the reasons behind his attention. As if her life wasn't complicated enough at the moment.

"Thana." Nineteen year-old Hart Crossman approached.

Robb immediately straightened when he saw his suite mate. "Hi, Hart." He crossed his arms over his chest, then immediately uncrossed them, as if he couldn't quite make up his mind. Behind Robb, Jozy mimicked the movement, and Thana could see Robb making a mental note to retaliate as soon as Hart left.

"Hey, Robb," Hart replied, glancing at the young man before returning her attention to Thana. "Thana, Uncle Roderick wants to see you."

"Thanks, Hart."

"See you later, Thana, Robb." Hart smiled at Robb before turning to go.

Robb watched until she disappeared, then leaned over and punched Jozy in the arm. The younger brother glared, but didn't say anything. "See you in history," Robb said to Thana as she stood.

Thana nodded and left the dining hall. She pointedly avoided making eye contact as she went and soon found herself in front of the headmaster's office. The doors creaked open of their own accord and Thana entered. She'd never been to the headmaster's office, but paid little attention to her surroundings, more curious as to why she'd been summoned. Headmaster Manu sat behind a large desk, its expansive top covered by stacks of papers and numerous, important looking writing implements. His cloak hung behind him on his chair. The headmaster motioned for Thana to take a seat in one of the two chairs opposite him.

"How have you been, Miss Decker?"

"I'm sorry?" Thana blinked at him.

"I know coming back to school must be difficult for you." Headmaster Manu pressed his fingertips together, hands at his chin. "Aside from all of the memories being here must bring, I have no doubt that the student body is buzzing with questions and speculations. Am I right?"

"You are," Thana admitted warily. She wasn't sure where the conversation was headed or how much she wanted to disclose. Not that she distrusted the headmaster, she just knew how secretive Jael had been about where she'd come from and what they were doing. If Jael had wanted the headmaster to know more, she would've told him.

"If you ever need to talk, I'm available." The headmaster tried for a fatherly smile, but it just ended up looking awkward and forced. "Anything at all. The journey back from wherever you were to the avalanche itself, or even the trip to where you were going or what you did when you were there. Anything you feel you need to share, please, feel free."

"Um, thanks." Thana kept her tone polite, but noncommittal. "I'll keep that in mind." She wasn't sure if it was her imagination or if the look of disappointment on Headmaster Manu's face was real. "May I go now, headmaster? I have Professor Fiat next and I don't want to be late."

"Oh, of course." Headmaster Manu nodded graciously. "And don't forget my offer."

"I won't," Thana promised as she stood. She felt the headmaster watching her as she left his office. Her thoughts buzzed as she hurried down the corridor, heading for her argumentative law class. Headmaster Manu suspected something about the public story was off, she was sure of it, but what he knew and how he knew it was still a mystery. She was so immersed in trying to unravel the reasoning behind the inquest she didn't notice Professor Durand until the professor spoke.

"Miss Decker," Morcades Durand regarded Thana with her strange silver-gray eyes. "What did the headmaster wish to discuss with you?" Her tone was cool.

Startled, Thana blinked, stopping dead in her tracks. She wasn't quite sure how to answer the question. As little as she knew Headmaster Manu, she knew Morcades even less. Just because she trusted the professor's nephews didn't mean she could trust Morcades herself. "Um, nothing really." Thana kept her face carefully blank. "Just wanted to see how I was doing.

You know, adjusting after everything that happened."

Professor Durand studied her for almost a full minute, and Thana fought to urge to squirm under the steady gaze. "You may go."

Thana hurried away, casting a glance over her shoulder before turning the corner. The professor hadn't moved, her face expressionless, limbs as motionless as stone. Thana shook her head. She considered the Durand boys, with all of their quirkiness, her friends, and wanted to get along with the rest of their family, but their aunt was downright odd. Thana picked up her pace as the warning bell rang. Professor Fiat was not known for being lenient with tardy students and Thana had no desire to spend a detention copying pages from *The Complete and Entire History of Law from Inception to Present* again. Two times through the book was enough.

***

Kase watched Thana as Professor Durand stopped her. He wasn't close enough to hear what was being said, but suspected it was the same thing he was wondering. Why had the headmaster called Thana to his office? Did he, like a few others, suspect Thana's story was incomplete? It seemed Morcades Durand certainly thought Headmaster Manu's questions may have been motivated by something other than concern. Judging by the expression on the professor's face as she watched Thana walk away, she wasn't going to let matters go.

Kase waited until Thana disappeared around the corner before heading for his Introduction to Healing class. He was going to need to step up his game. With so many unknowns, Thana was going to need protected now more than ever. Even as he entered his classroom, he didn't quite believe the lie he was telling himself that all of this was just about protecting Thana.

Chapter Five: Time is Moving

Vir faded to Animas without incident and Thana found herself putting aside all of the worry and anxiety as questions and comments about last year dwindled to practically nothing.

To mixed emotions, she regained her position on the Fuhjyn team after a stellar tryout during which she surpassed everyone else on the field. After fumbling the ball for the second time, Becca had ruefully commented that it was a good thing the captaincy hadn't been based on tryout performances. Most of the previous team had also returned, leaving only a few new faces to fill in for the missing. To Thana's annoyance, one of those new faces belonged to Kase.

The new Latet was bigger than Brina had been, but only by an inch or so in height, though he did outweigh the former Latet by almost forty pounds of pure muscle. Despite the extra muscle, he had a gracefulness to which, combined with his single-minded determination, Thana found herself attracted. She'd been intentionally avoiding him for the past month, purposefully ignoring his stares and refusing to yield to the temptation to watch him, even though he kept showing up in her thoughts. Only when he was on the field, and it was expected for the team members to observe their new teammates did she allow herself to give in to the desire to focus on him. If anyone noticed her unusual attention and silence, they didn't say anything. Then again, since she'd gotten back, most people didn't say anything to her outside of polite small talk. They may have quit talking about her, but no one seemed quite sure how to talk to her yet.

The Durand brothers were Thana's refuge. They never acted as if she'd suddenly grown a third arm. Well, except for the one time she actually had grown a third arm when one of Jozy's transfiguration spells had gone awry. He'd stopped laughing when Thana retaliated with a hex that made him speak in rhymes for an entire day. She found the brotherly banter and everyday problems a welcome distraction. When Robb had come to her for advice on how to ask out Hart Crossman, Thana had been all too happy to put aside her potions homework – she didn't understand why she needed to know the antidote for a *farflanx* bite when the creature had been extinct for twelve years – and help. Likewise, when Pepino had eaten a *ardarf* seed and gotten stuck against the ceiling in the corner of Professor Gibberish's classroom, Thana had climbed on Robb's shoulders to retrieve the hooting happyemo.

Then, at the end of Animas, something happened that made Thana wish she'd never returned to school.

"Did you hear?" Elle burst into their room, cheeks pink with excitement. She clutched a piece of bright yellow paper in one hand.

"Hear what?" Thana asked, curiosity piqued. She and Elle had established a polite, if somewhat distant, relationship. It wasn't because Thana didn't like the girl. In fact, it was virtually impossible not to like Elle, which was actually the problem. It hurt too much to think she could ever be as close to another girl as she had been to Brina.

"The headmaster let Librarian Beatus decide on the Gnaritas event and she's planning a ball!" Elle thrust the paper at her roommate.

"A what?" Thana wasn't sure she'd heard correctly. Surely Headmaster Manu hadn't agreed to a dance. He generally saw the monthly school events as frivolous. He'd never agree to something like a ball.

"On the fifteenth, we're going to have a masquerade ball, complete with fancy ball gowns and masks and music and dancing," Elle sighed. "I hope someone asks me."

"I'm sure someone will," Thana answered automatically, staring down at the flyer in her hand. She used to like social events and, while she wasn't exactly a great dancer, the chance to dress up and be around lots of glittering people would have been a dream come true. Once upon a time. Now, it just seemed like a waste of time, particularly for those pariahs like her who would spend the entire time wondering if charming a potted plant to carry on a conversation would be a good idea. She was still brooding over the upcoming event when she met the Durands in the common room half an hour later. They, like everyone else, had already heard the news.

"What's a masquerade ball?" Jozy didn't look up from where he was tossing mango chunks to Pepino. The happyemo hooted each time it caught one.

"It's a dance where everyone wears masks." Robb glanced at Thana. "Do you think Hart has a date?"

Thana grinned. "I'll be she's just waiting for the right person to ask her."

Despite Robb's dark skin, Thana could see the red rising to his cheeks. For a moment, she flashed back to the previous year, the memory of teasing Brina and Aidan coming back with a bitter sweetness that formed a lump in her throat.

"Are you okay?" Robb's concern cut through the reverie.

"Fine." Thana gave herself a shake. She was spared needing to explain further when, with a loud hoot, Pepino hopped off the table after a mango and ran straight into a chair. The older Durand boys laughed as Jozy immediately gathered the little fur-ball into his arms, making comforting noises that may or may not have been actual words. In a way, Jozy and Pepino were a lot like Professor Gibberish and Ziege.

Thana gave Robb a wan smile, but it didn't reach her eyes. The emotion evoked by the memory had taken precedence over her feelings about the ball. Part of it was the grief that still came when she thought of Brina. Another part was different, a new and strange tightness linked to Aidan. She'd been closer to Brina, but Aidan had been her friend as well. What Thana couldn't quite understand was the intensity of what she was feeling. It was sharper than anxiety, something she didn't have a name for, and it made her decidedly uneasy.

The bell rang for lunch, breaking through the brothers' bickering and Thana's introspection. She followed the boys into the dining hall, unusually somber. She had so many things on her mind, all vying for her attention. The past that wanted her to stay and wallow in self-pity and misery. Her present and unusually high level of concern for Aidan. The headmaster's strange questioning. And then, as she headed for her usual seat, the other person who'd been haunting her thoughts appeared at her side.

"Good afternoon, Thana." Kase sounded stiff, but not like he was upset.

Thana raised an eyebrow as she returned Kase's greeting.

"I was wondering." A red flush was creeping up his neck. "If you'd go to the ball with me?"

Thana stopped mid-stride, oblivious to the people behind her who nearly ran into her. She could honestly say she hadn't been expecting that. While he still watched her, he hadn't spoken to her outside of Fuhjyn practice since she'd yelled at him in class.

"Thana?" Concern changed Kase's tone and he reached for her.

The instant his fingers came in contact with her skin, a shock ran through them both, the charge nearly visible. Neither one jumped back, but their eyes locked and Thana felt a tug at her heart like nothing she'd ever felt before. It wasn't her thinking he was cute or wondering what went on in his head. This was a force beyond some sort of youthful attraction.

"Everything okay here?" Robb's deep voice broke the spell and Kase dropped his hand.

"I'm fine, Robb." Thana heard herself as if at a distance. Her whole body was humming, crackling with some foreign energy. She didn't even think twice about her answer. "Yes, Kase, I'll go to the ball with you."

"Thank you." Kase smiled, a shy expression mixed with something more intense in his eyes, something that reflected the things twisting in Thana's stomach.

Thana stared after the young man as he left, taking his normal seat. After a moment, Thana slid into her usual place, expression pensive as she ate. If she noticed the looks her friends were throwing her way, she didn't respond. Her head was swimming and the closest thing to a coherent thought she could form was "Elsali, what just happened?" But despite her repetition of the question, she didn't get an answer.

Almost a week passed and, aside from basic courtesy conversation, Kase and Thana didn't speak. The Durands, perhaps sensing Thana's conflicting emotions about the situation, made no mention of the upcoming date. Then again, the brothers had their own concerns at the moment, not the least of which was their aunt. The new professor had quickly gained the reputation of being the toughest educator in Audeamus. Even those who'd had the claim before seemed easy compared to Morcades Durand, and no one was more prone to receive a tongue lashing or a week's detention than the professor's nephews.

The thing Thana found the most disconcerting about the professor was the way those pale eyes followed her, seemed to find her wherever she sat. Something about the expression made Thana feel like Morcades knew more than she let on. Just how much, Thana wasn't sure, but it was certainly enough to make the girl wary. The question was, should she share her concerns with Professor Gibberish who was, after all, the only other person at Audeamus with whom she could speak relatively freely? Now didn't seem like the best time, however. From what she'd gathered, Corakin was attending the ball as a chaperone and was apparently out of sorts about it. Something about not wanting to dance. She wanted all of the professor's attention if she needed to discuss serious matters and the ball was proving to be a distraction for everyone.

Her concern was justified when, during the final class before the ball, Corakin's example Latin presentation was punctuated by three other languages, one of which he used to proclaim himself king of the barracudas. Fortunately, the only people who understood were the Durands who, in turn, shared the joke with Thana. The rest of the class simply stared blankly at the professor until the end of the very confusing speech.

"Um, so, Professor." Alyce Wellington finally ventured the question, absent-mindedly twisting a strand of straight black hair around her finger. "Does that mean we don't have any homework over our free week?"

"Oh, *nien, nien.*" Corakin's reply was airy as he waved his hands about. "Go. Have fun. *Carpe diem.*"

"Seize the fish?" Thana overheard one of the new students, seventeen year-old Ryan Johnson whisper to Alyce as they stood.

As the students filed from the classroom, Thana noticed Robb hanging back and a quick glance around gave her a glimpse of Hart Crossman lingering as well. She grinned as she followed the other Durands out of the classroom. About time, she thought.

"Where's Robb?" Jozy asked once they'd reached the hallway.

Thana's grin widened. "Asking Hart to the ball, I hope. If he doesn't and we have to listen to him whine any more, I may be forced to do something drastic."

"Really?" Jozy's voice held a combination of curiosity and excitement. "Like what?"

"Maurice might need to make an appearance, probably in the dining hall." After a moment, she added. "And I might have the sudden urge to reveal to our entire floor that Robb was once a proud fan of the New K—"

Robb's reappearance stopped any further discussion. Judging

by the huge smile spreading from ear to ear, Thana's threat was a moot point. When she caught Robb's eye, his nod confirmed her suspicions. She grinned. At least someone was sure to enjoy the ball.

Chapter Six: Sweet Surrender

The night of the masquerade arrived with much fanfare. The halls were buzzing as girls ran from room to room, sharing make-up and giggling over their dates. Most of the young men had gotten ready early and left the chaotic corridors for the relative safety of the dining halls to wait until it was time for them to pick up their dates.

In thirteen seventy-four, Elle and Thana were both putting the finishing touches on their outfits. Elle had chosen a sleek, elegant gown of pale green silk, her mask a matching shade. Her date was Rocco Parkman, a Praelia for the eleventh floor who'd gotten up the courage to ask her the day after the announcement had been made. Elle had been thrilled; it was the only time Thana had ever heard her roommate gushing. Deciding she wanted to at least look like she wanted to be there, Thana had opted for one of her favorite dresses, a soft dark blue velvet that made her eyes glow. The mask she conjured matched it perfectly, the silver edging complementing her jewelry. Elle had asked for help curling and styling her hair and, in turn, Thana had Elle arrange her hair in a complicated series of braids. The girls spoke little, but Thana was grateful for the companionship. She found being alone with her thoughts less appealing than ever, and Elle had no problem taking her cues from Thana regarding how much conversation was wanted. Had they met under different circumstances, Thana was certain she and Elle would have been great friends. As it was, she was thankful for the older girl's easy-going personality as well as the lack of questions. For a moment, a sad smile crossed her face. Brina would've liked Elle too. Then there was a knock at the door, and everything but nervous anticipation fled.

Elle and Thana exchanged eager and anxious smile, then Thana went to open the door. Rocco had arrived first, his cheeks flushed, a single red rose clutched in his hand. He gave a polite little wave to Thana, but only had eyes for Elle. They laughed nervously, talking over each other to compliment the other's attire. They were very sweet and cute, the embodiment of everything the night was supposed to be about. Thana was happy for her roommate, but couldn't quite ignore the wistful pang of how Brina and Aidan would've looked.

When the door closed behind them, Thana was alone again. Fortunately, it wasn't for long, and this time when the knock came, Kase stood on the other side of the door. His eyes widened as he saw Thana, and she felt a blush creep up her cheeks. Her own gaze ran over the young man in front of her. In the Audeamus tradition regarding formals, his school cloak was draped over his shoulders, but the black tuxedo he wore underneath drew attention to his athletic build and, unlike most of the other young men, he wore it all with ease. It wasn't until Thana reached his face that she saw the open admiration in his hazel eyes.

"You look very nice." Thana felt the compliment was a gross understatement, but somehow, she doubted babbling nonsense would've been appreciated. To her surprise, a pale pink flush stained the young man's neck at her words.

"You're beautiful." Kase's blush deepened, but he made no apologies for his boldness.

"Thank you." Thana was glad he didn't backpedal. Anyone who paid a compliment, and then retracted it didn't know his own mind. Wishy-wash people were one of her top pet peeves. "Ready to go?"

Kase nodded and held out a hand. When her fingers touched his, a jolt jumped from her skin to his. Thana's eyes darted to his face, the slight widening of his eyes telling her he'd felt it too. She let her fingers slide between his, the sudden charge becoming a dull tingle that spread from every point their hands touched. It faded quickly, but Thana remained aware that it had been there. As she and Kase walked down the hallway, she wondered if this was what Brina and Aidan had felt when they'd touched. And if it was, what did it mean? She'd been convinced the connection between Brina and Aidan had been all a part of Elsali's plan. If it was the same for she and Kase, it didn't bode well for a chance at a relationship, especially considering how Brina and Aidan's had ended.

She pushed her disturbing thoughts aside as they entered the auditorium. For the night, the magic-canceling enchantment had been lifted – something about magic being needed to hold some hairstyles in place – and she breathed a sigh of relief. Ever since she'd returned to the school, the sensation of her magic being blocked had made her nauseous for almost a full minute after going through the spell. She'd had to arrive early for every Fuhjyn practice and game just to make sure she was recovered by the time they started. She was thankful she didn't have to deal with any of that tonight. No memories, no worry. She just wanted to have fun with her friends and pretend, even if only for a few hours, that things were somewhat normal.

"There's Robb." She pointed as she saw her friend standing next to a smiling Hart Crossman. "He and Hart make such a cute couple, don't you think?"

"They do," Kase agreed. "Do you want something to drink?"

The change of subject caught Thana by surprise. "Sure."

"I'll be right back." Kase vanished into the crowd, heading for the punch bowl while Thana made her way toward Robb and Hart.

"Where are your brothers?" Thana had to shout to be heard over the music. She'd never really been a fan of The Natalion Complex, but tonight, everything sounded great.

Robb pointed across the room where Jozy was wrestling Pepino away from a plate of mangos while Jaiseyn and Henry were oblivious to their brother's plight as they carried on a conversation with new student, Tamara Smith, and sixteen year-old Sadie Matthews. Robb made no move to help his little brother either. "I told him to keep Pepino in the room, but he insisted."

"Are they always like this?" Hart whispered to Thana.

She grinned and nodded. "You should see their mom."

"Punch." Kase suddenly appeared at Thana's side.

She took the proffered glass and sipped at the mango-peach concoction, suddenly unsure of what she was supposed to do next. She'd never been on a date before. Face off against a dragon and its horde of followers, sure, no problem. Know how to behave at a dance with a boy? Forget about it.

Kase must have sensed her unease. He leaned over, lips close to her ear. "Relax. No expectations. Let's just have fun."

***

Thana looked stunning. There really wasn't any other word for it. In his whole life, Kase had never seen anything so beautiful. He was well aware that he sounded like a bit of an idiot, but this was all new to him. He'd had his fair share of female attention growing up and had even gone out on a few casual dates with different girls, but whatever this was with Thana was so far beyond his ability to understand.

He was a naturally quiet guy, the complete opposite of Thana's personality, but around her, he became even more reserved. He liked to watch the way she moved when she talked, as if her entire body was part of the conversation. And the way she never stood still, she reminded him of a hummingbird, flitting from flower to flower, never resting. She held a strength belied by her small stature and he wondered how much recent events had forged that strength.

Before he could muse too much on the past, Thana glanced over her shoulder at him, her dark blue eyes sparkling, and all he could think about was how much he wanted to kiss her. He'd actually been wanting to kiss her from the moment she'd opened the bathroom door, but things had been so tense between them he hadn't dared, even though he knew she'd felt the spark – literally. Tonight, however, he thought the timing might finally be right. Taking a deep breath, he smiled and crossed to Thana's side.

***

An hour had passed since they'd arrived and Thana now wondered why she'd been so anxious before. The Durands were their usual entertaining selves and, with Hart around, she had another girl to talk to. Then there was Kase. Once she'd gotten over the initial nervousness of being on a date, she found that if she let it, his presence actually put her more at ease. There was just a quiet steadiness to him that calmed her. His touch no longer gave her a shock, but she felt a warmth spread through her each time they made contact. As the night went on, she found herself saying less and less as she watched Kase interact with the others.

"It's getting warm in here." Kase surprised Thana by taking her hand. "Do you want to go for a walk?"

A snicker behind Thana made her turn before she answered. All four Durands were regarding her solemnly, their faces careful masks. Thana glared up at them until Jozy cracked. He pointed at Robb, then immediately cringed away from the inevitable. When Robb smacked the back of his brother's head, Thana couldn't maintain her annoyance.

"Too bad you think that's funny, Robb." Hart dropped Thana a sly wink. "I was going to ask if you wanted to go for a walk with me."

"Oh." Robb's eyes widened. "Well, I, uh, well..." He couldn't seem to find words.

Thana and Kase slipped away as the three younger Durand brothers teased the now stammering Robb.

"Your friends are quite entertaining." Kase broke the silence as he and Thana made their way up the hill. The sounds of the ball quickly faded as the pair distanced themselves from the main building. The moon was bright tonight, aided by hundreds of small globes of white-blue light scattered throughout the grounds.

"Yes, they are," Thana agreed absently. She'd just realized where she and Kase were headed.

The tree looked much different in the moonlight then it had the day Brina had climbed up to rescue Ziege. In hindsight, Thana could see how the events of that afternoon had set everything into motion. If she and Brina hadn't gone to walk the grounds, they wouldn't have seen Corakin trying to get Ziege down from the tree and Brina wouldn't have had to climb up after the badger. If Brina hadn't been in the tree, BD never would have hexed the branch, causing Brina to fall and break her arm. Aidan wouldn't have seen Brina fall and come up the hill to tell Corakin what BD had done. If Brina's arm hadn't broken, Aidan and Thana wouldn't have needed to take Brina to the healing wing...

"Thana," Kase said her name, the concern in his tone telling her it wasn't the first time he'd said it. He was a few steps behind her.

"Sorry, Kase." Thana flushed, grateful for the dusk that hid it. "Just lost in some memories."

"It must be difficult." Kase took the necessary steps to bring him within an inch of Thana. His voice was soft, understanding. "Being here, with all of the memories and no one who understands." His fingers found a few strands of her hair that had escaped her braids. He twisted the hair around his finger before tucking it behind her ear.

"It is." Thana surprised herself by her admission.

Kase's fingers lingered for a moment on her cheek, letting the tingling warmth spread from his touch. He didn't try to hide the amazement on his face, and Thana could see him gathering the courage to ask the question. For a moment, she wondered if she should introduce another topic, anything to distract him. The last thing she needed or wanted was romance making her life even more complicated than it already was.

Trust me.

Thana nearly jumped. She hadn't been praying, hadn't been asking for help, so Elsali's words came as a complete surprise. But what did they mean? What did He want her to do? Run away? Answer Kase's question before he asked it? Deflect and deny?

Ever think maybe I just want you to be quiet?

She barely repressed her scowl. She didn't like that response.

"Do you feel that?" Kase searched for the word. "This connection?"

Thana nodded.

"Have you felt it before?"

She shook her head. "No, but Aidan and Brina had one like it." She blurted it out before she could stop herself, then winced at the hurt of the memory. Even when the two of them had been fighting, she'd been able to see their bond. She'd seen it from the moment they'd laid eyes on each other. It had just taken them a little longer to figure it out. They'd completed each other, fixed whatever was broken in the other. Now she thought she understood her fear for Aidan. Without Brina, Thana feared he would break again, and even worse this time, and no one would be there to fix him.

Thoughts of Aidan flew out of her head when Kase put his hands on her cheeks, using his thumbs to tip her chin up. She had only a split second to realize what he intended before his lips were on hers.

It was a brief kiss, but Thana's first real one. More than just a brush of mouths between two giggling children, that short moment held heat and fire. When Kase took a step back, they were both breathing hard, cheeks flushed. Neither one said a word as Kase held out his hand. Thana threaded her fingers through his and they turned back toward the school.

***

The news that Thana Decker was with Kase Thorne made it around to both students and faculty before lunch the next day. The fact that Robb and Hart were also dating didn't seem to be of interest to anyone outside of their little group, with the exception of Professor Durand who showed up at breakfast to give her nephew a stern lecture about treating Hart well and not letting the relationship get in the way of his studies. The professor didn't say anything to either Thana or Kase, but the expression in those strange eyes when they landed on Kase was nothing short of loathing.

"What was that all about?" Thana whispered as the professor left.

Kase shrugged, watching Morcades walk away. "I don't know." His tone was even, his face carefully blank.

Thana's eyes narrowed. Kase was hiding something, she was sure of it. Before she could press him, however, Pepino leaped onto the table and stole a piece of Robb's bacon. The resulting chase – Robb after Pepino and Jozy after Robb – through the dining hall drove the questions from Thana's mind and she didn't think of them again until much, much later.

As the third month back at Audeamus turned into months four and five, Thana found herself with less and less time to brood on the few oddities that periodically popped up, and even less time to think about sharing her concerns with Professor Gibberish. The headmaster had tried questioning her twice more about what had happened to Jael and Brina, forcing Thana to resort to making excuses to dash away every time she saw him coming. Fortunately, her friends were more than willing to help her avoid Headmaster Manu, even if it meant creating a distraction that, at least once, resulted in them having to clean the language classroom after Jozy and Jaiseyn exploded a pumpkin.

Professor Durand had also been making unannounced visits that increased as Vita neared its end, and though her attention always seemed to be focused on her nephews, Thana had the uneasy feeling that the professor was keeping tabs on her and Kase. And, try as she might, she still couldn't shake her anxiety about Aidan. Any attempts to reach him were rebuffed by terse notes or flat-out refusals to communicate. Based on the lack of coherence in more than one of those notes, Thana suspected Aidan was spending most of his free time drunk.

Despite her concerns, her relationship with Kase, an increase in schoolwork and Fuhjyn practice left Thana with little time or energy to devote to anything else. In a way, Thana was glad. As much as she still missed Brina and Aidan, she was starting to believe her life could indeed return to some semblance of normal. It wasn't until late in Vita that she realized normal was still a long way off.

"Thana!"

Thana scowled. Of all the nights for Kase to miss Fuhjyn practice, it had to be this one. She understood why. Kase had wanted to be a Healer since he was a child and the opportunity to work with Healer Jacen while Assistant Healer Amari was away on personal business was one he just couldn't pass up. Unfortunately, that meant Thana was making her way up to the school alone when she heard Gray call out her name.

She didn't even break stride. "What do you want, Gray?" She slid her wand from her sleeve. Her patience was thin today for some unknown reason, and Gray's presence did nothing to make things better. In fact, she had a pretty good idea it was only going to get worse.

"I want to know how you can live with yourself."

So, it was that time again. Thana sighed. Every few weeks, Gray decided he needed to come after Thana. Judging on his haggard appearance and the very strong smell wafting off of him, Thana felt it safe to assume he'd been imbibing in the homemade alcohol some of the final year students had been known to mix up. She responded to his statement, knowing he'd just get angrier if she ignored him, and with him being drunk, Thana didn't know what he'd do. "What are you talking about?"

"Oh, nothing." Gray stuck his hands in his pockets as he matched his pace to hers. "I just find it funny how fast you seem to have forgotten your friend. Walking around, acting like nothing happened. Like she didn't matter to you."

Thana made a disgusted sound and started to walk faster, resisting the urge to explode at him.

"Don't you walk away from me, *kahaba*!" Gray's hand closed around Thana's arm.

Thana jerked her arm out of Gray's grasp, raising her wand as she took a step back. Her normally contained temper flared. "I've had enough of you acting like you and Brina were so close. She couldn't stand you!"

"How dare you point your wand at me!" Gray snapped as he drew his own wand. "You never have known your place."

Thana saw Gray start to move his arm and immediately reacted. "*Pavesco!*" She sent the spell toward Gray, gasping as a new flood of energy rushed through her.

Gray flew back several feet, hitting the ground with a sickening thud. Panic replaced anger and Thana ran toward her prone classmate. She hadn't meant to hurt him. His eyes were closed when she reached him and Thana quickly flicked her wand toward the school, sending a message to the healing wing. She needed help.

Chapter Seven: When the Darkness Comes

"Thana?" A familiar voice came out of the darkness, quickly followed by its tall, thin owner.

"Corakin?"

"I was just out looking for a lambton worm. They only appear during the last three days of Vita, during a full moon, two days after a thirty-hour rain." Corakin's voice faded as his gaze fell on Gray's still form. "What happened to Mr. Plumb? Did he perhaps encounter an angry beezlebear or some other malevolent creature?"

"I did it." Thana's voice, for the first time in her life, sounded as small as she was. "I was just so mad at him for talking about Brina, and I wanted to teach him a lesson. I just used *pavesco*. It's not like it was anything really dangerous. I've never felt anything like it—"

"Thana, you're babbling," Corakin said gently. His expression was unusually somber as he crouched next to Gray. "He doesn't appear to be suffering from any adverse side effects."

Thana gave Corakin a sharp look. Was he serious?

"Aside from the lack of consciousness, of course," Corakin added.

"Thana, are you okay?" Kase's voice reached the pair moments before he did.

"I'm fine," she said as she pointed at Gray. "My hex went a little overboard."

Kase immediately switched from concerned boyfriend to professional Healer. He withdrew his wand as he knelt next to Gray. He muttered something under his breath as he passed the tip of his wand across the unconscious young man.

Thana stood, unable to stay still. She needed to let Kase do his thing. "Cor... Professor, I need to talk to you." She glanced down at the two young men. "As soon as we're sure Gray's okay."

Kase spoke without looking up. "He's going to be fine. You just overloaded him, like when a potion explodes right in front of you, or you don't dilute it enough before using it. I'll take him to the healing wing for observation." Now he raised his head. "Though he may not remember what happened." A smile played across Kase's lips, telling Thana better than words that Gray really would be all right. He wouldn't look amused at all if something was seriously wrong.

"We can talk now, if you'd like," Corakin said.

"Yes, please." Thana nodded.

"Come with me." Corakin made a grand, sweeping gesture. "We will talk as we search for the elusive lambton worm."

This wasn't exactly how Thana had pictured talking to Corakin about all of the stuff that had happened over the past few months, but after what she'd just done, she didn't want to put it off any longer.

"You seem as if you've had something on your mind for quite a while now."

Sometimes it surprised Thana how observant Corakin actually was, no matter how absent-minded he appeared. "With Aidan not here, you're the only one who knows the truth about..." Her voice trailed off. Her statement wasn't entirely accurate, she realized. While Corakin had known about Brina, the truth about 'Professor Clio Penah's' real identity was still a secret to which very few had been privy.

"The truth about everything, right?" Corakin finished her statement, his voice gentle as he looked down at Thana. "Don't think you need to hide any of it from me. I know all of it."

Thana's eyes widened. He couldn't mean what she thought he meant, could he? How could he know Jael's secret?

Her questions must've been written on her face because Corakin continued as if she'd asked them. "While the four of you were gone, I spent quite a bit of time researching. You see, there were some things about my former colleague I had always found strange."

"What things?" Thana could hear her heart pounding in her chest. She'd always hated keeping secrets, and this past year had been chock full of them. To be able to be completely honest with Corakin would be such a relief.

He stopped and peered up at the moon. After a moment, he dove into a cluster of gooseberry bushes. Thana heard a muffled struggle and, moments later, he emerged with a wriggling lambton worm in hand.

"*Kazhah*! Once ground up, these are the only things that work on badger bites. Ziege's been naughty lately." He put the lambton worm into one of his cloak pockets. "Now, where was I? Ah, yes, I remember. Did you know my expertise with languages extends to studying the origins of speech?"

Thana wasn't thrown by the professor's rapid changes of focus. He was one of the few people whose mind worked like hers. It didn't mean, however, she understood where he was going with his question.

He continued. "I can hear someone speak and known where they were born as well as where they were raised."

Now she got it. "Something was off about Professor Penah's accent?" She still didn't say Jael's name, unsure just how far Corakin's knowledge went. She wouldn't be responsible for sharing a secret kept for thousands of years.

"I put the pieces together about where she'd spent her time and then delved a little deeper regarding a few other inconsistencies I'd noticed." Corakin began walking again and Thana hurried to catch up. "I won't bore you with the details from the mountains of ancient manuscripts I had to wade through to find the truth, but, three days before you kids were found, I learned that Clio Penah was, in fact, Jael, a member of the *Starateli*, the mythical Guardians."

"Why didn't you tell me you knew?" Thana asked.

Corakin shrugged. "Partly because the time wasn't right, but mostly much for the same reason you never told me, I assume. It was not my secret to tell." He stopped abruptly and Thana nearly ran into him. "Now, however, it looks to me like you have something you want to share that is your secret to tell and you needed to know you didn't have to hide anything from me."

Thana nodded, and suddenly didn't know what to say. How was she supposed to explain to him what was happening to her when she couldn't explain it to herself?

"You seem to be uncommonly taciturn this evening." Corakin pursed his lips, a thoughtful expression on his face. A minute passed and then he spoke again. "May I offer a speculation, a theory as to what this may be about?" He didn't wait for an answer. "Based on the prior events of tonight as well as the information you gave me in regard to the manner of Brina's death, I would say your magic has increased exponentially, a fact about which you were unaware until the fortunate – sorry, unfortunate – events with Mr. Plumb."

Thana stared, mouth hanging open. Gone was the scatterbrained professor who'd once accidentally transported a very confused elderly woman and her cat into the middle of a study session. This Corakin had just put together a logical and coherent explanation for something she'd been sure was unexplainable. Pieces of the puzzle fell into place. Granted, a lot was still missing, but she now understood why the magic-canceling charms and soft spots had affected her more strongly than they had in the past.

"How?" She found her voice. "How is that even possible? I mean, Brina and I were close, but it was nothing like the connection she had with Ai..." Her voice trailed off as the realization struck her. Aidan. "Brina healed Aidan too. Which means, if your theory is right–"

"Aidan will also be experiencing an increase in his abilities." Corakin finished.

"We have to tell him!" Thana remembered her previous feelings of concern for Aidan, the uncanny knowledge that something just wasn't quite right. Maybe, just maybe, if Brina's magic had increased their abilities when she'd healed them, it had also bound them.

"He's not at home."

"What?" The proclamation shocked Thana as much as anything else, perhaps even more.

"Several weeks ago, I suspected there might be repercussions to Brina's actions and sought to speak with Aidan. At first, he refused to speak with me. Then, just a few days ago, I contacted his house directly and was told he'd disappeared the night before, leaving behind a note saying he'd gone out to make sense of what had happened." Corakin frowned. "I do hope he remembered to take his toothbrush."

"Aidan disappeared, and you're just telling me this now?!" Thana couldn't believe what she was hearing.

Corakin seemed surprised by Thana's exclamation. "I've been looking for him, but there's no reason for alarm."

"'No reason for alarm'?'" She echoed. "Brina and Jael are dead and Aidan's missing. How is this not a perfect reason for alarm?"

"You do raise a valid point," Corakin conceded. "However, I have conducted numerous experiments on the note and determined that it was written by Aidan's hand and not under duress."

"Yeah, that makes me feel better," Thana said weakly.

"I believe we can trust the friends of the *Starateli* with him, do you not?"

"Who?"

"Oh, didn't I mention that the seal on the note was the ancient symbol for those who worked with the Guardians through the years?"

"No, Professor." Thana shook her head. "You didn't mention

any of that."

"Oops." Corakin at least had the grace to look sheepish.

And there was the Corakin Thana had always known. She sighed.

"Why don't you head back to your room and tomorrow, come to my house and I'll show you what I have. Then, the two of us – or more if you would like to include your friends – will figure out what's going on and why."

"Just us," Thana said quickly. "I don't want to get anyone else involved until we know more." Or ever, she added to herself. After everything that had happened, the last thing she wanted was her friends agreeing with everyone else's opinion that she was a freak. Her stomach churned. Silence might not be an option, she knew. Brina had predicted that killing the dragon wasn't the end, and now Thana had a feeling this latest twist was the beginning of the rest of the mission. "I'll come down after breakfast."

"I'll organize tonight." Corakin brightened. "And I'll make scones!"

***

Thana absently shoved another buttered tart into her mouth as she studied the positively enormous tome Corakin had given her ten days ago. He'd explained to her that this work was too important to be haphazard, and so he'd had the book charmed to meticulously record all of his findings in a through and organized manner.

Thana sighed. Thorough yes. Organized, yes. Interesting? That one she'd have to argue against. She'd been wading through paragraph after paragraph about the dragon, Jael, and the Guardians for the past seventy pages, and not one new piece of information had appeared. Granted, this was how Corakin had learned of Jael's identity, but it was all repetitious for

Thana.

She closed her eyes and pinched the bridge of her nose. She was getting a headache. She looked up, letters dancing like spots in front of her vision. At least she wasn't hungry. Corakin had been going overboard with the baking, and Thana had a feeling if he didn't stop, she was going to end up bigger around than she was tall. She'd always had a very high-running metabolism, but Corakin's cooking might be its undoing. Scones, tarts, cucumber sandwiches, roast potatoes with hand-churned sour cream – Thana just wished the circumstances were different. It was hard to appreciate even food this good while worried about magic making things explode. Sadly enough, explosion seemed to be a valid concern. The day after Thana's hexing of Gray, she'd tried a simple conflagration spell in potions class and almost set the entire classroom on fire. The professor had written it off as an excess of flammable things, but she'd caught Kase giving her a concerned look.

Which was, of course, the other reason she was feeling the strain of the situation. She hadn't wanted to tell anyone else what was happening, and that included Kase and the Durands. She still wasn't sure how she felt about what was happening, and she still had so many questions she didn't think she could handle any of theirs.

For right now, her vague story about study sessions with Professor Gibberish seemed to be working – score one for her bad language skills – but she wasn't sure how that excuse would work when they started on their off week in just a few days.

"Ah, ha!" Corakin shouted from where he sat behind what Thana could only assume was his desk. If judging by appearance alone, Thana would've said it was some sort of graveyard where manuscripts, odds and ends, and whatever else happened to be laying around, went to die. She was far from the tidiest of people, but this disorganization made her seem almost compulsively neat.

"Did you find something?" Thana asked, not daring to hope. The last two times Corakin had made a similar announcement had been false alarms. The first had been the discovery of a potpourri recipe for which Corakin had been looking for several months. The second had simply been in response to a bug he'd found crawling on his arm. Though, in hindsight, that particular sound most likely would have been clarified as a shriek rather than an announcement.

"Yes!"

Thana waited for clarification. The potpourri recipe had also received this answer.

"There is a passage here regarding the mysterious friends of the Guardians." Corakin pointed to a very ancient-looking manuscript.

Still trying to keep herself from thinking too much of Corakin's discovery – no need to risk disappointment – Thana crossed over to the professor. Since he was sitting, she was able to peer over his shoulder. As she looked down, however, she saw it didn't matter if she could see the paper. The writing looked like nothing more than a series of black squiggles on yellowed paper. She hoped Corakin could make sense of them; otherwise, they were going to have a very long night.

Without Thana having to ask, Corakin began to translate as he read. "'In the last days of the beast, one tribe stayed behind to help the others flee. When the creature arrived, it was too late for the people of Lyxena to escape. They held off the beast for the rise of seven suns, even as their people fell around them. As the eighth sun rose, only six of them remained. Just as they believed all hope was lost, the *Starateli* arrived and drove the creature back. When the war was over, those six pledged themselves to serve the *Starateli* until all was completed."

He fell silent and Thana waited patiently for him to continue. Even someone as proficient as Corakin could have trouble translating an ancient language. After a few minutes, however, he looked up at Thana.

"See? Everything is *bene*. Aidan is with them." He pointed to a symbol at the bottom of the manuscript.

"What else does it say?" Thana asked, her impatience getting the best of her.

Corakin looked surprised by the question. "That's all there is. The entry ends there."

Thana threw up her hands in frustration. "What good does that do us? It doesn't tell us where Aidan is or if he's got these weird new-whatever-you-want-to-call-them. It doesn't explain anything!" She could feel tears burning at her eyelids, and they just made her even angrier. "All of this is completely useless!" She had the sudden urge to throw something, preferably something breakable

"Thana." Corakin got to his feet, a concerned expression on his face.

It was as if a dam inside her had burst. Everything she'd been holding back since that first day now came flooding through her, and she was powerless to stop the words from pouring out.

"We fought a dragon for Elsali! We watched Jael and Lakyn die! We held Brina's dead body in our arms!" Thana was aware her voice was getting louder, but she didn't care. It felt good to finally say what she'd been thinking. She paced the floor, her movements frantic as she continued. "Everything Aidan and I have been through, and Elsali decides it isn't enough? We have to deal with more? I'm sick of dealing with it. I'm sick of having people look at me like I'm a freak and I'm sick of people talking about me! I just want to be left alone! I didn't ask for any of this! Why would Elsali put us through this after we've done everything He's asked?"

Corakin put his hands on Thana's shoulders and held her still. "Thana." His voice cut through the anger. "I won't pretend you and Aidan haven't been tested far beyond what many adults could bear. And I won't say I can understand Elsali's plan, but there is one thing I do know." His green eyes were bright. "You can complete any task before you, no matter how difficult it may seem at the time."

Thana shook her head as two tears finally spilled over. She wiped her hands across her cheeks. "I don't think I can."

"You can," Corakin assured her. "I believe in you." He paused for a moment, then added, "Now, why don't we stop for today. We've been working for hours. Go back to the school and relax. We'll start again tomorrow. *Zer diozu?*"

Thana sniffled and took a deep, shuddering breath. She nodded. He was right. She could do this. Her emotions were so close to the surface, as if something else were feeding them. With a start, she realized a possible explanation. "Corakin, do you think when Brina healed Aidan and I, that we..." She hesitated. This was going to sound crazy, she knew. "Do you think this connection goes deeper than me just worrying about him a lot? Is it possible what he's feeling could influence my own emotions?" She said the last question in a rush, afraid she wouldn't have the nerve to say it otherwise.

Corakin thought for a moment and then nodded. "I suppose it is possible, yes. In fact," an idea seemed to occur to him, "didn't you tell me it was your heart that had been damaged?"

Thana's blood turned to ice in her veins. She didn't like thinking about it. She didn't have a scar, but she remembered all too well what had happened. The pain going through her. The feeling of her heart trying to beat.

"Since Brina's healing would've had to focus on your heart, and she healed you first, perhaps some of her own connection with Aidan was transferred to you. From her heart to yours. You were already friends and you cared about him. The magic just gave you a different insight into him."

She felt light-headed. This just kept getting stranger and stranger. She bent to pick up a satchel so she could sit down. As she set it aside, a scroll tumbled to the ground. She almost ignored it, but something on the outside of the scroll caught her eye. "Corakin." She pointed.

The professor stopped and picked up the scroll. "That is the symbol of the *Starateli.* How did I miss this one?"

Thana was tempted to ask if he'd been distracted by something shiny, but she knew she wasn't exactly known for her own ability to focus.

"Shall we see what this one has to say before we finish for the night?" Corakin asked. "Or would you prefer to wait until morning?"

Part of Thana wanted to wait. She was mentally and emotionally exhausted. A night hanging out with the guys sounded really appealing, but, her intuition was telling her this was important. "Let's look now and if it seems like it's going to be too much work, we'll wait until tomorrow to analyze it, okay?"

"I concur." Corakin carefully unrolled the scroll.

As far as Thana could see, the black scribbles looked the same on this scroll as the dozens of others she hadn't been able to read. One look at Corakin's face, however, and she knew whatever language was on the scroll, it wasn't one with which the professor was familiar.

"The first bit here." Corakin gestured. "That's in the same language as the other scrolls, but it says that what follows will be in their most secretive language as it is the truth about the end."

"That doesn't sound good," Thana said.

Corakin shook his head. "No, it doesn't."

She sighed. So much for a relaxing night. "I guess we have work to do."

Chapter Eight: Don't Stop Believing

Thana let out an inarticulate cry of frustration as the rock she was trying to move from one side of the garden to the other went flying over the hedges. Every hour she hadn't been researching with Corakin over the past ten days, she'd been practicing small spells, trying to control this new, wild magic. Corakin had worked through the night, and was still working today on translating the scroll the two of them found. Since Thana was less than useless in that area, there'd been no point in her driving the two of them crazy, with her hovering and pacing around the professor's house, so she'd left. Now, she was driving just herself crazy in the garden.

She'd tried practicing other places, not wanting to deal with the memories this area held, but privacy and room in one place wasn't easy to come by. She'd also discovered it was her emotions that created the biggest and most intense bursts of power. The fountain was the best place for intense emotions.

She wanted to throw her wand to the ground, but she'd learned that lesson already, and if she started to forget it, a small patch of burnt grass a few feet away was there to remind her. She took a deep breath to try to calm herself and raised her wand again, but before she could try another spell, she heard a voice behind her.

"Miss Decker, may I have a word with you?"

Thana turned, already knowing who she was going to see. Her stomach twisted into knots as she faced the speaker. She had a feeling she was about to find out the reasoning behind the professor's strange behavior, whether she wanted to or not.

"How can I help you, Professor?" Thana managed to keep her voice even.

Morcades came further into the garden and crossed to a decrepit-looking bench. She kept her eyes on Thana as she sat. "I have been watching you for a while."

Thana started. She'd known it, of course, but she hadn't expected an out-and-out confession.

The professor continued, "I had hoped to win your trust as it appears Professor Gibberish has done, but the signs are all pointing to us running out of time before that would happen."

Thana was starting to wish she'd picked a less isolated place to practice. One where a lot of people would notice if something happened to her.

"I don't need you to say anything, just listen." Morcades folded her hands onto her lap. "Keep your wand in hand and remain standing if that is what you wish. All I ask is that you listen."

The internal debate was swift and decisive. Thana kept her wand out, but sat down on the grass, legs crossed. A compromise. "All right. Let's hear it."

"My brother and I share the same father, but not the same mother."

Thana's eyebrows shot up. Not exactly the sort of confession she'd been expecting. For once, however, she kept her mouth shut, letting the professor continue uninterrupted.

"Each of us was raised by our mothers after our father disappeared. Arthur's mother brought him up as a normal child, neither one knowing the truth. My mother, however, had been the last of her family line, just as my father had been. Both lines were descended from six surviving members of an ancient family sworn to serve those known in mythology as Guardians."

"You have Aidan?" Thana blurted out.

"No," Morcades said. "But I know where he is and he is safe." She held up a hand and Thana swallowed the questions she wanted to ask. "I assume this means you know of the debt my family owes to the *Starateli*, so I will not take the time to reiterate that. What you do need to know is that myself and one distant cousin are all that remain of our family line. When I learned of the death of my cousin's family, I knew I needed to reach out to the rest of my family. Arthur and I had always been close, despite the differences in our upbringing, and while my brother was not of an age to begin training, his sons were."

Thana couldn't breathe. Her friends had been lying to her this whole time. Were they even really her friends or had they just been trying to get out of her what had really happened last year? The thought made her sick to her stomach.

Morcades continued. "My nephews do not know of Jael's true identity or your involvement in the death of the dragon and the last *Starateli*. I never gave the boys the names of the surviving Guardians and they are unaware of my interest in you."

The icy hand around Thana's heart eased a bit.

"But now our time is short." Morcades stood. "Bring my nephews to my house in an hour. I will ask Professor Gibberish to join us as well. We must, as they say, lay all of our cards on the table."

***

Kase watched as Thana and the Durands made their way down the hill toward the row of professors' cottages. Ever since Thana had hexed Gray, she'd been acting weird. He knew she was hiding what had really happened the previous year, but this was something else. He'd tried to ask her about it, but she'd been purposefully evasive and any questions he'd asked Gray about that night had been answered with a mumble and a shake of his head. If Gray remembered anything, he wasn't talking.

Kase turned away. Since Thana would be down at either Professor Gibberish's or Professor Durand's house for a while, Kase headed for the garden to think. Not many people went there after the fountain had mysteriously been destroyed at the end of Fidelis, and since Pax and his girlfriend, a nice first year named Josie McDonald, were studying in the room, the garden seemed like the best place to be alone.

He barely noticed where he was walking, letting himself go on autopilot. His thoughts were chasing each other around, trying to make sense of everything. He and Thana had a connection like nothing he'd ever felt before, and he could see in her eyes that this was new to her too. He hadn't expected it to be like this. All he'd wanted to do from the moment he'd seen Thana was help and protect her, and because of what had happened with Gray, he was afraid he was going to lose her. At first, he'd thought she just needed space. Then she'd started spending all of her spare time with Professor Gibberish, even blowing off a Fuhjyn practice to do it. Kase had known the two of them were close, and had just assumed the professor was helping Thana with whatever was going on. Now, though, it looked like she was willing to let the Durand boys in on the secret. Kase liked the guys well enough, and had never considered being jealous of them until the moment he'd seen them all walking together. He didn't know if it meant Thana was just willing to share with them more than she was willing to share with him, or that she was involved with one of them. Both possibilities felt like a knife to the heart.

"Why'd you bring me here, Elsali, make me fall for her, only to put this wedge between us?" Kase spoke aloud. The concept of praying was still fairly new to him and he was never sure if he should just do it in his head or actually talk. At the moment, however, he was just going on instinct. "Couldn't I have just been her friend and helped her that way? And that's even if I can help, which I don't even know if I can."

Trust me.

"Easier said than done, isn't it?"

Tell her everything.

Kase froze. He'd been dreading those three words from the moment Elsali had told him to come to Audeamus, and even more so now that he cared so much about Thana. "If I tell her, she'll hate me. She won't understand."

Trust me.

***

The silence in the room spoke volumes. Even Jozy wore a serious expression. Well, Thana clarified, it really was more somberly overwhelmed than simply serious. In fact, all of the Durand boys looked like someone had just completely turned their world upside-down. In a way, she supposed, that's what had happened.

They'd been at the house for two hours and, once Morcades had started talking, Thana had ceased thinking about how different the place looked now than it had when Jael had lived here, and had been caught up in the story. The professor had gone into more detail than she had earlier, filling in a lot of the blanks between the bit of history Corakin and Thana had found and their present time. After nearly an hour, Morcades had finished, and then it had been Thana's turn. With Corakin's help, she'd told her part of the story, ending it with her magical problem and the discovery of a scroll Corakin was still trying to decipher.

That had been ten minutes ago and no one was talking yet. Thana understood. It was all almost too much for her and she'd already known most of it.

Robb was the first to regain his composure. "So, all this time, that's why you've been giving us these 'self-defense' lessons."

Morcades nodded. "And you've all done very well. Your ancestors would be proud."

"And we can't tell anyone about this?" Robb asked.

"No one. If any of the *Decazmaja* knew about us, we would be dead."

"How many more of them do you think are still out there?"

Thana finally asked the question that had been haunting her for almost a year. She still had nightmares about them. Sometimes they were just her memories replaying over and over again. Worse were the ones when her imagination took over and brought the *Decazmaja* back to life, chasing her until she inevitably stumbled and fell. Those usually ended when her screams woke her.

"Enough," Morcades said. "Some closer than you think." She started to look like she wanted to add more, but thought better of it. Instead, she changed the subject. "As you are all now aware of the nature of the threat, we will begin training again, this time with greater purpose."

"You kept Jael's training room," Thana said.

"Yes," Morcades replied as she stood. "Jael and I had planned for this contingency." She motioned for everyone to follow her. "Tonight, we refresh everyone's memory on the basics. Tomorrow, we choose weapons."

"Weapons?" Jozy perked up at the word. "Can I have nun-chucks?"

Everyone answered at the same time. "No!!"

"*No me grites*," Jozy grumbled. "I think I'd be good with nun-chucks."

***

Thana bit back a groan as she made her way through the dining hall. She'd assumed after last year, she'd be in great shape. She'd been very wrong. Muscles she'd forgotten she'd had were aching. Her first couple of knife throws had been so far off, she hadn't even touched the target, and she'd all but lost the ability to unsheathe a knife while on the move.

Her mind was so caught up in all she'd been doing that she almost missed Kase sitting near the entrance to their hallway. When he stood, she jumped back, a startled sound escaping.

"Kase, you scared me!"

"I missed you at lunch today," he said. "And at dinner."

"I'm sorry." Thana apologized. "I had a lot of work to do with Cor... Professor Gibberish."

Kase nodded. "You look tired."

Thana tried very hard not to squirm under his gaze. He had this way of studying people that made it feel like being under a microscope, or, at least what she imagined it would feel like to be under a microscope. "It was a long day." She started to move past him. "I just want to get a shower and go to bed."

"You know," he said as he followed her down the corridor. "That doesn't really look like mental tired. It more looks like physical tired."

"Get to the point, Kase." Thana sighed as she stopped outside of her door. She so did not have the patience for this right now.

"I'm just saying that I wasn't aware studying books could make you look like you'd spent hours on the Fuhjyn field." Kase crossed to his own door.

"Yes, Kase," Thana snapped. "I'm sweaty and gross and a general mess. Thank you for pointing that out. If you have any other rude observations to make, please save them until tomorrow because I'd really like to shower and go to bed."

She slammed the door behind her and stalked into the bathroom. She felt Elle's eyes on her, and was grateful her roommate didn't say a word. As she dropped her dirty clothes onto the floor, she was reminded of Brina and Aidan's fight after the Fuhjyn match. It had taken a near-death experience to get the two of them to stop being stubborn. She really hoped this wasn't going to be a pattern with her and Kase, following the same path as Brina and Aidan. As annoyed as she was at him at the moment, she really wanted a better ending for the two of them than the one her friends had gotten.

"What am I supposed to do?" Thana asked softly as she

tipped her head back to let the warm water wash the sweat and grime from her face. "I can't tell him about what's going on. I can't put him in that kind of danger, but, if I keep having to dance around where I've been and what I've been doing, I'm going to lose him. Elsali, didn't You bring him into my life? How am I supposed to keep him there if I can't talk to him?"

Trust me.

"Not really my strong suit, You know." Thana muttered as she poured her favorite scented body-wash into her washcloth.

I know. Just wait. You'll know when it's the right time.

"The right time for what?" She really hated cryptic messages.

Just trust me.

Thana scowled, but didn't argue as she continued with her shower. She'd learned a while ago that arguing really didn't do any good, not with Elsali anyway. She could only hope tomorrow would bring more answers and less pain.

When she opened her eyes hours later, she immediately found that the second part of her hope hadn't come true. She hurt. Even the movement to reach for her wand was painful. She'd never been great at healing spells, but she managed well enough to be able to get out of bed. She knew she could go to the healing wing for something to completely take away the lingering aches, but she didn't want to risk running into Kase there. She doubted he'd let last night go if he saw her going in for healing. Besides, if she took things slow, she was fine.

She'd barely had time to grab breakfast, so she didn't see Kase until she entered language class. One look at his face told her he hadn't forgotten their exchange the night before. She had a bad feeling it was going to be a long day.

By lunch time, Thana knew she was right. It felt like it should have been midnight rather than noon. She'd never had classes move so slowly before. If the rest of the day was like this, she didn't think she could survive it. When the noon bell rang, she hurried to the dining hall, grabbed whatever food she could carry and practically ran down to the garden. She knew the Durands would be looking for her, but she didn't even want to take the time to tell them where she was going. She just wanted to be away from people.

Unfortunately, it seemed she wasn't the only person to have that idea. As she stepped into the garden, she saw the last person she wanted to be alone with at the moment.

"Thana, wait." Kase stood. "Can we talk? Please?"

Thana set her food down on the bench. She didn't really have much of an appetite anymore. "Okay." She waited.

"You've been avoiding me," Kase made the statement flat out.

"Kase, I–"

"Just talk to me, Thana." His voice took on a pleading note. "Do you just not want to be with me anymore and don't know how to tell me? Maybe you want to be with Robb or Jozy–"

"What?" Thana would've laughed if Kase's expression hadn't been so serious. "It's not like that at all."

"Then tell me what it is like, Thana, because I've been going crazy this past week trying to figure out where things went wrong. What I did wrong." An expression akin to horror passed over his face. It was gone in a second, but Thana had seen it. "Did... did Professor Durand say something to you about me?"

"Professor Durand?" Now Thana was really confused. At least his question about Robb and Jozy made some sense. She did spend a lot of time with them. Professor Durand had never even mentioned Kase. "Why would she say anything about you to me?"

Kase ignored the question. "Just tell me what's going on. I'll stay out of it if you want, but I just need to know."

"I can't tell you." Thana didn't see a reason to keep pretending she didn't have a secret. If Kase was so sure she was hiding something that he'd think she wanted to break up with him, then she should at least acknowledge part of the truth.

"So, you are hiding something."

"It's complicated," Thana said.

"Let me guess. I wouldn't understand." Kase started toward the exit. As he passed Thana, he paused. "Let me know when you decide to trust me."

Thana sank down on the bench, suddenly weary. Maybe she shouldn't have gotten involved with Kase at all. With everything else going on, the last thing she needed was this emotional tangle.

Trust me.

She pressed her fingertips to her temples and closed her eyes. She was starting to have a new appreciation for what Brina had gone through keeping her secret for so long. It was exhausting.

"Thana Decker." The headmaster's voice boomed over the grounds. "Please report to my office. Thana Decker, please report to my office."

***

Kase was fuming as he left the garden. He started toward the Fuhjyn field, more for the walk than for any real desire to go inside. The day was cool and cloudy, the breeze welcome on his overheated face.

"How can I protect her if she won't tell me what's going on?" His voice was barely audible. "Elsali, why did You bring me here? She obviously doesn't trust me, and how am I supposed to trust her if she's keeping secrets?"

Aren't you keeping secrets from her?

Kase scowled. Yes, there was that. But it was different, he mentally argued. His secret was a lot more explosive than what Thana was hiding, he was sure of it. If he told her who he really was, he'd lose her for sure.

Do you think you'll keep her if things continue this way?
Valid point.

And is your relationship with her more important than doing as I've asked?

Kase raked his hand through his hair, surprised when he found it wet. He hadn't noticed that it was sprinkling. "No."

Then do what has been asked of you and leave the rest in My hands.

***

Thana was really beginning to hate the headmaster's office. It always looked the same and the questions he asked were always the same. Oh, he worded them differently, and sometimes couched them in some sort of flowery language, but the goal hadn't changed. He wanted to know what had really happened in the mountains.

Even after the second time he'd questioned her, she'd assumed it was just a morbid sense of curiosity. When he'd begun finding her in the hallways between classes to remind her that he was there if she needed to talk, she'd started to suspect his questions held more than simple curiosity. She still wasn't entirely sure what his angle was, but she knew she didn't trust it.

"Still doing well, Headmaster." Thana gave the headmaster a tight smile.

"Glad to hear it, Thana." Headmaster Manu returned the smile with one of his own.

Thana wasn't sure whose looked more fake, hers or his. She decided to cut to the chase. She was a busy person and the day had only so many hours. "Was there something specific you needed?"

"Yes, Thana." The headmaster folded his hands in front of him. "It's come to my attention that you've recently been spending quite a bit of time with Kase Thorne."

That was new. "Yes," she answered. Honesty with caution seemed like the best thing at the moment.

"That's good. He's a fine young man. His parents were close friends of mine."

Were? Was the headmaster saying Kase's parents were dead, or that they were no longer friends? Thana tried not to show her surprise at the statement.

Fortunately, Headmaster Manu continued without acknowledging any change of expression, his next words answering Thana's unspoken question. "It was tragic, really, what happened to them. An avalanche while they'd been skiing this past Fidelis. It's one of the reasons I was so glad I was able to get Kase off of the waiting list and into Audeamus. He's really had a tough time of it. I'm glad he has you. And, of course, that means you have him, if you ever need to talk about anything. After all, he understands tragedy as well as you do."

The bell signaling the end of the meal rang and Thana stood, grateful for the interruption. "Thank you. I need to get to class now." She didn't wait to be dismissed, her head spinning from what she'd just learned. She walked down the corridor, not really seeing where she was going, implications and accusations racing through her mind.

Was Kase asking her all of these questions so he could report back to Headmaster Manu? Had he been working with the headmaster this whole time? Did that mean was he only with her to get answers? And what about his parents? Was it possible Headmaster Manu was lying to her about how they died, or even that they were dead, just to get her to say something about the avalanche story used to cover up Jael's and Brina's deaths? And if their death wasn't a lie, had they truly been killed in an avalanche and that's why the headmaster suspected Thana and Aidan had lied about how Jael and Brina had died?

She needed to find Kase. She wouldn't be able to concentrate on classes or on training if she didn't have answers, and even then, she wasn't sure.

***

Kase saw her coming down the path and almost turned away. Only sheer stubbornness kept him walking back up toward the school. He'd gotten to the Fuhjyn field and realized it was pointless to try to get away from Thana in a place where they'd spent so much time together. Better to go to class and pretend to pay attention. At least he didn't have another class with her until the end of the day. His Introduction to Healing and Fourth Year Anatomy classes should provide some distraction. The moment, however, he'd realized Thana was coming toward him, all thoughts of distraction flew away.

It's time.

So not what he wanted to hear. Not right now.

You said you'd do as I asked.

Kase sighed. Yes, he had said that. He just hadn't imagined the opportunity would come up so suddenly. He was still trying to figure out how to broach the subject of his past when Thana's question caught him completely off guard.

"When did you decide that it'd be easier to get information out of me if I was your girlfriend? Was it before or after you figured out a way to shock me when we touched so I'd think we had some sort of connection?" Thana's voice was shaking and Kase couldn't tell what it was from. The moment he saw her eyes, he knew the answer.

Thana was furious.

***

She'd totally intended to play it cool, but when she'd seen Kase, she couldn't even keep her voice steady.

"When I... Thana, that wasn't me." Kase's eyes were wide. "I swear to you, I didn't cause the reaction between us. It's real."

"Is it?" Thana clenched her hands into fists to keep from reaching for her wand. "You mean to tell me you aren't working with Headmaster Manu to try to find out more about what happened to Brina and Ja – Professor Penah?"

Either Kase was a phenomenal actor or he really wasn't working with the headmaster. Thana hoped for the latter, but she was skeptical enough to need to disprove the former.

She continued. "And you're not keeping a secret from me?" This time, Thana saw the shadow pass over Kase's face and her stomach clenched. She had her answer. "All right then." She turned to walk away.

Kase's fingers closed around her arm, sending a current running through her, stronger than anything she'd felt before. He spun her around, and she had a moment to see fire blaze in his eyes before his mouth came down on hers.

If their first kiss had been the sweetness of a moment realized, then this was the bitterness of something that might be lost. One arm wrapped around her waist as the other moved to cup the back of her head, as if fearing she'd pull away. She should, she knew, but her hands clung to the front of Kase's shirt, trying to pull him closer as she pushed herself up on her tiptoes. Her heart was pounding, the blood rushing in her ears as warmth spread through her entire body. Thana could feel Kase's emotions flowing over and through her, a desperation and desire that matched her own as their lips moved together.

When she finally broke the kiss, Kase kept his arms around her. She could feel the tension radiating from him as he rested his forehead against hers. When he spoke, his voice was rough. "I do have a secret, though not what you think."

She stiffened, automatically trying to pull away. For a brief moment, she was afraid he wasn't going to let her go, then his arms dropped to his sides, and she took a step back. Her head was still muddled from the kiss, but she could think well enough to know what she wanted. "Then what is it?"

Kase paused, appearing to be unsure where to begin. He took a deep breath and ran his hands through his hair. Thana had a moment to think of how he needed a haircut and then he was speaking.

"I know a dragon was freed from these grounds last year. And I know the churches that have sprung up all around Ortus believe it was either a sign of the end times, or a being to be worshipped. None of these things are surprising to me because, as a child, I was raised to believe in the deity of dragons."

Thana caught her breath. He couldn't be–

"My parents were both descended from the founders of a group called The Children of the Dragon."

Everything swam in front of Thana's eyes and she clamped a hand over her mouth, certain she was going to be sick. This couldn't be happening. She sank to the ground.

"Thana!" Kase immediately rushed to her side, reaching out for her.

She jerked away, hating the flash of pain in his eyes, but unable to stop herself. "Finish your story." Her voice was weak.

Kase straightened, his face drawn. "One of the *Decazmaja* close to my family, Gilroy, had become disenchanted with the Children and, when I was fourteen, he began to tell me of the outside world and the reality of what we believed. Six months later, he ran and I went with him. We lived in Latro Fremo for a short time and then in Litaralis for two years before we were approached by a group of *Decazmaja* who had broken away from the main group. This group was led by my father's aunt, Dooriya. It didn't take long to realize she'd taken the teachings of the Children to a new extreme. She didn't just want to worship the dragon, she had plans, but what they were, I never found out. One night, after only a few weeks there, Gilroy told me he was going to join Dooriya. I left that night and never looked back."

The muscles in Thana's chest started to relax enough for her to breathe a little more easily. If he'd left both groups, then maybe, just maybe, things weren't as bad as she feared.

"I hadn't known Headmaster Manu was one of the *Decazmaja* until he called me into his office after bringing me here."

Thana couldn't even pretend that this particular piece of information surprised her. Instead, it just revealed more of the picture she'd been slowly putting together.

"He wanted to know what had happened to the dragon. When I refused to tell him, he threatened to kick me out of the school. I told him I had proof of his relationship to the *Decazmaja* and he let the matter drop. With me at least. I know he's been questioning you."

Thana cocked her head. Had she heard him correctly? "Why does Headmaster Manu think you'd know anything about what happened to the dragon?"

Color crept up into Kase's cheeks and he looked away again. "My parents, like many Children of the Dragon, placed an enchantment on me as a child, a spell that would allow me to see through their eyes whenever they chose. Last year, they activated the enchantment before going into battle to protect the dragon."

"I don't under..." Thana started to say, her voice trailing off as horror dawned with realization. *Elsali*, she prayed silently, *please let me be wrong.*

"My mother shot one of the arrows that killed the *Starateli*, Jael, and you killed her after she put a blade to your throat."

"Kase," Thana could barely manage a whisper.

He looked at her now, the pain in his eyes raw and she winced, hating herself for putting it there. He knelt in front of her. "I watched my father put a sword through your heart."

"I'm so sorry." Thana forced the words out, hardly able to

speak around the lump in her throat. She knew her actions had been justified, but her heart was breaking. She'd killed his parents. How could he stand to look at her, let alone touch her?

Kase reached out and gently cupped Thana's cheek. "No, Thana. Don't be sorry. I saw what they did, and I knew what they planned to do. I'm the one who's sorry because I know my parents' actions cost your friend her life."

It was then she realized that the expression on his face wasn't pain from his loss, but rather for what his family had done to her.

He continued. "I may not have seen what Brina did, but I saw what my father did to you. You shouldn't have been able to survive that wound, and I suspect Brina is the reason you're still alive."

Thana nodded as tears slipped down her cheeks. "She is." She took Kase's hand and pulled him down to sit next to her. The grass was still damp from the light afternoon shower, but she didn't think Kase cared any more than she did. "Now it's time for me to share my secret."

Chapter Nine: How It Starts

The rain had begun again by the time Thana had finished her story, but neither she nor Kase moved from where they were sitting. In the silence that followed her confession, only the sound of the drops pattering down on the grass could be heard. With their backs to the school, Thana could almost pretend she and Kase were the only two people in the world.

"So," he broke the silence. "What do we do now?"

"I don't know about you," Thana said as she looked over at him. "But I don't really think I'm going to be able to focus on class very well today."

Kase chuckled and it was only then that Thana realized just how much his secret had been weighing on him. She'd never heard his laughter so light. He wrapped his arm around her shoulders and pulled her against him. "I agree."

"But," Thana added with a sigh. "We should go to history. I'll need to tell Professor Durand that you're going to be joining us."

Kase stiffened. "I needed to tell you one other thing."

"The reason why Professor Durand keeps giving you dirty looks?" Thana tilted her head back to look up at Kase. "I figured it was because she knew who your parents were."

"Kind of." He grimaced. "About two years before my parents were married, Professor Durand and my father were engaged."

Thana's eyes widened. "But your father was a–"

"Yes."

"And she's a–"

"Yes." Kase explained. "When they discovered the truth about each other, it tore them apart. She almost killed him, but couldn't finish the job. I don't think she's ever forgiven herself for what she sees as a moment of weakness. When I first arrived, she confronted me and I told her what I told you, that I wasn't a member of the Children anymore. She didn't believe me, but because I didn't have the mark that's given to everyone who takes the vow, she couldn't hurt me. Instead, she just watches me. She's not going to be happy with me knowing about you, much less agreeable to letting me join your training."

"Well, she can either train you with the rest of us, or forget about me working with her." Thana got to her feet. "Did you tell the professor about your aunt's group?"

"No." Kase also stood. "Why?"

"Because I think it's time we all come clean with each other. We can't expect to be able to defeat the enemy if we're spending half our energy trying to keep secrets from each other. We need to start acting like an army rather than individual soldiers."

***

The unmistakable sound of a happyemo hooting in her ear woke Thana from a restless sleep. She opened her eyes and nearly fell off of her bed. Pepino was an alarming shade of orange, nearly glowing in the dim early morning light as it bounced up and down on Thana's pillow.

"Pepino," Thana groaned. "What are you doing here?" She sat up, glancing toward her roommate's bed before remembering that Elle had left the night before to go home and help her sister finish up the last-minute details for Andrea's wedding next week.

Pepino nudged Thana's hand with its head, and she absent-mindedly stroked its fur as she waited for her head to clear. It had been a rough night, her emotions skyrocketing before plummeting and nothing around to explain the change. It hadn't been until late that she'd finally dropped off.

Suddenly, a question occurred to her. "How did you get in my room?" Pepino cooed and hopped up on Thana's lap. "That's not really an answer." As she scratched the happyemo's neck, she spotted something hidden in its thick fur. She unrolled the tiny scrap of paper and read.

Headmaster Manu has begun monitoring communications within Audeamus. Come to Professor Gibberish's house immediately.

Not really the best way to wake up. Thana sighed and set Pepino on her bed while she dressed. When she turned around again, the happyemo was gone, apparently having left the same way it had arrived. Thana didn't let herself linger on the mystery. It wasn't important. Using all of her best shortcuts, Thana made her way down the hill to the cottages and knocked on Corakin's door.

The professor was unusually somber as he opened the door and led Thana inside. They walked in silence down the same hallway he'd led her and her friends down a little less than a year before. It was strange, Thana thought, how something could seem so similar and yet so strange at the same time. She and Corakin had studied in his office. This morning, however, he entered his living room. Thana hesitated for a brief moment before following him. She hadn't been there since the day Jael had shared her story.

The Durands were there, including the professor, as was Kase. He immediately stood and went to Thana, wrapping his arms around her in a quick hug. It wasn't until he stepped back that Thana saw the stranger.

She was tall and slender, but her bearing spoke of immense strength and power. Her eyes were so dark that they appeared black and her skin was dusky. Silver and gold braids stood out in stark contrast to the rest of her waist-length hair. Half a dozen small silver studs lined her ears and the backs of both wrists bore crosses. Her pants were black, her shirt a dark gray and purple camouflage. Though she appeared to be only a couple of years older than Thana, nineteen at the most, she carried herself like one who was used to being in charge.

"Thana Decker." The stranger stood and smiled. "It's nice to finally meet you. I'm Neysa Polyxena. Your friend Aidan has been staying with me."

"Aidan?" Thana squeezed Kase's hand. "Is he okay?"

"He's fine." Neysa gestured toward the two empty seats on the couch as she returned to the chair where she'd been sitting. Her expression was soft. "He's healing."

Thana leaned against Kase and he wrapped his arm around her shoulders. She leaned into him gratefully. She had a feeling she was going to need some support for what was coming next. Something about Neysa told Thana that she meant business, and not the good kind.

"Neysa is the cousin about whom I spoke before," Morcades said. "The only other descendant of the friends of the Guardians."

"I'm here for two reasons," Neysa said. "The first is for you, Thana." She studied Thana for a moment before continuing. "The second is to tell you about a mission for which I need your assistance."

"It's happening to Aidan too, isn't it?" Thana wasn't sure how she knew what Neysa was going to say, only that it just felt right. "His magic has... changed."

"Yes." Neysa seemed only slightly surprised by Thana's comment. "May I ask what made you say that?"

Thana glanced toward Corakin who nodded. "I've been... I guess sensitive is the word I'm looking for, when it comes to Aidan."

"The two of you are connected." Neysa exchanged looks with Morcades. "Then I was right to come here. Elsali has made it very clear that you are to join us in rescuing two young people who are going to be sacrificed by the *Decazmaja* in an attempt to bring back the dragon." Neysa's gaze turned to Kase. "My cousin has told me you grew up as a *Decazmaja*."

"Yes." Kase kept his face expressionless. "I left just after I turned fifteen."

"And you stayed with your aunt for a little while, with a group of *Decazmaja* who had broken away from the other Children?"

"Yes."

Thana could hear the undercurrent of tension in Kase's voice. She didn't blame him. She wasn't sure where this line of questioning was going.

"While you were with her, did you see a boy and a girl just a few years younger than you?"

Now Kase couldn't hide his puzzlement. "There were children and teenagers there, including my cousins."

"Your cousins?" Neysa asked.

"Distant cousins," Kase clarified. "My Aunt Dooriya's kids. Or, I guess maybe her adopted ones. I'm not really sure. I didn't know her very well."

"Were their names Adalayde and Callum?"

Thana watched the color drain from Kase's face.

"How did you know that?"

Neysa's expression was grim. "Get comfortable, because this is going to take a while."

Corakin bounced to his feet. "I'll get the scones."

By the time Neysa finished, Thana was glad Corakin had thought to bring in the food. They never would have had time to get breakfast and get to class on time. As it was, they were probably going to have to rush, especially if they didn't want to rouse the headmaster's suspicions. With everything Neysa had told them, Thana knew they all had to be very careful not to do anything to draw attention to themselves.

"So, what do we do now?" Robb asked.

"Well, I'm going to stick around for a while today," Neysa said. "I'll compare notes with Morcades and Corakin, see if they've found anything relating to what this group is trying to do. I'll head back home later this evening and work on training with Aidan and Carys. Morcades will continue your training here. I'll come back when I know more and we'll determine where we need to go from there."

***

A week and a half – fifteen days – and still, the most exciting thing that had happened was when Corakin announced that he and Morcades had successfully determined the scroll did indeed have something to do with the Children of the Dragon. They hadn't been able to translate anything more than basic articles since then. Not really much help.

Still, things hadn't been boring. Headmaster Manu appeared to be getting more suspicious with each passing day, making excuses to roam the halls between classes. He'd called the Durands, Kase and Thana into his office more than once, expressing concern over the fact they were spending a great deal of time by themselves. Thana's knowledge of the building had been helping them getting to and from the professor's cottage without being seen, but their absences had been noticed, though not as much as they would've been if the Thirteenth Floor's Fuhjyn team hadn't been eliminated in the first round of the finals.

Thana was back to her previous skill level with her knives. She'd been hesitant about continuing to practice with them around Kase, but he'd assured her that it didn't bother him. All five of the young men were proficient at hand-to-hand combat and had some skill with a sword, but Morcades had decided they each needed to have a specialty. She reminded them that they would need back-up if they ended up in a soft spot or another position where magic wasn't the best weapon.

Like Thana, Kase's talents ran toward blades, though he tended to lean toward ones just a bit longer than the average knife. Despite the trepidation of Jozy using anything even similar to nun-chucks, he'd shown a surprising proficiency at wielding a mace Morcades said once belonged to her father, his grandfather. Jaiseyn and Henry had both picked up archery, Jaiseyn with the crossbow, Henry with a longbow. Robb had chosen what Thana supposed was technically an axe, though she'd never seen one this large before. One side of the massive head was a traditionally rounded blade. The other side, however, could only be described as a hammer. When standing on end, the end of the handle was even with Thana's head. At least one of them didn't have to worry about someone taking their weapon from them. She doubted anyone else could lift the thing, much less swing it around with the same ease Robb did. The first time he'd tried to use it, he'd left a hole the size of... well, the size of something really big in the wall. Morcades had left it there as a reminder of what they were all capable of.

As Otium drew to a close, the nightly training session in what had been Jael's house was interrupted by a knock on the door. Neysa had returned. Over the next four days, she took over the training, giving Morcades the ability to run interference with Headmaster Manu. Based on what Thana overheard, communication in and out of Audeamus had become severely restricted. Neysa had been trying to contact the group for days with no luck. Whatever it was the *Decazmaja* had planned, Thana had a feeling its time was imminent. All they needed now was a break.

The first of Fatum brought, as it always did, the first snow of the season even though the weather had been unusually warm all year. Fat, lazy flakes drifted down from gray skies, melting just moments after touching the ground, but the air had the crisp, clean smell Thana had always associated with the coming of the cold. It didn't bother her as much as she'd thought it would.

As she stood at the dining hall window, looking out over the wet campus, Thana found herself wondering how long it would be before it would be time to leave again. Classes were back in session today, but Thana was having a difficult time keeping her mind on her studies.

"Care to share your thoughts?" Kase asked as he slid his arms around her waist.

Thana leaned back against him, taking comfort in the steady beat of his heart, in the strength of his arms. "I was just thinking about when we were going to be going on our little 'trip' and how, the last time I left with my friends, not all..." Her voice caught.

"We're going to be fine, *mi amor*." Kase pressed his lips against Thana's temple.

The warning bell sounded and Thana reluctantly straightened. As much as she wanted to stay there by the window, watching the snow with Kase, they had classes to get to. Professor Fiat wasn't any more lenient with her second year Argumentative Law class than she had been with her first, and Kase didn't want to be late for his Basics of Healing class. Even with everything else going on, they needed to maintain their grades, if only to keep the headmaster from getting involved.

When their final class of the day ended, however, something happened that drove all academic concerns from their minds.

"*Ich bin fertig!*" Corakin came rushing into the room, his normally pale face flushed.

All eyes turned toward him as Professor Durand stopped right in the middle of her last sentence in her lecture on the final days of the Great War.

"*Factum est!*" Corakin headed straight for Professor Durand's desk completely oblivious to the staring students.

As the bell rang, Morcades hurried everyone from the room, reminding them to read the next chapter in their history books. Thana hurried forward, Kase following her. The Durands were right behind him, none of them even giving a second look to their classmates hurrying for the halls. Morcades went to close the door, pausing only to let a cloaked figure slip inside. Neysa lowered her hood as she approached the desk.

"You completed the translation," Thana said. She reached over for Kase's hand. It was as cold as her own.

Corakin nodded. "The first part talks about a group of *Decazmaja* who have splintered from the main group and how, on the seventh day of Fatum of this year, they will bring about the beginning of the end."

"That's cheerful," Jozy muttered. He made a pained sound as Robb stepped on his foot. "What?"

"This part is an incantation." Corakin continued without acknowledging the brotherly exchange. "'*Raktadalli snana dryagan hrdaya jiva mattu savu mattu maya tumbisalpaṭṭa prani mattu manuṣyana rakta, yogya eradu marpaḍu.*'"

"What does it mean?" Robb asked.

"It's an ancient form of a nearly lost language, but I was able to translate it. 'Dragon heart, bathed in blood, blood of beast and of man, fed by life and death and magic, transform the worthy two.'"

"*Eso suena mal,*" Henry said seriously.

"I agree," Thana nodded. "That doesn't sound good."

"It's worse than you think," Neysa spoke up. Her dusky skin had taken on an ashen tone. "We were wrong. I don't think this group is trying to resurrect the dragon. I think they're trying to turn Adalayde and Callum into dragons."

Chapter Ten: The Last Time

"So, on the third, Neysa told us she got a message from you guys that you'd left the island and where you were going. We left the next day and here we are." Thana glanced up at Kase as she finished filling in Aidan and his friends about everything that had happened to bring them all to this point. "Did I miss anything?"

"No, you covered everything." Kase tightened his arm around her shoulders.

"I have to ask." Aidan gestured toward Thana's hair, or lack thereof. "When did you decide to do that?"

She ran a hand through her now-short locks. It still felt strange, having her hair cropped so close to her head. "The day before we left. It was constantly getting in the way and I figured this was easier than trying to tie it back."

"Well, I like it." Aidan gave her a fond smile.

Thana turned her gaze to Adalayde and Callum. "Are the two of you okay?" This was a lot to process for all of them and those two were getting all of it at once, including the fact that the woman who'd raised them had lied to them their entire lives. She may have been Kase's aunt, but she'd raised Adalayde and Callum as her own children. It couldn't be easy.

"Dooriya has a lot to answer for." Callum's expression was grim. "Adalayde and I will do our duty."

"It's nearly time." Neysa interrupted whatever else would have been said. "Is everyone clear on their part?" Everyone nodded. "Does anyone have any questions?"

Jozy raised his hand. "When we're done fighting, do you want to go out with me?"

"Seriously?" Robb turned toward his brother.

Jozy shrugged. "Seemed like a good time to ask."

Thana laughed. She couldn't help it. She clamped her hand over her mouth, but the giggles still escaped. One by one, the rest of the group joined in until even Adalayde and Callum were chuckling while Jozy looked around with a confused expression on his face. The tension eased to a more bearable level.

Neysa cocked her head to one side, a grin on her face. "Tell you what, *querido*, if we survive this, I'll let you take me out." She winked at him. "Just leave Pepino behind."

Jozy grinned and jumped to his feet. "*Kazhah!* Let's go!"

"Is he always like that?" Aidan asked in a hushed voice.

"Yes." Thana and Kase answered together.

"At least he broke the tension," Carys said as she got to her feet.

Aidan stood, his face serious as he put his hands on Carys's shoulders. Thana felt a sharp throb in her heart that had nothing to do with the upcoming battle. She'd guessed something more existed between them, but what she saw in Aidan's eyes said it went a whole lot deeper than she'd originally thought. It was good, she knew, for him to move on, but seeing his concern for Carys just made Thana think of the last time she, Aidan and Brina had been together. She silently prayed that this time, things would end differently.

"Hey." Kase pulled Thana into his arms. "We're all going to be okay. This isn't like before. No surprises here."

Thana nodded, wishing she could feel the same confidence. Then Kase's mouth was on hers and she stopped thinking, stopped worrying. It was only her and him and the heat of their skin. There was no urgency in the kiss, as if they could stay there forever, lips moving in their slow dance.

But forever wasn't an option, and the sounds of the others moving around them broke through, shattering the illusion. Thana looked up at Kase. The flecks of gold in his hazel irises were blazing as he brushed his thumb across her bottom lip, leaving a trail of heat on her skin.

"*Elsali vobiscum,*" She whispered.

"And He with you." Kase took a step back, letting his arms

fall back down at his sides.

"Archers, you're first out," Neysa said.

Thana ran her hands over her clothes, double-checking the placement of each of her knives. Thanks to an outfit Morcades had given her, Thana was caring twenty blades of varying lengths. Part of her wished the professor had been able to come with them, but she'd agreed with the decision to have Professor Durand to stay behind and keep an eye on the headmaster. If Headmaster Manu had figured out what was happening, Thana had no doubt he'd warn the other *Decazmaja*. She had a suspicion that subterfuge was only a fraction of the reasoning, however, and wondered if the headmaster would even be at Audeamus when they returned.

Aidan paused as he passed Thana. She could see her fears reflected in his eyes. They didn't say anything, but an understanding passed between them. They were going to keep their promise to Brina and see this finished, no matter the cost. He nodded once, and then turned to leave the protective circle.

As Thana waited for Neysa to call for her, she went over the strategy again in her head. The goal was two-fold. To stop the spell, the dragon's heart needed to be destroyed, but, since Dooriya was the leader, removing her was also necessary. Adalayde and Callum were certain once she was out of the picture, the rest of the *Decazmaja* would scatter. The pair had specifically requested they be the ones allowed to pursue the woman who raised them. Thana wasn't so sure it was a good idea, but Aidan and Carys had vouched for their twins and the matter was settled. While Adalayde and Callum went after Dooriya, Aidan and Carys would cover them from a small out-cropping of rocks. Jaiseyn and Henry had been assigned the other side of the clearing where the rest of the group would be coming in. It was closer to the ceremonial chest holding the dragon's heart, but was more heavily guarded.

Neysa had instructed the group she was leading to all work

their way toward the chest, saying whoever reached it first should destroy it, but Thana had her own plan. She needed to be the one to destroy the heart. She couldn't explain how she knew it, or why it had to be that way, only that it did. She didn't share her thoughts, knowing her friends would try to stop her. Instead, she followed the others and waited for the opportunity to move.

Thana peered out through the trees and her stomach clenched. She counted at least forty *Decazmaja*, all armed. Then, she saw it. Up on a small hill was the chest. The only part of the situation seeming to work in their favor was that the *Decazmaja* were facing away from the trees. They appeared to be more interested in what was about to happen than suspecting anyone would interrupt.

Neysa looked at each of them, the question written in her dark eyes. Thana took out her largest knife and saw Kase do the same. Robb's fingers flexed around the handle of his massive hammer and Jozy readied his mace. His mohawk had turned black and the expression on his face was more focused and determined than Thana had ever seen. So, she thought, a spell to transform two innocent people into dragons was all it took to make Jozy be serious. Then it was time to go and all of Thana's attention focused on what was about to happen.

They moved quickly and quietly with Neysa leading the way. Kase had explained that only the dedicated would be allowed to attend the ceremony so no one in the fight was a victim. Adalayde and Callum had confirmed this, but the first time Thana drove her blade into a man's back, she still couldn't keep herself from feeling sick. She didn't let herself dwell on it, though, moving on to the next target. The knife in her left hand severed the spinal cord as her right slit the man's throat, spraying her with blood as she let the body drop and kept going. Almost a dozen *Decazmaja* were dead before they realized something was happening and the real fighting began, magic mixing with weapons once the element of surprise was lost.

Thana had forgotten how the brain processed a battle, the images and the sounds. She moved instinctively, letting her muscles remember how to move as her knives found their targets. Without thinking about it, her hands called the blades back to her, the new magic surging through her stronger than ever before. She adapted into a new rhythm, following blades with bolts of magic powerful enough to knock her enemies back. Around her, the others were fighting just as hard. Robb's hammer sent *Decazmajas* flying and Jozy finished them off with surprising ferocity. Of Kase, she was acutely aware, her body shifting in response to his so that his back was never left vulnerable. Men and women dropped all around them and the ground grew slick with blood.

Thana almost slipped as she started for her next target. A sharp pain went through her side and she spun towards it, pushing aside the pain as she struck out with knife and magic. The blade went through her attacker's neck and lodged in the shoulder of the woman behind him even as he crumpled to the ground.

That's when she saw it, the opening to the chest. She heard Kase calling after her to wait, but she didn't listen. She needed to end this now. Arrows whistled over her head, and then thudded into the *Decazmaja* running toward her. Her side stung and she was vaguely aware of the hot liquid pouring down her side, but she didn't miss a step. She wasn't about to let a scratch keep her from doing what needed to be done.

Decazmaja were falling around her as her friends wielded their weapons with skill. She prayed it would be enough to keep them safe until she could end this. She didn't want to lose anyone else. Then the battle faded into the background as something else began to happen.

It was calling to her, calling to the dragon's magic inside her. She remembered how Brina's eyes had changed, marking her as the one who could kill the creature. Dragon eyes. Thana could smell and taste the copper tang of blood all around her, including the thicker, almost sulfuric scent that had haunted her nightmares, the scent of the liquid that had melted the snow around where Brina had died. Dragon blood. She could see every detail in the chest and knew what was inside, could feel her heart painfully pounding against her chest, as if trying to beat in time with something else. Dragon heart.

She had one knife left and she prayed it would be long enough. If it wasn't, they were all in trouble. She'd never get the chest open in time. She felt Aidan sending her strength through their connection as she reached the chest and her new magic filled every cell in her body.

"Elsali, help me," Thana said. As she raised her arms, she heard a woman scream. A second later, red-hot agony slammed into her chest and Thana cried out in pain. "*Fiat volvntas tua!*" The words spilled from her lips as she let the weight of her body take her down, hoping it would be enough. As she dropped to her knees, her knife cut through the ancient wood with relative ease.

An explosion of energy knocked her back and she knew she'd pierced the heart. The pain going through her was sharp and intense, every breath an agony, but she smiled. What had begun the day Brina had stepped onto the Audeamus ground, Thana knew, was finally over.

She heard familiar voices saying her name and opened her mouth to speak. Before a word could pass from her lips, the world began to gray. Kase was suddenly there, and his pale face was the last thing Thana saw before the world went dark.

Epilogue: Hope a Little Harder

Neysa's hand tightened around Jozy's as the pair walked toward the school. She still couldn't believe he'd talked her into this. She'd never gone to a formal school and never wanted to, and yet, here she was, ready to live in a dorm and take classes from real professors.

"Neysa!" Carys came running out of the front doors, Aidan just a few steps behind her. The girl's hair had grown longer, but it was the expression on her face that made her look different. With the rescue of her twin, and the support of Aidan, Carys had never looked so happy.

Neysa gratefully accepted Carys's hug, and then nodded at Aidan. The wound on his right cheek had healed nicely over the last four months. Despite the scar he would carry for the rest of his life, Aidan looked far more relaxed and content than he had in the time Neysa had known him.

"Corakin wanted to come out and talk to you guys, but Professor Durand is making him do meet and greets with the first-year parents." Robb spoke up from where he'd appeared behind them. Hart smiled in greeting, but she was still a bit awkward around the group since Robb had filled her in on the real reason his left arm now bore a mass of scar tissue. Neysa couldn't blame her. It was a lot to take in.

"Having them both take over as Headmaster was a great idea," Aidan said. "Combine Corakin's people skills with Professor Durand's good sense."

"Has anyone heard if they've found Headmaster Manu yet?" Jaiseyn asked.

Neysa shook her head. "Your aunt said he ran, so I'm guessing he doesn't want to be found."

"Jozy!" A short brunette approached with Henry. As they drew closer, Neysa recognized the eldest of the Durand girls. The younger of the twins, Janet, must still be unpacking. In

Julie's arms was a ball of bright pink fur.

"Pepino!" Jozy ran over to his little sister. "How did you get out of the car?"

Neysa grinned. She and Jozy balanced each other well. She turned to Carys. "How are Adalayde and Callum doing?"

"Adjusting," Carys said. "But if Mrs. Preston spoils them any more, they're going to be impossible to live with."

Neysa sobered. "What about Kase?"

Carys's face fell. "As well as can be expected. It was a tough loss." She glanced over her shoulder toward the school. "Here he comes."

Neysa followed Carys's gaze. Out of all of them, Kase had sustained the only real damage. Everyone else's wounds had healed, even if some of them had scarred, but there hadn't been anything anyone could do to help Kase. They'd all been so worried about Thana that no one had noticed Kase's injury until it was too late, and even then, he'd been reluctant to do anything that took him away from Thana. In the end, even with all of the healing skill in the group, none of them had been able to save his hand.

"I'm just glad he has Thana to help him through it," Aidan said as he watched Thana pull Kase's arm even more tightly around her.

"Has she had any side-effects?" Neysa asked.

Aidan shook his head. "Not really. She eats more, which I never would have thought possible." He grinned as he stepped out to hug his friend.

To Neysa's relief, Kase gave them all a smile that reached his eyes. When she saw his smile, saw the way he looked at Thana, she knew he would be okay. Her gaze traveled over each of them, watching as they talked and laughed. Her eyes met Aidan's, then Thana's, and she read in them what she now knew for sure. It was finished.